Patrick O'Brian

THE FORTUNE
OF WAR

Thorndike Press • Chivers Press
Thorndike, Maine USA   Bath, England

This Large Print edition is published by Thorndike Press, USA and by Chivers Press, England.

Published in 2001 in the U.S. by arrangement with W. W. Norton & Company, Inc.

Published in 2001 in the U.K. by arrangement with HarperCollins Publishers Ltd.

U.S. Hardcover   0-7862-2202-6   (Basic Series Edition)
U.K. Hardcover   0-7540-1588-2   (Windsor Large Print)
U.K. Softcover   0-7540-2449-0   (Paragon Large Print)

The text of this Large Print edition is unabridged.
Other aspects of the book may vary from the original edition.

Set in 16 pt. Plantin by Rick Gundberg.

Printed in the United States on permanent paper.

British Library Cataloguing in Publication Data available

Library of Congress Cataloging-in-Publication Data

O'Brian, Patrick, 1914–
    The fortune of war / Patrick O'Brian.
    p. cm.
    ISBN 0-7862-1927-0 (lg. print : hc : alk. paper)
    1. Aubrey, Jack (Fictitious character) — Fiction.
    2. Maturin, Stephen (Fictitious character) — Fiction.
    3. Great Britain — History, Naval — 19th century — Fiction.
    4. United States — History — War of 1812 — Fiction.
    5. Large type books. I. Title.
    PR6029.B55 F67 2001
    823'.914—dc21   00-068299

The Fortune
of War

The sails of a square-rigged ship, hung out to dry in a calm.

1 Flying jib
2 Jib
3 Fore topmast staysail
4 Fore staysail
5 Foresail, or course
6 Fore topsail
7 Fore topgallant
8 Mainstaysail
9 Main topmast staysail
10 Middle staysail
11 Main topgallant staysail

12 Mainsail, or course
13 Maintopsail
14 Main topgallant
15 Mizzen staysail
16 Mizzen topmast staysail
17 Mizzen topgallant staysail
18 Mizzen sail
19 Spanker
20 Mizzen topsail
21 Mizzen topgallant

Illustration source: Serres, Liber Nauticus.
Courtesy of The Science and Technology Research Center,
The New York Public Library, Astor, Lenox, and Tilden Foundation

AUTHOR'S NOTE

When history and fiction intertwine, the reader may well like to know how far the recorded facts have suffered from the embrace. In this book I have two historical frigate-actions, and when I describe them I keep strictly to the contemporary accounts, to the official letters on service, the courts-martial on the officers who lost their ships, the newspapers and magazines of the time, to James, the best of contemporary naval historians, of course, and to the biographies and memoirs of those who took part. It seems to me that where the Royal Navy and indeed the infant United States Navy are concerned there is very little point in trying to improve the record, since the plain, unadorned facts speak for themselves with the emphasis of a broadside; and the only liberty I have taken is to place my heroes aboard. And even so, although they are not quite as peripheral as Fabrice on the field of Waterloo, they do not play a decisive part nor bend the course of history in any way.

For those who might like to follow the second action in greater detail, may I recommend the *Memoir of Admiral Sir P. B. V. Broke, Bart., KCB, etc.* (London 1866), by the Rev. Dr Brighton, MD? It is something of a hagiography, and sometimes it is neither candid nor generous to the enemy; but the author was in touch with many of the survivors on the British side (including the Mr Wallis who appears in these pages as a youth and who lived on until he was a hundred years old, Admiral of the Fleet Sir Provo Wallis, still on the active list) and with a zeal perhaps more suited to the medical man than to the parson he accounts for every single shot, round, bar, or grape, that struck the embattled ships.

And just as my imagination could not outdo the facts in the matter of these actions, so it was incapable of producing a Frenchman's English of such value as that of Anthelme Brillat-Savarin, who took refuge in the United States at the time of the Revolution (he cooked squirrels in madeira during his stay) and whose outburst will at once be recognized by readers of his *Physiologie du Goût*, although I put it into the mouth of one of my characters.

Finally I should like to thank the Public Record Office and the National Maritime Museum for their help and kindness in sending me copies of the original log-books and the plans of the ships concerned: these are authenticity itself, and I hope that at least some of this quality may have carried over into the tale.

CHAPTER ONE

The warm monsoon blew gently from the east, wafting HMS *Leopard* into the bay of Pulo Batang. She had spread all the sails she could, to reach the anchorage before the tide should turn and to come in without discredit, but a pitiful show they made — patched, with discoloured heavy-weather canvas next to stuff so thin it scarcely checked the brilliant light — and her hull was worse. A professional eye could make out that she had once been painted with the Nelson chequer, that she was a man-of-war, a fourth-rate built to carry fifty guns on two full decks; but to a landsman, in spite of her pennant and the dingy ensign at her mizen-peak, she looked like an unusually shabby merchant ship. And although both watches were on deck, gazing earnestly at the shore, the extraordinarily bright-green shore, and breathing in the heady scent of the Spice Islands, the *Leopard*'s crew was so sparse that the notion of her being a merchantman was confirmed: furthermore, a casual glance showed no guns at all; while the ragged, shirt-sleeved figures on her quarterdeck could hardly be commissioned officers.

These figures all gazed with equal intensity down the bay, to the green-rimmed inlet where the flagship rode, and beyond it to the spreading white house that had been the Dutch governor's favourite wet-season residence: a union flag flew over it at present. As they gazed a signal ran up on a second flagstaff to the right.

'They desire us to heave out the private signal, sir, if you please,' said the signal-midshipman, his telescope to his eye.

'Make it so, Mr Wetherby, together with our number,' said the Captain; and to his first lieutenant, 'Mr Babbington, round-to when we are abreast the point and start the salute.'

The *Leopard* glided on, the wind singing gently in her rigging, the warm, still water whispering down her side: otherwise a total silence, the hands bracing her yards without a word as the breeze came more abeam. And in the same silence the shore contemplated the *Leopard*'s number.

She was abreast of the point; she came smoothly to the wind, and her single carronade began to speak. Seventeen feeble puffs of smoke, and seventeen little bangs like damp squibs over the miles of deep blue sea; when the last faint yelp had died away, the flagship began her deep, full-throated reply, and at the same time another hoist ran up on shore. '*Captain repair to flag,* if you please, sir,' said the midshipman.

'Barge away, Mr Babbington,' said the Captain, and walked into his cabin. Neither their landfall nor the presence of the flag was unexpected, and his full-dress uniform was laid out on his cot, scrubbed and brushed to remove the stains of salt water, iced seaweed, antarctic lichen and tropical mould until it was threadbare in some places and strangely felted in others; yet the faded, shrunken blue gold-laced coat was still honest broadcloth, and as he put it on he broke into a sweat. He sat down and loosened his neckcloth. 'I shall get used to it presently, no doubt,' he said, and then, hearing the voice of his steward raised in blasphemous, whining fury, 'Killick, Killick there: what's amiss?'

'Which it's your scraper, sir, your number one scraper. The wombat's got at it.'

'Then take it away from him, for God's sake.'

'I duresn't, sir,' said Killick. 'For fear of tearing the lace.'

'Now, sir,' cried the Captain, striding into the great cabin, a tall, imposing figure. 'Now, sir,' — addressing the wombat, one of the numerous body of marsupials brought into the

14

ship by her surgeon, a natural philosopher — 'give it up directly, d'ye hear me, there?'

The wombat stared him straight in the eye, drew a length of gold lace from its mouth, and then deliberately sucked it in again.

'Pass the word for Dr Maturin,' said the Captain, looking angrily at the wombat: and a moment later, 'Come now, Stephen, this is coming it pretty high: your brute is eating my hat.'

'So he is, too,' said Dr Maturin. 'But do not be so perturbed, Jack; it will do him no harm, at all. His digestive processes —'

At this point the wombat dropped the hat, shuffled rapidly across the deck and swarmed up into Dr Maturin's arms, peering at close range into his face with a look of deep affection.

'Well, I can keep it under my arm, together with my reports,' said the Captain, picking up a bundle of papers and carefully fitting them round his gold-laced hat to conceal the tear. 'What now, Mr Holles?'

'Barge alongside, if you please, sir.'

The *Leopard* in fact possessed no barge: nothing more than a little clinker-built jolly-boat, patched and pieced until scarcely an original plank was to be seen. It was rated barge for the occasion, but it was so small that the Captain's bargemen (once ten of the most powerful Leopards, all dressed alike in Guernsey frocks and varnished hats) amounted to no more than two, his coxswain Barrett Bonden and an able seaman by the name of Plaice: still, this was the Royal Navy, and the jolly-boat, like the *Leopard*'s deck, had been sanded and holystoned to a state of unearthly lustre, while the bargemen themselves had done all that naval ingenuity could devise in the article of whole duck trousers and white sennit hats. Indeed, the *Leopard* herself took on an almost naval appearance for a moment as her captain came on deck: the Marine officer and his few remaining men had put on their dim pink or purple coats, once a uniform scarlet, and they stood as straight as their own ramrods while the Captain went down the side to what remnant of ceremony the Leopards could provide.

'Aubrey!' cried the Admiral, rising as the Captain was shown in and taking him by the hand. 'Aubrey! By God, I am glad to see you. We had given you up for dead.' The Admiral was a stout, thickset sailor with a Roman emperor's face that could and often did look very forbidding; but it was now suffused with pleasure, and again he said, 'By God, I am glad to see you. When you were first reported from the look-out I thought you must be *Active*, a little before her time; but as soon as you was hull-up I recognized the horrible old *Leopard* — I sailed in her in ninety-three — the horrible old *Leopard* come back from the dead! And tolerably clawed about, I see. What have you been at?'

'Here are all my letters, reports, returns, and statements of condition, sir,' said Jack Aubrey, laying his papers on the table, 'from the day we left the Downs until this morning. I am truly sorry they are so tedious long, and I am truly sorry to have taken such a time in bringing you the *Leopard*, and in such a state, at that.'

'Well, well,' said the Admiral, putting on his spectacles, glancing at the heap, and taking them off again. 'Better late than never, you know. Just give me a brief account of what you have been at, and I will look through the papers later.'

'Why, sir,' said Jack slowly, collecting his mind, 'as you know, I was directed to come out by way of Botany Bay, to deal with Mr Bligh's unfortunate situation there: then at the last moment it was thought fit to put a number of convicts aboard, and I was to carry them out as well. But these convicts brought the gaol-fever with them, and when we were about twelve degrees north of the line and becalmed for weeks on end, it broke out in a most shocking fashion. We lost more than a hundred men, and it lasted so long I was obliged to bear away to Brazil for provisions and to land the sick. Their names are all here,' he said, patting one of the sheafs. 'Then, a few days out of Recife, and shaping our course for the Cape, we fell in with a Dutch seventy-four, the *Waakzaamheid*.'

'Just so,' said the Admiral, with ferocious satisfaction. 'We were threatened with her — a goddam nightmare.'

'Yes, sir. And being so short-handed and out-gunned, I avoided an engagement, running down to about 41° South, a long, long chase. We shook her off at last, but she knew very well where we were bound, and when we turned north and west for the Cape some time later, there she was again, to windward; and it was coming on to blow. Well, sir, not to be tedious, she ran us down to 43° South, the wind rising and a very heavy following sea; but by getting hawsers to the mastheads and starting our water we kept ahead, and a shot from our stern-chasers brought her foremast by the board, so she broached-to and went down.'

'Did she, by God!' cried the Admiral. 'Well done, well done indeed. I heard you had sunk her, but could scarcely credit it — no word of the circumstances.' He could see it all now: he knew the high south latitudes well, the enormous seas and the winds of the forties, the instant death of any ship that broached-to. 'Well done indeed. That is a great relief to my mind. Give you joy of it with all my heart, Aubrey,' he said, shaking Jack's hand again. 'Chloe, Chloe there,' — raising his voice and directing it through a partially open door.

A slim honey-coloured young woman appeared: she was wearing a sarong and a little open jacket that revealed a firm and pointed bosom. Captain Aubrey's eyes instantly fixed upon this bosom: he swallowed painfully. He had not seen a bosom for a very long while indeed. The Admiral had, however, and with no more than a benign glance he called for champagne and koekjes. They came at once on trays, borne by three more young women of the same mould, lithe, smiling, cheerful; and as they served him Captain Aubrey noticed that they brought with them a waft of ambergris and musk; perhaps of cloves too, and nutmeg. 'These are my cooks, by land,' observed the Admiral. 'I find they answer very well, for country dishes. Well, here's to you, Aubrey, and your victory: it ain't every day a fifty-gun ship sinks a seventy-four.'

'You are very kind, sir,' said Jack. 'But I am afraid that what I have to tell you next is not so pleasant. Having started all our water bar a ton or so, I stood south and east for floating ice: there was no point in beating back a thousand miles to the Cape, and with the wind steady in the west I hoped to push straight on to Botany Bay as soon as we had completed our water. We found the ice further north than I had expected, a very large island of it. But most unhappily, sir, we had scarcely filled more than a few tons before the weather grew so thick that I had to call in the boats; and then in the fog we struck stern-first upon the ice-mountain, beat off our rudder and started a butt under the larboard run. The leak gained prodigiously in spite of fothering-sails, and it was then, sir, that the guns were obliged to be thrown overboard, together with everything else we could come at.'

The Admiral nodded, looking very grave.

'The people behaved better than I had expected: they pumped until they could not stand. But when the water was well above the orlop, it was represented to me that the ship must settle, and that many of the people wished to take their chance in the boats. I told them we must try one more fothering-sail, but meanwhile I should have the boats hoisted out and provisioned. But I very much regret to say, sir, that a short while after this some hands broke into the spirit-room: and that was the end of all order. The boats left in a deplorable condition. May I ask, sir, whether any of them survived?'

'The launch reached the Cape — that is how I knew about the Dutchman — but I have no details. Tell me, did any officers or young gentlemen go with them?'

Jack paused, twirling his glass in his fingers. The girls had left the door open, and in the courtyard beyond he saw five tame cassowaries hurry across on tiptoe, as intent as hens and very like them; but hens five feet tall. This sight scarcely brushed his conscious mind, however: he said, 'Yes, sir. I had directly given my first lieutenant leave to go; and my words to the men certainly implied permission.' He was aware that the Admiral was watching him from under a shading hand, and he added, 'I must say this, sir: my first lieutenant behaved in a most officerlike, seamanlike manner throughout, I was perfectly satisfied with his conduct: and the water was knee-deep on the orlop.'

'Hm,' said the Admiral. 'It don't sound very pretty, though. Did any other officers go with him?'

'Only the purser and the chaplain, sir. All the other officers and young gentlemen stayed, and they behaved very well indeed.'

'I am glad to hear it,' said the Admiral. 'Carry on, Aubrey.'

'Well, sir, we got the leak under some sort of control, rigged a steering-machine and bore away for the Crozets. Unhappily we could not quite fetch them, so we proceeded to an island a whaler had told me of, that a Frenchman had laid down in 49°44′ South — Desolation Island. There we heeled the ship and came at the leak, completed our water, took in provisions — seals, penguins, and a very wholesome cabbage — and fashioned a new rudder from a topmast. For want of a forge we were unable to hang it; but fortunately an American whaler put in, that had the necessary tools. I am sorry to have to report, sir, that at this point one of the convicts managed to get aboard the whaler, together with an American I had rated midshipman; and they escaped.'

'An American?' cried the Admiral. 'There you are — all of a piece! Damned rascals — convicts themselves, for the most part, piebald mongrels for the rest — they lie with black women, you know, Aubrey; I have it on good authority that they lie with black women. Disloyal — hang the whole lot of them, the whole shooting-match. And so this fellow you had rated midshipman deserted, and seduced an Englishman too, into the bargain. There's American gratitude for you! All of a piece — we protected them against the French till sixty-three, and what did they do? I'll tell you what they did, Aubrey; *they bit the hand that fed them.* Scoundrels. And now here is your American midshipman luring one of your convicts away. A fellow condemned for parricide, or gross immorality, or both, I make no doubt — birds of a feather, Aubrey, birds of a feather.'

'Very true, sir, very true; and if you touch pitch, you cannot very well get it off again.'

'Turpentine will remove pitch, Aubrey: Venice turpentine.'

'Yes, sir. But to do the fellow justice — and I must say he did *us* justice during the pestilence, acting as surgeon's mate — it was a female American prisoner, a privileged prisoner, berthing alone, that he went off with, an uncommonly handsome young lady, Mrs Wogan.'

'Wogan? Louisa Wogan? Black hair, blue eyes?'

'I did not notice the colour of her eyes, sir; but she was an uncommonly handsome woman; and I believe her name was Louisa. Did you know her, sir?'

Admiral Drury went a dusky red — he had just happened to meet a Louisa Wogan — an acquaintance of his cousin Vowles, the junior lord of the Admiralty — an acquaintance of Mrs Drury — no possible connection with Botany Bay — a very common name: mere coincidence — not the same woman at all —

besides, now that the Admiral came to recollect, his Mrs Wogan's eyes were yellow. However, they would not go into all that now: Aubrey might carry on with his account.

'Yes, sir. So having shipped the new rudder, we proceeded to Port Jackson — to Botany Bay. Two days out we caught sight of the whaler, far to windward; but I was advised — that is to say, I considered it my duty not to chase, in view of the fact that Mrs Wogan was an American citizen, and that in the present state of tension, taking her off an American vessel by force might lead to political complications. I suppose, sir, that they have not declared war on us?'

'No. Not that I have heard of. I wish they would: they do not possess a single ship of the line, and three of their fat merchantmen passed Amboyna last week — such prizes!'

'To be sure, a prize is always welcome, sir. We proceeded, then, to Port Jackson, where we found that Captain Bligh's problems had already been dealt with, and that the authorities could not accord us a single gun, nor any sailcloth, and precious little cordage. No paint, neither. So despairing of getting anything out of the military men in charge — they seemed to have taken against the Navy since Mr Bligh's time in command — I discharged our remaining convicts and proceeded to this

24

rendezvous with the utmost despatch. That is to say, considering the state of the ship under my command.'

'I am sure you did, Aubrey. A very creditable feat, upon my soul, and very welcome you are, too. By God, I thought you had lost the number of your mess long ago — lying somewhere in a thousand fathoms and Mrs Aubrey crying her pretty eyes out. Not that she gave you up, however: I had a note from her not a couple of months ago, by *Thalia*, begging me to send some things on — books and stockings, as I remember — to send them on to New Holland, because you were certainly detained there. Poor lady, thought I, she has been knitting for a corpse. Such a pretty note; I dare say I have it still. Yes,' said he, rummaging among his papers, 'here we are.'

The sight of that familiar hand struck Jack with astonishing force, and for a moment he could have sworn he heard her voice: for this moment it was as though he were in the breakfast-parlour at Ashgrove Cottage, in Hampshire, half the world away, and as though she were there on the other side of the table, tall, gentle, lovely, so wholly a part of himself. But the figure on the other side of the table was in fact a rather coarse rear-admiral of the white, making a remark to the effect that 'all wives were the same, even naval wives; they all supposed there was a penny post at every station where a ship could swim, ready to carry and fetch their letters without a moment's delay. That was why sailors were so often ill-received at home, and blamed for not writing oftener: wives were all the same.'

'Not mine,' said Jack; but not aloud, and the Admiral went on, 'The Admiralty did not give you up, either. They have given you *Acasta*, and Burrel came out months and months ago to supersede you in the *Leopard*; but he died of the bloody flux, together with half his followers, like so many people here; and what I shall do with *Leopard* I cannot tell. I have no guns here but what I can take from the Dutch, and our balls, as you know very well, don't fit Dutch guns . . . and without guns, she can only be a transport. Should have been turned into a transport these ten years past — fifteen years past. But that is nothing to do with the present case: what you will have to do, Aubrey, is to get your dunnage ashore as quick as you can, because *La Flèche* is due from Bombay. Yorke has her. She just touches here, the time to pick up my despatches, and then she flies home as quick as an arrow. As quick as an arrow, Aubrey.'

'Yes, sir.'

'Flèche is the French for an arrow, Aubrey.'

'Oh, indeed? I was not aware. Very good, sir. Capital, upon my word. Quick as an arrow — I shall repeat that.'

'I dare say you will, and pass it off as your own, too. And if Yorke don't delay, if he don't hang about in the Sunda Strait, whoring after prizes, you should still have the monsoon to carry you right across — a famous passage. Now give me a quick idea of the state of your ship. Of course, she must be surveyed, but I should like to have a general notion at once. And tell me just how many people you have aboard — you would scarcely credit how hungry I am for men. Ogres ain't in it.'

There followed a highly technical discussion in which the poor *Leopard's* shortcomings were candidly exposed — the state of her futtocks, her deplorable knees — a discussion from which it appeared that even if the Admiral had had the guns to arm her, she could hardly bear them, her timbers being so strained, and the rot having spread forward from her stern to so shocking a degree. This discussion, though melancholy, was perfectly amicable: no harsh words were heard until they reached the subject of followers, the officers, young gentlemen, and hands who, by the custom of the service, accompanied a captain from one command to another. With a false air of casualness, the Admiral observed that in view of the exceptional circumstances he proposed retaining them all. 'Though you may take your surgeon with you,' he said. 'In point of fact I have had several orders to send him back by the first ship; and he is to report to Mr Wallis, my political adviser, at once. Yes: you may certainly take him with you, Aubrey; and that is a very great indulgence. I might even stretch a point and allow you a servant, though *La Flèche* could certainly supply any number you may need.'

'Oh, come sir,' cried Jack. 'My lieutenants — and Babbington has followed me since my first command — my midshipmen, and all my bargemen, in one fell sloop? Is this justice, sir?'

'What sloop, Aubrey?'

'Why, as to that, sir, I do not mean any specific vessel: it was an allusion to the Bible. But what I mean is, that it is the immemorial custom of the service . . .'

'Am I to understand that you are questioning my orders, Mr Aubrey?'

'Never in life, sir, Heaven forbid. Any written order you choose to honour me with, I shall of course execute at once. But as you know better than I, the immemorial custom of the service is that . . .'

Jack and the Admiral had known one another off and on for twenty years; they had spent many evenings together, some of them drunken; their collision therefore had none of the cold venom of a purely official encounter. It was none the less eager for that, however, and presently their voices rose until the maidens in the courtyard could clearly make out the words, even the warm personal reflections, direct on the Admiral's part, slightly veiled on Jack's; and again and again they heard the cry 'the immemorial custom of the service'.

'You always was a pig-headed, obstinate fellow,' said the Admiral.

'So my old nurse used to tell me, sir,' said Jack. 'But surely, sir, even a man with no respect for the immemorial customs of the service, an innovator, a man with no regard for the ways of the Navy, would condemn me, was I not to stand by my officers and midshipmen, when they stood by me in a damned uncomfortable situation — was I to let my youngsters go off to captains that do not give a curse for their families or their advancement, and desert a first lieutenant who has followed me since he was a reefer, just when I have a chance of getting him on. One stroke of luck with *Acasta*, and Babbington is a commander. I appeal to your own practice, sir. The whole service knows very well that Charles Yorke, Belling, and Harry Fisher followed you from ship to ship, and that if they are commanders and post-captains now, it is thanks to you. And I know very well that you have always taken good care of your youngsters. The immemorial custom of the service . . .'

'Oh, f— the immemorial custom of the service,' cried the Admiral: and then, appalled at his own words, he fell silent for a while. He could, of course, give a direct order; though a written order would be an awkward thing to have shown about. But then again, Aubrey was not only in the right, but he was also a captain with a remarkable fighting reputation, a captain who had done so well in prize-money that he was known as Lucky Jack Aubrey, a captain with a handsome estate in Hampshire, a father in Parliament, a man who might end up on the Board of Admiralty, too considerable a man for off-hand treatment: besides, the Admiral liked him; and the *Waakzaamheid* was a noble feat. 'Oh well, a fig for it, anyhow,' he said at last. 'What a sullen, dogged fellow you are to be sure, Aubrey. Come, fill up your glass. It might get a little common good nature into you. You may have your mids for all I care, and your first lieutenant too; for I dare say that if you formed them, they would wrangle with their captain on his own quarterdeck, every time he desired one of them to put the ship about. You remind me of that old Sodomite.'

'Sodomite, sir?' cried Jack.

'Yes. You who are so fond of quoting the Bible, you must know who I mean. The man who wrangled with the Lord about Sodom and Gomorrah. Abraham, that's the name! Beat the Lord down from fifty to five and twenty and then to ten. You shall have Babbington and your mids and your surgeon, maybe even your coxswain, but let us hear no more about your bargemen. It is great nonsense and presumption on your part and anyhow there ain't room for another soul in *La Flèche*, so that's an end on it. Now tell me, among your remaining people, can you scrape together a decent eleven for a game of cricket? The squadron is playing ship against ship, for a hundred pound a side.'

'I believe I could, sir,' said Jack, smiling: in the very instant the Admiral uttered the word, he resolved a minute problem that had been nagging some remote corner of his mind — what was that absurdly familiar sound that came from the spreading lawn behind the house? Answer: it was the crack of bat meeting ball. 'I believe I could, sir. And, sir, I believe you mentioned mail for the *Leopard*?'

The Admiral's political adviser was a man of singular importance, for the British government had a mind to add the whole of the Dutch East Indies to the possessions of the Crown, and not only did the local rulers have to be persuaded to love King George, but the well-entrenched Dutch and French systems of influence and intelligence had to be counteracted and, if possible, eradicated; but he lived in a small, obscure house and he assumed no state at all, not half as much as the Admiral's secretary; and he dressed his subfusc person in a snuff-coloured coat, his only concession to the climate being a pair of nankin pantaloons, once white. His was a difficult task; yet since the Honourable East India Company had a great interest in eliminating their Dutch rivals, and since several members of the cabinet were holders of the Company's stock, he was at least well supplied with money. Indeed, he was sitting upon one of several chests crammed with small silver ingots, the most convenient currency in those parts, when his visitor was announced.

'Maturin!' cried the politico, whipping off his green spectacles and grasping the doctor's hand. 'Maturin! By God, I am glad to see you. We had given you up for dead. How do you do? Achmet!' — clapping his hands — 'Coffee.'

'Wallis,' said Maturin, 'I am happy to find you here. How is your penis?' At their last meeting he had carried out an operation on his colleague in political and military intelligence, who wished to pass for a Jew: the operation, on an adult, had proved by no means so trifling as he or Wallis had supposed, and Stephen had long been haunted by thoughts of gangrene.

Mr Wallis's delighted smile changed to gravity; a look of sincere self-commiseration came over his face, and he said that it had come along pretty well, but he feared it would never be quite the member it was. He related his symptoms in detail while the scent of coffee grew, pervading the little dirty room; but when the coffee itself appeared, in a brass pot on a brass tray, he broke off and said, 'Oh, Maturin, I am a mere weak monster, prattling about myself. Pray tell me of your voyage, your shockingly prolonged and I fear most arduous voyage — so prolonged that we had almost abandoned hope, and Sir Joseph's letters, from ecstatic, grew anxious, and at last melancholy to a degree.'

'Sir Joseph is in the saddle again, I collect?'

'More firmly than before; and with even wider powers,' said Wallis, and they exchanged a smile. Sir Joseph Blaine had been the very able chief of naval intelligence; they both knew of the subtle manoeuvres that had caused his premature retirement, and of the even more subtle, far more intelligent manoeuvres that had brought him back.

Stephen Maturin supped his scalding coffee, the right Mocha berry, brought back from Arabia Felix in the pilgrim dhows, and considered. He was naturally a reserved and even a secretive man: his illegitimate birth (his father was an Irish officer in the service of His Most Catholic Majesty, his mother a Catalan lady) had to do with this; his activities in the cause of the liberation of Ireland had more; and his voluntary, gratuitous alliance with naval intelligence, undertaken with the sole aim of helping to defeat Bonaparte, whom he loathed with all his heart as a vile tyrant, a wicked cruel vulgar man, a destroyer of freedom and of nations, and as a betrayer of all that was good in the Revolution, had even more. Yet the power of keeping his mouth shut was innate: so perhaps was the integrity that made him one of the Admiralty's most valued secret agents, particularly in Catalonia — a calling very well disguised by his also being an active naval surgeon, as well as a natural philosopher of international renown, one whose name was familiar to all those who cared deeply about the extinct solitaire of Rodriguez (close cousin to the dodo), the great land tortoise Testudo aubreii of the Indian Ocean, or the habits of the African aardvark. Excellent agent though he was, he was burdened with a heart, a loving heart that had very nearly broken for a woman named Diana Villiers: she had preferred an American to him — a natural preference, since Mr Johnson was a fine upstanding witty intelligent man, and very rich, whereas Stephen was a plain bastard at the best, sallow with odd pale eyes, sparse hair and meagre limbs, and rather poor. In his distress, Maturin had made mistakes in both his callings — mistakes that might have been attributed to over-indulgence in the tincture of laudanum to which he was at that time addicted — and when it so happened that Louisa Wogan, an American acquaintance of Diana Villiers, was taken up for spying and sentenced to trans-portation, Stephen Maturin was required to go with her, as surgeon of the *Leopard*. The mission was of no importance compared with some he had undertaken, and at the time it seemed clear that Sir Joseph was merely putting him out of the way. Yet his connec-tion with Mrs Wogan had taken a curious turn . . . How much should he tell Wallis? How much did Wallis already know?

'You used the word ecstatic in alluding to Sir Joseph's letters, I believe?' he said. 'A warm expression.'

This was a signal for Wallis to display his

hand if he wished the game to continue on a reasonably candid level; he did so at once. 'None too warm, Maturin, I assure you,' said he, reaching for a file. 'Upon receiving your communication from the Brazils, from Recife, he wrote to say that you had brought off a splendid coup, that you had extracted all the information the lady possessed in far less time than he had expected; that he had a tolerably complete picture of the Americans' organization; and that he would endeavour to bring you back from the Cape by a despatch sent in the first ship bound for that station, but that even if that could not be accomplished, he should count the time of your absence well spent. This was already strong language from Sir Joseph, but it was nothing in comparison of the panegyric he wrote when your papers reached him from the Cape.'

'So the boats survived?'

'One boat. The launch, conducted by a Mr Grant, who delivered your papers to the naval officer commanding.'

'Were they damaged, at all? I was up to my knees when I wrote them.'

'There were water-stains, and there were blood-stains — Mr Grant had trouble with his people — but except for two sheets they were entirely legible. Sir Joseph extracted the main lines for my benefit, together of course with all that was relevant to the situation here. At the same time he sent you this letter,' — handing it to Maturin — 'and desired me to look upon you as an exemplar in deceiving and dividing the enemy. I was, said he, to emulate your proceedings, as far as it was possible in this sphere. Other despatches followed, each with a letter for you: their tone, as I said, changed to anxiety and, as time went on, almost to despair, but they always had the same tenor — you were to return at once, to exploit the confusion caused in the French services to the utmost, and to renew your activities in Catalonia. I have a condensed report for you, on the present situation there.'

Wallis was an old, tried colleague, with no vices but the parsimony, meanness, and cold lechery so usual in intelligence; it was clear that he was acquainted with nearly all the essentials; it was also clear that as Stephen Maturin had very nearly perished on the outward voyage, he might quite well perish entirely homeward-bound. The sea was a treacherous element; a ship but a frail conveyance — *fragilis ratis* — tossed by the billows at their whim, and subject to every wind that blew. It was as well that Wallis should know.

'Listen,' he said, and Wallis leant his best ear forward, his face expressive of the most intense interest and curiosity. 'Now the beginning of it you know, the arrest of Wogan with Admiralty papers in her possession?' Wallis nodded. 'She was an agent of no great importance, but a loyal, well-plucked one, not to be bought; and naturally she did her best to let her chief know how she had left the situation — who was compromised and who was not. It so happened that she had a lover aboard, a compatriot, an ingenuous scholarly young man by the name of Herapath, who had stowed himself away to be with her. She used him to convey her information: I intercepted it, at Recife. That was my first communication. At the beginning of the voyage I had an assistant called Martin, a Channel-Islander brought up in France: he died, and it occurred to me that with his antecedents he made a very convincing secret agent. I therefore fabricated a general statement of the position, purporting to have belonged to him and dealing with our intelligence in Europe, with references to the United States and to a separate document covering the East Indies. I did not possess enough information to make an East Indian report convincing to an expert, so I did not attempt it; but I flatter myself that my analysis of the European situation, and my passing remarks about the United States, would persuade even so sceptical a man as Durand-Ruel. I need scarcely tell you, my dear Wallis, that my paper contained details of double agents, of bribes, of sources of information in the various French ministries and those of their allies — indeed, it was calculated to confound their politics, to put their best men out of action, and to ruin their mutual confidence. This document was found among the dead officer's effects; it aroused suspicion; copies were to be made for the authorities at the Cape, to be sent home. Herapath and I were the only men aboard conversant with French; my time was taken up, and the task therefore fell to Herapath, who had become my assistant. I was convinced that he would tell his mistress and that Wogan's empire over him was such that in spite of his honourable reluctance, of his scruples, a copy would pass to her and that she would send it to America from the Cape. The copy did pass, and she encoded it — I have the key to their code, by the way — but we did not touch at the Cape, since at that time we were being pursued by a Dutch vessel of superior force. I comforted myself with the reflection that she would certainly contrive to send it from Botany Bay, and that the loss of those months, though infinitely regrettable, was not disastrous, since until there was a state of open, declared war between the United States and England, we could not be quite certain that the Americans would pass the information on to their French allies, or at least to their French co-belligerents. Though indeed it was probable, even in peace-time, that the usual good offices would convey the essence if not the entirety, in an informal way. Their Mr Fox sees a great deal of Durand-Ruel. But tell me, has this war been declared?'

'Not by our latest advices. Though I cannot see how it can be long delayed, if Government pursues its present course. We are strangling their trade, as well as abducting and abusing their seamen.'

'An absurd, unnecessary, immoral, blundering course,' said Stephen angrily. 'And apart from all other considerations a war would lead to a deeply stupid dispersal of our force and efforts. Can Government really mean to give that scoundrel Bonaparte a respite, merely to recover a few alleged deserters — who, by definition, are unwilling to serve — and to gratify an old ignoble spite? It is stark staring madness. But I wander. Mrs Wogan was to send the document from Botany Bay: excellent, had she ever reached that settlement. She did not. Our ship struck upon a mountain of ice and very nearly sank: some of the people went away in boats, and to these I entrusted what I could copy of my statement, so that in the event of their reaching the

Cape, Sir Joseph should have some notion of what was afoot, and take his measures accordingly. That was my second communication. At the time I had little doubt that Captain Aubrey would bring us through; but I must say that the delay was a torment to my heart. You may imagine my delight, therefore, when an American whaler put in to the island where we had taken refuge — Desolation Island, a place that I shall not attempt to describe — such birds, such seals, such lichens, Wallis! It was a Paradise to me. An American whaler, homeward-bound for Nantucket. With infinite pains I induced Herapath and Wogan to go aboard this vessel, carrying the report, and to sail away. The wear of spirit, as Herapath wavered between love and honour, you cannot easily conceive, Wallis; nor the extreme difficulty of concealing my manipulation of him from his mistress. And even then, the zeal of my captain very nearly defeated me: this whaler, clearly recognizable on the horizon, appeared early one morning before I was about, and it was only by representing to him that I should certainly hang myself from the mainyard-spritsail-gubbins or something of that sort if he did not desist that I persuaded him to resume our course for New Holland, that interesting continent. When we lost sight of her, the whaler was speeding, all sails abroad, in the general direction of America; and before now, I trust, Louisa Wogan will have presented her poisoned gift with the most perfect, and wholly convincing, conviction of good faith.'

'She has!' cried Wallis. 'She has, and its effects can already be discerned as I am sure you will see from Sir Joseph's letters. He tells me that Cavaignac has been shot; and that following up your hint he has sent tolerably easily detected presents to several members of Desmoulins's bureau by way of Prussia, for favours received; from which he confidently expects a pretty holocaust. Clearly, the good offices have been in operation. Lord, Maturin, what a coup!'

Stephen's eyes glittered. He loved France and the French idea of how life should be lived, but he hated Bonaparte's intelligence service with a consuming hatred: moreover, he had been interrogated by some of its members, and he would carry the marks to his grave. 'It was a happy chance that threw Louisa Wogan in my path,' he said, 'and I have not told you of perhaps the most important event in our intercourse. She was aware that I was a friend to liberty, but it may be that she placed a false interpretation upon the words, for just before she left she desired me, with a significant look, to call upon a friend of hers in London, Mr Pole of the Foreign Office.'

'Charles Pole — the American department?' cried Wallis, changing colour.

Stephen nodded. They exchanged a look, more significant by far than Mrs Wogan's, and Stephen stood up, quite satisfied with the effect of his words. 'May I beg you to give me Sir Joseph's other letters?' he said. 'I could wish to exult for a short while, in the privacy of my cabin.'

'Here they are,' said Wallis, passing the letters after a silent pause. 'Here they are. Your private post will be at the secretary's office. It is in the Residence, the large white house: should you like me to send a boy?'

'You are very good, but I believe I shall walk there myself,' said Stephen. 'I long to see a cassowary.'

'There is every likelihood of your seeing a whole drove, or company, of them at the Admiral's. His Dutch predecessor was a cassowary-fancier, and had them brought from Ceram. It is the large white house with the flag-poles; you cannot miss it. Lord, Maturin, what a coup!'

Stephen did not miss it, but he did miss his cassowaries; they were timid birds, and the sight of a party of seamen returning from the cricket-field had caused them to hurry away on their enormous feet and stand in the shade of the sago-palms. The sailors were nominally in charge of a stunted young gentleman from the *Cumberland*, but the democracy of the game was still upon them, and they called out 'What cheer, *Leopard*?' 'Do you want any paint?' and 'Borrow a couple of muskets off of us, and set up for a man-of-war, ha, ha, ha,' waving their bats and laughing at their own wit with a vehemence that drowned the midshipman's shrill piping, and caused the cassowaries (though tame from the egg) to retreat further into the shade, pursing their beaks.

The cricketers were scarcely out of sight before Stephen met Captain Aubrey, coming down the steps with a parcel under his arm. 'Why, Stephen,' cried he, 'there you are! I was just thinking about you. We are ordered home instanter. They have given me *Acasta*. Here are your letters.'

'What is *Acasta*?' asked Stephen, glancing at the meagre bundle without much interest.

'A forty-gun frigate, pretty well the heaviest in the service, bar *Egyptienne*; and *Endymion* and *Indefatigable*, of course, with their twenty-four-pounders. And the finest sailer of the lot, on a bowline. Two points off the winds, she could give even dear old *Surprise* foretopgallant, at least. A true, copper-bottomed plum, Stephen; I was sure the next would be some dull ship of the line, to and fro for ever off Brest, or polishing Cape Sicié. My time with frigates is pretty well up.'

'What is to happen to the *Leopard*?'

'She is to be a transport, as I have been telling you ever since Port Jackson. And when the Admiral sees the state of her futtocks, I doubt he will transport anything very valuable in her: the ice gave her as cruel a wrench as ever a ship could have and still swim. No, she will end her days as a transport, and God help the man who commands her if it comes on to blow.'

'Do you mean that we are to go home at once?' cried Stephen angrily.

'As soon as *La Flèche* comes in for despatches. Tomorrow or perhaps the next day she comes in, lies under the cape there, backing and filling, not to lose a moment of the monsoon, just long enough for Yorke to pull ashore to pick up the Admiral's *billets doux* and a couple of men that are invaliding and us, and then away, trembling in every limb.'

'A notoriously fragile ship, I find: very well — it is all of a piece.'

'Quivering, I meant to say. The arrow quivering. Do you smoke it?'

'How can you speak with such levity, when with the same breath you tell me that we are to go home without a chance to look at the wealth of the Indies — the flora and fauna passed by in frigid indifference, completely unexamined? The fabled upas-tree itself unseen. Can this be really so?'

'I am afraid it is. But you did have a fine run at 'em on Desolation, you recall — stuffed seals, penguins, albatross's eggs, those birds with curious beaks — *Leopard*'s hold is crammed with them. And you did not do so badly in New Holland neither, with your God-damned wombats and all the rest.'

'Very true, Jack: do not think me ungrateful. And to be sure, I shall be glad to get my collection home as soon as possible; the giant squid is already in an advanced state of decomposition, while the kangaroos grow fractious, for want of a proper diet. But I did long to see a cassowary.'

'I am sorry for it, indeed; but the exigencies of the service . . .' said Jack, who dreaded a fresh influx of Sumatran rhinoceroses, orang-utangs, and infant rocs. 'Stephen, I do not suppose you are much of a hand with bat and ball?'

'Why should you make any such injurious supposition? I had not my equal with the hurly, or bat as you call it, from Malin Head to Skibereen.'

'I only meant that you might be above such things; but I am very glad to hear what you tell me. The Admiral challenges us to a match, and there are precious few Leopards to make up the side.'

The Captain of the *Leopard*, though an early riser, did not find his surgeon at the breakfast-table: nor did he find the officer or midshipman of the watch. This was scarcely odd, since, being deep in his correspondence from home, he had for once invited neither; but Dr Maturin was his invariable companion, and he called out to learn the reason for his absence. 'Killick, there. Where's the Doctor?'

'Which he gone ashore in a bumboat before the crack of dawn,' said Killick with a lewd grin; in Killick's mind there was only one valid reason for going ashore, apart from getting drunk. He would have ventured some facetiousness had the Captain looked his usual pink cheerful morning self rather than grey-yellow and old, as though he had passed a sleepless night.

'Oh well, never mind,' said Jack, in such a tone that Killick glanced at him with real concern: he poured himself a pint mug of coffee, spread his letters on the table, and arranged them as nearly as he could in chronological order — a difficult task, for in spite of all his pleas Sophie rarely remembered to put the date. There were accounts among the letters, and from time to time he added up a sum, whistled, and looked graver still.

Killick sidled in with a dish of kidneys, the Captain's favourite relish, and placed it silently among the papers. 'Thankee, Killick,' said Jack, absently.

The kidneys were still there, as cold as the tropical sun would ever allow them to be, when Dr Maturin came aboard in his usual elegant manner, kicking the port-lids, cursing the kind hands that propelled him up the side, and arriving breathless on deck, as though he had climbed the Monument at a run. He was deeply laden, and his despondent shipmates thought they detected a python in one of the round flat covered baskets.

There were few shipmates to help him or to examine his baggage, however; only the maimed or crippled Leopards could be spared; the rest were busy. The ship's remaining midshipmen were gathered on the larboard gangway, furiously bowling spun-yarn sailcloth-covered balls at Faster Doudle, the *Leopard*'s wicket-keeper, who seized them as accurately as a terrier might seize a rat, and with much the same ferocious concentration, while the whole watch below and all the Marines passed sharply critical remarks. For although the *Leopard* might lack paint and even guns, as well as men, they were determined that she should come off creditably in the match with those sods of the *Cumberland* — they might even wipe the buggers' eye! There were several Kent and Hampshire men among them, nurtured on the green; and Mr Babbington, their first lieutenant, had distinguished himself by notching forty-seven runs against the Marylebone club on Broad Halfpenny Down itself. He was very active among them — the ordinary forenoon tasks had been laid aside — adjuring them 'to pitch it up, pitch it up' and 'for God's sake to keep a length'; and catching sight of Stephen, he cried, 'You have not forgot the match, Doctor?'

'Never in life,' said Stephen, waving a white, new-cut piece of wood. 'I have just cut my hurly from a noble upas-tree.'

He made his way to the carpenter's and thence to the cabin, and he was giving an account of the upas-tree — 'quite exploded, of course — not the least small smell of a corpse in the neighbourhood — but an interesting sight: he conceived it to be cousin to the fig' — when he noticed his friend's face, and broke off. 'I trust you have good news from home, my dear?' he said. 'That Sophie and the children are quite well?'

'Blooming, Stephen, I thank you,' said

Jack. 'That is to say, the mumps ravaged the nursery shortly after we left, and George had the red-gum at Christmas; but they are better now.'

'The mumps: very good. The earlier the better. Had we stayed longer, I should have suggested leading them all into some stricken cottage. I could wish that Government would infect every child, above all every male child, at a very early age. An orchitis that takes an ugly turn is a melancholy spectacle. And Sophie is quite well?'

'She was, by her latest letter — she sends you her love in each, as I should have said before — but it was wrote a great while ago, and how she has been standing the anxiety since then I cannot tell.'

'Had she heard of Grant's bringing the boat safe to the Cape?' Jack nodded. 'She had your letters from Brazil, so she knows that you were dissatisfied with Grant. She knows that he must represent the situation as having been desperate in order to justify himself: reasoning on the basis of these two facts, she will discount his words. She will have a total confidence in your dealing with the situation. She will, if anything, underestimate the peril.'

'You are quite right, Stephen. That is exactly what she has done, and she writes to me as though she had certain knowledge I was alive; and maybe she has, too. Never shows the least doubt of it, in any of these letters, bless her. And I hope to God that by now mine have reached her from Port Jackson. But even if they have, there is still the anxiety of this God-damned fellow Kimber. That is what I was really talking about.'

At these words Stephen's heart sank low. The God-damned fellow Kimber had led Jack Aubrey to believe that there was silver in the dross from the ancient lead-mines on his land; that this dross could be treated by a secret process so that it would yield the residual metals; and that if a certain amount of money were spent on the undertaking, the eventual returns would be enormous. From what little Stephen understood of metallurgy, the thing itself was not physically impossible, but both he and Sophie looked upon Kimber as an impostor, one of the many land-sharks who hung about sailors on shore. Stephen knew that on his element Jack Aubrey was immensely capable, and that in warfare he was as cunning and foresighted as Ulysses, often deceiving, rarely deceived; but he had little opinion of his friend's wisdom or even common sense by land, and he had done his best to warn him against the projector. 'You did tie him up very rigorously, however, as I recall,' he said, looking attentively at Jack's face.

'Yes,' said Jack, avoiding his eyes. 'Yes, I did follow your advice; or some of it. But the fact of the matter, Stephen — the fact of the matter is, that in the hurry of leaving, and of seeing to the horses and the new stables, I signed some papers he brought me after dinner without quite attending as much as I should have done. From the way he is carrying on — new roads, cuttings, drifts, steam-engines, buildings, even some idea of a stock company — you would think one of them was a power of attorney.'

'You did not read them through, I collect?'

'Not quite through, or I should have smoked it, you know. I am not such a flat as all that.'

'Listen, Jack,' said Stephen, 'if you brood upon it now, without all the data or learned advice, you will do no good, and you will make yourself sick. I know your constitution: who better? It is not one that can withstand prolonged, and above all useless, brooding. You must discipline your mind, my dear. For you are to consider, that thanks to this blessed order, you will be home sooner than the swiftest messenger — you are yourself the swiftest messenger — and that therefore it is your present duty to be reasonably gay, or at least to affect the motions of gaiety. You are to indulge in field-sports, such as the game this afternoon, until *La Flèche* comes in. Be not idle; be not alone. I speak in all gravity, brother, as a physician.'

'I am sure you are right, Stephen. Moping and cursing don't answer: I shall spring about on shore until *La Flèche* is on the wing. By rights I ought to sit mewed up with the ship's books, to pass my accounts — muster-book, slop-book, sick-book, gunner's, bosun's, and carpenter's returns, general and quarterly accounts of provisions, order-book, letter-book, and all the rest. But they went overboard: everything but the log and my remarks and a few others, that I took up to the Admiral. So I can play with a clear conscience, at least. Though I tell you what, Stephen, *La Flèche* can't come in too soon for me, though I dearly love a game of cricket. If it had not been that we are already ordered home, I should apply for leave, or invalid, or even throw up the service to be back.' He considered for a while, looking very grim; and then, with an obvious effort at disciplining his mind, he said, 'Is that your bat, Stephen?'

'It is. I have just roughed it out with the carpenter, and am about to work upon the distal extremity with a bone-rasp, to deepen the recess.'

'It is rather like my grandfather's bat at home,' said Jack, taking it in his hand, 'curl-

53

ing out sideways at the end like that. Don't you find it a trifle light, Stephen?'

'I do not. It is the heaviest hurly that ever yet was cut from the deadly upas-tree.'

The match began precisely on the hour, by Admiral Drury's watch: Jack won the toss, and elected to go in. The game was democratic, to be sure; but democracy was not anarchy; certain decencies were to be preserved; and the Captain of the *Leopard*, with his first lieutenant, led the way, while the Admiral opened the proceedings, bowling downhill to Babbington. He took the ball from his chaplain and polished it for a while, fixing the lieutenant with a steely glare; then, taking a skip, he bowled a wicked lob. It pitched well up outside the off stump, and Babbington played back; but as he played, so the ball broke in towards his vitals, and jerking back further still he spooned the ball neatly into the Admiral's hands, to a roar of applause from the assembled Cumberlands.

'How is that?' said the Admiral to the chaplain.

'Very pretty, sir,' said the chaplain. 'That is to say, Out.'

Babbington returned, downcast. 'You want to watch the Admiral,' he said to Captain Moore, of the *Leopard*'s Marines, who succeeded him. 'It was the most devilish twister you ever saw.'

'I shall play safe for the first hour or so, and wear him out,' said Moore.

'You want to dart forwards and catch 'em full-toss, sir,' said Doudle. 'That's the only way to knock him off his length — that's the only way to play them lobs.'

Some Leopards agreed; others felt that it was preferable to bide one's time, to get used to the feel of the wicket, before setting about the bowling; and Captain Moore walked off with a wealth of contradictory advice pursuing him.

Having never watched a cricket-match before, Stephen would have liked to see what course Moore pursued, and what indeed the game consisted of — it obviously differed in many respects from the hurling of his youth. He would also have liked to go on lying on the grass in the shade of the majestic camphor-tree, gazing at the brilliantly-lit expanse of green with the white figures arranged upon it in the pattern of a formal dance or perhaps of a religious ceremony — perhaps of the two combined — a resplendent field surrounded by a ring of figures, some all in white, some with blue jackets, some with brilliant sarongs; for the Cumberlands had already supplanted the Dutch soldiers in the affections of the local fair. But at this moment a messenger appeared with a note: Mr Wallis was truly grieved to importune Dr Maturin, but his confidential clerk had fallen sick; there was a most important despatch to be enciphered before the arrival of *La Flèche*; and if his dear Maturin were at leisure, Mr Wallis would be infinitely grateful for a hand.

'I am not quite at liberty, colleague,' said Stephen, reaching the dirty little office. 'My ship is engaged in a match of cricket, and I am to take my part. However, Captain Moore stated that he should play safe for an hour or so; though for the life of me, I cannot conceive how he can spend . . . Never mind: let you read it out *en clair* and I will cipher. You are using thirty-six with the double shift, I take it?'

Slowly the despatch rolled out; in a dull, toneless, uninterested voice it related the devious proceedings of Mynheer van Buren at the court of the Sultan of Tanjong Puding, the surprising steps that Mr Wallis had taken to counteract them — Stephen had never known that Wallis was quite such a man of blood, nor that he had such enormous sums at his disposal — concluding with an objective statement of the case for and against a British occupation of Java, from the political point of view. 'The ethics they may sort out for themselves,' said Wallis. 'That is not my concern. What do you say to a glass of negus?'

'With all my heart,' said Stephen. 'Thirty-six, with the double shift, is dry work.' But he was fated never to drink his negus.

'Sir, sir,' cried a scarlet young gentleman from the *Leopard* — an absurdly beautiful child called Forshaw who had always been very kind and protective towards Dr Maturin — 'I have found you at last. You are in! Doudle is out — you are in — and we are all at a stand — the Admiral told me to run — I ran to the hospital, and I ran to Madame Titine's — nine wickets down and we have only notched up forty-six — we are in a terrible way, sir, terrible.'

'Calm yourself, Mr Forshaw,' said Stephen. 'It is but a game. Forgive me, Wallis; this is the engagement of which I spoke.'

'How grown men can think of playing bat and ball in this weather,' said Wallis to the closing door, as he drank Stephen's negus, 'I cannot tell.'

'Oh pray, sir, come on,' cried Forshaw over his shoulder. 'The Admiral is skipping up and down: and we are in a dreadful way. Mind the branch, sir. Nine wickets down, and only forty-six. Mr Byron got a duck, and so did old Holles.'

'How came you to think I should be at Madame Titine's, Mr Forshaw?' asked Stephen. 'And you are never to go there yourself, either.'

'Oh pray do come on, sir,' cried the child again, dodging behind Stephen to urge him to a run. 'Let me carry your bat. We absolutely depend on you. You are our only hope.'

'Well, I shall do my best, sure,' said Stephen. 'Tell me, Mr Forshaw, the aim is to beat down the opposing wicket, is it not?'

'Of course it is, sir. Oh pray come on. All you have to do is to keep your end up and let the Captain do the rest. He's still in, and there's still hope, if only you will keep your end up.'

They emerged from the tropical vegetation, greeted by a general cheer. Stephen advanced, carrying his hurly: he was feeling particularly well and fit; he had his land-legs again, and no longer stumped along, but walked with an elastic step. Jack came to meet him, and said in a low voice, 'Just keep your end up, Stephen, until your eye is in; and watch out for the Admiral's twisters,' and then, as they neared the Admiral, 'Sir, allow me to name my particular friend Dr Maturin, surgeon of the *Leopard*.'

'How d'ye do, Doctor?' said the Admiral.

'I must beg your pardon, sir, for my late appearance: I was called away on —'

'No ceremony, Doctor, I beg,' said the Admiral, smiling: the *Leopard*'s hundred pounds were practically in his pocket, and this man of theirs did not look very dangerous. 'Shall we begin?'

'By all means,' said Stephen.

'You go down to the other end,' murmured Jack, a chill coming over him in spite of the torrid sun.

'Should you like to be given a middle, sir?' called the umpire, when Stephen had walked down the pitch.

'Thank you, sir,' said Stephen, hitching at his waistband and gazing round the field, 'I already have one.'

A rapacious grin ran round the Cumberlands: they moved much closer in, crouching, their huge crab-like hands spread wide. The Admiral held the ball to his nose for a long moment, fixing his adversary, and then delivered a lob that hummed as it flew. Stephen watched its course, danced out to take it as it touched the ground, checked its bounce, dribbled the ball towards the astonished cover-point and running still he scooped it into the hollow of his hurly, raced on with twinkling steps to mid-off, there checked his run amidst the stark silent amazement, flicked the ball into his hand, tossed it high, and with a screech drove it straight at Jack's wicket, shattering the near stump and sending its upper half in a long, graceful trajectory that reached the ground just as the first of *La Flèche*'s guns, saluting the flag, echoed across the field.

CHAPTER TWO

'The boat ahoy?' roared the *Leopard*'s Marine sentry, meaning 'What boat is that? Whom does it convey?'

The question was unnecessary, since *La Flèche* lay not a cable's length to windward, and all the Leopards with time to look over the side had seen her captain get into his gig in reply to the Admiral's signal, pull ashore in splendour, return an hour later with an official package, certainly despatches, go aboard on the larboard side of his ship, silently reappear with a parcel of quite a different shape, and pull straight for the *Leopard*. A question unnecessary for information, but nevertheless of great importance, since nothing but the coxswain's answering roar of '*La Flèche*' could set the proper ceremony in train.

The performers were pitifully shabby, the ship herself devoid of paint, but the rite was carried out in every detail, side-boys as brown as Malays and almost as bare darting down to offer the man-ropes with hands ludicrously gleaming in white gloves, run up by the sailmaker, the bosun's call wailing as he and

61

his mates piped the side, the rugged Marines presenting their bright arms as Captain Yorke set foot aboard and saluted the quarterdeck. Byron, the officer of the watch and therefore as respectable as his means would allow, received him, and a moment later Jack Aubrey, having had time to clear the cabin of wombats and to put on a pair of whole trousers, emerged from his cabin. 'Yorke!' he cried. 'Welcome aboard. I am delighted to see you.'

They shook hands, and Jack introduced his officers, Babbington, Moore, and Byron, and those of his midshipmen who were at hand, while all the time Captain Yorke studiously avoided seeing the *Leopard*'s squalor, and then led him aft. As soon as the cabin door closed behind them Yorke said, 'I have a letter for you, Aubrey,' — pulling it from his pocket — 'I took the liberty of waiting on Mrs Aubrey on my way down to Portsmouth, thinking that just in case the *Leopard* had — that is to say, had reached the East Indies, you might like news of her.'

'What a good fellow you are, Yorke, upon my soul,' cried Jack, growing suddenly red with delight. He took the letter and stared at it with his bright blue eye. 'You could not have given me greater pleasure, short of bringing her out to me yourself. Amazingly good-natured in you: I take it very, very kindly.

How was she? How did you find her? How did she seem to be going along?'

'Most uncommonly well, I do assure you. Overflowing spirits; came downstairs singing; I have never seen her look so well. She had a bran-new baby in her arms, and kept laughing at it for being so perfectly toothless and bald.'

'Oh,' said Jack.

'A new nephew or niece of yours; I forget quite which. I had put on a pretty solemn face, I can tell you, what with that ugly tale of the boats, and with *Leopard* being so damnably overdue; so I was taken aback to find her brimming over with spirits — even more so when she laughed and said she would be obliged to me if I would bring you out some warm stockings. Indeed, I was so put about, that I could hardly follow her explanation; but it seems she had had a letter from America to say that all was well. I forget the details, though she showed me the letter — she had it in her bosom. Not that she had needed it, she said; she had always known perfectly well you were safe. But she was infinitely obliged to the sender, and the moment she received it she had set to work on a new set of active-service linen and some more stockings: she had not needed the letter, however.'

'It must have been the American brig that put into Desolation Island, when we were trying to put ourselves to rights,' said Jack, laughing for joy. 'Honest, good-hearted fellows; though you would not think so to look at them. Ha, ha, ha! Bless 'em. There is good in everybody, Yorke, even an American.'

'Certainly there is,' said Yorke. 'I have half a dozen in *La Flèche* at this moment, and prime seamen they are, every man-jack of them. I pressed them out of a Salem barque, a little south of Madeira. They cut up rough at the time, but they soon made the best of it. Capital fellows.'

'You did not see the children, I suppose?' said Jack.

'No. But I heard them. They were singing the Old Hundredth.'

'Bless 'em,' said Jack again, and he cocked his head. 'That must be my surgeon coming aboard. You will like him; a reading man too, most amazing learned; a full-blown physician into the bargain, and my particular friend. But I must tell you this, Yorke; he is wealthy —' In point of fact Captain Aubrey had little idea of his surgeon's fortune, apart from knowing that he owned a good deal of hilly land in Catalonia with a tumbledown castle on it. But Stephen had done pretty well out of the Mauritius campaign; his manner of living was Spartan — one suit of clothes every five years and perhaps a couple of shirts — and apart from books he had no visible expenses at all. Jack was no Macchiavel, but he did know that to the rich it should be given; that capital possessed a mystical significance; that even the most perfectly disinterested respected it and its owner; and that although a naval surgeon was ordinarily a person of no great consequence, the same man moved into quite a different category the moment he was endowed with comfortable private means. In short, that whereas an ordinary surgeon, living on his pay, might not readily be indulged in room for exotic livestock, an imperfectly-preserved giant squid, and several tons of natural specimens, in a stranger's ship, a wealthy natural philosopher might meet with more consideration; and Jack knew how Stephen prized the collection he had made during their arduous voyage. '— he is wealthy, and he only comes with me because of the opportunities for natural philosophy; though he is a first-rate surgeon too, and we are very lucky to have him. But this voyage the opportunities have been prodigious, and he has turned the *Leopard* into a down-right Ark. Most of the Desolation creatures are stuffed or pickled but there are some from New Holland that skip and bound about: I hope you are not too crowded in *La Flèche*?'

'Not at all,' said Yorke. 'We brought out a

quantity of soldiers and their stores for Ceylon, and now there is plenty of room. Plenty, that is to say, for a twenty-gun post-ship.'

'So that is a twenty-gun post-ship,' said Stephen Maturin to Babbington, as they stood by the rail, looking out over the sea at *La Flèche*: she was unusually beautiful in her pure lines, unbroken by quarterdeck or forecastle — a flush-decked ship — and her strongly-raked masts gave her a dashing air. She had recently been repainted with a blue streak, slightly darker than the perfect sea, up to her ports, then a band of white with the black port-lids dividing it, and then a lighter blue, while discreet gold twinkled with the ripple at her head and stern. She had been titivated off to the nines for the Admiral's inspection, scrubbed by the lifts and braces, sails furled in a body with never a wrinkle; and as she lay there, framed by the wooded Kampong headland a mile or so beyond her starboard bow and a low sandy island with a few palm-trees far on her quarter, she might have been something without weight or earthly substance, ideal, self-existing, belonging to another dimension. 'Ten port-holes I see on this side,' he went on, 'and no doubt there are ten more on the other, which makes the same number of guns as she is alleged to carry, for once. But as for the post, I cannot make it out at all, unless it is that odd slender pole at the back.'

'No, sir,' said Babbington. 'That is the en-sign-staff, I believe. We all have them, you know. No: they call her a post-ship because she is commanded by a post-captain — I mean she is a sixth-rate, the smallest ship a man can be posted into, you follow me?'

'Imperfectly. She has a curious touching beauty of her own, however. But tell me, Mr Babbington, is she not very small?'

'Why, I should imagine she would gauge about four hundred and fifty ton to our thou-sand or so. I dare say you are thinking about your collection, sir?'

'I am, too. Yet perhaps there are not many people in her — perhaps room can be found. The sea-elephants can be unstuffed and folded up.'

'Her complement would be a hundred and fifty-five, including the boys. And then of course there are all of us, the passengers.'

'Oh dear, oh dear,' said Stephen in a low voice, and he was about to suggest that the *Leopard*'s midshipmen would be far better off running about in the sun and fresh air of the East Indies than moping themselves into a phthisis in an overcrowded berth when Babbington left him at a run. Captain Yorke was leaving the ship, the usual compliments attending him: stepping into his gig he called up. 'At the turn of the tide, then? She should cast pretty, at the turn of the tide; and I should not like to lose a moment of this monsoon.'

'At the turn of the tide,' answered Jack, looking at his watch. And then turning to Stephen he said, 'Captain Yorke is very handsomely clearing his whole forepeak for you, and all your dunnage must be aboard within the hour. Mr Babbington will give you a party to rouse it out, and you must supervise its stowage. *La Flèche*'s boats will be alongside as soon as I am relieved. There is not a moment to be lost.'

Stephen was used to the shocking abruptness, the inhuman promptitude of naval decisions — the cry of 'Lose not a minute' had echoed in his ears from his first day in the service — but never had he been expected to be required to transfer the fruit of so many months of patient toil from one ship to another in fifty-three minutes. The minerals alone weighed several tons. His mouth opened in protest but he knew that there was no hope, closed it again, and stared distractedly around.

'This way, sir,' said Mr Forshaw in his clear treble pipe, leading him to the fore hatchway. 'I know just where the sea-elephants are stowed. Mind the step, sir, and clap on with both hands.' Mr Forshaw often protected Dr Maturin, whom he regarded as a worthy man, but quite unfit to be let out alone. Yet in spite of the young gentleman's protection, and that of the first lieutenant, and the willingness of the party, and the kindness of a great many other Leopards, who lent a hand as soon as their own messmates' property was shifted — no great task, since they carried almost all of it on their backs, and the rest would scarcely fill a ditty-bag, while a single sea-chest was enough for two officers — in spite of all this, the Doctor spent a most hellish afternoon, hot, hurried, stifling, and above all extremely anxious. He never even noticed the arrival of the Admiral's nominee, who took over command when the ship abruptly turned into a sloop, being now in charge of a lieutenant. Cheerful hands whipped the never-ending giant squid to the topmast yardarm, burst into ribald laughter, words and gestures at the appearance of the male, the very male, sea-elephant, tossed jars of animals in spirits from hand to hand — irreplaceable specimens of incredible rarity. And aboard *La Flèche* it was worse, far worse. Here the people did not know him; here the first lieutenant, instead of being a young man Stephen had known since Babbington's precocious puberty, a steady friend, was a grey, severe disciplinarian who took it very ill that the squid should leave a long greenish-yellow trail on his topsail, his main-course, and the attendant rigging, and that a wombat should have forgotten itself on the quarterdeck; and here what he had always feared would happen did in fact take place — in the darkness of the forepeak the seamen got at the double-rectified spirits of wine in which his specimens were preserved, and presently their mirth increased extremely, while at the same time their dexterity diminished. At one point Forshaw plucked him by the sleeve and told him to come and say goodbye — they were off, they were homeward bound. He scrambled up from the gloom to the brilliant sunshine, and there, broad on the starboard beam, lay the poor battered old ship that had so very nearly been their coffin. She was already further off, and as *La Flèche* sheeted home her topsails the remaining Leopards uttered a thin cheer. 'Huzzay, huzzay, and give them our love on Portsmouth Hard.' Stephen waved his wig — his hat had long been lost from sight — and watched her as the turn swept her aft and far astern; then he plunged below. It was worse than ever; the smell was like Gin Row, mingled with something of Billingsgate (many of the specimens being fish); the voices were louder; the fooling more evident. Two ship's boys were openly playing tug-of-war with a sealskin. By a violent exercise of authority, together with a few hearty kicks and blows, Stephen rescued the skin and a basket of albatross eggs that was within an ace of being trampled underfoot as *La Flèche*, under topgallants now, heeled to the monsoon. Yet no sooner had he preserved one basket, one penguin, one blue-eyed shag but another was in danger, either from mere levity or from mistaken blundering goodwill; and now the ship was out of the sheltered anchorage — now she was taking the swell on her larboard bow, so that the forepeak and all within it was in a state of perpetual motion. In his anguish Stephen did not hear the tall master's mate say, 'The Captain's compliments, sir, and he begs the favour of your company at dinner.

'Silence, fore and aft,' roared the young man, and in the pause he repeated the invitation, adding, 'That will be in three and twenty minutes, sir.'

'I cannot conceivably leave my collections tossing to and fro; they cannot possibly be secured before nightfall. Pray tell the Captain, with my compliments, that I shall be glad to wait upon him at any other time. Honoured. Happy. You, sir!' — projecting his voice into the darkest corner — 'Put it down this minute.'

Five minutes later the grey lieutenant appeared. When he could command Dr Maturin's attention he said, 'There must be some mistake, sir. The Captain invites you to dinner. It is the *Captain* who invites you to dinner.' He had changed his fine coat for a round working jacket, and in the gloom Stephen did not recognize him. 'My dear sir,' he said. 'You see the state of affairs in this Bedlam, this Purgatory. Surely you must perceive that it is impossible for me to abandon even what is already here, let alone all that is still upstairs. First things must come first.'

Mr Warner remonstrated, spoke of 'an appearance of disrespect — unintentional, he was sure', and referred to 'natural curiosities' in an unfortunate manner. The tone rose, until Stephen, having himself cracked one of his very few whale-bird's eggs, turned on him and said, 'You are importunate, sir. You are indiscreet. You oppress me with your civilities. I beg you will go about your affairs, and leave me to mine.'

'Very good, sir. Very good, Mr —,' said the first lieutenant, swelling and at the same time growing even more rigid. 'Your blood be upon your own head.'

'What blood, now, I wonder?' muttered Stephen, returning to his fragile crates. 'Double, double, toil and trouble. Oh, you infernal set of maniacs — brute-beasts.'

The next to interrupt his anxious busyness, his inefficient attempts at tying down cases, baskets, chests with string, and at controlling his helpers, was Captain Aubrey himself. Jack did not address him first, however: to the oldest seaman there he said, 'What is your name?'

'Jaggers, your honour, carpenter's crew, starboard watch.'

'Very well, Jaggers: jump up to the main-deck with your mates. Tell my coxswain and steward I want them here at once.'

'Aye aye, sir.'

The sailors vanished silently upwards, like bulky, inebriated mice, not a hoot nor a halloo until they were well out of sight.

'Stephen,' said Jack, quickly tricing a wandering basket to a stanchion, 'you are in a sad way, I see.'

'So I am too,' cried Stephen, 'with these bestial Goths, these drunken Huns all about me — I could weep from mere vexation — so much to be preserved, so much already lost — would you have another piece of string in your pocket, at all? — and there was a prating fellow that would insist on my dining with the captain of this vile machine. I sent him about his business; told him to go trim his sails.'

The vile machine took a lee-lurch and the

female sea-elephant slid to starboard. Jack waited for the weather-roll, heaved it back, passed a line round its middle, made all fast, and said, 'Yes: that was Warner, their first lieutenant. Stephen, there is something about the Navy I should have told you before. A captain's invitation cannot be refused.'

'Why not, for all love? Oh, for a decent ball of string.'

'The immemorial custom of the service requires that it should be accepted. It is as who should say a royal command; and a refusal is near as a toucher mutiny.'

'What stuff, Jack. In its very nature an invitation implies an option, the possibility of refusal. You can no more compel a man to be your guest in the sense, the only valid sense, of a willing commensal, a glad partaker of your fare, than you can oblige a woman to love you. A prisoner is not a guest; a raped wench is not a wife; an invitation is not an ukase.'

Jack abandoned the immemorial custom of the service, though it had answered well before: there was only four minutes to go. 'Hold fast,' he called up the scuttle, and in a low voice he said, 'I should take it as a particular favour if you were to come. Yorke has asked you out of kindness to me. It would be a most unfortunate beginning to the voyage if there were any appearance of slighting him, unfortunate for me and all our shipmates.'

'But, Jack,' cried Stephen, waving hopelessly at his tumbled collections, most in uneasy movement, all threatening decisive motion, 'how can I leave all this?'

'Bonden and Killick will be below directly, both sober and both carrying any amount of cordage. And all the other Leopards will give you a hand as soon as dinner is over. Pray be a good fellow for once, Stephen.'

'Well,' — with an unwilling look at all he was leaving — 'I will come so. But mark you, brother, it is only in compliment to you. I do not give a fig for your immemorial tyranny and oppression, nor for his Czarish Majesty back there.'

'Bonden, Killick,' called Jack.

They instantly dropped through the scuttle, Killick carrying what remnants of uniform Dr Maturin still possessed, a clean shirt and a comb, for he knew perfectly well what was afoot. *Leopard*'s surgeon, mad with drink, had refused the Captain's invitation. It was confidently expected that Mr Warner would have him brought aft in irons, that his jaws would be prised open with a handspike and his dinner poured down his throat, whether or no; that he should be placed under close arrest, forbidden to move from his cabin for the remainder of the voyage and court-martialled the moment *La Flèche* reached Pompey. It was with a certain feeling of disappointment, of anticlimax, therefore, that they saw him pass at a shambling run, square-ribbed and fairly trim, in his own captain's wake, at one minute to the hour.

'You will be civil?' Jack whispered in his ear at the cabin door.

Stephen's noncommittal sniff gave him no comfort, but immediately afterwards, he was relieved to see Stephen's courtly leg and bow, to hear his urbane 'Your servant, sir'. Stephen was, after all, a man of high breeding, though wonderfully ignorant of seafaring ways: once, when he was attending a levee, Jack had seen him walking about, perfectly at home, familiarly known and indeed caressed by a surprising number of people, some of them very grand.

Ignorant though he was of naval customs, Stephen did at least know that guests under the rank of captain were not expected to speak to the commander of the ship until they were spoken to; it was an extension of the court etiquette. He sat mute, therefore, looking amiable, while they drank a pint of sherry and ate up their fresh turtle soup: he looked round the cabin, the only book-lined cabin he had ever seen — row after row of books, and low down, built in among the quartos, the sheet-music, and the incongruous nine-pounder gun, a small square piano: Jack had said that Captain Yorke was a musician: and evidently he was a reader too — no man carried books to sea for show. He could make out some of the nearer titles: Woodes Rogers, Shelvocke, Anson, the immense *Histoire Générale des Voyages*, Churchill, Harris, Bougainville, Cook, all natural enough in a sailor; then Gibbon, Johnson, and stretching away and away the Kehl edition of Voltaire. Above Voltaire an even greater number of small octavos and duodecimos whose labels he could not distinguish: novels, in all likelihood. He looked at their owner with greater interest. A dark man, rather plump, with a clever face; about Jack's age; by no means so obviously a sailor. He looked capable, but Stephen had the impression that he loved his ease.

'We were very nearly late,' said Jack. 'I absolutely burst a stocking, pulling it on, the yarn completely rotted — those that you brought out could not have come at a better moment — and the Doctor was having a devil of a time stowing his philosophical creatures and their eggs.'

'*J'ai failli attendre*, as Lewis XIV put it,' said Yorke with a smile. 'How deeply shocking. I

77

dare say you have noticed, Dr Maturin, that sea-captains assume a kind of regal state; it may at times seem rather comic. But I am sorry to hear that your creatures were giving difficulty; and even sorrier when I reflect that perhaps my invitation was ill-timed. Can my people be of any use? Our Jemmy Ducks was a sow-gelder on shore, and he is a great hand with both bird and beast.'

'You are very good, sir, but my living specimens are perfectly well behaved; they are sitting in my cabin in rows, staring at one another. No, it is the inanimate objects that caused me some anxiety, as they tossed about.'

'But that is all in hand now,' said Jack. 'My coxswain is in the forepeak, seeing to the stowage; it will be perfectly safe now. And most fortunately the Doctor did not trust all his eggs in one basket, ha, ha, ha! Oh no, there are dozens of 'em, each with a different kind — albatrosses', petrels', penguins' . . .' Captain Aubrey could not finish: his mirth choked him. 'All his eggs in one basket' was not perhaps the very highest point of wit; but it was pretty lofty for him, and it was his own; and he drew so much honest merriment from it that his face, already mahogany-red from the sun and the wind, turned purple. His eyes vanished, and he laughed his deep, intensely amused laugh until the glasses rattled. Yorke watched him affectionately, and Stephen, noticing this, warmed to the Captain of *La Flèche*.

'You have not changed much since the old *Reso*, Aubrey,' said Yorke at last. 'I hope you still play your fiddle?'

'Yes, I do,' said Jack, wiping his eyes. 'All in one basket, ha, ha, ha! Lord, I must remember to tell Sophie that, when I write. Yes, I do: and I see you have risen to a pianoforte. How do you keep it in tune?'

'I don't,' said Yorke. 'I have a key, and I make my attempts; but it is a sad jingling little box, after all. How I wish I could press a piano-tuner. Yet I could not do without it; I could not do without some sort of music, all these months at sea.'

'I am entirely to your way of thinking. The Doctor and I scrape away, although his 'cello and my fiddle have suffered cruelly — glue and varnish almost gone, and our bows obliged to be replenished from the longest pigtails the crew could provide.'

'You play the 'cello, sir?' Stephen bowed. 'I am delighted to hear it, and I very much hope we may have some music together. I am sick of the sound of my own voice; and a captain, you know, hears little other.'

The dinner wound its comfortable course

— Captain Yorke had a far better cook than most — and while the sailors sat with their port Stephen wandered among the books.

'Where do you stow them all when you clear for action?' asked Jack, following him with his eye.

'They are in interlocking boxes, you see,' said Yorke. 'It is my own invention! You only have to turn the toggle behind Richardson, and they are all free. The bar in front of each keeps the books from falling out, and the boxes can be struck down into the hold in a moment. Well, in a couple of moments. Though to tell you the truth, I do not make a clean sweep fore and aft quite as often as I ought. Certainly not as often as my first lieutenant would like. If he had his way, we should be as bare as a barn every time the drum beat for quarters — not a cabin, not a bulkhead standing — everything in fighting-trim.'

'Is he a great fire-eater, then?'

'Oh, he longs for action, of course. He would give an arm and a leg to be made, like all of us before we reached post rank, and an action is his only chance. He had no interest at all, poor man, and the years are going by.'

'You spoke of Richardson, sir,' said Stephen, who had taken down the first volume of the *Histoire Générale* and who was looking at the Abbé Prévost's round, cheerful face. 'Some months ago I learnt that the Abbé Prévost translated him into French. I was astonished. It was a lady who told me this,' he added, nodding to Jack.

'I am astonished too,' said Yorke. 'I should never have thought he could find the time, with his own splendid works and all those voyages too; Richardson is thousands and thousands of pages long — a *travail de Bénédictin*. Yet if I remember right, Prévost actually *was* a Benedictine, though perhaps somewhat irregular at times; but in any case, who more suitable than the author of *Manon Lescaut* for *Clarissa Harlowe*? Such penetration, such awareness of the mind that is not aware of itself. You have read Richardson, sir, I make no doubt?'

'I have not, sir. The lady of whom I spoke urged me to do so, and I did indeed look into the first volume of *Pamela*; but the ship was sinking, the Captain in a state of wild alarm, continually turning to me for advice; and it did not seem to me that the time was quite propitious for such an enterprise.'

'Certainly Richardson calls for a long period of calm; he is not lightly to be embarked upon. But now you have it, my dear sir! Months of calm before you — I touch upon wood: *absit omen* — months of mental calm, with only your few Leopards to look after, since for ourselves we have an excellent surgeon in young Mr McLean. Let me entreat you to launch into *Pamela* again, and then *Clarissa. Grandison* I cannot quite so heartily recommend. But I believe that even Dr Maturin's understanding of human nature might be increased by the first two. Pray take the first volume of *Pamela* with you now — it is just above your head — and come back for the others when it is done.'

'I never was a great reader,' said Jack. His friends looked down at their wine and smiled. 'I mean I never could get along with your novels and tales. Admiral Burney — Captain Burney then — lent me one wrote by his sister when we were coming back with a slow convoy from the West Indies; but I could not get through with it — sad stuff, I thought. Though I dare say the fault was in me, just as some people cannot relish music; for Burney thought the world of it, and he was as fine a seaman as any in the service. He sailed with Cook, and you cannot say fairer than that.'

'That is the best qualification for a literary critic I ever heard of,' said Yorke. 'What was the name of the book?'

'There you have me,' said Jack. 'But it was a small book, in three volumes, I think; and it was all about love. Every novel I have ever looked into is all about love; and I have looked into a good many, because Sophie loves them, and I read aloud to her while she knits, in the evening. All about love.'

'Of course they are,' said Yorke. 'What else raises your blood, your spirits, your whole being, to the highest pitch, so that life is triumphant, or tragic, as the case may be, and so that every day is worth a year of common life? When you sit trembling for a letter? When the whole of life is filled with meaning, double-shotted? To be sure, when you actually come to what some have called the right true end, you may find the position ridiculous, and the pleasure momentary; but novels, upon the whole, are concerned with getting there. And for that matter, what else makes the world go round?'

'Why, as to that,' said Jack, 'I have nothing against the world's going round: indeed, I am rather in favour of it. But as for raising your spirits to the highest pitch, what do you say about hunting, or playing for high stakes? What do you say about war, about going into action?'

'Come, Aubrey, you must have observed that love is a kind of war; you must have seen the analogy. As for hunting and deep play, what is more obvious? You pursue in love, and if the game is worth engaging in at all, you play for very high stakes indeed. Do you not agree, Doctor?'

'Sure, you are in the right of it. *Intermissa, Venus diu, rursus bella moves.* And yet perhaps full war, martial war, may wind even more emotions to the breaking-point — the social emotions of comradeship, extreme joint endeavour, even patriotism and selfless devotion may be involved; and glory rather than a humid bed may be the aim. The stakes are perhaps higher still, since physical annihilation accompanies defeat. But how is this to be encompassed in a book? In a venereal engagement between a man and a woman the events occur in turn, in a sequence of time; each can be described as it arises. Whereas in a martial contest so many things happen at once, that even the ablest hand must despair of drawing the appearance of a serial thread from the confusion. For example, I have never yet heard two accounts of the battle of Trafalgar that consist with one another in their details.'

'You was at Trafalgar, Yorke,' said Jack, who knew that if Stephen were not brought up with a round turn he might go on for hours and hours. 'Pray tell us how it was.' He turned to Stephen, adding, 'Captain Yorke was second of *Orion*, you know, a line-of-battle ship.'

'Well, as you know,' said Yorke, 'I was in

84

charge of the slaughter-house guns, so I did not see a great deal once the fun began, and I dare say my account will conflict with all those Dr Maturin has heard hitherto. But up until then I had a wonderful view, because we held our fire longer than any ship in the fleet, and Captain Codrington called us up to see it all. *Orion* was in the rear of the windward division: we lay ninth, with *Agamemnon* ahead and *Minotaur* astern, and as we bore down I could see the whole of Collingwood's division and the enemy's line clear from the *Bucentaure* down to the *San Juan de Nepomuceno*. They lay thus,' — placing a series of biscuit-crumbs — 'and these are their frigates . . . No, I will fetch a box of tooth-picks, and cut them in half for the frigates.'

Two weevils crept from the crumbs. 'You see those weevils, Stephen?' said Jack solemnly.

'I do.'

'Which would you choose?'

'There is not a scrap of difference. *Arcades ambo*. They are the same species of curculio, and there is nothing to choose between them.'

'But suppose you had to choose?'

'Then I should choose the right-hand weevil; it has a perceptible advantage in both length and breadth.'

'There I have you,' cried Jack. 'You are bit

— you are completely dished. Don't you know that in the Navy you must always choose the lesser of two weevils? Oh ha, ha, ha, ha!'

'I like your friend,' said Stephen, rejoining Captain Aubrey after a hurried visit to the forepeak, where he found all the Leopards sitting companionably among the perfect order of the collections.

'I was sure you would. There is not a better-hearted fellow in the service than Charles Yorke. Do you know, he called on Sophie on his way down to the ship, although it was out of his way and he was in a hell-fire hurry, posting down with despatches, merely to bring me news of her in case we had survived — a damned unlikely chance. But she knew we had! Don't that amaze you, Stephen?'

'It does. Yet from your overflowing spirits, your inordinate amusement at a couple of wretched clenches, and your general boisterous conduct, I was aware that something had pleased you. Will you tell me how she knew?'

Jack hesitated for a moment. 'Diana told her,' he said in a strange, awkward tone, entirely at variance with what had gone before.

'Diana Villiers?'

'Yes. I hope I have not wounded you, Stephen? I thought it better to be frank.'

'Never in life, my dear. I am exceedingly happy to hear it; and to hear of her. Will you tell me more, now?'

'Well, it seems that the Mrs Wogan who gave us the slip with Herapath on Desolation was acquainted with Diana, and that on getting back to the States she told her all about her adventures and about us — about the ice-mountain, the boats going off, the reaching Desolation, the coming of the whaler, the then state of the ship and so on. And Diana smoking what the state of affairs must be at home with us so long overdue, sat down without losing a moment and dashed off a letter to Sophie, telling her that all was well. I take it very handsomely in her, after all that has passed. So does Sophie: swears she will never again say an unkind word — however, that is to say, she takes it very kindly too. I have her account here,' he said, tapping his pocket. 'Only a quick scrawl, wrote while Yorke was waiting, but full of love and joy. And she sends both to you, Stephen — longs to see you safe at home.'

'Sweetheart,' wrote Jack in his daily letter, a letter that now amounted to a moderate book, since, unless his ship were either sinking or in action, he could not go to sleep without adding to it, and since he had not been able to

87

send any part of it away since the remote days of Port Jackson — a letter that was quite pointless now that in the natural course of events he would be his own postman. 'Sweetheart, I had your dear letter this morning, brought me, together with the very welcome stockings, by that fine good-natured fellow Yorke. I have never been so pleased in all my life, as in knowing that you and the children are well and that you are not fretting your heart out after that unhappy business with the boats and the rumours that must have gone about when Grant brought the launch to the Cape. It was very kind, very handsome and considerate in Diana to write so quick. I had misjudged her: she has a good heart, and I shall always value her for it. I told Stephen straight out, and he said he should have expected it of her — she was a gentlemanlike creature, he said, with no pitiful spite or rancour about her. For his part he is in fine spirits, and better than I have seen him for years: he had a splendid run ashore, for a man of his tastes, on Desolation and then again at Botany Bay and some other parts of New Holland where we touched, and he filled the *Leopard* with some very curious animals indeed. But *Leopard* is mine no more. The survey proved she could not carry anything above a few nine- or six-pounders without she was rebuilt, so she is to be a transport; and since they have given me *Acasta* I am coming home as fast as *La Flèche* can fly, with Stephen, Babbington, Byron, my remaining mids, and Bonden and Killick. You would laugh to see Killick looking after Stephen, as he has been doing ever since Stephen's servant — a half-wit — went away in the boats. Stephen is very unwilling to be looked after, but Killick has taken it into his head that it is his duty, and sews on buttons, washes and darns his two and a half shirts, irons his neck-cloth, brushes his only decent coat, and makes him shave at least once a week by steady nagging in that grating voice of his, in spite of any amount of abuse — it is like an old angular mother-hen with a fractious chick. He turned him out quite presentably for dinner with Yorke today, and he is working on what he thinks is the proper kind of wig for a doctor to wear, making it out of spun-yarn crimped at the galley fire: perhaps it will be an improvement on the horrible old scratch-bob that has survived so many storms and broken eggs and dank mossy plants. Yorke gave us a capital dinner, with roast buffalo, a pair of ducks, a ragoo, and a roly-poly pudding; and he and Stephen got along famously, as I hoped they should. People may say that Yorke is no great seaman, but he is a very good fellow, and he drank his two bottles without turning a hair; and in any case he has an excellent premier, a man by the name of Warner, who drives the ship at a tremendous pace — almost as fast as I could wish to see her eat up the fifteen thousand miles between us. They will be two hundred and fifty less at noon tomorrow, believe, for now we have sunk the land we have the full monsoon, and Warner is on deck at all hours, in jib, out jib, wetting the royals and top-gallants as though we were in chase of a golden fortune, and leading the foremast jacks a pretty dance of it. *La Flèche* was always a good sailer, like so many of your French flush-deck corvettes, but Warner gets more out of her than I should have thought possible: he may have persuaded Yorke to give her foremast a trifle more rake than is quite right, but he is a fine seaman, and at the moment we are making eleven knots one fathom. It is a pity that he and Stephen should have contrived to fall foul of one another, but so it is: there was some disagreement before dinner, and then a kind of hairy thing between a bear and an ape behaved unsuitably on the quarterdeck. And then there is a rule here that no smoking is allowed anywhere but in the galley, and Warner pointed it out: it is a good rule, but perhaps he might have put it more tactfully. Still, we have thousands of miles of sweet sailing before us (I hope), and being homeward bound, with everybody in a good humour, no doubt they will come to love one another before we reach soundings. I was amazingly witty at dinner, for your letter was as good as wine to me, and there was wine as well.' There followed a description of the wit, and Jack went on, 'As for that damned fellow Kimber, sweetheart, never let your mind be tormented: if the worst comes to the worst, and if he ruins us, the girls' portions are safe, and I always have my pay. The moment I am home I shall call him to a pretty sharp account, I promise you; until then I intend not to vex my spirits but to indulge in idleness, high living, sweet sailing, and music. And perhaps I shall attend to my youngsters more than I have been able to do up to the present: in the nature of things they have necessarily come to some notion of practical seamanship by now, but their notions of navigation are very strange. Young Forshaw is a good boy — far prettier even than his sisters, though no doubt adolescence will soon cope with that — but sometimes I doubt he knows the odds between east longitude and west, which would be a disadvantage to a mariner, particularly to a mariner in hurrying round the world to his wife. And so good night, my dearest soul.'

In another part of the ship Stephen Maturin, having no one to confide in, wrote to himself, to the Stephen Maturin of some future period, who alone could read this private, encoded diary: 'So Diana wrote. A generous, handsome motion on her part should not surprise me, since it is perfectly in character; meanness was never among her faults. Yet I am absurdly pleased. Herapath said of his Louisa Wogan that even when she was lying with other men she still remained his friend; and either he or I observed that deep friendship as men understand it is rare in women of the common sort. On a smaller scale Wogan resembled Diana in many ways: perhaps also in this. I like to persuade myself — I easily persuade myself — that Diana Villiers retains a friendship, even a tenderness for me.' A pause, and he wrote, 'Wallis's report on the situation in Catalonia is the most interesting I have ever read. If only half of what Mateu states is true, the prospect has never been so full of promise; but how they need a man they can all trust, to act as a link between the different movements and to coordinate their efforts with those of the British government — in this case the government as represented by the Navy. Now that the French have killed En Jaume, I do not think there is a man better qualified than myself. I long to be there. But longing will not affect the countless miles of intervening sea, and I shall spend these months with my collections, happy in possessing such a wealth of time (though years would not be too long for a sound, scientific description of all the specimens). Some music and reading too, I trust. Captain Yorke seems a polite, amiable, and literate man, no mere sea-officer; he has neither read nor travelled in vain. My companions in the gunroom I have scarcely met. I hope they will prove more like their Captain than their first lieutenant; for on them the social comforts of this voyage must in a large degree depend.'

The social comforts of the gunroom were meagre enough, and after the *Leopard*'s spacious, well-lighted wardroom the place itself seemed cramped. Warner *was* a mere sea-officer: his one aim in life seemed to be to make *La Flèche* run through the water at the greatest possible speed consistent with the safety of her masts, and although he was not one of those spit-and-polish first lieutenants whom Stephen looked upon as the bane of the Navy, he was no very good company either, except perhaps for those who could speak knowingly of kites, moonsails, and stargazers. He seemed to take no pleasure in anything; and in him the naval love of punctuality reached something not far from mania. He was far older than any other officer in the gun-room, and he ruled its proceedings with a firm and gloomy authority. Like the second lieutenant and Marine officer, Warner was a tall man; and since *La Flèche* had been designed for swift-sailing stunted Frenchmen as far as her tween-decks was concerned, Stephen's first impression of the gunroom was that of a low thin shadowy place inhabited by three unnaturally large bowed figures, all looking at their watches. A fourth walked in immediately afterwards, bringing with him the smell of stale tobacco, alcohol, and unwashed clothes, a man even taller, even more bowed beneath the beams; and Warner introduced McLean, the surgeon. He was a young man and he seemed almost paralysed with shyness; at all events he remained profoundly silent, apart from an awkward plunge and grunt when Warner pronounced his name. Presently the drum beat and the room quickly filled, and when all were present, with their servants standing behind their chairs, there was scarcely room for the gunroom steward to carry in the pease-pudding and salt pork. The purser, the last man in, received a significant look from Mr Warner, a look that moved slowly from the purser's face to the watch still exposed in Warner's hand; but there were no harsh words, perhaps in honour of the guests. Babbington and Byron brought the sun with them, or if not the sun itself (for the gunroom had no stern-window) then at least some of the warmth and cheerfulness that Stephen had always associated with any gathering of sailors. They found a fellow-spirit in the master, and presently their end of the table was in a fine flow of conversation, reminiscence, anecdote, and laughter — former shipmates recalled, other commissions compared. Stephen laid out some pains in being agreeable to McLean, who sat by him, eating voraciously with a good deal of noise; but until half way through the meal there was little or no response. Then at last persuaded that Dr Maturin was neither going to snub or scorn him, McLean said, 'I hae your bukes,' adding something that Stephen could not catch, the accent being so strong, the voice so lowered in embarrassment. But judging by the young man's expression, the words were obliging, so Stephen bowed, murmuring, 'You are very good . . . too kind. I believe, sir, you are a naturalist yourself?'

Yes. As a wee bairn McLean first skelpit a mickle whaup his Daddie had whangit wi a stane, and then ilka beastie that came his way; comparative anatomy had been his joy from that day to this, and he named some of the beasties whose inward parts he had compared. But since the scoutie-allen, the partan, the clokie-doo and the gowk seemed not to convey any precise idea, he followed them with the Linnaean names; Stephen did the same for the creatures he referred to, and from this it was no great way to Latin descriptions of their more interesting processes. McLean was fluent in the language, having been to Jena, and Stephen found him far more comprehensible; presently they were talking away at a great rate, with barely a word of English but Och aye, and Hoot awa. They were deep in the caecum of Monodon monoceros when Stephen, becoming aware of a silence on his right, looked up and met the delighted grin of Babbington and Byron.

'We had just been boasting about you, sir,' said Babbington. 'We said you could talk Latin to beat a bishop, and these fellows would not believe it.'

'Dilke,' cried Warner, obscurely displeased by all this, 'draw the cloth.' And as soon as the execrable port had appeared, 'Mr Vice, the King.'

Stephen blessed His Majesty, mastered an involuntary grimace, felt in his pocket for an Amboyna cheroot, recollected himself, and said, 'When you are at leisure, Mr McLean, I should be happy to show you some of my collections.'

McLean stood up at once: he was the Doctor's man directly, he said, if he might but have leave to pass by the galley for a pipe, this last with a nervous glance at Mr Warner.

'The galley? To smoke tobacco? I will join you,' said Stephen. 'Please to lead the way.' And to himself he added, 'There is some inherent imbecility in my will. No sooner have I rid myself of one addiction, than I plunge into another. How I long for my cheroot! I will return to snuff.'

They were not wanted in the galley. All the smokers of the watch below were already there and an awkward silence greeted the arrival of the officers. Silence and disapproval. Their own Doctor they were used to; they did not cordially like his presence in the galley at any time, since it stood to reason he clapped a stopper on any kind of free conversation; but they were used to him. They might not always like what they were used to, but it was dead certain that they would always loathe what they were *not* used to: and they were not used to this new Doctor. The Leopards might crack him up, and he might in fact be handy with both saw and pill, but at present the Flitches (for Flitches were they called) only wished that he might fall down dead.

In time this was borne in upon Dr Maturin, not by any words or even by wry looks, but by sheer moral force alone; he threw his half-smoked cheroot into the galley range and said, 'Come, colleague; let us go.'

This was the beginning of a close association; it was also the beginning of the pleasantest voyage that Maturin had ever made. The monsoon bore them steadily west and south over a limitless and amiable sea, with never an island, never a ship, and rarely a bird to recall them to any sense of the terrestrial, clouds their only companions. It was a sea-borne life, ordered by an exact sequence of bells and of naval rites: the sound of the decks being holystoned, swabbed, and flogged dry in the early morning, hammocks piped up, the forenoon tasks, the ceremony of noon itself, when a dozen sextants shot the sun from *La Flèche*'s crowded quarterdeck and Captain Yorke said 'Make it so, Mr Warner', the bosun and his mates piping the hands to dinner, the fifer fifing them to grog; then the drum for the gunroom's meal, the quiet afternoon, and the drum again for quarters and for retreat, the piping down of hammocks, and the setting of the watch. All these were perfectly familiar to Stephen; but what was less familiar, and what in time came to have a hypnotic effect, as of living in the heart of an illusion, was the fact that these rites were never interrupted by the usual emergencies of the sailor's life: no sudden squalls, no untoward calms broke the smooth run of days. *La Flèche* sailed across the ocean, across a vast disc of sea whose limits always remained the same, neither nearer nor further; she sailed untroubled by the enemy, by storms, by crime aboard; and presently she might have been sailing for ever. Stephen was cut off from the past, and the future lay at so great and indeterminate a distance that it had little reality. His Leopards and McLean's Flitches were healthy, and however unreasonable it might appear, salt beef, salt pork, dried peas, hard work, far too much rum, stifling quarters, and little sleep kept them so; their surgeons had little to do in the physical line, and every morning after breakfast they repaired to the forepeak, where they sorted, classified, and described the wealth of Desolation and New Holland, discovering fascinating analogies between these forms of life and those with which they were more nearly acquainted. On occasion they withdrew to a lair behind the bitts, McLean's own domain, where by powerful lanterns they dissected, sometimes far into the night, amidst a strong smell of alcohol and other preservatives. McLean was not a drinker — the spiritous reek he carried with him was innocent — but he was a smoker, a very heavy smoker, and it was in his lair that he told Stephen how he defied the first lieutenant, keeping his pipe perpetually lit. McLean was a respectable young man, the son of a crofter, who by extraordinary perseverance and exertion had acquired enough knowledge of medicine to qualify himself for a naval surgeon's career, and a much greater fund of anatomy, which was his delight. He was an admirable colleague for this kind of work, accurate, conscientious, learned, and wholly devoted to his chosen pursuit; he had studied under the illustrious Oken at Jena, and he knew an immense amount about the bones of the skull, of all skulls, considered as highly developed vertebral processes. He was prodigiously ignorant of literature, music, and the common graces, but he would have been ideal, from the scientific point of view, if he had not absorbed so much of the learned German's metaphysics that even his respect for Dr Maturin could not keep him from emitting them, together with clouds of smoke. On the more human plane, he could be a tedious companion. He rarely washed, his table manners were offensive, he was extremely umbrageous; and finding that Dr Maturin was an Irishman, he gave full vent to his dislike for the English. Thon southron loons didna ken cleanliness; nor, it seemed, did they ken anything else, much, until the Hunters had taught them anatomy; they profited shamelessly from the Union; and they despised their betters. A puir wambly set of boggarts: where would they be without Scotch generals?

Stephen had no great love of the English government in its dealing with Ireland; in fact he had actively conspired against it. But he was deeply attached to individual English men and women, and in any case he did not like anyone to abuse the country but himself. 'You are mistaken, Mr McLean,' he said, 'in supposing that the English have no generals. They have; and the truth of the matter is that all of them who accomplish anything, such as Lord Wellington, are Irish. Much the same applies to their writers. Let us return to the parietal foramen and the anomalous carnassial teeth of this Otaria: at the present rate we shall not have described half the Phocidae before we reach the Cape. Nay, before we reach England! And they are decaying fast. Pray, take care of your tobacco-pipe, Mr McLean. It is leaning on the spirit-pot; and you are to consider, that should it take fire, all the specimens we have already described must infallibly be lost.'

Stephen's days were busy, and in spite of

the gloom of the gunroom and of McLean's shortcomings most unusually enjoyable. His evenings were usually spent in the cabin, playing music with Jack and Captain Yorke as the ship ran on and on, urged by Warner's unremitting zeal. He often dined there too, escaping the gunroom's purely naval conversation and Spartan fare; for whereas *La Flèche*'s officers had nothing but their pay, Yorke was possessed of comfortable private means. He kept a table, and nearly every day invited two or three of his officers or young gentlemen. After one of these dinners, at which the first lieutenant, the master, and Forshaw had been present, Stephen was walking on the quarterdeck to air his mind and to dispel the fumes of the Captain's port before rejoining McLean in the depths. The fine quartering breeze had slackened, and it had also drawn more astern, so that there was little refreshment in it; and in spite of the awning the sun beat down with more than common force. It was a make-and-mend day, and the Flitches were scattered about the deck forward of the mainmast, quietly sewing and darning, but Warner had scarcely taken a couple of turns, looking up at the rigging and laying his hand on the braces, before he gave an order: the placid groups among the guns broke up in an apparent chaos. Three sharp pipes of the bosun's call; the chaos resolved itself into a pattern; another pipe, and the ship spread her studdingsails. The booms bent, settled to the strain, and the speed increased perceptibly; at the same time what little refreshment there had been died quite away. Stephen took off his coat and folded it absently, his mind dwelling on the question of the anomalous Otaria, with *four* roots to its carnassial teeth: if in fact it should prove to be a distinct species, which seemed likely, he should name it after McLean. That would be a handsome compliment, a gleam of fame more valued than an appointment to a line-of-battle ship; it would also far outweigh the short answers Stephen had given recently, when McLean had been more than usually wearisome about the English. Like some other Scots he knew, McLean seemed to labour under some sense of inferiority; and to labour rancorously. Strange: it could never occur to an Irishman. And yet the situation of the two countries — here a cascade of small coins, a snuff-box, a tinder-box, a spunk-box, a penknife, two lancets, a cheroot-case, a duodecimo Horace, some pieces of rosin, a variety of small bones and mammalian teeth, and a partially-eaten biscuit fell from his inverted coat pockets on to the deck. Forshaw helped him pick them up, gave him some advice on the proper, the seamanlike, way of folding a coat, warned him against creasing it and against undue exposure to the sun, and said he should carry the coat down for Killick to hang it up in the Doctor's cabin. The cabin was of course below, but Forshaw's road took him by inconsequential leaps along the top of the hammock-cloths with nothing between him and the white racing water but a little slippery canvas: just as he was about to dodge between the forecourse and its deeper studdingsail he lost his footing in a way that would have made Mrs Forshaw turn deathly pale and that did make Dr Maturin feel anxious for his coat. But he seized the sheet and hung there for a moment, laughing up at a friend in the foretop, before vanishing between the sails, as safe as a young ape in its native wood: and as he balanced there in his best cabin-going uniform of silver-buckled shoes, white breeches and blue coat, with his teeth flashing in his sunburnt face and his hair streaming in the wind, he looked uncommonly fetching.

'Can you imagine anything more beautiful?' said Warner, in his harsh, grating voice.

'Not readily,' said Stephen.

'Cracking on when the sun is bright has always been a joy to me,' said Warner quickly, 'and now we have just about everything abroad that she can bear.'

'A noble spread of sails, upon my word,' said Stephen; and indeed he was by no means unmoved by the beauty of sail above sail, sail beyond sail, taut, rounded, and alive, nor by the huge curved shadows, and intricate geometry of line and brilliant surface. But whereas he had often seen a ship under royals and studdingsails aloft and alow, tearing through the deep blue sea with a bone in her teeth, he had rarely seen such a look of hunger, of hunger combined with something else — admiration or rather wonder, affection, tenderness.

'Poor man,' he reflected. 'The instinct so very strong, so very nearly unconquerable even in a phlegmatic. If he is, as I suppose, a paederast, small wonder he should be glum. When I consider what desire has done for me, how it has torn my heart — and mine an avowable desire, glorified by specious, heroic names — I am astonished that such men do not consume themselves entirely. A hard fate, to be shut up day after day with such a longing in a ship, where everything is known; and where this must not be known; where there must be no approach to an overt act.'

The Flitches were no brighter than the next ship's company, but as Dr Maturin observed there was little they did not know of what went on aboard. They knew the nature of Warner's inclinations, for all his ceaseless, rigorous control. They knew that their Captain was an indolent, easy-going, good-natured man, with little ambition to rise and shine in his profession or anywhere else; that he would fight like a good 'un if called upon to do so — he had given proof of that — but that he had no restless urge for action, that he was quite content with a small post-ship rather than a dashing frigate; and that although he would rather have been sent up the Mediterranean, where he could contemplate the Greek remains, he was happy to carry despatches to and from the Indies, leaving the running of the ship to his capable first lieutenant. They knew that the bosun and the carpenter had contrived to move a surprising quantity of the ship's stores to unfrequented places, and they had little doubt that these objects would vanish once *La Flèche* reached the Cape: the only question was, who shared? They knew a great many other things, some of no importance whatsoever, such as that the *Leopard*'s midshipmen were finding the voyage a burden to their spirits.

Jack Aubrey was a conscientious captain; he thought it his duty to form his youngsters, most of whom had been entrusted to him by friends or relations, not only into officers who understood their profession but into reasonably moral and socially presentable beings as well. During the first part of the *Leopard*'s voyage he had delegated much of this to the schoolmaster and the chaplain; then from the time these men vanished he had had little leisure for education; but now the whole day was his own, and he devoted far more of it than they liked to leading his reefers through Robinson's *Elements of Navigation*, Norie's *Epitome*, and Gregory's *Polite Education*. For his part Jack had received precious little education, polite or otherwise, and he learnt a great deal from Gregory as he went along — an exact list of the kings of Israel, among other things. There were no doubt conscientious captains at the time of the Spanish armament, when he first went to sea; but those he had sailed with had confined themselves to seeing that their midshipmen's drinking and whoring were kept within limits, limits that varied according to the captain. Only one of his early ships had carried a schoolmaster, a gentleman who passed his waking hours in an alcoholic haze; so that apart from a term or two at school by land, where a little Latin had been beaten into him, he was, from the point of view of literature, as the beasts that perish. Seamanship, of course, had come naturally to him — he was a born mariner — and then he had fallen in love with mathematics, a late love, but fruitful. Yet in the new, smoother, more scientific Navy that was coming into being this was not enough: his youngsters must add a powerful dose of Gregory to their Robinson. He made them read *The Present State of Europe, Impartially Considered*; he saw that the journals they were required to keep would meet the inspection of the severest board of examiners; he stood by while his coxswain taught them the finer points of knotting and splicing. It was a pity that his material was so indifferent, so refractory to anything but the knots and splices; for his intentions were of the best. In some commissions he had had midshipmen who loved the mathematics too, who doted upon spherical trigonometry, so that it was a pleasure to teach them navigation; it was not the case at present.

'Mr Forshaw,' he said. 'What is a sine?'

'A sine, sir,' said Forshaw, speaking very fast, 'is when you draw a right line from one end of an arc perpendicular upon the radius from the centre to the other end of the arc.'

'And what is its relation to the chord of that arc?'

Mr Forshaw looked wild, gazed about the day-cabin that Captain Yorke had given over to his guest, but found no help in its neat fittings, its skylight, nor in the nine-pounder gun that took up so much of its space, nor in the blank and hideous face of his companion, Holles, nor in the title of the novel *The Vicissitudes of Genteel Life*: life aboard *La Flèche* might not be particularly genteel but it was certainly full of vicissitudes. After a long pause he still had no views to offer, other than that the relationship was no doubt pretty close.

'Well, well,' said Jack, 'you must read page seventeen again, I see. But that is not what I sent for you for — that is not the reason for which I sent for you. There was a great deal of correspondence for me to attend to at Pulo Batang, and I have only now reached this letter from your mother. She begs me to take great care that when you brush your teeth you will brush them up and down, and not only sideways. Do you understand me, Mr Forshaw?'

Forshaw loved his mother dearly, but at this moment he wished she might be deprived of the power of holding a pen for ever. 'Yes, sir,' he said. 'Up and down it is, not only sideways, sir.'

'What are you tittering at, Mr Holles?' asked Captain Aubrey.

'Nothing, sir.'

'Now I come to think of it, I have a letter from your guardian, Mr Holles. He wishes to be assured that your moral welfare is well in hand, and that you do not neglect your Bible. You do not neglect your Bibles, any of you, I dare say?'

'Oh, no, sir.'

'I am glad to hear it. Where the Devil would you be, if you neglected your Bible? Tell me, Mr Holles, who was Abraham?' Jack was particularly well up in this part of sacred history, having checked Admiral Drury's remarks on Sodom.

'Abraham, sir,' said Holles, his pasty, spotted face turning a nasty variegated purple. 'Why, Abraham was . . .' But no more emerged, other than a murmur of 'bosom'.

'Mr Peters?' Mr Peters expressed his conviction that Abraham was a very *good* man; perhaps a corn-chandler, since one said 'Abraham and his seed for ever'.

'Mr Forshaw?'

'Abraham, sir?' said Forshaw, whose spirits had recovered with their usual speed. 'Oh, he was only an ordinary wicked Jew.'

Jack fixed him with his eye. Was Forshaw making game of him? Probably, judging from the extreme innocence of his face. 'Bonden,' he called, and his coxswain, who was waiting outside the door with sailcloth and rope-yarn to learn the young gentlemen to make foxes, walked in. 'Bonden, seize Mr Forshaw to the gun, and knot me that rope's end.'

'Golden days, Doctor, golden days,' said the master of *La Flèche* to Stephen Maturin. Far, far to leeward an enormous dust-storm in Africa had raised such a veil that the sun, setting behind it, suffused the clean sea-air with an amber light, turning the waves jade-green; though in a few minutes it was to make one of its more spectacular disappearances in crimson glory, when the same waves would show deep amethyst. Stephen was standing on the quarterdeck with his hands behind his back, his lips pursed, his eyes fixed, wide open, seeing nothing, upon a ring-bolt. He uttered a low whistling sound. 'I said these were golden days, Doctor,' said the master rather louder, smiling at him.

'So they are too,' cried Stephen, starting from a dream of Diana Villiers and staring round. 'Such a light as Claude might have painted, had he ever been to sea, the creature. But you are speaking figuratively, no doubt? You refer to the ease of our progress, the prosperous gale, the ocean's amenity?'

'Yes. I never touched sheet or brace right through the middle watch, and not a hand but took a caulk, bar the lookouts and the man at the wheel. Never was there such a run: at least two hundred mile logged regular from noon to noon without a break. Golden days — though maybe it has been a bloody day for him,' — nodding towards Forshaw, who walked slowly, awkwardly towards the forehatch, his chin trembling, his companions urging him in a whisper 'to bear up, old chap, and not let those —ing Flitches see', for a knot of grinning reefers stood by the larboard rail.

'There is always something in the misfortune of others that does not displease us,' observed Stephen. 'Will you look at the wicked malicious glee of those snotty midshipmen, now? Poor child, I shall poultice him with the best linseed mash; and a comfortable analgesic too.' A pause. 'But golden days, as you so rightly say, Master. Now that I reflect, I cannot remember ever having passed my time so pleasantly, at sea. If it were not for the health of my marsupials, I could wish nothing changed at all.'

'Do they pine, sir?'

'They miss their filth. That is to say, the wombats miss their filth. Their quarters are cleaned out most rigorously twice a day, and sometimes, I have reason to believe, by night. Now I am aware that in a man-of-war there is no place for filth — perhaps no place for a troop of wombats either — yet I cannot but regret it, and shall be glad when we reach the

Cape. I have an excellent friend at Simon's Town, that keeps a number of contented aardvarks in purely nominal captivity: to him I shall confide my marsupials. Do not think, however, that I intend the least reflection on *La Flèche* — a most —' he had been about to say 'commodious machine', but the sight of well over a hundred Flitches swarming about the narrow deck with a great number of empty water-casks made him change the word to 'well-conducted'.

'It will not be long, Doctor. For although it looks bloody in the west just now — Lord, how the deck shines red! — I think I can promise you the breeze will hold; and unless my reckoning is sadly out, tomorrow we shall raise the land.'

The master's reckoning was true. *La Flèche* made as pretty a landfall as could be wished, and the following dawn she glided in under topsails with the tide, right down Simon's Bay to the well-remembered anchorage; a wonderfully silent progress after all these weeks of strong winds loud in the rigging and the water racing along her side. Silence, with the shore moving past; a prolonged and dream-like silence shattered at last by *La Flèche*'s salute, the roaring acknowledgment, and the splash of her best bower.

From that moment on all peace was at an end. A ship carrying despatches was required to come and go with even greater haste than the ordinary man-of-war. *La Flèche* set about completing her water as though her life depended on catching the next tide but two; stores and wood and provisions flowed into her, and some flowed secretly out; again and again Stephen heard the words 'Lose not a minute'; again and again he fagged along the dusty road to Cape Town in a rickety cart full of wondering marsupials, confined beneath a net, until he found them a suitable haven; for his friend van der Poel had moved house, aardvarks and all. He was so active on shore that it was not until *La Flèche* was standing out to sea and her captain sitting down to his dinner that he heard of the United States' declaration of war.

The news was received with mixed feelings aboard *La Flèche*: some of the officers who still felt strongly about the War of Independence welcomed it; others, who had American friends or who thought that the whole affair had been shockingly bungled by the Tories and the army and that in any case a desire for independence was natural, regretted it. Others again left politics to politicians, but supposed that if they had to fight the Americans as well as Bonaparte and his allies, then it was all part of their calling; and at least there might be some hope of prize-money. The glorious days of Spanish treasure-ships were gone for ever; French prizes were precious thin on the ground; but American merchantmen had taken to carrying much of the world's trade, and they might be met with anywhere at all. Bonden told Stephen that upon the whole the lower deck was not pleased: apart from the regular man-of-war's men, they were mostly hands taken out of merchantships or pressed on shore; many had sailed in American vessels and all had had American shipmates. Although they liked the notion of prize-money, they could not see much sense in fighting Americans: there were half a dozen Americans aboard at this moment, and they were practically the same as Englishmen — no airs or graces about them — and you could not say fairer than that. Fighting the French was different; they were foreigners, and somehow it came natural. But generally speaking the whole ship's company looked upon this new war as a matter of no great importance; there might be some advantage in it, but as a contest it was neither here nor there, compared to the war with France. No details had reached the Cape, but everybody knew that the Americans did not possess a single ship of the line, whereas the

Royal Navy had over a hundred actually at sea, to say nothing of those building or in reserve.

Yet although the issue of the war as far as it concerned the sailors was a foregone conclusion — the Royal Navy had, after all, spent the last twenty years beating every fleet that was brought against it, taking, burning or sinking the enemy in the mass or in detail wherever he floated — Captain Yorke for one was doubtful, if not despondent, about the outcome on land. If the Americans had beaten the British army in eighty-one they might do so again, particularly as so many of the best regiments were engaged in the Peninsula; and then the French in Quebec could scarcely be expected to show much zeal on the English side. What he feared was a sudden crossing of the border to take the naval base of Halifax from behind. That would be extremely inconvenient; but even so he was quite happy about the naval side. There were the West Indies, there was Bermuda, there were of course the home bases, and he and Jack fell to working out the composition of the squadron required to keep the American navy in check or to destroy it, in the event of a general engagement, on the assumption that Halifax was gone.

They had always taken a keen professional

interest in the navies of other powers, even of so young a power as the United States, and when Stephen asked 'What does the American navy consist of, pray?' they were able to answer him at once.

'Apart from their sloops and brigs, they have only eight frigates,' said Yorke. 'Eight, no more. It would be stark staring madness to declare war with only eight frigates when your opponents have more than six hundred cruisers at sea, if you meant to do anything in the naval line; but of course their real aim is Canada — they cannot mean to do anything at sea, except for snapping up a few prizes before their ships are taken or blockaded in the Chesapeake.'

'Eight frigates,' said Jack. 'Two of them we should scarcely call frigates at all, nowadays; a thirty-two and a twenty-eight by the name of *Adams*; then three eighteen-pounders, rated thirty-eight guns apiece, much the same as ours though perhaps a little beamier, *Constellation*, *Congress*, and *Chesapeake*; and then three more, heavier than anything we have, *President*, *Constitution*, and *United States*, all rated forty-four guns and all carrying twenty-four-pounders. I dare say *Acasta* will be ordered to the American station to cope with them, together with *Endymion* and *Indefatigable*. I shall like that; there is splendid shooting behind Halifax.'

'When you say heavier than anything we possess, do you mean in physical bulk, or in the magnitude of their artillery?'

'I really meant the guns. They have long twenty-fours as opposed to our eighteens — they fire balls that weigh four and twenty pounds, rather than eighteen. Six pound more, do you see?' said Jack kindly. 'But, of course one goes with t'other. The American forty-fours must gauge about fifteen hundred ton, while our thirty-eights are only a trifle over a thousand. *Acasta* is one thousand one hundred and sixty, if I don't mistake, and she carries forty eighteen-pounders.'

'Would not this preponderance give the enemy a great advantage? Suppose he were to dash his beakhead against you, would not his greater mass bear you down, as the Turks were borne down at Lepanto?'

'Dear Doctor,' said Yorke, 'those are galley tactics. In modern scientific war mere weight does not signify, except that the thickness of your scantlings is some protection to your gun-crews at long range and enables you to carry heavier guns. Yardarm to yardarm, it does not make much odds: an eighteen-pound ball will do just about as much damage as a twenty-four, if the guns are well pointed and well served. When I was third of the

Sybille, thirty-eight, we set about *La Forte*, of forty-four twenty-four-pounders, and when we took her we found we had killed and wounded a hundred and twenty-five of her people, while they only killed five of ours. We dismasted her entirely, too, and lost not one of our own. That was in ninety-nine.'

'And then in Trafalgar year,' said Jack, 'Tom Baker — you remember Tom Baker, Stephen, the very ugly, carroty-haired man with a pretty wife that dotes upon him — Tom Baker, in *Phoenix*, thirty-six, and an uncommonly small thirty-six, took *Didon*, forty, in a very bloody fight. But I tell you what, Yorke, it will never do to send too many liners; you cannot expect any frigate, forty-four or not, to come out and engage with a ship of the line. Now I suggest *Acasta*, *Egyptienne* . . .'

Stephen's attention wandered, and presently he took up his 'cello, whispering over the strings. He had made his views on this hurtful, unnecessary war — unnecessary and yet, with such a ministry, perhaps inevitable — clear to Wallis long ago: he was not going to repeat himself. What preoccupied him was the effect it might have upon Diana Villiers, pinned in what was now an enemy country; and upon intelligence. Yet from the point of view of intelligence, he was infinitely more concerned with Catalonia; he longed to be there, and although *La Flèche* was at present dashing into the south Atlantic in the same magnificent style as that with which she had traversed the Indian Ocean, he was obliged to command his mind with unusual force to prevent it breaking out into sterile impatience and complaints. He thought that Yorke might well be right about Canada, but he could not care a great deal about the hypothetical naval war. If it took place, many men on both sides would no doubt be killed or cruelly maimed, a great many women would be made bitterly unhappy, a great deal of energy, material, and treasure would be wasted — diverted from the only real contest — but whatever the event the war would remain a side-issue, a piece of wanton, bloody foolishness. He wished Jack and Yorke would be less prolix, less inclined to neglect music for the American navy: he was tired of their ideal squadrons, their strategy, and their new naval bases.

The American navy was the staple diet of conversation: the American navy day after day after day. To escape it he spent more time on deck or in the mizentop. They were in albatross waters now, running up the cold current to the west of Africa, and long did he gaze for those splendid wings over the long greenish swell. But when the darkness or the cold — and it was unusually cold, so cold that he blessed the day he had landed his marsupials, creatures subject to bronchial complaints — drove him down to the gunroom, there he always found the Americans again, and not only their frigates but every one of their eight brigs and sloops from the *Hornet*, twenty, to the *Viper*, twelve, with every wearisome detail of shifting guns and boat-carronades, swivels in the tops and along the gangway.

Here the feeling was quite different. Mr Warner had no fear for Canada, no fear for Halifax; nor did he give a rap for the American navy. And as he was the only man aboard who had fought the Americans, his opinion carried weight. 'When I was a midshipman in the year eighty, sir,' said he, 'serving under Foul-Weather Jack Byron on the American station, we saw a great deal of them. Contemptible, sir, contemptible: they never fought a single action with any credit. Filthy ships: more like privateers than a real navy. But what can you expect of people who think Commodore is a permanent rank, and who chew tobacco on the quarterdeck, squirting their spittle right, left and centre?'

'Yet perhaps they may have improved with the passage of time,' said Stephen. 'I seem to remember that during their abortive little war with France in seventeen ninety-nine their frigate *Constellation* took *l'Insurgente*.'

'Very true, sir; but you are forgetting that *Constellation* carried twenty-four-pounders and *Insurgente* twelves. You are forgetting that *La Vengeance*, who carried eighteens, knocked *Constellation* all to pieces. And, Doctor, you are forgetting that in both these actions the Yankees were engaged with foreigners, not with Englishmen.'

'Ah,' said Stephen, 'that I cannot deny.'

'My brother Numps —' said the purser.

'*Vengeance* carried forty-two-pound brass carronades,' said the second lieutenant, 'and that I know very well, for I was third of the *Seine* when we took her in the Mona Passage.'

'My brother Numps —' said the purser.

'And these carronades were mounted on a new non-recoiling principle: let me draw it on the cloth.'

Despairing of a wider audience, the purser turned to Stephen and McLean; but Stephen, feeling that no good could come of brother Numps, nor of the non-recoiling principle, glided from his place.

The discussion carried on in the gunroom without him, still on the subject of the Americans, for it seemed that Numps had visited the United States: and it continued in the cabin, perhaps at a slightly higher level, but still very tedious for one who was not a sailor. There were times when it seemed to Stephen that they would never stop, and that boredom would be the death of him, since to escape their endless prating he was obliged either to pace the deck in the cold dampness or to take refuge in the forepeak, which was equally cold and damp, with the reek of a charnel-house added. His cabin was not altogether without comfort, but it was separated from the midshipmen's berth by so thin a bulkhead that even the stout balls of wax that he thrust into his ears could not keep out their din. 'As I grow older,' he reflected, 'I become less tolerant of noise, boredom, and promiscuity; I never was well suited to a life at sea.'

Then abruptly, from one day to the next, *La Flèche* was in deep blue water; the early morning air was warm; waistcoats and comforters were stowed away, and the noonday sun was observed by a quarterdeck full of men and boys in light round jackets. Soon the jackets disappeared, and they passed under Capricorn in shirt-sleeves: dinner with the Captain, which entailed full uniform, was no longer looked forward to so eagerly, except among the midshipmen, a penurious, hungry crew, whose small supply of private stores, bought at the Cape, had long since been squandered in high living, and who were now growing thin on salt horse and biscuit, no more.

It was well north of Capricorn that their fantastic luck with the wind deserted them. The south-east trades had had so little south in them that *La Flèche* was nearer Brazil than she had intended to be when they died away altogether, leaving her wallowing on a heavy swell under a sun so huge, so very near, and so furious that even at first dawn the metal of the guns was still quite hot.

After a week of this, when all real recollection of the cold had vanished, when even coolness seemed to belong to some ideal existence, a faint breeze, coming down from the equator, directly against their wishes, filled the sails at last, giving the ship life and motion. Now Warner could exert all his seamanship, the parboiled hands all their zeal, in beating slowly north.

He did so with admirable skill, applauded by those, such as Captain Aubrey, who could appreciate his endeavours, ignored by others, such as Stephen and McLean, who cared for none of these things. They had some interesting sunstrokes in their sickbay now, together with the usual diseases that some of the hands had found time to acquire in their few moments of free or stolen time at Simon's Town; but still their main preoccupation was what remained undecomposed of the treasures in the forepeak, mostly bones, salted skins, and small creatures or organs in alcohol . Everything was at least catalogued by now, and much was fully described. McLean was a fanatical describer, a dissector of wonderful dexterity: a most dogged, stubborn worker. After a day of such heat that tar dropped from the rigging and the pitch in the deck-seams bubbled under foot — perhaps the twentieth of such days in succession, with all the ship's boats towing astern to keep them watertight — Stephen left him down in his private lair, dissecting an eared seal's foetus, the pride of their largest jar of spirits. Although this was probably the foetus of the new species that was to be called Otaria macleanii and that was to win them undying glory, Stephen could no longer bear the dense cloud of tobacco-smoke (for McLean worked with his pipe in his mouth), the fumes of alcohol, and the enclosed, fetid heat, after the gunroom supper of pease-pudding. He wished McLean good night, warned him not to overtax his eyes, heard his abstracted grunt, and groped his way up ladders to the deck. The watch had been set long since, and the ship was very quiet: she was slipping along under topsails alone with the wind one point free, making perhaps a couple of knots through the long easy swell. The master had the watch, and he was not one to badger the hands with jib and staysails after a wearing day hogging and boot-topping the ship's weed-grown sides for some minute increase of speed. Stephen could see him, as his eyes grew accustomed to the dark, standing near the quartermaster at the con, in the glow of the binnacle light. Beyond him, by the taffrail, Jack was showing his midshipmen the stars, and Forshaw's high young voice could be heard piping about the Southern Cross. Such stars! The young moon had set, and they blazed there in a velvet sky, hanging, he would have sworn, at different heights, with Mars a startling red among them. A certain refreshment rose from the sea, a damp exhalation almost cool, and Stephen walked forward across the space amidships where in ordinary times the boats stood on their chocks and which was now strewn with sleeping or at least recumbent figures, their heads enveloped in their jackets. He made his way through them to the bows, then carefully out along the bowsprit as far as the spritsail yard. There he turned, and sitting easy, let himself go to the smooth motion of the ship, gazing now at the ghostly foretopsail, now up at the masthead describing intricate regular curves among the stars, and again down at the cutwater, perpetually advancing, never reaching him, shearing the black sea with a faint white gleam. There was a continual living sound of blocks heaving, the strain and slight creak of wood and cordage, the hiss and ripple and surge of the water: he was very tired, quite why he could not tell, unless it was the effort of keeping his mind from anxious, fruitless worrying about Diana — she was very present to his inward eye these days — and the events in Catalonia. Back there in the ship the bells struck one after another, and every time the sentinels called 'All's well' from their various stations. Perhaps it was their reiterated cries that impressed their sense upon his unreasoning part, perhaps several of a thousand other causes, but after some time his tiredness was no longer a jaded, harassed fatigue but mild, calm, physical weariness, a comfortable desire for sleep. He crept back, holding his breath and any rope that came to hand: if Jack or Bonden should discover him he would have to endure their reproaches: he would be harshly blamed. However, he managed the descent and walked aft; Jack and his star-gazers were no longer there, so after a word with the master and a long stare at the wake, the faintly phosphorescent starlit wake with the boats black in it, like little whales, he went below.

Unfortunately the midshipmen were still keeping it up. The liveliest of the ship's young gentlemen had been brought up by his uncle, an Oxford don, and he had instituted gaudy nights. This was one of them, and through his wax Stephen could hear

Our Captain was very good to us,
He dipped his prick in phosphorus;
It shed a light all through the night
And steered us through the Bosphorus.

Again and again they sang it, and again and again there was the howl of laughter at the end: it seemed to grow funnier with each repetition, and by four bells they could not get beyond 'was very good to us' before they were overcome by mirth.

'Four bells, the vile brute-beasts,' said Stephen, ramming the wax still further home. But five bells he never heard. He was deep, deep down; and his next impression was one of extreme, general, incoherent violence — Jack shaking him, pulling him bodily out of his cot, shouting 'Fire, fire, the ship's on fire. Get up on deck.'

He could see almost nothing for the smoke, but snatching up a book and writing-case he followed Jack's fleeting lantern along the deserted orlop to the forehatch. The whole deck was aglow with a rosy light reflected from the smoke and the sails, and an occasional tongue of flame could be seen above the main hatchway. Hoses were playing, half-naked men heaving strongly at the pumps. He stood there for a moment in his shirt, grasping the situation; then he turned to dart down to his cabin, but the scorching smoke drove him back directly, and as he emerged so a fountain of brilliant flame shot up from the cabin sky-light. The main and mizen topsails and all their tarred rigging took fire at once: blazing pieces fell on the deck, starting other fires — coils of rope, wood tinder-dry all flared with an extraordinary speed and brilliance — and now there was a vast omnipresent roar as the main fire took an unconquerable hold.

The men started from the pumps and ran to the side, all looking at Captain Yorke. 'Starboard watch away,' he cried. 'Easy, easy, there. Leopards to the blue cutter.'

There was a rush for the bows, where the boats had been hauled alongside: not an un-disciplined panic-stricken rush, but violent enough for Stephen to be thrown down and trampled upon. He found himself picked up, heard Bonden's strong voice cry 'Make a lane, there', and there was Babbington, grasping his legs and guiding him into the boat.

'Pull clear ahead,' shouted Yorke, and a moment later, 'Larboard watch away.'

Now the flames roared higher still. There

was some confusion, men throwing themselves into the water, shouts of 'Come on, sir, come on'. But in the glare Yorke, Warner and the gunner could be seen racing about the deck, firing the guns so that they should not go off at random as the heat reached them, perhaps hitting the boats. The last three guns all together, and Yorke came down the side, the last man off the ship. 'Give way,' he called, and his gig shot forward, passed through the rest, and led the way, pulling very fast. Presently they rested on their oars and gazed back at their ship: they gazed and gazed, with never a word, and in half an hour she blew up, a vast crimson lasting flash that grew with enormous speed, covering the sky, followed by a total darkness and the sound of timbers, masts, spars plunging from the darkness into the empty sea.

CHAPTER THREE

The blue cutter was eighteen feet long, and with thirteen men in the boat it was uncomfortably crowded, dangerously low in the water. They were silent and for the most part motionless, squeezed into what little shade they could find — precious little, under the high tropical sun, but more now that it was fast declining from its height, well down the western sky ahead. A sensible relief, for the blaze directly overhead at noon might have been called intolerable but for the fact that they had borne it. They had a good deal to bear, apart from the heat and the overcrowding: fear, hunger, thirst, and sunburn, and of these sunburn was the most immediate.

Their shirts now formed the small shoulder-of-mutton sail that was to carry them across the ocean to Brazil, and although their faces and forearms were tanned beyond the reach of any sun their backs were not: those with pigtails had unplaited them and spread the long hair as some kind of a shield, but that was not much use against such a blaze and their backs were fiery red or purple, cracked

131

and peeling or quite raw; for although the cutter was properly fitted with its oars, stretchers, mast and cordage, its sails had formed part of the bosun's perquisites at the Cape, the loss being disguised by a small piece of canvas stuffed with junk. There were a few jackets in the boat, and these were passed, wetted, to those that took their places on the sunward side, turn and turn about at each hypothetical bell. As for fear, it had always been present from the moment it replaced their intense relief at escaping from the burning ship; and it had increased during the blow that separated the boats the very night *La Flèche* took fire — a series of squalls that cut up such a sea that they all sat on the weather gunwale to keep the waves out with their close-pressed backs, bailing furiously the while, one bailer and a couple of hats between them. After that fear had dropped to something more like a steady anxiety, tempered with confidence: Captain Aubrey had stated that he knew where they were and that he would take them to San Salvador in Brazil; and if any man could pull them through it was he. Yet it had revived these last few days, with the biscuit and the water dwindling so, and never a fish, never a turtle on the vast expanse of deep blue sea. Even Captain Aubrey could not bring rain out of this implacably pure sky, nor increase the small parcel of biscuit that lay by him as he sat in the stern-sheets, steering the cutter westwards. Beneath him, carefully wedged and covered, stood the mess-kid with the few remaining pints of water. He would serve out a third of a mug at sunset, together with the third part of a biscuit; the Doctor would add a certain quantity of sea-water; and that would be all, the kid quite empty. There might be dew to lick from the mast and gunwales and to suck from the sail — it happened sometimes — but that would not keep them going long, any more than the urine they had been drinking this last week. Since Wednesday the Doctor had been pointing out birds that he said were never seen more than a few hundred miles from land, and they had all felt encouraged; but with these light variable airs a few hundred miles might mean another week, and they no longer had the strength to pull for any length of time if the breeze failed them: they had chewed all the goodness out of their leather belts or shoes, and when the biscuit was gone, all was gone. No one complained, but each knew very well that he could not last a great while now; and though hope was not gone, nor nearly gone, the anxiety weighed very heavy in the boat.

'Change over,' said the Captain in a hoarse croak. The jackets were wetted and passed to the men who were to take their place in the bows, and there was a general post. Yet even with this moving around the main order did not vary: the Captain sat in the stern-sheets, the two lieutenants by him, the midshipmen further forward, then the Leopards, and then the three Flitches they had picked up — men who had flung themselves over the side in the confusion and had lost their own boats. Each man sat by his belongings, such as they were: sometimes they were the effect of chance, of what happened to be at hand in the last moment, but sometimes they seemed to show what each man had valued most. Jack Aubrey had his chronometer beside him, next to the biscuit, the heavy cavalry sabre he had used for many years, and a pair of pistols. He had come off better than most, since Killick, having a few minutes longer warning, had also caught up a sheaf of the Captain's papers, his best telescope, and half a dozen of his best frilled shirts, fresh from the ironing-board; but the shirts were now part of the sail's after-leach. Babbington had preserved his commission; Byron the official journals and certificates he would need if his acting-rank were to be confirmed, and a sextant. One midshipman still had his dirk, and the two others their silver spoons. Several of the foremast-hands had saved their ditty-bags, often beautifully embroidered, their hussifs, and of course their knives. Dr Maturin's locked writing-case stood on his diary, and his new wig on that: he himself could not be seen, except for his fingers clinging to the gunwale, because he was hanging in the sea. Sweat could not evaporate in water, and there might possibly be some penetration of the pure fluid through the pervious membrane of his skin.

'Will you give me a hand, now?' he said, heaving himself to chest-height on the side.

Bonden stood up, and as he did so the breeze caught his long loose hair, covering his face. He turned to windward to blow it back, stiffened, stared, and said to Jack, 'A sail, sir, right on the starboard beam.'

No discipline on land or sea could withstand this. As Jack stood up, so did every other soul in the boat. The cutter took a wild weather-lurch and very nearly shipped a sea. 'Sit down, you God-damned lubbers,' cried Jack — a loud, inhuman sound.

They sat down at once, for they had seen all that mattered, a ship on the northern horizon, topsails up. Jack stood on the midships thwart, steadied himself, and looked long and hard with his glass. The light was perfect: three times on the rise he saw her hull. 'Probably an Indiaman,' he said. 'Bonden, Harboard, Raikes, sit on the larboard gunwale. Ready about.'

The distant ship was sailing on the opposite tack, something south of east, with the wind at north, making six or seven knots. He put the boat about and steered a course to intercept her. The question was, could he do so before nightfall? The sudden tropical nightfall with no twilight to prolong the day?

Could he urge the cutter through the sea so as to get within view of the look-outs before the sun went down? It would be a near-run thing. The same thought was in every mind, and many an eye glanced at the sun. The men on the weather-gunwale leaned out to make the boat more stiff; and already the other hands were dashing water against the sail so that no breath of air should pass through it and be lost.

'Killick,' said Jack, 'do what you can by way of a staysail with handkerchiefs, ditty-bags, anything at all.'

'Aye aye, sir.'

The precious bags were handed over without a murmur; knives slit their seams; some men twisted rope-yarn into thread, others sent needles running through and through — a cruel task, since the sailmakers and their mates could not take more than an occasional glance at the ship.

'Mr Babbington,' said Jack again, 'spread

out the powder in my flask to dry.' There was little need for this in so blazing hot a boat, but he wanted to be quite certain of a signal at the last extremity.

Their courses were slowly converging; now even without standing up the men in the cutter could see the ship's black chequered hull as she rose. And a kind of parched cheer went up as the tiny new sail, a particoloured triangle, climbed the stay and all hands felt the very slightly greater thrust. But God, the sun was sinking so — every time they looked astern, a handsbreadth lower — and though no man spoke, they felt that the breeze was sinking too.

The lively run of water down the side was dying away. There was no need for anyone to lean out to keep the boat stiff to the wind, for wind there was almost none. Yet she was well within a mile — maybe a mile and a half — and still on their larboard bow. She had not crossed them yet; she was not going from them yet. The distance would still diminish till she crossed, and the look-outs must see them any moment now.

Jack stared at the sea, the sky, sinking sun, the uncertain signs of wind. 'Out oars,' he said, naming the strongest men. 'We must make a dash for it.'

Another half-mile and the most careless

look-out could not miss them. Another half-mile and they would be within hail — within the sound of pistol-shot. And the sun was still clear of the sea.

'Stretch out, stretch out,' he cried, right into the labouring stroke-oar's agonized, contorted face. They stretched out: and now the water raced foaming down the side. The ship came nearer fast, and right ahead he could see men moving on her deck. Had they no look-out at all? 'Stretch out, stretch out.

'In oars and face about. Now all together hail. One, two, three ahoy!'

'Ahoy, ahoy, the ship ahoy.'

The ship let fall her topgallants, sheeted home: she gathered way, her bow-wave increasing with her speed. The sea's blue darkened fast with the setting of the sun.

'Ahoy, ahoy.' Jack fired both pistols, a fine ringing crack. 'Ahoy, oh Christ ahoy, the ship ahoy,' quite desperate now. The ship crossed the cutter's bows at half a mile, her bow-wave rising much whiter now, her wake stretching far.

Every second the distance grew. 'Ahoy, ahoy!' tearing their throats in fury; and the quick darkness spread. Stars beyond the ship: she lit her stern-lantern, a top-light; and the top-light moved fast away among the stars.

Silence, but for the painful gasping of the

men who had pulled so hard, rowing their hearts out, and for the dry sobs of the youngest reefer. The rowers lay in the bottom of the boat. One of them, a big, heavy-boned man named Raikes, stopped breathing for a moment; Stephen leant over him, massaging his chest and throwing water on his face. After a while he revived, and sat there, bowed, without a word.

'Do not be downhearted, shipmates,' said Jack at last. 'She is carrying a top-light, as you see. That proves we are in the track of shipping. Now I shall serve out supper, and shape course for land. I will lay any man ten guineas to a shilling we see a ship or land or both tomorrow.'

'I will not take you, sir,' said Babbington, as loud as his racked voice could speak. 'It is a certainty.'

A little after moonrise Stephen woke. Extreme hunger had brought on cramps in his midriff again and he held his breath to let them pass: Jack was still sitting there, the tiller under his knee, the sheet in his hand, as though he had never moved, as though he were as immovable as the Rock of Gibraltar and as unaffected by hunger, thirst, fatigue, or despondency. In this light he even looked rock-like, the moon picking out the salient of his nose and jaw and turning his broad shoulders and upper man into a single massive block. He had in fact lost almost as much weight as a man can lose and live, and in the day his shrunken, bearded face with deep-sunk eyes was barely recognizable; but the moon showed the man unchanged.

He saw that Stephen was awake, and a white flash appeared as he smiled. He leant forward, patted Stephen's shoulder, and pointed north. 'Ducking,' was the only word he uttered — all his parched tongue could do.

Stephen followed his pointing arm, and there to windward he saw no stars, but a prodigious blackness, shot with inward lightning.

'Soon,' said Jack. And half an hour later he brought out an inarticulate bellow near enough to 'All hands' to rouse those that could be roused. Raikes, the big quarter-gunner belonging to *La Flèche*, was dead; and the other rowers were likely to follow him quite soon unless they had some relief. He had died with a startled gasp, and uncomprehending stare, as supper was serving out, and they had not put him over the side, although no man had yet spoken of eating his body.

'Sail,' croaked Jack. 'Funnel: kid.'

Abruptly the northern breeze veered due south: a pause on the uneasy sea while the darkness raced across the sky. The first drops fell as hail, great hail-stones that drew blood; and then, driving from the north once more the sheets of rain came down, filling their open, offered mouths, washing their upstretched arms, their burnt, salt-crusted bodies. 'Quick, quick,' cried Jack, much louder now, as he directed the flow of water from the horizontal sail into the kid and every other receptacle they possessed. But he need not have troubled; long after they were filled the rain went on, pouring down so that they could hardly breathe as they wallowed in the pure luxury, absorbing it at every pore, pouring down with a universal hiss and roar so that they even had to bail it out, throw the precious stuff over the side to keep afloat.

It was while they were bailing that Babbington called out 'Oh!' and then, 'It's something soft'. This was the first of a shower of flying squids, hundreds and hundreds of them that passed all round and over the boat, some hitting the men and falling into the fresh water in the bottom of the boat, glowing with a faint phosphorescent light, coupling in an intricacy of arms. Too many for any call to share. The men hunted them down, scrabbling fore and aft, scrabbling under the dead man's legs, and ate them alive.

The darkness was gone; the moon shone out again and in the north the stars were brighter still. Stephen found that he was cold, even shivering; his belly was like a filled sack, heavy, as if it were a foreign body. 'Here, sir,' said Forshaw in his ear. 'Here's my jacket. Stretch out on the thwart and take a caulk. It will be dawn in an hour or two. And now we can hold out for another week at least; you will be quite all right.'

Dawn: the first light rising to the zenith . A pure sky over a sea swathed in white, swirling mists, mists filled with changing dream-like shapes, some in the form of clouds. Then all at once the sun's upper limb; then the whole sun itself, flattened like a lemon, but a lemon of enormous, blazing power that rounded as it climbed, dispelling the mists with its horizontal rays. And there, where the mists had been, lay not one ship but two, directly to leeward, two miles away.

The nearer had backed her foretopsail to speak the other; and yet it was terribly like a mirage. No one uttered any distinct, firm word until Jack had put the boat before the wind and they were running down at four or five knots on a true, steady breeze. There was no chance that the ship could escape them — for ship she was: no mirage could hold so still so long — and almost no chance that they had not already been seen, since the ship was a man-of-war, her pennant streaming in the wind. Nationality unsure, for her colours, British, French, Dutch, Spanish, or even American, were blowing from them — a hint of blue, no more — but in any case a present Paradise. Yet no man dared tempt fate: they sat rigid, staring with all their force across the sea, willing the boat on. Total silence until Jack handed the tiller to Babbington, crept stiffly forward with his glass, and almost instantly said, 'Ours. Blue ensign. *Java*, by God. Yes, *Java*. I should have known her anywhere. T'other's a Portuguese.'

A hum of talk: *Java* — all the Leopards who had served with Jack before knew her well; she had been the French *Renommée*, taken off Madagascar, a fine plump thirty-eight-gun frigate.

'They have seen us,' said Jack. He had the officer of the watch in his objective glass, and the officer, telescope levelled, was looking straight at him.

The question arose, should they now slip Raikes over the side? It seemed more proper, in a way — it was bad luck to keep a corpse aboard — *Java* might still fill her topsail and away. Besides, he had swollen shockingly; and although no one mentioned it, part of his left thigh had been eaten in the night: the squids were a thin unsubstantial fare, to fill such an enormous hunger. No, said his shipmates from *La Flèche*: no, now they had got him so far, he should have a parson. It should be done right, with a hammock and two round-shot, and the words read over him.

'Quite right,' said Jack. 'But cover him decently for now. And, Doctor, I will trouble you to put on your apron.'

In the last thousand yards, when they could see the *Java*'s side lined with watching figures, they suddenly became self-conscious. Tie-for-tie pairs formed, plaiting pigtails: the officers plucked at what clothing they possessed and fingered their beards.

Nearer, and nearer still; and at last the hail 'What are ye?'

In the sudden gaiety of his heart, now that the last tension was gone, Jack thought of facetious replies, such as 'The Queen of the May' or 'The Seven Champions of Christendom'; but this would not do, not with a corpse aboard. He called out, 'Shipwrecked mariners,' let fly the sheets, and brought the boat kissing up against the *Java*'s side.

No side-boys, no bosun's call for Captain Aubrey this time; but seeing the state of the cutter's crew the officer sent a couple of powerful men down with man-ropes, and one of these said to Jack, 'Can you get up the side, mate?'

'I believe so, thankee,' said Jack, springing

for the cleats. His head felt very strange when he stood up, but he felt that at all costs he must go aboard correctly — the point of honour was concerned. Fortunately the *Java* had a fine tumblehome — her sides sloped steeply in from near the waterline — and with a couple of heaves and the help of the roll he was on the quarterdeck, the unusually crowded quarterdeck. He straightened, though his knees trembled beneath him — reaction was fast setting in — touched his hat to no particular person but rather to that august sweep of deck, concentrated his gaze on the advancing officer, and said, 'Good morning, sir. I am Captain Aubrey, late of *Leopard*, and I should be obliged if you would inform your captain.'

The young man's face expressed wonder, astonishment, perhaps incredulity, but before he could speak a small round brisk man stepped from the group of figures somewhat aft and cried, 'Aubrey? By God, so it is — I did not recognize you — thought you was lost a great while since — how come you here? — Your Excellency —' to a tall figure in white just behind him — 'allow me to name Captain Aubrey of the Navy — General Hislop, Governor of Bombay.'

Jack's head swam, but he managed a civil bow, a 'Your servant, sir', and a kind of smile at the Governor's words '. . . knew your father

. . . delighted . . . most interesting occasion'. Then unable to recall the name of the familiar face before him, he said, 'Captain, may my men be seen to? They are quite knocked up. My surgeon will need a bosun's chair. And we have a corpse with us. Pray tell me, have you any news of boats from *La Flèche*?'

No news alas; and Captain Lambert — for Lambert was his name — having given orders, urged Jack to come below. 'Come, take my arm. A glass of brandy . . .'

'I will just see my people aboard,' said Jack. He would have given the world to sit on the carronade-slide just by him, but he stood there while the Leopards and the Flitches reached the deck; he introduced his officers; and he even noticed that the Javas made a poor fist of hoisting the boat on deck. When he reached the cabin, and when Captain Lambert was calling for 'a glass of brandy, there, and mince pies; but only small ones, d'ye hear me, only small ones,' he was obliged to steer his way, half-blind, to the quarter-gallery, and there he fell. 'The fall very nearly came before the pride,' he said to himself as he half-lay, half-reclined there — no room to measure his unusual length — wonderfully comfortable and relaxed. And much later, 'What did he mean by mince pies? Lambert is his name, Harry Lambert: he had *Active* in

146

the year two: cut out the *Scipion*: married Maitland's sister. Mince pies. Why, of course: it must be Christmas in a day or two.'

It was indeed, and in spite of the enormous sun the *Java*'s galley turned out puddings and pies in prodigious quantities, enough for well over four hundred men and boys with healthy appetites and for twelve whose lust for food was barely human. She was a fine dry quick-sailing weatherly ship, with plenty of head-room between decks, and she would have been called roomy, by naval standards, if she had carried only the normal complement for a thirty-eight-gun frigate; but she was bound for Bombay, and she had the new Governor aboard, with his numerous suite; and as though that were not enough, drafts for the *Cornwallis*, *Chameleon*, and *Icarus* had been joined to them, so that where three hundred men could have turned and breathed and fed with something like ease, four hundred could not — on punishment days there was scarcely room to swing the cat effectively — and the accommodation of twelve more presented se-rious difficulties. Difficulties in the matter of volume, not of victuals; the *Java* was a well-found ship, her lower depths still crammed with sheep, swine and poultry in addition to her ordinary stores, and although her captain was known to be poor, she had a comparatively wealthy gunroom, and the catering-officer at once ordered a massacre of geese, ducks, sucking-pigs.

Yet in spite of the season and the rich smell of festivity, there was no Christmas spirit in the ship at all. Stephen's first impression was that she was the gloomiest vessel he had ever known. Her people were kind, none kinder: they re-rigged their guests in the most open-handed way: the tallest lieutenant provided clothes for Captain Aubrey, and Captain Lambert provided the marks of splendour due to his rank, while the *Java*'s surgeon gave Stephen his best coat and breeches, to say nothing of the anonymous linen that appeared in his cabin. But there was no merriment aboard, and when, after a long night's perfect sleep, a shave, a visit to his worst sunburns in the sickbay, and a turn on deck, Stephen made acquaintance with the gunroom as a body at breakfast he thought them a strangely mumchance crew: never a smile, never a single one of those flights of naval wit, flabby puns, traditional jokes, proverbs, saws, to which he was accustomed and which he now so curiously missed. It was not that they were short of talk; on the contrary, there was a great deal of conversation; but it was all dogged, glum, declamatory, indignant, or angry. It was all highly professional, too, and it seemed to him that he had only exchanged the boredom of *La Flèche* for a greater boredom still, since here too it was all about the navy of the United States, and here there were twice as many men at table.

'Oh for women at sea to obviate the eternal crosscat-harpings,' he said to himself, 'to do away with the grumlin-futtocks, and to inject a little civilization, even of an equivocal nature, even at the risk of moral deviation.'

He was the first of the Leopards to appear, and apart from offering him coffee, tea, mutton chops, bacon, eggs, soused herrings, cold pie, ham, butter, toast and marmalade, and seeing to his comfort, few people spoke to him. He was obviously still much reduced by his ordeal; he was thought to be deaf; and their surgeon had told them that he was not to be excited — 'He has an ugly livid countenance that argues some damage to the heart.'

The master did ask him what he thought of the *President*, but he replied, 'A most unfortunate choice, sir. No bottom, weak, easily blown from side to side.'

'Indeed, sir?' cried the master: and several other officers paid close attention.

'He may be a tolerable Hebrew scholar; he may have genteel insinuating manners and a handsome wife; he may overflow with private virtues. But there is the evil corrupting love of power, the consuming lust for office —'

'I was referring to the ship, sir, to the frigate *President*.'

'Oh, as for the ship, I am not qualified to form any opinion, at all.'

The master turned to his neighbour, who had something to offer on the subject of scantlings, as they were understood in the United States; so, as neither Babbington nor Byron was yet afoot, Stephen escaped the American navy by swallowing his breakfast in a few quick snaps, in spite of his colleague's warning 'not to eat too much — to chew every mouthful forty times', took a couple of pinches of fortifying snuff, returned to the deck, and asked for news of Captain Aubrey. Captain Aubrey too was still asleep; and pleasantly enough the words were uttered in a little above a whisper, in spite of the hullaballoo that filled the ship from stem to stern.

Stephen took a few more turns in the brilliant morning sun, revelling in the luxury of clean linen — of any linen at all. The others on the quarterdeck watched him with discreet curiosity, and he watched the working of the ship: even to his unprofessional eye it seemed a little haphazard. Surely there was more noise, more instruction, more pushing men into place than was usual? Forshaw interrupted his thoughts, a strangely transformed Forshaw, not only in that he was clothed, and clothed in garments far too big for him, but in that he had never a smile: his face looked as though he had been crying, and in a low voice he told Stephen that 'if he were at leisure, Captain Aubrey would be glad to have a word with him'.

'I hope that child has not had bad news,' said Stephen to himself, walking to the cabin. 'Some letter announcing death, sent out and here received. On top of what he has experienced, it might have very ill effects. I shall give him half of a blue pill.'

But the look of grief was not peculiar to young Forshaw; it was plain upon Jack's face too, and even more pronounced, a look of shock and deep unhappiness. Captain Lambert, already straitened for room, had moved the *Java*'s master from his day-cabin for his latest guest, and here Jack sat, wedged between an eighteen-pounder gun and the chart-table, with a pot of coffee on the locker beside him. He gave a poor smile as he wished Stephen good morning, asked him how he did, and invited him to share his pot.

'First show me your tongue and let me take your pulse,' said Stephen; and a moment later, 'You have had bad news, brother?'

'Of course I have,' said Jack in a low, vehe-

151

ment tone. 'Surely you have heard?'

'Not I.'

'I will put it in half a dozen words: it don't bear dwelling on,' said Jack, putting down his untasted cup. 'Tom Dacres, in *Guerrière*, thirty-eight, met the American *Constitution*, forty-four, brought her to action of course; and was beat. Dismasted, taken, and burnt. Then their sloop *Wasp*, eighteen, tackled our brig *Frolic*, of almost exactly the same weight of metal, and took her too. Then *United States*, forty-four, and our *Macedonian*, thirty-eight, had a fight off the Azores, and *Macedonian* struck to the Americans. Two of our frigates and a sloop have struck to the Americans, and not one of theirs to us.'

In his diary that night Stephen wrote, 'I do not believe I have ever seen Jack so moved. If he had heard of Sophie's death he would no doubt have felt an even keener, even crueller emotion; but it would have been a personal grief, whereas this is beyond self, except in so far as he is entirely identified with the Royal Navy — it is, after all, his life. This series of defeats, without a single victory, in the first months of a war, is striking enough, particularly since the frigate is the very type of the fighting ship; but it is of no real consequence. This whole American war and *a fortiori* these defeats which scarcely affect the enormous

British naval force at all, is essentially irrelevant: furthermore, the defeats themselves can readily be explained (and I have no doubt the ministry is busily explaining them at this moment to a shocked, an outraged public opinion). The Americans brought larger frigates with more and heavier guns to the task: their ships are manned by volunteers, I understand, and not by what the press-gang, the quota-system, and the gaols can provide. But no, this will not do; there is no comfort for the sailors here. The British army may be defeated again and again; that can be accepted; but the Navy must always win. It always has won these last twenty years or so; nor is there any record of serious naval defeat since the Dutch wars. The Navy has always won, and it must always continue to win, to win handsomely whatever the odds. I remember the unfortunate Admiral Calder, who, with fifteen line-of-battle ships, met M. de Villeneuve with twenty, and who was disgraced because he took only two of them. Twenty years of victory and some inherent virtue must offset heavier guns, larger ships, more men. And although I have hitherto regarded the Navy more as a medium in which to work — although I do not feel that the heavens have fallen, nor that the foundations of the universe are subverted — I must confess that I am not unmoved. I feel no hint of animosity against the Americans, except in so far as their action may to some degree help Bonaparte, yet it would do my heart (as I term the illogical area of my being — and what an expanse it does cover, on occasion!) it would do my heart good to hear of some compensating victory.'

Christmas Day, and Jack, Stephen and Babbington dined with Captain Lambert, General Hislop, and his aide-de-camp. It was a creditable spread and they ate a good many geese, pies, and puddings; but Jack caught Lambert's anxious eye on the wretched wine and his heart was moved for him: Jack too had been a captain with nothing but his pay, compelled to entertain voracious, thirsty guests. The soldiers were gay enough, although General Hislop did refer to the unfortunate effect these recent events would have in India, where moral force counted for so much. And the others did their best; yet upon the whole, with its factitious merriment, it was not a very successful feast and Stephen was glad when Captain Lambert suggested showing them the ship.

A long tour it was, with Jack and Lambert pausing by each of the eighteen-pounder guns, each of the thirty-two-pounder carronades, and by the two long nines, discussing their qualities; yet this too had its end. Jack and Stephen retired to the master's day-cabin, where they sat eating ship's biscuit from their pockets: they could both eat without a stop, and they both did so almost automatically.

Their future was clear. The *Java* had taken a prize, a fair-sized American merchantman that was to meet her off San Salvador, where they were both to water. This prize, the *William*, was a slow-sailing vessel, and Captain Lambert had left her behind while he went in chase of the Portuguese ship the *Java* had brought to when the cutter saw her. They would move into the *William* in a few days' time and either take passage in her to Halifax or go straight to England in some other ship from San Salvador. *Acasta* was still on the Brest blockade, and she had a jobbing-captain, Peter Fellowes, to keep her warm for Jack.

'I am glad Lambert has a decent prize at last,' said he. 'He has always been a most unlucky wight, and never was there a man who needed money more — half a dozen boys and an invalid wife. No luck at any time: if ever he took a merchantman it was re-taken before it reached home, and of the three enemy ships he captured, two sank under him, and he had battered the third so hard that Government refused to buy her for the service. Then he was on shore for a couple of years, living in lodgings in Gosport with all his brood, a damned uneasy life; and now they have given him *Java*, about as expensive a command as you could wish. Burning to have a go at the Americans, like all of us, and then to be sent off to Bombay, with a shipful of guests, no chance of distinguishing himself, and precious little of any prizes. They might have sent Hislop in an Indiaman; it was cruel to tie up a fellow like Lambert, as good a fighting captain as any man afloat. And what a crew!'

'What is the matter with them? Are they disaffected? Mutinous?'

'No, no. They are honest creatures, I believe, God help them; but I doubt he has a hundred real seamen aboard. How they contrived to take the *William* I cannot imagine, with so many landsmen and assorted vermin in the ship — such a Bartholomew Fair, striking topgallantmasts, I have rarely seen. It reminded me of our early days in *Polychrest*. And as for the forward guns at quarters . . . but it is not fair to judge Lambert or his officers. She is only forty-odd days out of Spithead, and she had foul weather for the first twenty of them; so they have not had time to work up their gun-crews. They will come to it in time, I dare say; Lambert has a very good notion of gunnery, and Chads, his first lieutenant, is a very scientific officer. He dearly loves a gun.'

'What did Captain Lambert mean by saying, when you suggested a real discharge, a live discharge, that you were to remember the regulation, and that he had already been rapped on the knuckles for exceeding his allowance?'

'Why, there is a strict rule that for the first six months of a commission no captain is allowed to fire more shot a month than a third the number of his guns; and after the first six months, only half as much.'

'Then you must have infringed the regulation almost every day; I scarcely remember quarters without the firing of guns. Sometimes all of them, on both sides, with small-arms and swivels from the tops as well.'

'Yes, but that was powder and shot I had either captured or bought. Most captains who can afford it and who care for gunnery get round the regulation that way. Lambert cannot afford it; and although Chads might be able to, he could not possibly put himself forward.'

'Mr Chads is wealthy, I collect. Did he do well in prize-money?'

'Not that I have ever heard of. He went a far more compendious way about it — cut out the only daughter of a Turkey merchant in very dashing style with a chaise and four. A thirty thousand pounder, I have heard tell.'

Mr Chads might be rich, but he was not proud; nor was he impatient. Early in the morning some days later, when they had raised the high land of Brazil and were in hourly expectation of the *William*, Stephen came across him in the bows, showing a particularly stupid, though willing, gun-crew how to point their weapon. Again and again he made them and their midshipman heave it in and out, go through the motions of loading, taking aim, and firing: he clapped on to the tackles himself, plied the handspike, tried to make them understand the ideas of elevation, point-blank range, line of metal, the differencc between firing on the upward and the downward roll. He praised their real efforts, saved two of the duller landsmen from having their feet crushed off by the moving carriage, and promised they should fire a live round at a target presently. He showed them how to bowse their gun tight against its port and make all fast, so that the two tons of concentrated weight should not start lurching about the deck; and then, wiping his face, he joined the Doctor, saying, 'They will do very well. Good, sensible, steady men.'

'Surely, sir,' said Stephen, 'it must call for a

very nice appreciation of distance, of angle, and of direction, to judge the right moment for firing off a piece, when both the deck and the target are in motion?'

'It does, Doctor, it does indeed,' said Chads. 'But it is wonderful what use will do. Some men get the knack of it very soon — a matter of eye and tact — and they will fire amazingly well at a thousand yards after a couple of months.'

'On deck, there,' hailed the look-out from on high, in an unemphatic tone. 'Sail fine on the starboard bow.'

'Is she *William*?' called the officer of the watch.

'*William* she is, sir,' replied the look-out, after a considering pause. 'And a-closing of us fast.'

Chads glanced towards the remote loom of Brazil to the westward, and said, 'I shall be glad to have her alongside again. There are three of my best gun-captains in the prize-crew, and one landsman who has come along amazingly. But we shall be losing you and the other Leopards, sir, and we shall all be sorry for that.'

'I shall be sorry too: I should have liked another view of your ingenious sight. There were some points that I did not quite apprehend.' Mr Chads had invented a device, designed to take some of the uncertainty out of gunnery at sea and adapted to the meanest understanding: and he had spent the evening hours of Thursday explaining it to Stephen. 'But I suppose that I must pack up my belongings.'

They were not inconsiderable; the *Java*'s gunroom had done the Leopards proud, and Stephen for one had never possessed so many handkerchiefs in his life. But the word brought his vanished collections to his mind. He dismissed them at once. A woman whose acquaintance he greatly valued had once remarked that it was foolish to reflect on the past except where that past was agreeable: he did his best to observe the precept, but it was not much use — a sense of bereavement would keep breaking in. Nor had it been much use to the lady in question; she had withered away after the death of his cousin Kevin, a young man in the Austrian service.

A slow packer he was, and inefficient; if Killick had not come to him, having stowed the Captain's sea-bag, Stephen might have gone on staring at the handkerchiefs, the neckcloths, and the warm-weather drawers until the drum called him away to dinner.

'Come, sir, show a leg,' said Killick angrily. '*William*'s alongside. We'll never get a decent cabin without you show a leg — Mr

Babbington and Mr Byron and all them wicked reefers nipping aboard of her like ferrets, swiping all the decent berths. This is no good at all —' upending the sailcloth bag and starting again. He packed with quick, deft movements, and grew more nearly amiable. 'There's a fine howdy-do on deck, sir,' he said. 'A sail in the offing, and the whole quarterdeck a-staring through their spy-glasses. Some say she's a Portuguese razee —'

'What is a razee?'

'Why, a cut-down ship of the line, in course. Upper deck cut off, and all her guns behind one line of ports. Surely you know that, sir? Howsomever, Bonden been up at the jacks this last glass, and swears she's their *Constitution*, which he saw her and went aboard to visit his friend Joe Warren when they were in the Med, tickling up the Barbary States. But never mind, sir; you're quite safe. You'll be aboard *William*, and in a decent berth too, in five minutes, or my name's not Preserved Killick.'

No one on the quarterdeck was as positive as Bonden; the nature, the relative size of a ship might easily be mistaken at such a distance, and there was a strong likelihood of her being the Portuguese razee that was known to be in these waters; but Stephen walked into an atmosphere of eager hope and confident expectation. His colleague Fox, for example, was transformed from a bowed, depressed, though kindly, middle-aged man to an upright, bright-eyed creature, no older than his assistants; he turned his flushed face to Stephen and cried, 'Give you joy, Dr Maturin; I believe we have the enemy under our lee.'

Stephen stared over the water south and west at the white glint of sails, and he heard Captain Lambert say to Jack, 'It is no more than a possibility, of course, but I shall run down and take a look. Perhaps you and your people would like to go into the *William* now: I shall send her into San Salvador.'

'I think I may speak for all the Leopards when I say we should be wretchedly disappointed to be put out of the ship,' said Jack with a smile. 'We had very much rather stay.'

'That's right, sir,' said Babbington; and Byron said, 'Hear him, hear him.'

Lambert had expected no less, but the words gave him pleasure; he acknowledged them with a chuckle and gave orders to wear ship.

Round she came in a long smooth curve and steadied on the larboard tack, the same tack as the stranger, who was heading out to sea. The *William* also wore, since their courses would be much the same until the southern cape was weathered, but she was a dull sailer, and the *Java*, letting fall her topgallants and crossing her royal yards, left her far behind.

The *Java* had plenty of right seamen to sail her, that was clear: the royal yards fairly raced aloft. Jack stepped below for his telescope, and when the rigging was tolerably clear of hands he went up to the crosstrees to view the distant ship. He paused in the maintop, for although according to the purser's scales he had lost four stone he seemed to be heaving a most uncommon weight: obviously his strength had not yet come back, in spite of these days of good eating. However, from the maintop he could see nothing, because of the foretopsail, so after a while he climbed again: the crosstrees at last, and he found that he was in a muck-sweat. 'What a flat I should look, was I to drop down among them like an act of God,' he said, glancing at the remote, crowded quarterdeck, so narrow from this height, flecked with the red coats of the Marines, the white shirts of hurrying foremast hands, blue-coated officers, the parson's black, all sharp in the brilliant sun. There was not much chance of his dropping, however; these airy regions had been his so long that his hands moved as surely as an ape's: without thinking of it, he took up the comfortable position he had learnt as a mastheaded midshipman, and unslung his glass. The *Java* was lying over with the brisk north-eastern breeze, making something better than nine knots; and as he pulled the telescope to its full length he wondered how long Lambert would keep her under royals. She was somewhat by the head, like all French ships he had ever sailed in, and for his part he would have preferred lower and topmast studdingsails: but that was Lambert's business. He knew how to sail his own ship: and fight her, too.

Ducking to see under the taut arch of the foretopgallant, he fixed the stranger, focused, and stared long and hard. Yes. She was a frigate, of that there was no doubt. She bore on the *Java*'s starboard bow, sailing into the offing, going from her on the same tack, and he could not count her ports, but a minute examination showed him that she carried these ports high — a strong presumption of her being a heavy, stout-built ship. And although she too was under royals she did not lean from the strengthening breeze: another mark of a heavy ship. She was probably sailing about as fast as she could go; yet judging from her broad, turbulent wake, that was not very fast. *Java* would have the legs of her in a long chase. On the other hand, she had not set her lower weather studdingsails, nor anything in the way of bonnets or sky-scrapers: the *Java* was not in fact in pursuit of a fleeing ship, but of one that meant to draw her away from the land, away from the *William*, a possible consort, a possible man-of-war — to draw her far out into the offing, where there was all the sea-room in the world. Jack nodded: it was a sensible move. The man over there handled his ship well.

But so did Lambert. The *Java*'s fore and main studdingsails appeared, aloft and alow; and on his high perch Jack felt the ship respond with a beautiful eager living thrust: she was a fine sea-boat, and not only that, but a very much finer ship altogether than the poor old shattered *Guerrière*, all paint and putty over her shaky timbers, over-gunned, under-manned . . . It appeared to him that they were gaining on the chase, and that in perhaps three or four hours they would be within gun-shot: and then, if she proved to be an American — and he was intimately convinced she was an American — they would put it to the test. He found that his heart was beating so hard that he could scarcely keep the long glass steady. That was no state for going into action, although he was only a mere passenger: coolness was all. The question was, were they in fact going into action? Was the *Java* gaining, and if so, by how much? He clapped the glass to, and heaviness forgotten he shot down on deck like a boy to join Chads on the forecastle. The first lieutenant and Babbington were busy with their sextants, measuring the angle subtended by the chase's masthead, leaning right over on the sloping deck: spray from the fine bow-wave swept over them each time the *Java* pitched, but they had much the same results. The *Java* was gaining, but only by a little under a mile in one hour. At this rate, and if the chase spread more canvas, they could not bring her to action much before nightfall. And then again, was she an American at all?

'We must presume she is,' said Chads, 'even if it means losing a spar or two.' He looked anxiously up at the whipping studding-sail-booms.

'Just so,' said Jack. 'And suppose what we hope proves to be the case, may I suggest you give us a pair of guns? We are used to working together.'

'If you would take over the forecastle battery, sir, I should be infinitely obliged, with numbers six and seven for your own. I had to entrust those two to the Marine recruits. Seven kicks a little, but we renewed the breechings last week, and the bolts are sound.'

'Six and seven: very good. I take it that Captain Lambert will manoeuvre to cross her wake and hang upon her starboard quarter,' said Jack. 'So we must get our hand in with the larboard gun first.'

'Why no, sir,' said Chads. 'The Captain was speaking of his plan of action not five minutes ago — the General asked him how we set about these things at sea, lines of approach and so on. The Captain quoted Lord Nelson's "Never mind manoeuvres, go straight at 'em", declaring that since we had the weathergage, that was exactly what he meant to do — to go straight at 'em, batter 'em yardarm to yardarm for a while, and then board in the smoke.'

Jack was silenced. He could not contradict Lord Nelson, whom he adored, nor could he utter the least criticism of the *Java*'s captain, who had carried a French corvette with a broadside half as heavy again as his own, in just that determined manner. He himself, commanding a ship that moved faster through the water than the chase, would certainly have manoeuvred, playing at long bowls with the enemy, probing him, hitting him on the quarter, endeavouring to rake him, and taking advantage of the leeward attack, with the rising breeze laying the enemy's ports low to the water, perhaps even smothering his fire. On the other hand, in a close engagement the leeward ship often could not see her opponent through the enormous clouds of smoke. Yet clearly this was no time for expressing his views on the subject, above all since the word was being passed for Mr Chads. They walked back to the quarterdeck, and a moment later the private signal broke out at the *Java*'s masthead. No reply. The Spanish and Portuguese signals followed. Still no reply, and conviction grew.

Conviction grew still stronger, doubting voices were silenced, when the stranger took in her studdingsails, hauled her wind and came about, standing north and west on the starboard tack, apparently to cross the *Java*'s bows. The precision of her turn was impressive; so was the long row of gun-ports it revealed: without any question she was a forty-four-gun frigate, tall and stiff.

Captain Lambert put his ship about to keep the weathergage, and steered a course parallel to the American's. They were so close now that he could force an action in the afternoon, even if the big frigate wished to decline it; but for the moment he chose to bide his time, and the ships sailed side by side, with a great stretch of sea between them.

Jack gathered his Leopards, and they looked to their guns, number six to starboard and seven the other side, just under the over-hang of the forecastle: each crew fought a pair of guns except in those few ships with a super-abundance of hands, and in the unlikely event of their being engaged on both sides at once the crew ran from one to the other, firing them alternately. The Leopard quickly settled who should be first and second captains — Bonden and Babbington — who should be boarders, fireman, sponger and so on; checked the breeching, drew the charges, having little faith in any loading but their own, recharged, ran the guns in and out half a dozen times, and drew breath. Those were the familiar eighteen-pounders, five hundred-weight a man, and they offered no problems, though the Leopards did not much care for the way *Java*'s jollies had arranged the swabs and rammers, and though in their weakened state they did find the starboard gun heavy to heave inboard against the slope of the deck: but as Bonden observed, once the dust started flying, the recoil would look after that.

Forshaw darted below to report that the chase had worn and shown a waft, thought to be a private signal, and that the *Java* was about to wear likewise. He was in a state of shrill glee, and his voice went so high that it almost vanished. He looked so frail, so very childish in his over-sized borrowed clothes that the older man looked at him quite piti-fully, and Jack thought, How I hope that boy don't stop a ball. 'House your guns,' he cried aloud, glancing at his watch, which said one minute before noon.

Immediately afterwards the hands were piped to dinner, and at the same time the drum beat for the officers. This pleased Jack: Lambert meant to take advantage of the last minutes before the galley fires were put out in clearing the ship for action. He and Jack might differ about manoeuvring, but they were of the same mind about going into battle with a full belly.

The *Java* was already almost entirely cleared, and although there was not yet a clean sweep fore and aft — some of the immense amount of baggage belonging to the Governor and his suite had still to be struck down into the hold — the cabin bulkheads and furniture were gone, and her captain, General Hislop, Jack, and the captain of the Marines, sitting at a grating slung between two guns, could see their probable, their almost certain adversary, as they ate. They were all men who were thoroughly accustomed to fire and they ate heartily; but rarely did they take their eyes from the American.

'As I was telling Chads,' said Lambert to Jack, 'my intention is to go the plain, straightforward way about it: to bear down, lay the ship alongside her, hit her as hard as we can, and then board her in the smoke.'

'Yes, sir,' said Jack.

'We have plenty of willing hands for the job, with all our supernumeraries; and I fancy they will make a better fist of it with the cutlass than playing long bowls with the guns. And now I come to think of it, Chads tells me you have very handsomely offered to fight a pair of guns yourself and to keep an eye on the forward battery. I am very much obliged to you, Aubrey: I am a lieutenant short, and most of my youngsters are on their first voyage; and six and seven were served by the Marines. Not that they did not serve them pretty well, but Captain Rankin here will be happy to have his small-arms men back again.' Rankin agreed, observing that the tops were not nearly as full of sharp-shooters as he could wish, if the action became really close. One bell struck, and Lambert continued, 'I think it is very nearly time: so, gentlemen, I will give you the King, and confusion to his enemies.'

The officers walked out on to the quarterdeck: the chase lay about two miles ahead, to leeward, and both ships were running at a good ten knots; but now the *Java* was labouring under her royals and Captain Lambert had them taken in. Yet even without them she gained perceptibly: and so they ran eastwards, each drawing a long white furrow in the sparkling sea. An empty sea: nothing to windward, nothing to leeward, and the *William* had vanished astern long since, while Brazil was no more than a faint cloudlike band from the masthead.

And now the stranger — a stranger no longer, nor a chase — displayed a commodore's broad pendant on the main, together with the colours of the United States. Bonden had been right: she was indeed the *Constitution*.

A few moments later her royals too came in, followed by her fore and mainsail, and she hauled to the wind, her speed dropping immediately. It was clear that she meant to fight and that she had always meant to fight, but to fight as and when it suited her: she had drawn the *Java* from the land and from the *William*, and now she was content. An intelligent opponent, reflected Jack; cool and calculating.

The *Java* replied to the American colours with her own, and a union flag high in the leeward rigging as well, so that there should be no mistake; and she too stripped to her fighting sails — no sound on board but the brief orders, the bosun's call, the run of seamen's feet, the creaking of blocks, and the song of the wind in the rigging. With the main and foresails hauled up, every man on deck had a clear view of the American as she lay there, her head a little off the north-north-eastern wind: and now in total silence Captain Lambert took the *Java* down as he had promised, slanting across the wind straight for the enemy's larboard quarter. Half an hour would bring them into battle.

For those with no immediate tasks at hand, ten of these thirty minutes passed in a state of suspended activity, the wheel unmoved by so much as a spoke, scarcely a word on the crowded, gravely attentive quarterdeck. Then Captain Lambert nodded to Mr Chads, and the drum volleyed and thundered fore and aft. Most of the officers and midshipmen ran to join their divisions at the guns; the master stepped behind the wheel to con the ship; three parties of Marines climbed into the tops, trailing their muskets; the surgeons went below, down, down, under the waterline; and silence fell again. Everything was ready. All along the clean, neat deck, brilliant in the sun, the powder-boys stood with their cartridges behind the guns; the shot-racks and garlands were full; thin smoke streamed from the match-tubs; the bosun had long since secured the yards with puddening and chains; deep in the magazine the gunner waited among his open powder-kegs; the fearnought screens were laid over the hatchways.

Jack walked into the comparative darkness of the forecastle, and there at the open port his gun-crew was waiting for him: they were stripped to the waist, showing their appalling burns, and most had tied handkerchiefs around their heads against the sweat. They looked at him with a serious though confident expression; the neighbouring crews with curiosity and a kind of hopeful deference — few, apart from the captains, had ever seen a great gun fired in anger, and Captain Aubrey was known to be a master of his trade.

Blazing sun beyond the port, and there, exactly framed, the *Constitution*. A heavy frigate indeed; now he could gauge the true size of her massive spars, the unusual height of her ports, well clear of the choppy sea breaking white against her side. A tough nut to crack, if the Americans could fire their guns as well as they could sail their ship. American seamanship he knew; but could a fighting ship be improvised? Could four hundred officers and men be taught their duty in a few months? A few months as against the continual practice and tradition of twenty years of war? Unlikely, but not impossible; after all, a great many Americans had learnt gunnery, often much against their will, in the Royal Navy — he had had scores under his command in one ship or another. He hoped Lambert would board as soon as possible: there was something very daunting about the determined attack of hundreds of men swarming over the side with cutlasses and tomahawks. Few ship's companies could withstand it.

Behind him Forshaw, who, being too light to heave upon a tackle with any effect, acted as their powder-boy, was explaining to one of the *Java*'s midshipmen that he would feel quite different, quite easy, once the dust began to fly. 'I generally chew a quid of tobacco while we are going into action,' he added, 'and I encourage my men to do the same; it makes the awkward waiting pass much quicker.'

In the cockpit, where, by the light of three hanging lanterns, the surgeons were putting a final razor edge on their instruments by means of an oiled silk-stone, Stephen said to Mr Fox, 'Do you not find, sir, that your perception of time is strangely altered on these occasions, when — that rat, Mr McClure, you may certainly strike that rat, if you are brisk.'

Mr Fox was obliged to admit that he had not experienced such an occasion before; but he hoped that presently the dispersion of stimuli would have a lenitive effect, that the din of battle and the necessary activity would dispel a certain illogical uneasiness, or rather impatience.

'There,' cried Stephen, flinging a retractor at a particularly bold rat. 'I very nearly had him, the thief. Surely, Mr Fox, you have more than your fair share of rats aboard? Have you thought of introducing a parcel of weasels? We find them answer admirably, in Ireland.'

'I thought you had no weasels, no serpents, no salamanders, in your country.'

'No more we have; the Irish weasels are all stoats. But they are the devil for rats.'

A tremendous triple knock, a bang or crash reverberating along the cable-tiers, cut off the surgeon's reply: the *Constitution* had opened fire at half a mile, and three of her round-shot had struck the *Java*'s side on the ricochet.

'Good practice,' observed Jack; and as he watched, bent low to see through the port, he saw another jet of smoke from one of the American's after-guns. The shot struck the sea, skipped three times, with each splash in a direct line for his eye, came aboard — a muffled thump in the tight-packed forecastle hammocks — and could be heard rolling about overhead. Forshaw darted out and came back with the ball, a twenty-four-pounder.

'A pity it is so big,' said Jack, turning it over. 'I remember when I was a boy in *Ajax*, and the *Apollon* was blazing away at us like Guy

Fawkes's night, a spent eighteen-pound ball came in at our port. The lieutenant — it was Mr Horner: you remember him, Bonden?'

'Oh yes, sir. A very sprightly gentleman, that loved his laugh.'

'He picked it up, called for a piece of chalk, wrote Post Paid on the ball, rammed it down our gun, and so sent it back in double quick time.'

'Ha, ha, ha!' went the gun-crew and their neighbours on either side.

'And not long after that, he was made a *post*-captain, ha, ha, ha!'

Nearer, and the *Java* was almost on the *Constitution*'s larboard beam. The American's side vanished in a cloud of smoke: her broadside, some seven hundred pounds of iron, ripped up the water, a series of white fountains short of their mark by a hundred yards; and a few harmless balls struck the *Java*'s side.

Nearer still. Little more than musket-range, and they could see their enemies' faces. They stood poised and tense over their guns, waiting for the order to fire, Bonden glaring along the barrel, perpetually shifting it with his handspike as the *Constitution* came full in the beam. Point-blank range, but still no order. The Americans were running out their guns: Jack had been counting the seconds from the first broadside, and he reached a hundred and twenty before the vast thundering eruption hid the enemy again, all but her topgallantmasts, that could be seen high above the smoke, quivering from the shock. This time the whole well-grouped broadside raced humming deep far overhead. Two minutes; quite good gun-drill, though he had managed seventy seconds. And they had misjudged the —

'Fire as they bear.'

The welcome order came as the *Java* reached the top of her roll and was just beginning to lean to leeward. The whole of her starboard broadside roared out and instantly the deck was filled with smoke, with the marvellous powder-smell. Laughing aloud, Jack and his mates clapped on, ran the gun in, sponged, reloaded, rammed home the charge, working like powerful machines, and as the smoke cleared they saw that they had hit her hard — gaps in the hammocks, the wheel destroyed, some shrouds and a backstay hanging loose. On either side the Javas cheered like fury; and as they heaved so they came closer still, within pistol-shot of the *Constitution*'s bow. And at pistol-shot the *Constitution* fired again. A few splintering crashes aft, but nothing to interrupt the cheers forward as they ran their guns out, thumping them hard against the sills. Yet as they peered into the dense cloud of American smoke to point their loaded guns, staring and ludicrously fanning with their hands, the sail-trimmers were called. The *Constitution*, having fired, had instantly filled her headsails and put before the wind: she had worn, and the *Java*, without waiting to catch her and rake her on the turn, was wearing after her: the starboard guns no longer bore. The Leopards exchanged a glance.

The smoke cleared entirely, drifting away in a solid bank and showing the *Constitution* well to leeward, with the *Java* coming up fast on her quarter but still turning with her as she hauled up on the other tack, presenting her undamaged starboard ports. In the long pause Jack hurried up and down the forecastle battery, making them stop their noise, house the starboard guns safely and cast loose those on the other side. The two *Java* midshipmen, first-voyagers, had no notion of anything beyond the formal movements of the great-gun exercise. His heart was still beating high with the immense vitality of battle, and this violent activity — heaving, shoving men into their places, checking the tackle-falls, breeching, cartridges, grape and round-shot — covered the uneasy feeling in the back of his mind. Lambert might have missed one golden chance, but there would soon be another.

Very soon. The *Java* was ranging up on the *Constitution*'s starboard side. The larboard guns, trained hard forward, began to bear; and as they bore, so they fired. One; three and five together; and as Bonden fired number seven he saw the shot strike the *Constitution*'s mainchains, just before the smoke swept down. But now there were orange flashes in the smoke as the American after-guns replied; and after a few savage moments both full broadsides were at work, a continuous bellowing roar, punctuated by the even louder crashes of the next-hand guns and the carronades overhead. A prodigious omnipresent din, and in it the kicking number seven broke its breeching after the fourth discharge. Worse than that, number three had been dismounted and there were several men lying on the deck, including both midshipmen. Leaving the practised Leopards to their tasks, Jack ran to trip and secure the gun. Its crew had little notion of what to do, but by gesture and bellow and example in the incessant roar and clangour he got them to make it fast, slid a dead man through the port, and made them carry the wounded below.

The fire was very hot, with a furious discharge of musketry as well, almost as hot as he had known it; and there were three of the maindeck guns knocked out — perhaps some of the larboard carronades too. Amidships and aft the pattern of the *Java*'s fire was gone. An officer, running to deal with the confusion, was shot dead from the *Constitution*'s tops, and the next moment his body was struck, jerked against the starboard rail by a twenty-four-pound ball. But that was the last shot from the *Constitution*'s great guns, the last for this bout; an eddy cleared the smoke and they saw her wearing once again, wearing very fast.

This time Lambert quickly let fly his topsail sheets, checking the *Java*'s way. Jack smiled: clearly Lambert meant to cross the *Constitution*'s wake, raking her from stern to stem, the most damaging fire a ship could receive.

'Sir, sir,' cried the midshipman from number eleven, the gun to which poor Broughton had been running, 'what shall we do? The shot is jammed.'

Jack had taken three strides aft when he fell — it was nothing, he found, scrambling up and slipping again in Broughton's blood — a musket-ball had grazed his head. But now the *Java* was beginning her turn: in less than a minute she would cross the *Constitution*'s wake right under her stern — a beautifully calculated move — yet most of these poor brave willing silly fools were milling about to port, unaware that the starboard guns would be engaged.

'T'other side, t'other side,' he roared, on his feet at last. They raced across the deck, willing and eager in spite of the hail of small-arms fire; but to his utter horror he realized that on quitting them they had not reloaded their starboard guns. The turn continued: the *Constitution*'s tall, unprotected, naked, infinitely vulnerable stern was right before the *Java*'s broadside, the *Java* so beautifully steered that her main yardarm crossed the *Constitution*'s very taffrail: and only a single gun went off.

Cursing did no good; blasphemy brought bad luck. Jack split his remaining crew — Mr Byron had copped it with a nasty splinter in his chest, Bates the Flitch had lost the number of his mess — divided them among the other forward guns, and helped load two or three. There was no time for cursing, either: the *Java* was running alongside the *Constitution*, and now the fire resumed its utmost fury, firing, reloading, firing again as fast as the powder could run up from the magazine. And all the time he had to try to stop the Javas from madly overcharging, from ramming two cartridges into their guns, and any bits of metal they could find.

The Americans' aim was better now, and they were firing low; the twenty-four-pound balls sent splinters racing across the deck in clouds, great jagged lumps of sharp-edged wood, and one of these struck Bonden down. Jack heaved him out of the way of the recoiling gun, and when it had fired knelt by him on the deck and shouted into his deafened ear, 'Only a handsbreadth of scalp; your pigtail's all right. Get you below for a stitch.'

'Bowsprit's gone, sir,' said Bonden, peering through his blood, and following his gaze Jack saw the jib and forestaysail blowing free.

'Give the Doctor my regards,' said he, and ran along the deck, checking each gun, helping to point, cheering the men. Not that they needed much cheering: they were firing much better, much faster, now they had the hang of it, and they roared like devils as their shot went home. No sign of flinching from the guns, though three ports were battered into one, and amidships the dead and wounded lay by the score, blood oozing thick.

'Heave, heave,' bawled Jack at number three, and as the gun ran up he stared into the smoke to place his shot, waiting for the roll with his mates poised over the scorching barrel; but this time there was no shifting hint of the enemy's side. The roll came: again: and still the thick smoke lay. Nothing beyond it as it cleared — the American had worn again.

'Hands about ship,' came the cry; and then, 'Ready, oh!'

The sail-trimmers ran to their stations and in the silence Jack moved back to the forward scuttle-butt and took a long, long-needed drink. Lambert was going to tack rather than wear, so as to cut the *Constitution* on her turn — to cut across her stern. A fine move, if only the *Java* could make it quick enough; there was little way on her, and her headsails were gone.

Here was Bonden, a reddening bandage all round his head. 'All right, sir?' he asked.

Jack nodded, and said, 'Warm work, Bonden. How are things below? How is Mr Byron?'

'Mr Byron looks a bit old-fashioned, sir, as far as I could see. Powerful lot of work down there — Doctor's as busy as a bee. Sends his love, though. Their premier, Mr Chads, he got a nasty swipe.'

The Leopards had no stations for tacking ship: they gathered round their Captain and drank deep from the scuttle-butt as the *Java* swung up into the wind. Slowly, slowly.

'I have no notion of all this wearing,' said Babbington.

'He may do it once too often,' said Jack. 'The most dangerous movement I have —'

'Christ, we're going to miss stays,' whispered Babbington. And indeed, with neither jib nor forestaysail it looked as though the *Java* could not cross the wind's eye, but must fall off, stern to the enemy, now a quarter of a mile to leeward. Jack glanced aft, and there she was, luffing up to show her starboard broadside. In another minute the *Java* would be raked.

'Lie down,' he said, pressing on Forshaw's shoulder: and the broadside came, striking the *Java*'s stern and tearing the whole length of her deck. But in the same moment her backed foretopsail filled, and slowly she began to pay off — she was round.

'Larboard guns,' cried Jack, springing up, and now the Javas scarcely needed any teaching. They flew to their guns and as the ship turned a little further they returned the fire, a hearty though ragged volley that went right home; and once again the *Constitution* wore.

The *Java* came straight down for her, ranged alongside, received her fire, returned it, the guns so hot that they leapt clear of the deck at each discharge. Rough work, rough work: the difference between twenty-four and eighteen pounds was telling now, and the *Java* could not stand much more of it. In the short seconds between guns, between making the cheering men reduce their charge, fire low and steady, and swab clean, Jack saw the enormous wreckage amidships, the shattered boats, the grim wounds in the mainmast and above all in the unstayed foremast. 'We must board,' he said to himself. 'We still have about three hundred men'; and as the words formed he heard Lambert roar, 'Boarders away.'

The *Java* bore up, heading straight at the *Constitution*'s side. The boarders swarmed on to the forecastle, cutlasses, pistols, axes ready. Chads was there again, pale at his Captain's side; both of them caught Jack's eye — a savage, eager grin. A few yards more and there would be the crash of impact, the spring aboard, the hot work hand to hand. The Americans were firing from their tops as fast as they could load: it made no odds to the furious impatience of the crowd of men poised for their leap.

But then over all the din, cutting clear through, the high shrieking hail from the *Java*'s foretop, 'Stand from under', and the mast, the towering great edifice of the foremast with all its spreading yards, its fighting-top, its sails, its countless ropes and blocks, came crashing down, the lower part kicking aft to cover the maindeck, the upper covering the forecastle.

There was an immense amount of rigging, of spars over them and over the forward guns;

there were some men pinned, others wounded; and for the next few minutes, in the fury of clearing so that the guns could fire, Jack lost all track of the relative position of the ships. When at last the forward battery was to some extent restored he saw the *Constitution* well ahead, in the act of wearing across the *Java*'s bows. Not a gun could the *Java* fire in this position, and the *Constitution* raked her deliberately from stem to stern, killing a score of men and bringing down her maintopmast.

Once again the wild labour of clearing, slashing at the wreckage with axes, anything that came to hand; and now the *Constitution* lay on their starboard quarter, pouring in a diagonal fire; lay there a moment before bearing up and giving the *Java* her full larboard broadside.

'Captain's down,' said a Java, having carried a wounded mate below. 'But Mr Chads is back.'

'Never say die,' cried the captain of his gun, and firing he knocked away the *Constitution*'s maintopsail yard to a frenzy of cheering all along the deck.

Yet at the same time the *Java*'s gaff and spanker-boom went by the board, and a little after the mizenmast followed them. The Javas, undismayed, fired like demons, streaming with sweat under the smoky sun, often with blood; and the stabbing flames from almost every shot they fired set light to the tarred wreckage hanging over the side: fire-buckets, powder, fire-buckets, powder, the remaining officers had them running in a continual stream. At one point the ships were side by side again, and the *Java*'s great guns gave as good as they got; or at least did all they could to do so; and she being low in the water now, some of her round-shot made cruel wounds. But the *Java* lacked her fighting-tops — fore and mizen were gone and the maintop was a wreck — whereas the American did not. Her tops were filled with marksmen, and it was one of these that brought Jack down. The blow knocked him flat, but he thought nothing of it until on getting up he found that his right arm would not obey him, that it was hanging at an unnatural angle. He stood, swaying, for with two masts and all but one sail gone the *Java* was rolling very heavily; and as he stood amidst the din, still shouting at the crew of number nine to depress their gun, an oak splinter knocked him down again.

He had a vague awareness of Killick's voice swearing at a Marine — 'Handsomely, handsomely, you fat-arsed, Dutch-built bugger' — and then he came fully to his wits as Stephen leant over him, searching the wound. 'Stephen,' he said. 'Quick, just bind it up, splint it up. You shall have it off afterwards if you wish. I must go on deck.'

Stephen nodded, splinted and bound the arm, and turned to a man lying on his own liver while Jack made his way through the long, long rows among the smell of blood to the ladder. On the quarterdeck he found Chads, equally bandaged, equally pale, with a fine determined light blazing in his eye: Chads was now in command of the ship. He was getting the wreckage of the mizen free, before the heavy floating mast should ram the *Java* with its butt end, sending her to the bottom a little before her time. The carpenter and the gunner and the armourer were all standing by him, waiting for the chance to have a word. 'Pray go forward, sir, if you can,' he said to Jack. 'If we can get her before the wind we'll board her yet.'

Forward he went along the bloody deck, lurching on the enormous roll and watching the *Constitution*: she had run ahead out of gunshot and her people were busy knotting and splicing. The thin gun-crews he passed were in high spirits, bawling after the American, challenging her to come back and have it out.

'Game young cocks,' he reflected, hurrying faster. With such men, if only they could get before the wind, and if only they could fall aboard the American, they might carry her yet. He had known victory snatched from a situation worse than this, with an over-confident enemy making a mistake. *Constitution* had already made at least two very dangerous moves: she might make another.

On the forecastle Babbington and a party of seamen had roused an almost undamaged topgallant mast from the wreckage of the booms and they were trying to make a jury foremast of it. But the *Java*'s roll and even more her pitch was so violent that they were having a cruel time with it; and at every pitch wreckage from the maintop showered down on them, while the remnant of the mainmast itself, with never a shroud on either side and backstays gone, threatened to fall outboard at any moment.

'The mainmast must go,' said Jack. 'Forshaw, jump to the quarterdeck and ask Mr Chads for permission and for the carpenter's crew. Forshaw — where is Forshaw?'

Nobody answered for a moment, and then Babbington said, 'Gone, sir. Blasted over the side.'

'Oh Christ,' said Jack: a very slight pause, and then, 'Holles, cut along.'

Holles came back with the carpenters and their axes. The mast was gone, clean over the side, and the ship was steadier. Chads and all the seamen from aft were now on the forecastle, working on the jury foremast with intense effort and concentration; and all the time the gun-crews cheered and called after the *Constitution*. The jury-mast rose up, straight up; they made all fast, rigged out a lower studdingsail-boom. The awkward sail rose, filled, and the *Java* gathered way, answering her helm. She turned, bringing the wind a little abaft the beam, and moved towards the distant *Constitution*, her tattered ensign flying from the mizen's stump.

With only one arm, and that his left, there was little that Jack could do at this point. He stood by Chads as they turned aft, considering the situation: the deck before them was a shambles; they could see a dozen guns dismounted, and there were others they could not see; the boats were all shattered; and then of course there was the blood. But it was not a hopeless shambles; the one pump that had not been destroyed was pumping hard; the crews stood by their guns, ready and eager; all the boarders had their weapons there at hand; a Marine stepped forward to strike one bell in the first dogwatch — a cracked and tinny sound. Jack fumbled awkwardly for his watch with his left hand, automatically checking the time — a vain attempt: all he brought out was a twisted gold case and a handful of glass and little wheels. The carpenter stepped up to Chads and said, 'Six foot four inches in the well, sir, if you please, and gaining fast.'

'Then we had better go aboard the American at once,' said Chads, with a smile.

They looked forward, and there was the American: she had completed her repairs, and as they watched she filled, wore, and came towards them on the starboard tack.

Now was the time to profit from a God-sent mistake: now or never. If the *Constitution* would only neglect the weathergage, would only come close enough to allow them to board in a last dash through her fire . . . but the *Constitution* intended nothing of the kind. Deliberately and under perfect control she crossed the *Java*'s bows at rather more than two hundred yards, shivered her main and mizen topsails, and lay there, gently rocking, her whole almost undamaged larboard broadside looking straight at the dismasted *Java*, ready to rake her again and again. With her single sail right forward the *Java* could not move into the wind — could no longer approach the *Constitution*; all she could do was to make a slow starboard turn to bring her seven port guns to bear: by the time they could fire she would have been raked three times at point-blank range — in any case, the

Constitution would not wait until they bore, but fill again and circle her. The *Constitution* lay there: with evident forbearance she did not open fire. Jack could see her captain looking earnestly at them from his quarterdeck.

'No,' said Chads in a dead voice. 'It will not do.' He looked at Jack, who bowed his head: then walked aft, as a resolute man might walk to the gallows, walked between the sparse gun-crews, silent now, and hauled the colours down.

CHAPTER FOUR

The *Constitution* was sailing northwards with a flowing sheet, helped on her way by the great current that flowed from the Gulf of Mexico; and Dr Maturin stood at her taffrail staring at the wake, white in the indigo blue. Few things could be more favourable for the easy run of a retrospective mind, and Stephen's flowed as free as the stream itself.

The recent past was immediately present to his eye, his mind's or inner eye; it saw the various incidents reenacting against the background of white water, sometimes blurred and fragmentary, sometimes as sharp as an image in a camera obscura. The ferrying of all the prisoners of war across the heaving sea in the only boat left to the other side, a leaking ten-oared cutter, over a hundred of them wounded. Bonden's cry of 'Why, Boston Joe!' as the American seaman, a former shipmate, put the manacles on him. The burning of the *Java*; the vast pall of smoke that rose over her as she blew up; the horrible journey to San Salvador in the enormously overcrowded ship on a blazing day with a lifeless following breeze, the *Java*'s unwounded hands in irons and battened down in case they should rise upon their captors — the captors themselves furiously busy with their own repairs. The *Constitution*'s cable-tier turned into one long sickbay, and many shocking wounds to deal with. It was here that he had met Mr Evans, the *Constitution*'s surgeon, and learnt to esteem him: a bold, deft operator with a firm mind, a man whose sole aim was to preserve life and limb and who fought very hard to do so, with great skill, learning, and devotion — a man who made no difference between his own people and the prisoners, and one of the few surgeons he had known who considered the whole man, not only the wound itself. Between them they thought they had saved Captain Lambert, although they very nearly despaired of Jack when the high fever and the look of gangrene appeared: yet in both cases they were wrong — Lambert died the day he was carried ashore and Jack survived, although he was too near death to be moved before the *Constitution* sailed.

'Lambert died more of misery than of his wounds,' reflected Stephen. 'The third frigate to strike to the Americans! I believe it would have killed Jack, in his already weakened state, had he been in command: even so, he smelt of death.' He contemplated for a while upon stimuli, positive and negative; upon that which had filled the much weakened Leopards with prodigious strength and activity during the battle; upon that which had struck them back to a state of extreme, listless fatigue. 'He has survived, sure, and his functions are much what they should be; but he has had a shocking blow. Sometimes he is positively humble with me, diffident and as it were apologetical, as though detected in false pretences, while with others he is cold, reserved, and on occasion arrogant, so unlike his usual open friendly candour; and a relapse would not surprise me. At present, now that he can defecate with ease, his greatest difficulty is maintaining the dogged mechanical cheerfulness intended to show the American officers that he does not mind it, that he can lose as well as win. I have seen him succeed to admiration when taken by the French; but here the case is altered: these gentlemen are Americans, and the *Java* was the third frigate their little navy has taken, without a single victory to set off against the defeats. They are indeed a gentlemanly set, with one or two exceptions (for I cannot think highly of those who squirt tobacco-juice past my ear, however skilfully), but they would be more than human if they could conceal their cheerfulness, their sense of well-being, I might even say their perfect happiness at having defeated the first naval power on earth; and even if they could, there would be no hiding the rustic merriment of the ship's company, the jolly carpenters, the facetious men with the caulking-irons.'

A gang of these jolly carpenters moved him over to windward so that they could get at a gaping wound in the deck, hitherto covered with a tarpaulin — moved him quite gently. 'Mind where you put your foot, squire; there are holes enough to fill a wagon.' Plenty of holes indeed; the ship had been filled with the sound of hammering ever since they left San Salvador; but he was so used to it by now that this fresh outburst close at hand did not interrupt his thoughts. A gentlemanly set: he recalled their extreme care that nothing belonging to the *Java*'s officers should be lost or looted. He remembered a huge American midshipman appearing with his diary and Jack's sheaf of papers folded into it and asking 'who the black book belonged to?' He not only still possessed his diary and his writing-case but every last handkerchief and pair of stockings bestowed upon him — some of the givers now dead, alas, more than three thousand miles astern. The word 'diary' made him frown, but the perpetual streaming wake carried his thoughts along, or rather the succession of images, and against that churning whiteness he once again beheld the ceremony in San Salvador at which the American commanding officer, Commodore Bainbridge, had addressed all his captives who were in a fit state to hear him, stating that if they would give their word not to serve against the United States until they were duly exchanged they might go straight home to England in two cartel ships. Then the more private ceremony at which General Hislop, in his own name and in that of *Java*'s surviving officers, presented the Commodore with a handsome sword in acknowledgment of his kindness to the prisoners — a kindness that extended not only to their ordinary belongings but even to the Governor's magnificent service of official plate, a circumstance that may have added to Hislop's eloquence.

Diary: the word jagged at his consciousness and he returned to consider it. He had given way to two dangerous indulgences in his time: laudanum was one, the bottled fortitude, the nepenthe that had tided him over some of his worst times with Diana Villiers and that had then turned into a tyrannical master. Diary-keeping was the other: a harmless and even a useful occupation for most, but unwise in an intelligence-agent. To be sure, in most places the manuscript was encoded three deep, in a cipher so personal that it had baffled the Admiralty's cryptographers when he challenged them with a sample. Yet there were some purely personal parts in which he had used a simpler system, one that an ingenious, puzzle-solving mind with a knowledge of Catalan could make out, if he chose to spend the necessary labour. It would be labour lost, from the point of view of intelligence, since these sections dealt only with Stephen's passion for Diana Villiers over all these years. Yet even so he was very, very unwilling that any other eye should see him naked, see him exposed as a helpless tormented lover, a nympholept furiously longing for what was beyond his reach; and even more unwilling that any man should read his attempts at verse, Catullus-and-water at the best. A very great deal of water, though the fire might perhaps be the same: *nescio, sed fieri sentio et excrucior.*

He did not really fear that any important part could be deciphered, but it would have been wiser to toss the diary overboard with a weight attached, as Chads had thrown the *Java*'s signal-book in its leaden covers and General Hislop his despatches; and although he valued it extremely (apart from anything else he often needed a portable, infallible, artificial memory) he probably would have done so, if he had not had seven amputations on his hands. A foolish slip: an intelligence-agent should carry nothing that did not bear its apparent explanation on its face, nothing that could arouse suspicion of a code. He had not claimed the book until they were in San Salvador, and when he did so the Commodore asked him whether the book had anything to do with the *Java*'s cipher or signals, or whether it was of a private nature. Mr Bainbridge was sitting in the great cabin, obviously in considerable pain from his wounded leg, with Mr Evans and a civilian beside him; and it appeared to Stephen that the three Americans looked at him very attentively as he assured the Commodore that the entries in the book were of a purely personal, medical, and philosophic nature.

'And what of these papers?' asked Bainbridge, holding up the sheaf.

'Ah, those have nothing to do with me,' said Stephen carelessly. 'I believe Captain Aubrey's steward brought them aboard: one looks very like his commission.' He leafed through the diary and showed Mr Evans various anatomical drawings — the alimentary tract of the sea-elephant that covered two pages, the whale-bird's oviducts, the flayed hand of a man suffering from calcification of the palmar aponeurosis, some dissected aborigines.

Mr Evans expressed his admiration: the civilian said, 'May I ask, sir, why the text appears to be disguised?'

'A personal diary, sir,' said Stephen, 'is best considered as a mirror in which a man may see himself: few men, who set down their shortcomings with the utmost naked candour, would wish to have them read by others. A medical diary, recording the symptoms, sufferings, and treatment of named patients, must also be secret: Mr Evans will support me when I say that secrecy, total discretion, is one of the most important duties of our profession.'

'It is part of the Hippocratic oath,' said Mr Evans.

Stephen bowed, and went on, 'And lastly, it is notorious that the natural philosopher is extremely jealous of his discoveries; he wishes to have the credit of first publication; and he would no more share the glory of a new-found species than a naval commander would wish to share his capture of a ship.'

The argument went straight home, and the Commodore handed over the book. The civilian appeared somewhat less satisfied, however: who was he? The consul? He was neither named nor explained. He said, 'I believe you belonged to the *Leopard*, sir?'

'Just so, sir,' said Stephen, 'and it was

aboard her, in the high southern latitudes, that I made the greater part of these discoveries, and these drawings.'

He had the diary back: but although he retained it he had in some degree taken against the book and illogically he no longer set his private mind on paper, as he had done for so many years. Apart from notes recording the appearance of various birds, his last entry was that of many days ago: 'Now I know what Jack Aubrey will look like when he is sixty-five.'

He had the diary back: yet an uneasiness remained. Had not the Americans been strangely ready to grant his request when he asked leave to accompany those patients who were too sick to be moved from the *Constitution*, Jack and the two quarter-gunners who had been buried at sea a week ago, the ship heaved to and her bell tolling as they went over the side? Had he put his head into a trap? What was the true nature of the passengers the ship was carrying from San Salvador to Boston? One was certainly a consular official, a foolish little man whose only care was his luxuriant whiskers, a tiny politician for whom the world might fall apart so long as the Republicans remained in power. The other two were Frenchmen; the first a small, subfusc, grey, middle-aged man with a liverish face who wore grey small-clothes, the kind of stockings that Franklin had made fashionable in Paris many years before, and a blue-grey coat; he was almost never seen on deck, and when he was, he was always being sick over the side, usually the windward side. The other was a tall, military-looking civilian, Pontet-Canet, who seemed at first sight to be as vain as the consular young man, even more loquacious and quite as silly; yet Stephen was not sure. Nor was he sure that he had not seen Pontet-Canet in some other place. Paris? Barcelona? Toulon? If he had, then it was certainly without those jet-black whiskers. But he had seen so very many people, and there were innumerable tall vain Frenchmen who dyed their hair and spoke with a strong Burgundian accent. A secret agent needed a prodigious memory: he also needed a diary to supply those inevitable gaps and failures.

Stephen had recently been looking into the Bible that a Boston society had placed in his cabin, as in every other part of the ship, and he had fallen upon two verses that stuck in his memory: *the wicked fleeth where no man pursueth,* and *the fall of a liar is as from the housetop.* A secret agent was not necessarily wicked, but an undue portion of his life was necessarily a lie. Once again Stephen felt the sickened weariness rising up, and he was not sorry to hear Pontet-Canet's voice wishing him good day.

The Frenchman messed in the gunroom and he often engaged Stephen in conversation, speaking a fluent though curious and heavily-accented English: now, having dealt with the weather and the probable nature of their coming dinner, they spoke of America, of the New World, comparatively empty, comparatively innocent.

'You have been in the States before, sir, I collect?' said Stephen. 'I dare say you know the country and the people well.'

'Perfectly,' replied Pontet-Canet. 'And I was very well received, for when I arrived among them, I spoke like them, I dressed like them, I bewared to have no more wit than them, and I found that all they did was good, ha, ha, ha!'

'Sometimes I think of retiring there,' said Stephen.

'Ah?' said Pontet-Canet, looking at him sharply. 'You would not object to the regime — you would not object on the national grounds?'

'Never in life,' said Stephen. 'Europe is so old, so tired, so wearisome, that one longs for the simplicity of . . .' He would have added 'the noble Huron, and for the vast range of unknown birds, mammals, reptiles, plants', but he had rarely finished a sentence when talking to Pontet-Canet, and now the Frenchman broke in with a strong recommendation of such a course. America was the Golden Age revived: 'I myself was in the Connecticut, in the back grounds of the state, hunting savage turkeys with a veritable American farmer, and he held me the following discourse: "In me, my dear sir, you see a happy man, if such is to be found under the Heaven. Everything you see about you comes from my own land. These stockings — my daughter knitted them. My shoes and clothes come from my herds; and these herds, with my poultry-yard and my garden, provide a solid, simple nourishment. The taxes here are almost nothing, and so long as they are paid we can sleep on both ears." There is Arcadian simplicity, *hein?*'

'Certainly,' said Stephen. 'Pray, sir, did you find your turkeys?'

'Yes, yes!' cried Pontet-Canet. 'And some grey squirrels. I was the one that shot them all, ha, ha, ha! I was the best fusil of the party; and, I allow myself to say without forfantery, the best cook.'

'How did you dress them?'

'Sir?'

'How did you cook them?'

'The squirrels in madeira; the turkey roast.

And all round the table was heard "Very good! Exceedingly good! Oh, dear sir, what a glorious bit!" '

'Please to describe the turkey's flight.'

Pontet-Canet spread his arms, but before he could take to the air Mr Evans appeared: the other Monsieur, in conference with the Commodore, needed an interpreter.

'I hope Mr Bainbridge is well?' said Stephen.

'Oh yes, yes, yes,' said Mr Evans. 'A little laudable pus, no more. The wound is healing very prettily. Some pain, of course, and some discomfort; but we must learn to put up with that without growing mean or snappish.' A pause. 'They tell me we are nearing the edge of the stream,' said the surgeon, 'and that presently we shall see green water to larboard, and Cape Fear.'

'Ha,' said Stephen, 'the green water in with the land. How I hope that we shall also see a skimmer.'

'What is a skimmer?'

'It is one of your sea-birds. It has a singular beak, the lower mandible being longer than the upper: with this it skims the surface of the sea. I have always longed to see a skimmer.'

'I guess you must be a considerable ornithologist, Dr Maturin. You made some uncommon drawings of the far southern birds in your journal, I recall.' There were no birds on the pages Stephen had exhibited: clearly the book had been studied for some time. Mr Evans seemed quite unaware of his slip, however, and he now proposed that they should finish their game of chess, a match that had reached a desperately congested middle-game with almost all the pieces on the board, not one of which could be moved without the utmost peril.

'By all means,' said Stephen. 'But do you think it would be possible to play on deck? Then, while you attempt to delay your inevitable defeat, I may keep my eye upon the sea. I should be loath to miss my skimmer.'

Mr Evans looked doubtful, but said he would have a word with the officer of the watch. 'All is well,' he said, coming back. 'Mr Heath has every sympathy with your wish: if you want to see a skimmer, you may play chess in any part of the ship, he says; and he will give orders that you be told if skimmers appear. He thinks there is a fair chance, once we are close in with the cape, and out of the blue water.'

Some minutes later he brought the board, saying, 'I love this game. Apart from anything else, it is agreeable to my sentiments as a citizen of a republic, since it always ends with the discomfiture of a king.'

'I too was a republican in the frothy pride of my youth,' said Stephen, inspecting the position, while an awning was being stretched to protect them from the sun. 'And had I been out of coats at the time, I should have joined you at Bunker Hill and Valley Forge and those other interesting spots. As it was, I cheered the taking of the Bastille. But with age, I have come to think that after all a monarchy is best.'

'When you look about the world, and view the monarchs in it — I do not refer to your own, of course — can you really maintain that the hereditary king cuts a very shining figure?'

'I cannot. Nor is that to the point: the person, unless he be extraordinarily good or extraordinarily bad, is of no importance. It is the living, moving, procreating, sometimes speaking symbol that counts.'

'But surely mere birth without any necessary merit is illogical?'

'Certainly, and that is its great merit. Man is a deeply illogical being, and must be ruled illogically. Whatever that frigid prig Bentham may say, there are innumerable motives that have nothing to do with utility. In good utilitarian logic a man does not sell all his goods to go crusading, nor does he build cathedrals; still less does he write verse. There are countless pieties without a name that find their focus in a crown. It is as well, I grant you, that the family should have worn it beyond the memory of man; for your recent creations do not answer — they are nothing in comparison of your priest-king, whose merit is irrelevant, whose place cannot be disputed, nor made the subject of a recurring vote.'

Six bells struck; the awning was finished; Mr Evans said, 'Good Dr Maturin, you will not take it amiss, if I point out that your priest-king is on the wrong square.'

'So he is, too,' said Stephen; and having put it right he fell to studying the position again. While he did so, a shadow crossed the board. He made his move and looked up: it was Pontet-Canet, surveying the game with pursed lips and narrowed eyes. The oblique sunlight fell on his black whiskers, showing an odd rusty tinge beneath the dye: or perhaps caused by the dye? Where had he seen the man before?

His eyes wandered beyond the whiskers, beyond Mr Evans's bowed cogitating head, swept the sea for skimmers, and returning beheld Jack Aubrey. Jack kept out of the way of his captors as much as he decently could — the necessary cheerfulness was burdensome to him, far more burdensome than the truly shocking pain in his shattered arm; but now that he was well enough to come on deck he could not decently sit moping in his cabin. He paused at the top of the ladder, and Stephen saw his keen gaze run round the horizon in search of a British man-of-war, preferably an exact match for the *Constitution*, ideally his own *Acasta* (though she only carried eighteen-pounders). Having searched in vain he cast an automatic glance at the sails and the sky to windward, and walked aft to watch the game.

'I have moved, sir,' said Mr Evans, disguising his triumph in a tone of false meekness.

He had indeed. Stephen, intent upon his own attack, had overlooked that odious knight. Whatever he did he must lose a piece, and against a player as strong as Mr Evans that must mean losing the game: unless . . . He advanced a pawn.

'No, no,' cried Pontet-Canet. 'You must —'

'Hush,' cried Evans, Jack and Stephen.

Pontet-Canet glared, particularly at Jack, sniffed, and walked away; but presently he was back, his fingers fairly itching to put the chessmen right.

The pieces fell, a brisk massacre; the board was almost clear, and Evans, one piece and two pawns up, fell plump into the trap. 'Oh,' cried he, striking his forehead, 'a stalemate!'

'Morally you won,' said Stephen. 'But at least this time my king was not discomfited.'

'What you should have done,' cried Pontet-Canet, 'was to take the fool.'

Evans and Stephen were too busy telling one another how they had contrived to lose, each having an impregnable position, an invincible plan of attack, to pay much attention to the others; but they were soon obliged to do so. The tone had risen far beyond that of ordinary disagreement; it had risen to acrimony; and at the same time it had so increased in volume that the American officers who were on the quarterdeck looked round in surprise.

'I must insist that you have placed the pieces wrongly,' said Jack again in a strong voice, unaccustomed these many years to contradiction from any but admirals and his wife. 'The queen's rook was here.' He tweaked the piece from the Frenchman's hand, and firmly leaning across him, put it down, not without some emphasis.

'Do you believe to bully me?' cried Pontet-Canet. 'You damned rogue. By God, it will not be so . . . I'll overboard you like a dead cat . . . if I find you too heavy, I'll cling to you with hands, legs, nails, everything; my life is nothing to send such a dog to hell. Now, just now . . .'

Fortunately his words came tumbling so fast, and in so very strange an accent, that

Jack did not understand much of what he said; and fortunately, as Stephen and Mr Evans interposed, the quarterdeck filled for the solemn noonday observation of the sun — a ceremony as grave here as it was in the Royal Navy — and the moment Commodore Bainbridge decreed that the hour was twelve the uproar of All hands to dinner drowned all private dissension. Stephen and Evans led Jack below for the dressing of his arm, and made him lie down to rest before dining with the Commodore.

'Shall we save it, do you suppose?' asked Evans as they returned to the open air.

'I doubt it,' said Stephen, 'and sometimes I am much tempted to cut. It is this clammy heat that does so weigh against him. And of course the mental agitation: he *will* accept Mr Bainbridge's invitations, his very kindly-intended invitations, though it kill him.'

'As for the heat,' said Mr Evans, 'once we round Cape Hatteras and stand inshore for the stream, there will be no more of that. And as for the agitation, might not we add the inspissated juice of lettuce to our present measures? The pulse is light, quick, and irregular; and there is an uncommon degree of nervous excitement and irascibility, in spite of the apparent stoicism. Another such scene as this morning's may have very grave effects.

Obnoxious fellow, with his "what you ought to have done"! I would not lose a game of chess to that man for the world. With no fever, no pain, no weakness, I found it hard enough to govern my tongue. In peacetime I should have kicked him; but war makes strange bedfellows.'

'A ludicrous exhibition,' said Stephen. Too ludicrous, perhaps: perhaps too much of the excitable passionate Frenchman, whom no one would take seriously. With his foot on the top of the ladder, Stephen remembered where he had seen him before: it was at a little inn high above Toulon, much frequented by the greedier part of the French navy. A French officer, Captain Christie-Pallière, had taken Jack and Stephen to dinner there, during the peace of Amiens, and this man, passing by their table, had spoken to Christie-Pallière. Stephen remembered his Dijon accent: he was about to eat a 'côôôôq au vin' and the rest of his party a 'rrâââble de lièvre'; and he had taken particular notice of Jack, who was speaking English.

'Do you see a skimmer, sir?' asked Mr Evans, blocked behind him.

'I doubt it,' said Stephen.

They took several turns, up and down past the repairing parties and the line of carronades, a neat line now, although two had broken trunnions and one had received a ball full in the muzzle, while many of their slides were deeply scored and wounded. If an English man-of-war were to appear, she would find that the *Constitution* already had several of her teeth drawn. But it was too early for much hope of that: the cruisers were much more likely to be off the Chesapeake, or Sandy Hook, or in Massachusetts Bay, at the entrance to Boston itself; for Boston was their destination. The *Java* may have been destroyed, but at least she had prevented the *Constitution* from going on to cruise in the Pacific as she had intended, and obliged her to return to her home port to be overhauled. Boston was her port, and at Boston, unless the blockading squadron captured her, the future would begin: for this voyage was no more than a transition, a curious long-continued present.

'That is Cape Fear,' observed Mr Evans, pointing. 'And now you can see the division between the Gulf Stream and the ocean clearly. There, do you see, the line running parallel with our course, about a quarter of a mile away.'

'A noble headland,' said Stephen. 'And a most remarkably clear division: thank you, sir, for pointing it out.'

They paced on in silence. No skimmers: no birds of any kind. With his mind reverting to chess, Stephen said, 'Your republic, now, Mr Evans: do you look upon it as one and indivisible, or rather as a voluntary association of sovereign states?'

'Well, sir, for my part I come from Boston, and I am a Federalist: that is to say I look upon the Union as the sovereign power. I may not like Mr Madison, nor Mr Madison's war — indeed, I deplore it: I deplore this connection with the French, with their Emperor Napoleon, to say nothing of the alienation of our English friends — but I see him as the President of the whole nation, and I concede his right to declare it, however mistakenly, in my name; though I may add that by no means all of my Federalist friends in New England agree with me, particularly those whose trade is being ruined. Most of the other officers aboard, however, are Republicans, and they cry up the sovereign rights of the individual states. Nearly all of them come from the South.'

'From the South? Do they, indeed? Now that may account for a difference I have noticed in their manner of speech, a certain languor — what I might almost term a lisping deliberation in delivery, not unmelodious, but sometimes difficult for the unaccustomed ear. Whereas all that you say, sir, is instantly comprehensible.'

'Why, sure,' said Evans, in his harsh nasal metallic bray, 'the right American English is spoke in Boston, and even as far as Watertown. You will find no corruption there, I believe, no colonial expressions, other than those that arise naturally from our intercourse with the Indians. Boston, sir, is a well of English, pure and undefiled.'

'I am fully persuaded of it,' said Stephen. 'Yet at breakfast this morning Mr Adams, who was also riz in Boston, stated that hominy grits cut no ice with him. I have been puzzling over his words ever since. I am acquainted with the grits, a grateful pap that might with advantage be exhibited in cases of duodenal debility, and I at once perceived that the expression was figurative. But in what does the figure consist? Is it desirable that ice should be cut? And if so, why? And what is the force of *with?*'

After barely a moment's pause, Mr Evans said, 'Ah, there now, you have an Indian expression. It is a variant upon the Iroquois *katno aiss' vizmi* — I am unmoved, unimpressed. Yes, sir. But speaking of ice, Dr Maturin, have you any conception of the cold in Boston during the winter months? It may well do good to our patient's arm, but on the other hand, it may carry off the rest of him. Has he no other clothing but what I see? And you, my dear sir, have you cold-weather garments?'

'I have not; nor has Captain Aubrey. In our earlier mishap we lost all our possessions that we did not carry in our hands. All of them,' said Stephen, looking down as the piercing memory of his collection filled his mind. 'But it is of no great consequence. In a few days we shall be exchanged, and for a few days Captain Aubrey and I can very well brave the northern blizzard in the manner of the Iroquois, or the noble Huron, wrapped in a blanket. And in Halifax, I understand, there is every commodity to be had, from fur hats to the ingenious paddles used for walking on the snow.'

A shade of embarrassment crossed Mr Evans's face; he coughed once or twice and said, 'Are you not perhaps reckoning without your host, Dr Maturin? Exchange is sometimes eternal slow with us; and your officials in Halifax do not always seem to be much brighter than officials in other parts of the world, nor more active at their work. Surely it would be wise to lay in flannel shirts and woollen drawers, at least? They will always serve.'

Stephen promised to bear what he said in mind, and indeed it was impossible for him not to do so. When the *Constitution* was north of the Chesapeake, a screeching north-wester laden with snow and ice-crystals stripped her to close-reefed topsails; and under these top-sails alone she stood on, close-hauled, for Nantucket Island.

Blue noses and red hands were the order of the day; so was an uncommon alacrity and good humour, super-added to the cheerfulness of victory, for these were home waters for half of the hands. Many of them hailed from Nantucket, Martha's Vineyard, Salem, or New Bedford, and as they jumped to round in braces or to hale upon the bowlines they laughed and called out to one another, in spite of the piercing cold and in spite of the fact that this was the most dangerous part of the voyage, since the Royal Navy was block-ading Boston.

All hands were in tearing spirits; they knew that they would have a heroes' welcome as well as all the delights of home, prize-money, and the diversions of Boston; and officers and men did all that superb seamanship could do to drive the ship onwards through the wicked gale. All hands, except of course for the pris-oners of war, particularly Captain Aubrey. Al-though he knew very well that this wind must blow the British cruisers off the coast he was perpetually on deck, chilled through and through apart from his burning arm, whose pain stabbed so hard from time to time that he was obliged to cling to the rail not to cry out or fall down. He was sick, grey, and weak; he repelled any attempt at help or kindness, any supporting arm, with a curtness that soon did away with any sympathy there might have been, and he stared through the squalls and the thick weather for the relief that never came. Not that there was much sympathy for him to lose, at least among the foremost hands: he was known to have commanded the *Leopard*, and the *Leopard*, that unhappy ship which had made the *Chesapeake* bring to in peace-time to take British seamen, alleged deserters, out of her, and which had fired into her, killing and wounding a score of Americans, stood for all they hated in the Royal Navy.

The north-wester blew on and on, and the *Constitution* lay to under Cape Cod, waiting for it to blow out, so that she could slip round into Massachusetts Bay and so home before the blockading squadron returned. Ice formed thick on the yards and rigging; snow drove aboard by day and night. He stood there still, though he could hardly hold his telescope, nor see when he had it firm, a tall and wretched figure. Once an empty beef-cask came alongside, instantly recognizable from its marks: it must have been thrown overboard from a British man-of-war within the last few days.

The doctors ordered him below, but he repeatedly escaped their vigilance, and the day before the wind veered far enough into the north for the *Constitution* to round the point, her bowlines as taut as harp-strings, the hands learnt, with general indifference, that the Captain of the *Leopard* had been laid low with pneumonia.

'We must get him across at once,' said Stephen, raising his voice. The *Constitution*, home at last, was rapidly filling with friends and relations, and the increasing roar of New England voices, familiar and at the same time exotic, made it hard to hear. 'Perhaps that ship could be induced to come alongside, and then we could pass him across on a stretcher, without the inevitable agitation and disturbance of a boat.' The ship in question was a cartel filled with English prisoners to be exchanged; she was bound for Halifax, in Nova Scotia, there to pick up an equivalent number of Americans, and she would drop down the Charles river with the tide.

'I am afraid we cannot bundle him across just like that,' said Evans. 'I must have a word with the first lieutenant.'

It was not the first lieutenant who appeared, however, but the Commodore himself. He came limping in and said, 'Dr Maturin, this matter of exchange is not in my hands. Captain Aubrey must be taken ashore, and he must stay there until the proper authorities have made their decision.' He spoke in a strong, authoritative voice, as though he had an unpleasant duty to perform, and as though the doing of it called for a harsher tone than was natural to him. During the voyage he had always been considerate and polite in his intercourse with Jack, though somewhat remote and reserved, perhaps because of the pain in his wounded leg, and this new tone filled Stephen with uneasiness. 'You must excuse me,' said the Commodore, 'there are a thousand things that must be done. Mr Evans, a word with you.'

Mr Evans came back. 'It is much as I feared,' he said, sitting down by Stephen in the sickbay. 'Although I know nothing officially, I collect that there is likely to be a long delay over the exchange of our patient.' He leaned forward and raised Jack's eyelid: no comprehension in that blank, unseeing gaze. 'If, indeed, he is to be exchanged at all.'

'Have you any notion of why this should be so?'

'I believe it may have something to do with the *Leopard*,' said Evans hesitantly.

'But Captain Aubrey had nothing to do with that disgraceful affair, that firing into the *Chesapeake*; the ship was under the command of another man. At that time Aubrey was five thousand miles away.'

'It was not that affair I meant. No. But it seems that when he *was* in command of that wretched vessel . . . but you will forgive me. I must say no more. Indeed, I have no more to say. I have only heard rumours to the effect that someone, somewhere, seems to have taken exception to his conduct — a misunderstanding, no doubt — but he is likely to be detained until it is cleared up.'

Jack's noisy, laboured breathing stopped; he raised himself, called out 'Luff and touch her', and fell back. Stephen and Evans heaved him up on his pillows, and each took a pulse. They exchanged a look and a confident nod; the patient's heart was bearing up to admiration.

'What is the best course to follow?' asked Stephen.

'Well, now,' said Evans, considering, 'most of your officers put up at O'Reilly's hotel on parole; the men are kept in the barracks, of course. But that would not do in the present case; and I cannot conscientiously recommend the new hospital. The plaster is scarcely dry on its walls, and I would not see even a simple pneumonia, affecting no more than the apex of the right lung, subjected to those unwholesome damps. On the other hand, my brother-in-law, Otis P. Choate, who is also a medical man, has a small private establishment that he calls the Asclepia, in a dry, healthy location near Beacon Hill.'

'What could be more eligible? Would you — would you know the nature of his terms, at all?'

'They are very moderate: they are obliged to be very moderate, for I must tell you frankly, sir, that my brother-in-law is a man with strong notions of his own, and his Asclepia is not a paying proposition. Otis P. Choate is a good sound physician, but he riles his fellow-citizens: for one thing, he is opposed to alcohol, slavery, tobacco, and war — all wars, including Indian wars. And I must warn you, sir, that most of the attendants he employs are Irishwomen, Papists I regret to say; and although for my part I have not noticed the drunkenness and profligacy associated with that unhappy pack of barefoot savages, and although the majority of them speak English of a sort, and at least seem clean, the circumstance has of course made the Asclepia unpopular in Boston. So it is filled, as far as it is filled at all, with lunatics whose friends do not choose to keep them at home, rather than with the medical and surgical cases for whom it was designed. It is commonly called Choate's mad-house, and people affect to say that with such nurses and such a physician, no one can tell the odds between the patients and their attendants. I put this fairly before you, Dr Maturin, because I am aware that some people might object to such an establishment.'

'I honour your candour, sir,' said Stephen, 'but —'

'Never mind Maturin,' said Jack, suddenly speaking in a deep hoarse voice out of some partially lucid interval. 'He is an Irish Papist himself, ha, ha, ha! Drunk as a lord every morning by nine o'clock, and never a shoe to his name.'

'Is that so, sir?' whispered Mr Evans, looking more wretched and distressed than Stephen would have thought possible: for in general the *Constitution*'s surgeon, a man of somewhat formal, even ceremonious manners, presented a calm and impassive face to the world, an expression of grave, benign dignity. 'I had no idea — I was not aware — your sobriety, your — but apologies can only make the blunder worse. I beg you will forgive me, sir, and believe that no personal reflection was intended.'

Stephen shook him by the hand and said

that he was sure of it; but Mr Evans found it difficult to recover his composure, and eventually Stephen said, 'Dr Choate's Asclepia sounds almost ideal.'

'Yes,' said Mr Evans. 'Yes, yes. I will go and speak to the Commodore at once, and ask for his permission for the removal; he, of course, is responsible for your custody, for the production of your bodies on demand. I have no authority in the matter.'

A short pause, in which Stephen took a blanket from an empty cot and wrapped it round his shoulders against the damp and penetrating cold, and Evans returned. 'All is well,' he said, 'I found the Commodore very busy, surrounded with officials and people from the Yard, as well as half Boston's leading citizens; he merely called out "Do as you think fit", caught up this,' — showing a small packet — 'and desired me to deliver it to you.'

Stephen read the hastily-written note wrapped about the banknotes: 'Commodore Bainbridge presents his compliments to Captain Aubrey, begs he will accept the enclosed to bear his charges ashore for the time being, hopes to have the pleasure of seeing him fully recovered very soon, and asks his pardon for not waiting on him at present: he flatters himself that Captain Aubrey, from long experience, will understand the many preoc-

cupations that attend the docking of the ship.'
'This is exceedingly handsome in the Commodore,' he said. 'A most gentlemanlike, elegant gesture: I accept it for my friend, with the
utmost pleasure.'

'We are all subject to the fortune of war,'
said Mr Evans, visibly embarrassed as he produced a smaller packet. 'You will not, I am
sure, condemn me to being behindhand with
my shipmates. Come, sir, I do not need to tell
you, that there is a generosity in acceptation:
and it is, alas, no more than twenty pounds.'

Stephen acknowledged Evans's kindness,
accepted his loan, and said all that was proper
with real gratitude, for not only did the action
please him extremely, but he did not in fact
possess a single coin of any kind, great or
small, and he had been wondering how the
terms of Choate's mad-house could be met,
however moderate they might prove to be.

'You said twenty pounds, Mr Evans,' he remarked, after they had been talking for some
time about the apex of Jack's right lung,
enemata, and the care of the mentally de-
ranged. 'Is it usual, in your country, to use the
old names for money?'

'We often speak of pennies and shillings,'
said Evans. 'Sometimes of pounds, but far
more rarely. I caught the habit from my father
when I was a boy. He was a Tory, a Loyalist,

and even when he came back from Canada and learnt to live with the Republic, he never would give up his pounds and guineas.'

'Were there many Loyalists in Boston?'

'No, not a great many; nothing to compare with New York, for example. But still we had our sheep, black or white according to your point of view: perhaps a thousand out of some fifteen thousand, which is what I reckon the town held at that time.'

'A desperate state of affairs it must be, when a man finds himself torn between conflicting loyalties . . . Tell me, did you ever hear of a Mr Herapath?'

'George Herapath? Oh yes indeed. He was a friend of my father's, a fellow-Tory; they were in exile together, in Canada. He is quite a prominent citizen. He always was, being a considerable ship-owner and trading with China more successfully than most; and now that the Federalists and the old Tories have come together he is more important still.'

'I am a child in American politics, Mr Evans,' said Stephen, 'and cannot readily see how the Federalists and Tories can have come together, since, as you so kindly explained to me, the Federalists maintain the sovereignty of the Union, of the State as opposed to the states.'

'What brings them together is a common

dislike for Mr Madison's war. I am betraying no secrets when I say that this war is unpopular in New England: everybody knows it. And although there are no doubt higher motives, money speaks in Boston, whether you call it dollars and cents or pounds, shillings and pence; and the merchants are being ruined — their foreign trade is strangled, sir, strangled. But the Republicans —'

What the Republicans were about Stephen never learnt, for the *Constitution*'s starboard timbers uttered a long, concerted groan as she eased up against the wharf.

'We are alongside, gentlemen,' said the first lieutenant, looking into the sickbay. 'I have laid on a sleigh for Captain Aubrey: we aim to shift him in half an hour. And Dr Choate sends to say that all will be ready, sir.'

'Strangled, sir,' said Mr Evans, when they were alone again. 'George Herapath, for example, has three fine barques tied up here, and two more at Salem: his China trade is at a stand.'

'Mr Herapath has a son.'

'Young Michael? Yes. A sad disappointment to him, I am afraid, and to all his friends. He was bright enough as a boy — he was at our Latin school with my nephew Quincy — and he studied hard. Then he learnt Chinese, and it was thought he would be a great help to his father in business; but no, he went off to Europe and became a rake. And what some people think much worse, a spendthrift. I am told he is come back from his travels, bringing a drabbletail with him, a wench from Baltimore, a Romanist — not,' he cried, 'that I mean the least connection, my dear sir. I only mean to emphasize Mr Herapath's misfortune, he being a staunch Episcopalian.'

'Poor gentleman,' said Stephen. 'I met Michael Herapath in his travels; indeed, he acted as my assistant for a while. I valued him much, and hope I may see him again.'

'Oh dear, oh dear,' said Mr Evans. 'I seem fated to move from one blunder to another today. I shall hold my tongue for what remains of it.'

'Where would conversation be, if we were not allowed to exchange our minds freely and to abuse our neighbours from time to time?' said Stephen.

'Very well: it is very well. But I shall go and borrow a buffalo-robe for Captain Aubrey's journey, and say no more. The sleigh will be here at any moment now.'

Stephen was pleased with the Asclepia; it was dry, clean, and comfortable, and the kind gentle Irish voices made him feel that the pervading warmth must come from turf-fires — he could almost have sworn he caught that exquisite home-like scent. He was pleased with Dr Choate, as a physician, pleased with the design of the establishment and its many private rooms, its domestic air. Dr Choate's care and treatment of his many half-wits and lunatics was as far removed as possible from the chains, whipping, bread-and-water, barred-cell usage that Stephen had so often seen, and so often deplored; yet it might be that he carried the open-door principle a little too far. More than once Stephen had seen a potentially dangerous case wandering about the lower corridors, muttering, or standing rigid, motionless in a corner. But for Dr Choate's ordering of his sick-rooms Stephen had nothing but praise; these were in the central block, and Jack's was a fine light airy place with a view over the little town to the navy yard and the harbour. This central block, whether it was on purpose or by chance, seemed to be arranged in an ascending order of cheerfulness: the rooms on either side of Jack's were occupied by the few surgical or medical cases in a fair way to mending, and not far from them were those patients in the mildly exalted or elevated phase of the *folie circulaire:* they met in a common sitting-room where they played cards, sometimes for several hundred thousand million dollars, or played music, often surprisingly well; Dr Choate himself joined them with his oboe whenever he could, observing that he looked upon it as his most valuable therapeutic instrument. There were of course the usual heart-breaking melancholias: people who had committed the unpardonable sin, had done the everlasting wrong; others whose families were poisoning their food or who were going about to do them evil by means of Indian smoke; a woman whose husband had 'put her to a dog' and who sobbed and sobbed, never sleeping and never to be consoled. There were the senile dementias, and mad paralysed syphilitics and the nasty idiots, the despair of the world: but they were on the lower floors and in the wings.

Jack saw none of this. He was in the cheerful part, and this was appropriate, for superficially he was himself a cheerful patient; his arm, though still painful in some places and numb in others, was almost certainly saved; he had recovered from his pneumonia; and he had learnt of the Americans' reverses in their attack upon Canada. The army had done well, and to some extent that was a compensation for the Navy's failure. He was still weak, but he ate voraciously: clam chowder, Boston beans, cod, anything that came his way.

'My dear,' he wrote to Sophie, 'you know I have always wanted to imitate Nelson (except in the marital line) as much as ever I can, and here I am, dashing away with my left hand, and writing much the same kind of scrawl as he did. But in a month or so Dr Choate tells me I may try the right. Stephen says he is a very clever fellow . . .'

Clever, yes: and most unusually kind. Stephen admired his learning, his skill in diagnosis, and his wonderful handling of his lunatics; Choate could often bring comfort to those who seemed so deeply sunk in their own private hell as to be beyond all communication, and although he had some dangerous patients he had never been attacked. Choate's ideas on war, slavery, and the exploitation of the Indians were eminently sound; his way of spending his considerable private means on others was wholly admirable; and sometimes, when Stephen was talking to Choate he would consider that earnest face with its unusually large, dark, kindly eyes and wonder whether he was not looking at a saint: at other times a spirit of contradiction would rise, and although he could not really defend poverty, war, or injustice he would feel inclined to find excuses for slavery. He would feel that there was too much indignation mingled with the benevolence, even though the indignation was undeniably righteous; that Dr Choate indulged in goodness as some indulged in evil; and that he was so enamoured of his role that he would make any sacrifice to sustain it. Choate had no humour, or he would never have linked drink and tobacco to issues so very much more important — Stephen liked his glass of wine and his cigar — and he was certainly guilty of deliberate meekness on occasion. Perhaps there was some silliness there: might it be that silliness and love of one's fellow men were inseparable? These were unworthy thoughts, he admitted: he also admitted that he would rely implicitly upon Choate's diagnosis rather than his own; and Choate was more hopeful than he about Jack's arm.

Jack's letter crept on: 'I shall send this by Bulwer, of *Belvidera*, who was caught when one of her prizes was retaken and who is to be exchanged directly — he goes aboard the cartel that I can see from my window this evening. My exchange still seems to be hanging fire, though I cannot tell why; but I dare say it will come as soon as I am fit to travel, which will be in a week or two, at the prodigious rate I am gaining weight and strength. Bulwer has very kindly been coming to sit with me, and so have several other officers, and they have told me the most encouraging news about our successes in Canada: I expect him shortly, and must bring this sad scribble to a close. But before I seal it up, I must tell you of another visitor I had today: he often looks in, in the most friendly, free and easy way, and so do many of the other patients, to ask me how I do. Indeed, this is a very free and easy place, not to say haphazard, quite unlike Haslar or any hospital I have ever seen; visitors wander in and out as they please, and they are almost never announced. The one I am talking about is a fine stout rosy gentleman, the Emperor of Mexico in fact, but here he only uses the title of Duke of Montezuma, and today he let me into a great secret, known to very few: the whole world has gone mad, it seems, but they are too far gone to know it — a kind of sudden epidemic, caused by drinking tea. It began with our poor King and then burst out with the American election, when President Madison was chosen; now it covers the whole world, said he, laughing extremely and skipping. "Even you, sir, even Captain Aubrey, ha, ha, ha!" But he comforted me with a grant of fourteen thousand acres on the Delaware, and the fishing-rights on both banks of the Gulf of Mexico, so we shall not go short of victuals in our old age. He and many of the others, do you see, are somewhat astray in their wits; yet I have noticed a curious thing, which is that the sort I see, the patients that Dr Choate lets wander about and gather in the parlour, are not nearly so much astray as they seem. Much of it is play. They are persuaded that I am one of them, that I only pretend to be a post-captain R.N. for fun, and so we humour one another, each playing at being madder than the next. And there are certain unspoken rules —'

'Come in,' he cried.

The door opened and three men appeared. The first, a man in sad-coloured clothes with a large number of dull metal buttons, seemed to be all trunk, so very short were his legs, and those legs almost hidden by his long coat. His large fat glabrous face was pale and shining; his watery eye had the glare that was now so familiar to Jack: he wore his grey hair long. The other two were less striking: meagre fellows in black, but equally insane. He hoped they would not be tedious, or lewd.

'Good afternoon, sir,' said the first. 'I am Jahleel Brenton, of the Navy Department.'

Jack knew Jahleel Brenton quite well, a distinguished post-captain in the Royal Navy, an unusually religious man, a friend of Saumarez and other blue-light admirals — had been made a baronet quite recently — born in America, hence the curious Christian name. He said, 'Good afternoon to you, gentlemen.

I am John Aubrey, grandson to the Pope of Rome.'

After a slight pause Mr Brenton said, 'I was not aware that Romanists were allowed in your service, sir.'

'Never you believe it, sir. Why, half the Board of Admiralty is made up of Jesuits, though it don't do to let it be generally known. Pray take a seat. How is your brother Ned?'

'I have no brother Ned, sir,' said Mr Brenton crossly. 'We are come here to ask you some questions about the *Leopard.*'

'Ask on, old boy,' said Jack, laughing at his approaching wit. 'All I know is, she can't change her spots, ha, ha, ha! 'Tis in the Bible,' he added, 'and you can't say fairer than that.' A pause. 'What about the tiger? Should not we be happier with the tiger? I could tell you any number of tales about the tiger.'

One of Jack's madder neighbours thrust his head in through the partly-open door, and cried, 'Peep bo.' Then, seeing that the Captain had company, he withdrew it. The smaller dark man whispered to Mr Brenton 'Zeke Bates the butcher' in a tone that quivered with horror. But after a moment, unable to resist, Mr Bates slid his portly form through the crack, and with his finger to his lips glided up to Jack's bedside, taking long undulating steps. There he produced a butcher's knife, wrapped in a handkerchief, showed Jack how it would shave the hairs from his forearm, laid his finger to his nose, gave Jack a knowing, private wink, and glided silently off again.

The middle-sized dark man looked about, but finding no spittoon he stepped to the window and squirted a stream of tobacco-juice into the garden. 'You, sir,' cried Jack, who disliked the habit extremely, 'put that damned quid out of your mouth. Toss it out of the window, d'ye hear me? Close the window, sit down, and tell us what you know about the tiger.'

The man tiptoed to his chair. Mr Brenton wiped his glistening face and said, 'It is not the *Tiger* that is in question, Captain Aubrey, but the *Leopard*. Is there a key to that door?' he cried, his eye on the gently moving handle.

'You surely do not think I am going to allow myself to be locked in with you?' said Jack, a cunning leer. 'No. There ain't.'

'Mr Winslow,' said Brenton, 'go put your chair against the door and sit on it. Now, sir, it is alleged that on or about twenty-fifth March last year, when in command of HBM ship *Leopard*, you fired upon the American brig *Alice B. Sawyer*. What have you to say to that?'

'I confess all,' cried Jack. 'I shifted

backstays, I slept out of my ship, I kept false musters, I failed to submit my quarterly returns, I allowed stove casks to be thrown overboard, and I blasted *Alice B. Sawyer* from the water with both my broadsides, treble-shotted. I throw myself upon the mercy of this honourable court.'

'Note that,' said Brenton to one of his assistants; then, 'Captain Aubrey, do you recognize these papers?'

'Of course I do,' said Jack, in an ordinary voice. 'The one is my commission and the others — let me have a look at them.' They looked very like the packets that Admiral Drury had asked him to take home, together with some of his own victualling notes. The smaller dark man brought the sheaf, and Jack, who had noticed that he was writing, plucked the notebook from his hand and read 'The prisoner, apparently in liquor, acknowledges that he is Captain Aubrey, states that he is a Roman Catholic and makes similar allegations about the British Board of Admiralty; admits that when in command of the *Leopard* he fired both broadsides at the brig *Alice B. Sawyer*.'

The door gave a sudden jerk, butting against Winslow's chair: Winslow leapt up with a tremulous howl: the door opened wide, and Mr Bulwer of the Royal Navy appeared.

'Bulwer,' cried Jack, 'I am delighted to see you. Now, gentlemen, you must excuse me: there is an urgent letter that I must finish.'

'Not so quickly, Captain Aubrey; not so quickly, if you please,' said Mr Brenton. 'I have a whole raft of questions yet. You, sir,' — to Bulwer — 'you may wait in the lobby.'

Jack had made an awkward movement in shaking Bulwer's hand; his arm hurt damnably. The peevishness of convalescence rose in a sudden tide: and in any case these were dreary lunatics, not nearly so quick or lively as Butcher Bates; Sir Jahleel Brenton was not a patch on the Emperor of Mexico, and this was a dreary game — he was tired of it. 'Mr Bates, there,' he cried. 'Friend Zeke, Brother Zeke.' The huge mad glowing face instantly showed at the door, excited, all alive, growing rather wild, a white line of spittle between its grinning lips. 'Good Mr Bates, pray show these gentlemen the door. Show them the way to Mrs Kavanagh: she will give them all a comfortable warm draught.'

'Jack,' said Stephen, coming in with a parcel, 'I have bought us woollen undergarments, just one set apiece — the winter is passing fast — and bonnets with flaps, to protect the ears. Why, Jack, what's amiss?'

'I must tell you some damned bad news,'

said Jack. 'Did you hear the bands playing all over the town, and the people cheering, this afternoon?'

'How could I miss it? I thought they were celebrating the capture of the *Java* all over again: it was much the same din, with three bands playing "Yankee Doodle" and three "Salem Heroes, Rise and Shine".'

'They were celebrating a victory, true enough; but it was a different victory, a fresh victory. Their *Hornet* has sunk our *Peacock*. Engaged her off the Demerara river and sunk her in fourteen minutes.'

'Oh,' said Stephen. There was a curious stab at his heart: he had not known how much he felt for the Navy.

'You may say what you like,' went on Jack, in a flat, dogged voice. 'You may say their *Hornet* — you remember her, Stephen, the little ship-sloop that was lying in San Salvador — that their *Hornet* had a two hundred and ninety-seven-pound broadside and the *Peacock* only one hundred and ninety-two, but it is still a very bad business. To sink her in fourteen minutes! They killed young Billy Peake, too, and knocked out thirty-seven of his men, as against only three Americans. No wonder they are thumping on their drums. And anyhow, the whole point of war is to bring more guns to bear on your enemy than he can bring to bear on you; or to point them better. The whole point is to win: it is not a game. Bulwer brought the news, so upset he could hardly speak; and he showed me this paper.'

Stephen looked at it: a card addressed to Captain Lawrence of the *Hornet* by the five surviving officers of the *Peacock* and repro- duced by the Boston newspaper: '. . . we ceased to consider ourselves prisoners; and everything that friendship could dictate was adopted by you and the officers of the *Hornet* to remedy the inconvenience we would other- wise have experienced from the unavoidable loss of the whole of our property and clothes owing to the sudden sinking of the *Peacock*.' He said, 'I am sure that what they say is very true: but it makes a somewhat abject publica- tion.'

Jack stared out of the window: he could see the American men-of-war down there, dressed all over for the victory; and it was only by the grace of God that he did not see the American flag flying over the British — the *Peacock* lay in five-fathom water in the mouth of that distant river, the *Guerrière* and *Java* at the bottom of the Atlantic; and the *Macedo- nian* was in New York. He thought of elabo- rating his ideas on the nature of war — on the change that had come over the Navy since

Nelson's time — the wanton stupidity of the administration — the over-confidence of well-connected commanders — the God-damned spit-and-polish — a whole series of reflections that had filled his mind for a great while now; but he was too weary, too low. He said, 'Oh, there was another damned thing that happened today. Some officials from their Navy Department came to see me. They were not announced and I thought they were just some more of our lunatics, particularly their leader, a Dutch-built civilian with a wall-eye; and when he said he was Jahleel Brenton I was sure of it. So I humoured them and played the fool with their questions until Bulwer came, and then I put them out, because I wanted to finish a letter to Sophie for Bulwer to take.'

'You gave him my parcel, I trust?' asked Stephen. He was speaking of his diary, packed, sealed, and addressed to Sir Joseph Blaine at the Admiralty, together with a covering note to his colleague in Halifax.

'Oh yes. I could not forget your parcel. I wrote my letter on it, and when I watched Bulwer going aboard, through my glass, I noticed he had it under his arm. It was he who told me they really had a Jahleel Brenton, a man who has to do with the exchange of prisoners. Apparently the name is quite usual in these parts; our Brenton came from Rhode Island, I believe.'

'What was the nature of their questions?'

'They wanted to know whether the *Leopard* had fired on an American merchantman to bring her to: the *Alice B. Sawyer*, as I recall. I don't think we did, but I should have to look at the log to be sure. And then they wanted me to explain some papers I had wrapped up in my commission: victualling notes, as far as I recollect, and some private letter the Admiral asked me to carry home.'

They sat there in the gathering twilight: sounds of rejoicing and the occasional roar and crack of a rocket reached them through the window: and at last Jack said, 'Do you remember Harry Whitby, who had *Leander* in the year six? You treated him for some complaint or other.' Stephen nodded. 'Well, when he was off Sandy Hook, he fired to bring some American merchantmen to, to see whether they had any contraband aboard. A man was killed, or died, or at all events lost the number of his mess: Whitby swore it was not *Leander*'s fault, because her shot passed a full cable's length ahead of the American's bows. However, the Americans swore it was, and they moved heaven and earth to have him brought to trial for murder in their own country. It seems that the ministry even thought of handing him over, but in the end they only had him court-martialled. He was acquitted, of course, yet to pacify the Americans he was never given another ship, not for years and years. He was on shore, unemployed, until in some way he came by proof that the man had not in fact been killed by *Leander*'s fire. Now it occurs to me, that they might be trying the same kind of caper in this case: but in this case there is no question of their having to persuade Government to hand me over — I am here.'

'Such inveterate malignance, brother? I find it hard to credit. I do not believe you made any American ship stop this last voyage at all.'

'Oh, I dare say it is only because I am hipped — the blue devils put such ideas into your mind. But still, it would explain the delay in exchanging me; and then again, they hate the very name of *Leopard*, naturally enough. I am connected with her; and any stick will do to hang a wicked dog. The American sailors we have met are good seamen, brave fellows, and generous — generous to a fault: I should never suspect them of anything like that. But these civilians, these officials . . .'

'Lord, they are sitting in the dark, the creatures,' cried Bridey Donohue. 'Doctor, there is a lady for you. Will I light the lamp, now?'

Through the open door, from some way away, came the sound of a laugh, a gurgling laugh, intensely amused, that went on and on. They both smiled, quite involuntarily; but then Jack, sinking back, said, 'That is Louisa Wogan. I should have known that laugh anywhere. But, Stephen, I could not cope with visitors just now. Pray be a good fellow, and make my compliments and excuses, will you?'

CHAPTER FIVE

Louisa Wogan had been put into a waiting-parlour: for once Dr Maturin's visitor was not wandering about the corridors in the Asclepia's usual haphazard way. But the door had been left open and the Asclepia had come to her; the Emperor of Mexico and a couple of millionaires were gathered in the parlour, laughing merrily. They were polite lunatics, however, and when Mrs Wogan sprang up, ran to Stephen, took him by both hands and cried, 'Dr Maturin, how glad I am to see you!' they filed out on tiptoe, each with his finger to his lips.

'How are you?' she went on. 'You have not changed in the least.'

Nor had she: still the same pretty young woman — black hair, blue eyes, lithe, like a plump boy, lovely complexion: she was wearing the sea-otter furs that Stephen had given her on Desolation, down there towards the southern pole, and they had the happiest effect upon her looks. 'Nor have you, my dear,' said he, 'except to improve in bloom: your native air, no doubt, and proper nourishment.

246

Tell me, how did you support the voyage?' He had last seen her in a tolerably advanced state of pregnancy, and he feared for the child.

'Oh, pretty well, I thank you. The baby was born in a most appalling tempest, while we were going to and fro off Cape Horn — the men were all aghast — kept the deck, all of them, though the weather was quite unspeakable. But Herapath was very good; and afterwards everything was delightful. Such a pleasant run northwards from Rio, and the baby was so good. She had long curling dark hair from the very start!'

'And Mr Herapath?'

'He is very well: but he dared not come to see you, and I have left him at home with Caroline. But come, we cannot talk here; I mean to take you back. They do let you out, do they not?' Stephen nodded. 'Then let someone fetch your greatcoat; it is amazingly cold outside, with a biting wind.'

'I have no greatcoat. We are to be exchanged so soon that it is not worth the while; and I feel no inconvenience from the cold. Captain Aubrey charges me with his best compliments, and he is much distressed at being unable to pay them himself.'

'Oh, him,' said Mrs Wogan, in a tone which made it clear to Stephen that the visit was intended for Dr Maturin alone: at the same time he recalled that the conditions of Mrs Wogan's captivity aboard the *Leopard* were such that she could have no conception of their intimacy. But recollecting herself she asked politely after Captain Aubrey's health, and hoped that he should soon be well.

They went out into the front hall, where the porter came from his booth to open the door for them, an immensely tall and massive Red Indian, dressed in a suit of European clothes, one of the few unsmiling faces that worked in the Asclepia: invariably grave, sculptured, and apparently mute. Stephen addressed a civil 'Ugh' to him, and as usual he received no reply, not even the slightest change of expression; but for the first time he did notice the lever that controlled the door, a comparatively simple arrangement, yet presumably enough to keep the madder patients in.

Spring had come to Boston, spring at its most virulent, and as they walked across the Common an icy wind from Cambridge blew small shattered green leaves into the half-frozen mud, while nearly all the Americans they passed, red, black, or bluish-grey, had streaming colds: but neither Maturin nor Wogan noticed it. They were lost in a flood of reminiscence — their voyage, the comforters she had knitted him, the stockings; the battle, the ship near sinking, the frigid refuge of Desolation Island; seal-skins, warmth and food at last; the coming of the American whaler in which Wogan and Herapath had made their escape. How was Mr Byron? Mr Babbington? Mr Babbington's dear fool of a dog? Eaten, alas, by the natives of the Friendly Islands; but they had offered a maiden in exchange. What had happened to the Gypsy woman and her baby, and to Peg? The one had found her husband at Botany Bay, the other a dense pack of lovers, women being in such short supply. And as they talked Stephen observed that Mrs Wogan showed no reserve of any kind towards him; she spoke as to an old friend, with the same openness and confidence of their days aboard the *Leopard*: with even more, perhaps, as though their friendship had matured with time. He was glad of it, because he was really fond of Wogan; he admired her courage, he liked her prattle, and he found her an agreeable companion; but he was surprised. She was after all an intelligence-agent (though not a very good one) and he had, in the naval phrase, 'stuffed her up' with false information of a singularly lethal nature: and as far as he could tell, this stratagem had borne fruit in the form of a trail of dead or discredited spies. Yet there she was, warm, pressed close to his side, leaning on his arm, apparently devoid of resentment.

Then, partly as a result of what she let fall, and of what she did not say, and partly from his own reflections, it came to him that this was because she thought him guiltless: he had been an unwitting tool, manipulated by the wicked Captain Aubrey, that bluff-seeming Macchiavel. Or had she never even learnt from the vague, the woollen-minded Herapath that the papers had passed to him through Stephen's hands?

'Watch out!' she cried, plucking him from under the wheels of a dray. 'Really, my dear, you must watch out, and keep to the sidewalk.' They returned to that interesting period of their stay on Desolation when the whaler was ready to depart: she described her preparations with the utmost candour and with a reminiscent glee, and she said, 'I so very nearly told you: I was sure you would not mind, being an Irishman and a friend to liberty — to America. Did you not guess, when you saw my seaman's trousers? Would you have helped me, if you had known?'

'I believe I should, my dear,' said he.

'I was sure of it,' she said, squeezing his arm. 'I told Herapath so, but Lord, what a fuss he made about it — his honour, you know, and all that. Apart from anything else he said he owed you money: I always knew Northerners worshipped the dollar, but I would never have believed anyone could have made such a coil about small change — in the South, of course, it is quite different. I had to screech and bawl like a fishwife to shift him: oh Lord!' At the recollection she began to laugh, that absurd infectious laugh of hers that always gave Stephen pleasure; and now people turned in the street and smiled at her. A pause, with a few more inward gurgles of mirth, and then suddenly she cried, 'But you never told me you know Diana Villiers!'

'You never asked,' said Stephen. 'You know her too, I collect?'

'Heavens, yes,' said Mrs Wogan. 'I have known her this age and more. We are amazingly close friends. Well, we were in London, anyway; and I love her dearly. As I dare say you know, she is the particular friend of Harry Johnson, a man I know very well; we both come from Maryland. They will be in Boston on Wednesday. I long for you to meet him: he loves birds, too. When I reached the States at last I told them all about you, and Diana cried out, "But that is my Maturin!" and Harry Johnson said, "It must be the same Maturin that wrote the paper about boobies" — could it be boobies?'

They passed O'Reilly's hotel, and two British officers, who knew Stephen, looked at him with open envy. They saluted, and Mrs

Wogan gave them a flashing smile. 'Poor fellows,' she remarked. 'It is dreadful being a prisoner. I must get Mrs Adams to invite them.'

'It is not so much the Englishmen that you dislike, then, but rather their Government?'

'That's right,' said Mrs Wogan. 'Though of course I hate some Englishmen too: but it is really their Government I detest, and I dare say it is the same with you. Do you know, they hanged Charles Pole, the friend of mine in the Foreign Office I told you about long ago. Such a cowardly, despicable thing to do — they might have shot him. Here we are,' she said, steering him into a muddy street of small brick houses with lean hogs searching along its gutter. 'Are we not squalid? It is the best poor Herapath can do, for the present.'

Poor Herapath was waiting for them in a sparsely furnished room, little less squalid than the street, and full of smoke. He greeted Stephen with a painful mixture of embarrassment and affection, hesitating to offer his hand until Stephen grasped it. He had aged since they parted on Desolation Island and from his emaciated appearance Stephen supposed that he had returned to the abuse of opium. Yet he was essentially the same Herapath, and while Louisa went to fetch their baby he showed Stephen his translation of Li Po with an eagerness that brought the days of the *Leopard*'s sickbay vividly to mind.

The baby was an ordinary specimen of its kind, probably good at bottom; but it was angry at not having been fed, and while its parents argued the point in voices necessarily raised above the usual tone, it roared and howled again. Stephen gazed at its red and angry face, the successive or sometimes mingled expressions of woe and rage, and reproached himself for wishing it never had been born; he also noticed that Herapath was somewhat less inept at handling it, and that the little creature paid more attention to its father than its mother. Eventually, after the usual compliments, delivered in something near a shout, it was carried away, and Herapath said, 'I am exceedingly concerned, Dr Maturin, that I should have left you without paying my debt.'

'Not at all,' said Stephen. 'I seized upon your property and sold your uniforms to Byron, who was naked, and much of your size; you left me the richer for the bargain.'

'I am glad of that: it preyed upon my mind. After all your kindness . . .'

'Pray, Mr Herapath, do you spend all your hours with Li Po? I had hoped you might perhaps study physic on your return: you have a real gift for medicine.'

'And so I should, if I had the means. As it is, I have read Galen and what other books I can come at. But I hope that when my translation is published, the profits will allow me to return to Harvard and qualify myself as a physician. I have great hopes: Louisa has a friend, a childhood friend from the South, who has made interest with a Philadelphia publisher, and he gives me every reason to suppose that all will be well. The book may come out in a handsome quarto next year, with an octavo edition to follow, if the demand is great enough! In the meantime we live upon an allowance that my father is good enough to make me. But if only he would —' Herapath checked himself, coughed, and said, 'My father desires me to make you his best compliments, and he hopes for the honour of your company at dinner tomorrow.'

'I should be happy to wait upon him,' said Stephen, rising, for Mrs Wogan had come back, followed by a slatternly black woman and two small black boys with the tea-tray and its grubby appurtenances.

'I do hope it will be to your liking,' said Mrs Wogan, looking anxiously into the pot. 'Sally is better at mint-juleps than tea.'

At one time Stephen had been marooned on a bare rock in the south Atlantic, and his only drink was the warm rainwater that remained in the guano-filled hollows: it had been more disagreeable than Mrs Wogan's tea, but only very slightly so. The taste of his bitter cup stayed with him the rest of the day, although he had endeavoured to qualify it by eating lumps of an amorphous grey substance, said to be spoon-bread, a Southern delicacy.

He was conscious of it when he woke in the morning, and he could still readily evoke the curious mixture of tar, molasses and perhaps verdigris when Herapath came to the Asclepia to fetch him.

'Do you think, sir,' said Herapath uneasily, 'that I should pay my respects to Captain Aubrey?'

'I do not,' said Stephen. 'He would consider it his duty to hang you for having run from the *Leopard*; and the excitement, the agitation, in his enfeebled state, would be very bad for him. I have just agreed with Dr Choate that no visitors should be allowed, particularly the people from the Navy Department who so upset him the other day.'

The Navy Department had upset Jack Aubrey, but not very much: not nearly so much as that distant victory off the Demerara river. Not nearly so much as the view from his windows, one of which commanded the harbour and the other the moorings of the American men-of-war. It was not that a great deal happened, since all the merchantmen were tied up, sometimes two deep, all along the wharves and little was to be seen in motion apart from small craft and fishing-boats; but what did happen moved him as he had very rarely been moved before.

Apart from the intervals of meals and medical care and the cleaning of his room, he spent the daylight hours with his telescope to his eye. He knew the powerful American frigates intimately well — he even knew a great many of their officers and men, quite apart from those officers from the *Constitution* whose acquaintance he had made during the voyage and who came to visit him — and he watched them with passionate intensity. Three of them: *President*, a forty-four-gun twenty-four-pounder, wearing a commodore's broad pendant; *Congress*, thirty-eight; and of course his own dismantled *Constitution*. And he had but to swing round and steady his glass on the other windowsill and there in the offing he would catch the topgallantsails of the blockading squadron. Sometimes a frigate, *Aeolus* or *Belvidera* or *Shannon*, would come right into the outer harbour and reconnoitre, and his heart would beat so that he had to hold his breath to keep the glass from moving

— beat with wild notions of a cutting-out attack or a landing to carry the forts from behind.

Constitution was undergoing massive repairs and alterations: he could not flatter himself that this was all owing to the damage that *Java* had inflicted, but she had certainly made her contribution, and the *Constitution* would not be a fighting ship for some months to come. The *President* and *Congress*, however, were rapidly preparing for sea, and he watched every move: he saw their rigging new set-up, noted the seamanlike way in which the *President* re-rove her bowsprit gammoning in a single afternoon, saw their stores come aboard, hundreds and hundreds of casks, saw them complete their water, exercise their hands aloft, take in their powder from the hoy. They were almost on the wing, waiting perhaps for no more than a brisk south-wester and the ebbing tide to shift the blockading ships far enough north and east to let them slip out into the Atlantic.

It was when his glass had been long focused on *President*'s quarterdeck, trying to make out the exact nature of her carronades, that he heard a remote cheering from the harbour. He turned quickly — he was nimble enough now, and every day he felt his strength returning — and there was another American frigate, standing in under topsails and jib. Somehow she had evaded the blockading squadron although the wind was moderate, a little south of east, and had been so all day: perhaps they were manned entirely by blind lunatics. But this was no time for recrimination; he levelled his telescope and stared, his whole being concentrated in that eye.

A thirty-eight-gun frigate; fine entry, smooth run; twenty-eight long eighteen-pounders, twenty-four thirty-pound carronades; two traversing long eighteen-pounders on her forecastle and another on the quarterdeck; deck priddied to the nines, falls flemished. The *Chesapeake*. As he watched, an officer on her quarterdeck raised his speaking-trumpet: before he could hear the order the frigate's jib and topsails vanished in one movement; she glided on in a long curve, stemming the tide, and picked up her moorings just as the way came off her. At the same moment her starboard quarter-boat splashed down, the bargemen jumped into it, and her captain pulled ashore. It could not have been done better in any ship that Jack had served in, not even when Old Jarvie had the Channel Fleet. The only thing that he could have taken exception to was the spectacle of three tall midshipmen leaning on the rail in nonchalant attitudes, chewing tobacco and squirting the juice over the side.

'Will you take your dinner now, sir?' asked Mary Sullivan. ' 'Tis twice Bridey has been up, and you looking at your old boats. Do you wish it cold, for all love, the good codfish? Well, well, eat it up while there's some warmth to it still. There, now. And the Doctor is having his dinner in the town, so he is, God bless him.'

Mr Herapath senior was a big, authoritative man, big in his chest, shoulders, and belly, with a large florid face and even larger features: his hair was powdered, and he wore a black velvet coat with blue collar and cuffs, a combination of colours that brought Diana Villiers even nearer to the forefront of Stephen's mind. In a little less than twenty-seven hours, he reflected, glancing at a handsome English clock, she would be in Boston. Mr Herapath's manner was firm and assured; he was obviously accustomed to command, and both his son and the elderly lady who kept house for him sank into mute insignificance; but to Stephen he was markedly amiable, welcoming, and even deferential.

He apologized for not having come to the Asclepia to pay his respects to Dr Maturin and to thank him for his great goodness to Michael; he had been kept withindoors by a wretched colic, but it was gone now, and he was very happy to have this opportunity of making his acknowledgments — he could never sufficiently congratulate himself upon Michael's having been honoured with the acquaintance and of having come under the influence of such a distinguished man. Dr Rawley had spoken to him of Dr Maturin's valuable publications on the health of seamen, and he understood that Dr Maturin was a Fellow of the Royal Society; he was only a merchant himself, but he honoured learning — useful learning.

Dinner was a long, slow, massive affair, and the conversation was almost entirely carried on by Mr Herapath and Stephen; Michael Herapath said very little, and Aunt James confined herself to asking Stephen whether he believed in the Trinity.

'Certainly, ma'am,' he replied.

'Well, I am glad someone does,' said she. 'Nearly all those scoundrels at Harvard are Unitarians, and their wives are worse.'

After that, she produced no more than hissing noises at the servants: but although she was no great conversationalist she was clearly a notable housekeeper. The fog outside made the whole day dim, yet the big, comfortable dining-room was alive with the subdued gleam of polished wood; the noble fire, flanked by brass that would have done credit to the Royal Navy, lit up a great expanse of Turkey carpet, red and blue; they ate their good sober dinner off uncommonly massive plate; and when she left them Stephen observed that she passed into an equally agreeable drawing-room. It was not an elegant house, although there were some fine things in it, but it was discreetly rich and above all comfortable; he might have been dining with a long-established merchant in the City of London. This impression was much strengthened, startlingly strengthened indeed, when Mr Herapath filled his glass, passed the decanter, rose to his feet, and proposed the health of the King. Michael Herapath drank the toast with an abstracted look, and Stephen perceived that he was gliding a silver table-spoon into his pocket, the pocket away from his father's chair.

Mr Herapath then proposed 'a decent end to Mr Madison's war, and may it come very soon,' and Stephen followed him with 'trade's increase', which Mr Herapath drank in a bumper, thumping his glass three times on the table to show the heartiest agreement.

In the drawing-room Stephen eyed the silver urn with some apprehension, but it appeared that in Boston they knew how to make tea, and he drank it gratefully, for his head was not unaffected by the amount of claret and port he had drunk. Only two cups, however, for Mr Herapath was restive: he asked Aunt James whether it were not time for her nap, and upon this the poor lady walked straight out of the room without a word, leaving a half-mumbled piece of muffin. Then he told Michael that it was high time he returned to Caroline, since that Maryland Sally could not be trusted to feed her regularly, nor could anyone else; that he would see Dr Maturin back to the Asclepia himself; and that Michael had better look sharp — the fog was getting thicker still.

'There, Dr Maturin,' he said at last, leading his guest into a small room, presumably his study, for there were half a dozen books in it, as well as ledgers, 'let me draw your chair to the fire. I cannot tell you how pleased I am to see you here.' After a pause during which he looked at Stephen with a bright and eager eye, he stated that in the War of Independence he had been a Loyalist, and that although to protect his interests he had returned from Canada, compounding with the Republic, his heart remained where it had always been. 'My conduct may not have been very heroic, sir; but then I am only a merchant, not a hero. Heroism can, I believe, be very safely left to you gentlemen who serve the Crown.' Still, he and his friends had done all they could to prevent Mr Madison's war — here followed some pretty bitter remarks about Mr Madison, Mr Jefferson, and the Republicans — and now they were doing all they could to hamper its progress and to bring it to an early close. He would have invited some of his friends, Tories and Federalists, to meet Dr Maturin today, but that he wanted to express his gratitude first, and Dr Maturin might have found that embarrassing in the presence of company.

'And because you wanted to weigh me up, old fellow,' thought Stephen. He wondered at Herapath's simplicity in expecting to be accepted at his own self-declared value, yet he also found it quite agreeable, since he had independent evidence of its truth; and he waited, nodding, agreeing, for the proposition that he sensed at no great distance.

'I am always glad to see a British officer,' said Mr Herapath, 'and I and my friends have had the honour of entertaining several; but none has been of your weight and seniority, my dear sir. And none has had such claims on my esteem and gratitude. When my son returned, sir, he talked perpetually of you, of how you had raised him from the lowest rank to the quarterdeck, and of your kindness to him on all occasions. He was particularly unhappy that he should have left you without a word and that he should have run away when he was in your debt. Would to God he had stayed . . . however, you must allow me to settle his debt at once. May I ask . . . ?'

'He owed me seven pounds,' said Stephen.

Mr Herapath heaved sideways to reach his pocket, laid down the sum, and said, 'Let me add, sir, that my purse is always open to you. Within reason,' he added automatically, and went on. 'At least he was my son in hating debt: but in everything else, good Lord above . . . He spent years studying the Chinese language, sir; but will you believe me when I say it was the Chinese of a thousand years ago, of no use to man or beast? He cannot even make out a bill of lading. And there were some other most unfortunate events . . . Then to crown all he comes home from his travels not only naked but with a drabbletail wench from Maryland into the bargain, and a bastard child. I ask you, sir, what can I make of a son like that?'

'You can make him a physician, sir. He has considerable natural gifts in the physical line, and a keen intelligence. I was much impressed by his cool capability when he served as my assistant in the *Leopard*, often in very trying circumstances; and I do most earnestly beg you will consider the suggestion.'

'Is he really capable of becoming a physician?' asked Mr Herapath, looking pleased. 'He often spoke of it when he first came home.'

'Certainly he is,' said Stephen. 'His Chinese may be a thousand years old, but you are to consider, that Greek and Latin are older still. They are required in a physician, because the wisdom of ages has found that they give a nimbleness of mind. They supple the mind, sir; they render it pliant and receptive. He has Latin and Greek, and he has Chinese too: there is suppleness, there is pliability and receptiveness, I believe.'

'He often spoke of going to medical school. But to be frank with you, Doctor, I did not like to trust him with the money. His connection with Mrs Wogan is very painful to me: and since I believe that she has interested motives, I mean to starve her out. I should go a more decided way about it and have her taken up as a vagabond, if it were not for what is after all my grandchild, Caroline. A most remarkable baby, Dr Maturin.'

'I had the pleasure of seeing her yesterday.'

'Ah, had you known her dear great-grandmother, you would have seen the likeness directly; you would certainly have remarked upon it. A delightful child — such pretty ways. So, you understand, sir, I am obliged to make Michael an allowance, not to lose Caroline; and although of course I cannot receive Mrs Wogan publicly, I do see her from time to time. But my visits are very rare, and the allowance is very small. Do you think my course is well advised, sir? I should be grateful for your opinion.'

Stephen considered. He could do no harm: he might possibly do some good. He said, 'I believe you are wise, sir. Yet I believe you would be wiser still in sending Michael to the medical school.' And then, since the words might reinforce the possible good, although they were blasphemy to him as a lover, hc added, 'A connection of this kind rarely fails to die away when it is coupled with possession and with prolonged discouragement, and above all if an engrossing new interest, such as medicine, enters into competition with it.'

'Perhaps you are right. Yes, yes, I believe you are right. Dr Herapath, ha, ha! But do you really suppose he could qualify himself?'

Stephen spoke of medical studies, instanced men barely capable of telling right from wrong who had passed through them with success, and stated that he had no doubt but that one who had mastered Chinese could do as much and more. He felt that he had made his point, and when Mr Herapath moved on to some tolerably illiberal abuse of

Mrs Wogan and of women from the Southern states in general — Mr Herapath would not say this except to a physical gentleman, but it seemed that they were insatiable, sir, insatiable — he listened without contradicting.

'Yet has Mrs Wogan no sources of income other than the allowance you mention?' he asked after a while. 'I noticed that she kept three servants, which in England would argue a certain modest ease.'

'That vile Sally and the foot-boys? Oh, they are only slaves, sent up from her cousin's place near Baltimore. She would sell them if she could, but that is not so easy in Massachusetts; and anyhow, who would buy such a parcel of slubberdegullions? And so I have to feed the whole eternal pack of bone-idle good-for-nothing brutes.'

'Baltimore is in Maryland, is it not?'

'Yes, sir: right up the Chesapeake. Good tobacco-land and worthless people.'

'Do you know of a Mr Henry Johnson, who comes from those parts?'

'Why do you ask?' said Herapath sharply. 'Have you heard anything about him?'

'Mrs Wogan mentioned his name. It appears that he is acquainted with friends of mine.'

'Oh, I thought maybe . . .' Mr Herapath's voice died away; he coughed, and went on,

'Well, now: Mr Harry Johnson is a very wealthy man; he probably owns more slaves than anyone else in the state. He is a great Republican, and many of his friends are in power; he is counsellor to the Secretary of State, and he is often here in Boston. I keep my eye on him, because he knows Louisa Wogan. And to tell you the truth, sir,' — lowering his voice — 'I hope he may rid me of her; he is the greatest whoremaster in the South. But at the same time, I am very much afraid she might take my Caroline with her.'

'I have a certain, perhaps unfounded impression,' said Stephen, 'that Mrs Wogan is a somewhat detached parent. There may be a relative lack of that instinctive *storgé*, which equally binds the she-bear and the matron to their puling young.'

'She is an unnatural cat,' cried Mr Herapath, and there the conversation languished: Mr Herapath fell to poking the fire with savage stabs. 'I mentioned my friends some time ago, Dr Maturin,' he said at last. 'Much good may come of a meeting, since they are all gentlemen of a like mind with me. Would you come tomorrow? We should like to make our sentiments known in Halifax as soon as possible — to convey them by means of a man of real weight and consequence — and you will be exchanged very soon, as I suppose. We have information to give, not indeed of a military but rather of a political nature that may be of the first importance in bringing this war to an end. Some of my friends are among the most important merchants in New England, and they know a great deal in the political and commercial line; we are all suffering from this war — for example, I have three ships tied up here in Boston and two more at Salem. But do not suppose, sir, that our motives are entirely selfish. We *are* concerned for our trade, it is true, but there are motives far higher than any trade.'

'I am convinced of it, sir,' said Stephen. 'Yet, Mr Herapath, you are a former Loyalist: your opinions cannot be unknown to the authorities, and the most elementary prudence requires that they should watch your house.'

'If they were to watch all the households in Boston that are opposed to Mr Madison's war, they would need a couple of regiments.'

'But not all these households include an eminent citizen, the proprietor of five considerable vessels. I should be happy to give your friends the meeting, but I had rather it took place in some discreet tavern or coffee-house.'

'I own more than that,' said Mr Herapath. 'However, you may be right; it may be wiser. I honour your caution, Dr Maturin. It shall be so.'

In order that it might be so he walked Stephen home a roundabout way that took them past the harbour. He pointed out two of his barques, tied up against the wharf, their tall masts reaching up until they were no more than a faint trace in the fog. 'That is *Arcturus*,' he said, 'seventeen hundred tons burden, and the other *Orion*, a little better than fifteen hundred. If it were not for this damned war, they would be plying to the Far East and back, out by the Cape for Canton, and home by the East Indies and the Horn, with three thousand tons of silks and tea and spices, with china under all; but much as I respect the gentlemen of the Royal Navy I cannot afford to offer them prizes of that value. So here they lie, with nothing but a couple of ship-keepers in them. Joe!' he shouted.

'What now?' called Joe from out of the fog.

'Mind your fenders.'

'I am a-minding of them, ain't I?'

'God's my life,' said Herapath to Stephen, 'to speak to the owner so, and a black man at that! It could never have happened in the old days. With his democratical notions, that wicked fellow Jefferson has rotted the moral fibre of the whole country.'

Jefferson, who had prompted Joe's reply,

lasted until they reached a tavern, a quiet, respectable place frequented by shipmasters, which would do very well for their meeting, and then, having impressed the place on Stephen's memory, Herapath led him up the hill, through a series of alleys. 'How well you know your way,' said Stephen.

'It would be strange if I did not,' replied Herapath. 'My sister Putnam has been in Dr Choate's care these many years, and I visit her every new moon. She is a werewolf.'

'A werewolf,' said Stephen to himself, and he turned it over in his mind until they went up a flight of steps and the familiar building came in sight. At the gates of the Asclepia they uttered expressions of mutual esteem, and Mr Herapath left his best compliments for Captain Aubrey if, in view of his son's conduct, they should be acceptable, together with an offer of any assistance that the Captain might stand in need of. 'I should dearly love to show my gratitude,' he said, 'for although Michael may not be all I could wish, he is my son, and Captain Aubrey preserved him from drowning.'

'Perhaps you would like to walk in for five minutes?' said Stephen. 'The Captain is not well enough for a longer visit, but I believe it would do him good to see you. He loves to talk of ships with those who understand them, and in spite of the circumstances to which you refer, he retains an affectionate memory of your son.'

The Captain was asleep when they came into the room: asleep, with a look of deep unhappiness on his face, and the face was pallid, unhealthy, the long-established tan faded to a nasty yellow, the breathing laboured, with a râle that Stephen did not like to hear at all. 'What you need, my friend,' he said to himself as they stood there, 'is a victory, even quite a small victory, by sea; otherwise, you will eat your heart out — pule into a decline. Failing that, I believe we must try more steel and bark . . . steel and bark.'

'Why, Stephen, there you are,' said Jack, opening his eyes, wide awake at once, as he always was.

'So I am, too; and I have brought Mr Herapath with me, the father of my assistant who behaved so very well during our epidemical distemper. Mr Herapath also served the King in the former war, and he is the owner of several eminent ships, two of which you have remarked upon — they can be seen from this window here.'

'Your servant, sir,' said each, and Jack went on. 'Those two fine barques with the Nelson chequer and pole topgallantmasts, the finest in the harbour?'

Mr Herapath made his acknowledgments for Jack's preservation of his son, and they fell to talking of the ships: Herapath had made several voyages; he loved the sea, and he was a more amiable person here than in his own house. Their conversation was animated, and free.

Sitting by the window and looking at the fog, Stephen drifted far away: in less than four and twenty hours Diana would be here. Images of her moving, walking across the room, riding, setting her horse at a fence, flying over with her head held high. A distant clock struck the hour, followed by several more.

'Come, gentlemen,' he said.

'What a fine fellow!' cried Herapath as Stephen led him down the stairs. 'The very type of the sea-officer when I was young — no coldness, no pride, nothing like those army men. And a prodigious fighting-captain! How well I remember his action with the *Cacafuego*! Oh, if only Michael could have been like him . . .'

'I liked that man,' said Jack. 'He did me good. He knows his ships from stem to stern, and he has sound political ideas: he hates a Frenchman as much as I do. I should like to see him again. How did he ever contrive to have such a son?'

'Your own may turn into a book-worm or a

273

Methody parson,' said Stephen. ' 'Tis just as the whim bites, no more; for as you know, one man may lead a horse to the water, but ten cannot make him think. But tell me, Jack, how do you feel, and how did you spend your afternoon?'

'Pretty well, I thank you. I saw the *Chesapeake* come in, one of their thirty-eights; a beautiful ship. I suppose there must have been fog out there too, beyond the bay — anyway, she passed our squadron and came in in fine style. She is lying beyond the *President*, near the ordnance quay: you will see her when it clears.' While Stephen took his pulse he told him more about the *Chesapeake* and about the progress on the other frigates, and then he said, 'By the way, I had a luminous idea. Those Navy Department fellows are all to seek. I have been working it out with an almanack and I find that at the time I am supposed to have brought their *Alice B. Sawyer* to, *Leopard* was tearing along at twelve or thirteen knots with the Dutchman in her wake. It is materially impossible that I should have brought anything to. I am quite easy in my mind.'

'Bless you,' said Stephen. And in one of his very rare bursts of confidence he went on, 'I wish I could say the same. Diana will be in Boston shortly, and I am wondering what course to pursue — whether to inflict myself upon her, perhaps unwelcome, perhaps untimely; or whether to affect a frigid indifference and let her make the first step, always provided that she should choose to do so, and that she knows of our being here.'

'Lord, Stephen,' cried Jack, but no more, until recollecting himself he sat up and reached for a letter on his bedside table. 'Speaking of the devil, here is a note for you, perhaps it is from her. Our capture was in the papers. Though I must not say the devil,' he added, after a pause. 'She behaved very handsomely, writing home to tell Sophie we were alive, and I shall always think kindly of her.'

It was not from Diana. Louisa Wogan asked dear Dr Maturin to call on her; she would be alone any time after ten o'clock, and she had a great deal to say to him. But before Stephen had time to make any comment, Dr Choate and his patients, two doors away, struck into the triumphant opening bars of the Clementi C major quintet, playing with a sustained virtuosity and joy that kept their listeners silent until the sombre disenchantment of the finale.

Mrs Wogan was as who should say alone, since she did not count the occasional presence of her slaves, and Michael had taken

Caroline to see her grandfather. She had, rather touchingly, dressed for the occasion, and Stephen noticed an emerald ring of surprising size and beauty.

Their conversation was long, and on Louisa Wogan's side remarkably frank. She reminded Stephen of the growth of their friendship, of his distress at the prospect of war between England and the United States, of his support for liberty in Ireland, Catalonia, Greece, and any country where freedom was threatened, of his abhorrence of the English way of pressing American sailors, and of his kindness to the American whalers on Desolation Island — they were, she said, much attached to him. She then went on to say that, as Stephen knew, she had been educated in France and had lived much in Europe; she had been intimately acquainted with some of the most interesting and influential men in Paris and London, and for this reason she had been able to advise certain American representatives abroad. She possessed the languages, local information, and introductions that were valuable to them; they had consulted her, and they had even given her confidential missions to perform. Their aim had always been the maintenance of peace and of their country's liberty. It was in the course of one of these missions that she had fallen foul of the English law: that was why she was sent to Botany Bay. The English had wanted to hang her, but fortunately she had friends who saved her neck. Botany Bay was an amazingly savage punishment for what in fact amounted to very little, yet at least she had thought she was shot of those odious British intelligence people: but not at all — their malice pursued her even aboard the *Leopard*. Did Stephen remember some papers in French that were supposed to have been found among a dead officer's belongings and that the Captain gave to Michael Herapath to write out? Stephen had a vague recollection of such a task.

'You would not remember, would you?' she said, with an indulgent smile. 'You were too busy with your stormy petrels.' But then her face grew dark, and she said, 'They were completely false. I have a pretty good idea of who fabricated them, with the help of the people in London — and indeed in my own heart I am quite sure he is one of them, though I did not suspect him at the time, with his open, rather stupid seadog airs. Most of them are Freemasons, you know. Anyhow, it was my obvious duty to get copies, and so I did: and when I went off in the whaler there they were in my bosom, and I was so pleased and proud.' She began to laugh, low and then fuller and fuller, so amused at the backward sight of herself, ridiculously pleased and proud of her poisoned documents. Sally looked in, grinned, and withdrew. Stephen contemplated Mrs Wogan, and Mrs Wogan's heaving bosom: she might be an inept intelligence-agent, but he admired her dash and courage, he loved her acute, her wonderfully rare sense of humour, he had a real affection for her, and, at present, a distinct carnal inclination for her person. The long, long chastity of these recent voyages weighed upon him; he was particularly conscious of her scent, her supple roundnesses, her propinquity on this shabby but convenient sofa. Yet something told him that this was not the moment; that if in former times he might have risked no very severe rebuff, he certainly risked it now. He neither stirred nor spoke.

'But it was no laughing matter,' she said at last. 'When I reached the States with my papers, everyone was delighted, amazed and delighted. But then dreadful things began to happen — I will not go into all that now — but Charles Pole was hanged and Harry Johnson very nearly lost his place. He fairly hates Captain Aubrey and the *Leopard*.'

'The Mr Johnson who knows Diana Villiers, and who is to come so soon?'

'Yes. They always take the first floor of Franchon's hotel; it is being cleared out for them at this very minute — such a *remue-ménage*. I long for you two to meet. I am sure Harry Johnson would value your advice; he would love to consult you. When we parted, and when you gave me those lovely furs, I so very nearly told you about him. I wish I had.'

'I should be happy to meet Mr Johnson,' said Stephen.

'I shall take you to see him tomorrow.'

Emerging from Wogan's warren, Stephen reached a broad street, full of citizens in greatcoats and fur caps, chewing tobacco: there was one, however, a middle-aged man in a sheepskin cloak and a broad-brimmed hat, who was not doing so, and as Broad-brim paced soberly between the jets Stephen asked him the way to Franchon's hotel.

'Come, friend, and I will show thee,' said the American. 'Thou dost not seem to feel the cold,' he observed, as they walked along.

'I am not insensible to it, however,' replied Stephen, 'having recently come from a warm climate.'

'There,' said the American, stopping opposite a large, white-painted, elegant building with balconies running across its front. 'That is the house of the Whore of Babylon. Thou art neither so young nor so foolish as to enter into it: but if thou dost, friend, mind thy poke.'

'He that is down needs fear no fall,' said Stephen. 'He that is low, no pride. My poke is empty, and no man can rob me.'

'Art in earnest, friend?' said the American, looking at him attentively.

Stephen nodded: but then, seeing the man's hand go to his pocket, he cried, 'No, no, I have plenty in a drawer at home. Thank you, sir, for having shown me the way; and thank you for what I believe to have been your kind intent.'

Stephen stood there for a while after the American had left him. All things being considered, the Whore seemed to do herself pretty well. A comfortable place, no doubt, though somewhat richer than he would care for for himself; the kind of place where he might eat if invited by wealthy friends, but not alone. The first floor was indeed being turned inside out; pieces of furniture, carpets, rugs, appeared on the long balcony, moving from room to room; and judging by the passionate cries that accompanied every movement the hotel was run by French people. Good food and wine, in all likelihood, if one did not mind the cost. It would suit Diana perfectly.

As he watched he saw Pontet-Canet come out, pause on the sidewalk and call up to a man on one of the upper balconies, 'Yankee Duddle,' he cried, and laughed aloud. 'Yankee Duddle, *souviens-toi.*'

Stephen melted into the crowd and hurried off to his meeting at the quayside tavern, where, as he had expected, nothing awaited him at this stage but circumspection, generous sentiments of no binding quality, and vehement abuse of Mr Madison. The only solid information he received was that *Constellation*, a thirty-eight-gun frigate of 1265 tons, cost $314,212 to build at Baltimore, whereas the *Chesapeake*, also of thirty-eight guns, cost only $220,677 at Norfolk. 'Sixty-one thousand two hundred and ninety-nine pounds two shillings,' said Mr Herapath, looking at his notebook, 'and a dead waste of public money.' For his part Stephen was perfectly noncommittal: who could tell what private animosities there might be among these merchants, to say nothing of the possible agent provocateur?

As he walked back to the Asclepia his mind ran chiefly upon Mrs Wogan. She intended to present him to Johnson as her new recruit: 'consultant' was the term she used, nothing so coarse or injurious as 'spy' — adviser in the cause of peace. He had expressed nothing but a general interest, but her wishes had outrun her judgment, and she was almost sure of him. Mistakenly, as it happened, since he did not intend to play the double agent. He had seen it done, sometimes with spectacular results. But it was not for him, even if he had the necessary skill, which he doubted. There was the danger of being caught by friendship on the other side or by scruples, and above all there was the obligatory extreme depth of dissimulation and he was sick of it, sick of it all. He was sick even of simple dissimulation, dissimulation at one level, and he longed to be shot of it, to be able to speak openly to any man or woman he happened to like: or to dislike, for that matter. Yet he would have to see Johnson . . . Again, just as pretty Wogan had now persuaded herself that he would be an adviser, so in the past her partiality for him had blinded her, so that Jack appeared as the villain of the piece. A belief that was apparently shared by her superiors and that would account for many things: their unwillingness to let him go, their retention of his papers, the odd business about the *Alice B. Sawyer*, which might be a blundering first attempt at a trumped-up charge. He wondered what they might possess in the way of scruples: some intelligence services he had known let their desire for revenge and further information carry them very far indeed: Bonaparte's agents had no limits at all. He twitched his hands, still crooked and twisted from a French interrogation many years ago.

As far as the nations went, he did not think that there was the least parallel between the United States and France. The States had an active and vocal public opinion — he had read their papers, mostly written in a steady shriek of indignation, with astonishment — whereas the extremely efficient tyranny in France had almost entirely gagged it, and in any case the whole concept of government and of public morality was so entirely different. Yet intelligence services were something else again, little worlds of their own, often inhabited by strange, extreme beings: he knew something of the French and Spanish; he had seen the English in the Dublin of 1798, and the riding-school in Stephen's Green, where suspects were put to the question. Infamous creatures, most of the questioners; but even honourable, humane men were capable of almost anything for unselfish motives. On the other hand, the effects of the bomb that Wogan had so proudly carried home would have been felt primarily in France; it was essentially directed at Bonaparte, and only incidentally at the Americans, as his potential allies. The American agents would have suffered in their pride, not in their persons.

He found Jack Aubrey sitting on a chair by the window, surveying the harbour with his telescope. 'You have just missed Mr Andrews,' he cried, on seeing Stephen. 'If you had been a few minutes earlier, you would have caught him: indeed, I wonder you did not run into him on the stairs.'

'Who is Mr Andrews?'

'He is the new agent for prisoners of war, and he came to deliver a protest. He came from Halifax in that slab-sided ketch by the red buoys, and he brought some papers and this note for you: no letters from England yet, at least not for us.'

The note was from Stephen's colleague in Halifax: to all appearance it contained no more than a brief account of the death of a common friend; in fact it told him that Jean Dubreuil was in Washington. Jean Dubreuil was an important man in Paris and he was one of those Stephen had hoped to kill or disable with his bomb. He put the letter back in his pocket and attended to Jack, who was telling him about the blockade.

'*Africa* is laid up,' he was saying, 'and *Belvidera* sprung her mainmast a little above the partners; so we only have *Shannon* and *Tenedos* in Massachusetts Bay. Just those two and a tender, a sloop, to watch their *President*, *Congress*, *Constitution*, and now *Chesapeake*. To be sure, *Constitution* is laid up and *Chesapeake* is alongside the sheer-hulk, getting in a new main and mizen, but *President* crossed her royal yards this afternoon and *Congress* is pretty well ready for sea — she has her powder in, as I told Mr Andrews.'

'Did you tell him much?'

'Every single thing I have learnt with all this staring; and since, thank God, I have a very good glass, I have learnt a great deal. For example, *Chesapeake* landed four carronades and an eighteen-pounder, but she still has her full armament for a thirty-eight: I fancy she must have been over-gunned, and worked heavy in a sea. But there were several things I forgot while I was talking to him; I must note them down in future.'

'Jack, Jack, do nothing of the kind,' cried Stephen, and moving over to sit by him he went on in a low voice, 'Put nothing whatsoever down on paper, and take great care how you talk. For I must tell you this, Jack: the Americans suspect you of being concerned with intelligence. That is why the exchange is delayed. Do not, for God's sake, give them a handle to proceed against you — this is spying. But do not be too concerned, however; do not let it disturb your mind. It will all blow over, I am convinced. Even so, you would be well advised not to show too much blooming health: you must keep to your bed, and you may exaggerate your weakness — you may *swing the lead* a trifle. You must not see these officials, if it can be avoided; I will have a word with Dr Choate.' He gave some quick, expert hints on malingering. 'But do not be concerned: as I say, it will soon blow over.'

'Oh,' said Jack, laughing heartily for the first time since their captivity, 'I am concerned. If they suspect me of intelligence, I am sure it will soon blow over, ha, ha, ha!'

'Well,' said Stephen, smiling, 'you are not above playing on words, I find. So good night to you, now: I am going to turn in early, because I too wish to be intelligent tomorrow.'

CHAPTER SIX

It was with a feeling not unlike dread that Stephen followed Mrs Wogan into Franchon's hotel. The people behind the desk were talking French and this, together with the European atmosphere of the place, brought about an odd shift in his sense of time and country; he had not seen Diana Villiers for a great while, yet it was much as though he were returning to the field of yesterday's encounter — an action from which he might have retired intensely happy or with a lacerated heart. She had treated him abominably, at times: he dreaded the meeting, and he had got ready for it two hours before the appointed time. He rarely shaved more than once or twice a week, nor did he pay much attention to his linen; but now he was wearing the finest shirt that Boston could afford, and the keen though foggy Boston air had so heightened the colour of his double-shaved face that it was no longer its usual lifeless olive-brown but a glowing pink.

They were shown upstairs into an elegant drawing-room, and there was Mr Johnson.

Stephen had not seen him for many years and then only once: the American had ridden up to Diana's house in Alipur on perhaps the most beautiful horse that ever was; he had been denied, and he had ridden away again. A tall, capable-looking man, handsome too, though now there was something of a paunch, something of a jowl, that had been lacking in the young horseman on the chestnut mare: a lively eye, and somewhat lickerous: a jovian temperament, no doubt. How much did he know of Stephen's former relationship with Diana? Stephen had asked himself that question before: now, while Johnson was greeting Mrs Wogan, he asked it again.

Mrs Wogan made the introductions and Johnson turned all his attention upon Stephen, looking at him, as he bowed, with particular interest and as it were benevolence — a kind, polite, and deferential look. He was obviously a man of very good company and he had an agreeable way of making his interlocutor seem a person of real importance. 'I am exceedingly happy to meet Dr Maturin,' he said. 'Mrs Wogan and Mr Herapath have often spoken of your kindness during their voyage, and I believe you have been acquainted with my friend Mrs Villiers since she was a girl; and even more than that, sir, it is to you that we are indebted for the splendid monography on boobies.'

Stephen said that Mr Johnson was too kind, too indulgent by far: yet it was a fact that in the matter of boobies he had been more fortunate than most men — the merit, if merit there were, lay in circumstances, not in himself. He had been marooned on a tropical island during the height of their breeding-season, and he had of necessity grown intimate with most of the species.

'We are very poor in boobies, alas,' said Johnson. 'With great good fortune, when I was off the Dry Tortugas, I managed to secure one of the blue-faced sort, but the white-bellied I have never seen, far less your red-legged species, or the spotted Peruvian.'

'Yet on the other hand, you have your skimmers — you have your wonderfully curious anhinga.'

They talked of the birds of America, those of the Antarctic and the East Indies for some time, and it became apparent to Stephen that in spite of his modest disclaimers Johnson knew a good deal: he might not be a scientific observer — he knew little or nothing of their anatomy — but there was no doubt that he loved the creatures. He spoke in much the same slow soft voice as Mrs Wogan, rather like a Negro, yet this did not conceal his enthusiasm when they came to the great albatrosses, which he had seen when he was going to India. She, for her part, listened to them for a while, then lapsed into a good-tempered silence, gazing out of the window at the people passing by below, dim in the swirling fog. Eventually she walked right out on to the balcony.

'When I learnt that there was a possibility of meeting you,' said Johnson, bringing a portfolio from beside his desk. 'I put these in my baggage.' They were extraordinarily exact and delicate paintings of American birds, among them the anhinga. 'And here is the very fowl you were speaking of,' said Johnson, when they reached it. 'Do let me beg you to accept it, as some slight acknowledgment of the pleasure your monography gave me.'

Polite but steady refusal: Johnson urged the picture's trifling commercial value — he would be ashamed to say how little he gave the artist — but he was too well-bred to insist beyond a certain point and they moved on to the painter himself. 'A young Frenchman I met on the Ohio river, a Creole, very talented, very difficult. I should have ordered a great many more, but unhappily we fell out. He was a bastard, and bastards, as no doubt you have observed, are often more touchy than ordinary beings; one sometimes offends them without meaning to; and sometimes indeed they seem to trail their coats.'

Stephen was himself a bastard, and at the word his hackles rose; yet he could not but admit the justice of the remark, and what was much more to the point, a man as polite as Johnson would never have made it if he had known that it could have any present application. Clearly, Diana had been discreet: uncommonly discreet, since a friend's bastardy, divorce, or deformity was so often the earliest point of description, the earliest sacrifice to the candour of intimacy.

A servant came in and spoke to Johnson in a low tone. 'You will excuse me for two minutes, Dr Maturin?' he said. 'Just for two minutes, while I get rid of these people?'

'By all means,' said Stephen, 'and in the meantime I believe that I shall pay my respect to Mrs Villiers; for I understand that she is in the same hotel.'

'Oh yes, yes. Do — she will be delighted. Hers is the red door at the end,' said Johnson on the threshold. 'Straight down the corridor. You will find your way? I stand on no ceremony with you, as you see, my dear sir: and I will join you as soon as I have sent these men away.'

Along the passage: the last steps quite slow, and a pause before the red door. He tapped, heard a voice, and walked in. He had unconsciously composed his face so that it bore a civil unassuming old-acquaintance look, and he was surprised to find the effort that had been required when the expression fell apart on his seeing not Diana but a black woman weighing twenty stone.

'Mrs Villiers, if you please?' he said.

'What name shall I say, sir?' asked the black woman, smiling at him from her splendid height and bulk.

'Stephen!' cried Diana, running in. 'Oh, how glad I am to see you at last.' The same step, the same voice; and he felt the same blow about his heart. He kissed her warm dry hand and felt its responding pressure. She was telling the black woman to hurry down and bring up the best pot of coffee that Madame Franchon could make. 'And some cream, Polly.' The veil of tears cleared from his eyes; he recovered his composure and said, 'What a magnificent creature.'

'Yes, yes,' said Diana in a kind of quick parenthesis, holding his hands and looking him full in the face, 'Johnson has dozens like that — he breeds the house-slaves for size. Stephen, you have come at last! I was so afraid you might not — I waited in all the morning — had everyone denied.' She drew him nearer and kissed him. 'You did not get my note? Stephen, sit down: you are looking quite pale. How are you, and how is poor Aubrey? The coffee will be here directly.'

'No note, Villiers. Was it discreet?'

'Oh, just compliments and begged you would call.'

'Listen, my dear, Johnson will be here in a minute. What does he know about us?'

At another time this question would probably have received a very fierce and disconcerting answer, but now she only said, 'Nothing: old acquaintance, practically childhood friends. Oh, Stephen, how glad I am to see you, and to see a British uniform, and to hear a British voice. I was so sorry, so very sorry about Clarges Street and all that wild dashing out of town — out of England — without even seeing you.' The coffee came, with cream and *petits fours*, and as she poured it out so she poured out her words, pell-mell — the *Leopard*'s voyage, the wreck on Desolation Island, news of it all from Louisa Wogan; this dreadful, dreadful war, her mad decision to go back to the States; the loss of *Guerrière*, *Macedonian*, *Java* — how was Jack Aubrey bearing it? With Polly's return she had switched into French, and with astonishment Stephen observed that she was calling him *tu*. He was astonished too by her loquacity. Both she and her cousin Sophie had always talked at a great pace, but now Diana's words tum-

293

bled over one another; few sentences reached their end; and the connecting association of ideas was at times so tenuous that although he knew her very well he could scarcely follow. It was as though she had recently taken some stimulant which so hastened her mental processes that they outran even her outstanding powers of articulation.

He had known her in a great variety of moods — friendly, confidential, perhaps even loving for one short period; certainly, and for much longer periods, indifferent, impatient at his long dumb importunity, sometimes exasperated, hard, and even (though more through the force of circumstances than her own volition) very cruel — but never in this.

He had the strangest impression that she was clinging to him. And yet no, not to him but to some ideal personage who happened to have the same name; or at least to a mixture of this shadow and himself. And quite apart from that there was some essential change.

He felt the edge of a desperate coldness overcome his first agitation as she talked and as he covertly examined her, sipping his good coffee. The last time he had seen her he had been struck by the brilliance of her complexion; now it was comparatively dull. Otherwise, in spite of the years, there was little physical change: still the same splendid carriage of her head, the same great misty dark-blue eyes, the same black hair sweeping up. Yet there was some lack that he could not define, some discordancy. His eye moved beyond her to one of the many tall looking-glasses in the room and he saw her fine straight back, the perfect rise of her neck, the graceful movement of her hands, and in the reflection he also saw himself, a squat figure in the small gilt chair, looking crushed. He pulled himself upright, and as she said, with a smile, 'Why, Stephen, where is your tongue?' he heard steps outside and murmured, 'In English, now, my dear.'

The door opened and Mrs Wogan walked in, followed by Johnson. The women kissed each other; Madame Franchon and her tiny husband brought another pot of coffee, received congratulations on their *petits fours;* a general din of talk, and what seemed like a great crowd of people. Polly, reaching behind Johnson for an empty cup, dropped it on the floor; Johnson whipped round, and Stephen saw her face turn grey as she stared in naked terror, her arms down by her sides; but Johnson turned back to Stephen with a laugh — 'Where would the china-makers be, if no cups were ever broke?' — and went on talking about the ivory-billed and the pileated woodpeckers. Another man came in, an American:

introductions, though Stephen only caught the Mr Secretary part of the name. A great deal of conversation, dominated by the harsh metallic voice of the newcomer. Stephen wanted to observe them, but here was Mrs Wogan talking to him, very pleased, even triumphant, and so pretty; and now Diana; and presently it appeared to him that a dinner-party had been arranged and that he was invited. 'I shall so look forward to it,' said Diana, as he took his leave.

He walked out of the hotel into the fog, fog that thickened as he wandered down towards the harbour: fog in his mind as he tried to interpret the strong and sometimes contradictory emotions that overlapped and mingled in his unreasoning part — grief, disappointment, self-accusation, loss: above all irreparable loss — a cold void within.

A moderate breeze off the shore blew windows in the fog, and strange turbulencies; out over the sea it formed again, but on the landward side it was low-lying and patchy. Over the harbour and the navy yard the upper masts thrust up into clear air, and in many places the hulls of the nearer ships could be seen. Neither Jack Aubrey nor Mr Herapath, who was sitting with him, had missed a move as the *President* and *Congress* got under way.

They had been lying at single anchor throughout the morning's flood tide, and now at slack water the *President*'s fife could be heard through the silence, squeaking 'Yankee Doodle' to encourage the hands at the capstan-bars. The big frigate, looking perfectly enormous in the fog, moved steadily across the smooth harbour: a freak of the breeze or some odd echo brought the cry 'Up and down, sir' clear to the open window, and it was followed by the crisp orders.

'Hook the cat.'

'Man the cat.'

'Off nippers.'

'Away with the cat.'

'Hook the fish.'

'Away with the fish.'

'Haul taut and bitt the cable.'

In a single movement the *President* dropped and sheeted home her topsails; and the *Congress* did the same.

'There they go,' murmured Jack, as the dim, ghostly sails vanished in the fog: but a moment later both ships set their topgallant-sails, and these rose well above the bank, so that the frigates' course could be followed far along the intricate, turning fairway. As they went, Herapath named the shoals and banks until he came to Lovell's Island, where first the *President* and then the *Congress* faded quite away. 'At this rate, you should hear the great guns in about an hour,' he said. 'If the squadron is close in.'

Jack sighed. The American commodore had chosen the perfect moment for slipping out, and unless he ran bodily into the Royal Navy there was very little chance of his being seen. Herapath knew it too: but for some time they both listened, their heads cocked sideways, against all reason. 'It seems a wicked thing to say,' observed Herapath at last, 'wicked to wish for battle and death, yet if those two ships were taken now, it might bring this accursed war to an end — shorten it in any case — and prevent still more waste of blood and treasure. Well, sir,' he said, standing up, 'I must leave you: and I trust I have not stayed too long or tired you. The Doctor spoke of five minutes and no more.'

'Not at all, my dear sir. It was most benevolent in you to come; your visit has set me up amazingly, and I hope that your good nature may induce you to look in again, when business does not tie you to your desk.'

When Mr Herapath was gone Jack listened to the silence for a while, then slipped out of bed and began to bound about the room. He was naturally a very powerful man, and heavy, his strength was coming back, and although his right arm was still painful, its muscles flaccid, his left had grown much more deft with exercise, and now he whirled a ponderous chair over his head, thrusting and cutting, backhand and fore, with a wicked lunge from time to time, and all this in deadly earnest. He was a ludicrous sight, leaping to and fro in his nightshirt, but if he were to obey Stephen's orders to the letter — if he were to lie there a mere hulk, doing nothing to prepare for the day when he might be of some use — his heart would surely break. Presently the Emperor of Mexico joined him, and they pranced and sparred together; but not for long. Captain Aubrey's madness, his savage grunting as he lunged, his red and sweating face, frightened most of his neighbours; and they sensed the savage grief behind his cheerful front. Behind his back they tapped their foreheads, and said that there were limits — this was not a lunatic asylum. Some of the younger nurses were not too well assured, either; and when Maurya Joyce, a faint slip of a girl that a breeze might carry away, came in and bade him 'put it down now, Captain dear, and go back to your bed this minute,' she did so in a squeak. However, he obeyed at once, and seeing him docile she went on in a firmer tone, 'You know very well you are not allowed up, for shame, oh fie, Mr Aubrey. And three gentlemen to see you too.' She tweaked him into respectability, smoothed his sheets, put on his nightcap and whispered, 'Will I fetch you a p-o-t before they come, at all?'

'If you please, my dear,' said Jack. 'And my razor too, while you are about it.' He expected some of the *Constitution*'s officers — Mr Evans was particularly attentive, and the other officers looked in when they were not busy with their gutted ship — or some of the captured English: the daily management of the Asclepia was such that all these people, especially Mr Evans, were found to be exceptions to the rule that forbade him visitors. But following the chamber-pot and the razor, it was Jahleel Brenton who walked in, accompanied by his secretary and a strong, surly man in a cocked hat and a buff waistcoat with brass buttons, presumably a constable or a sheriff's man.

Mr Brenton began in a conciliatory tone; he begged Captain Aubrey not to be agitated — there had been some misunderstanding last time — this visit had nothing to do with the *Alice B. Sawyer*; it was only to check a few particulars that had not been fully noted down before, and to ask for an explanation of a few sheets that had been found among his papers. 'Our office is required to check all documents found on prisoners of war before any exchange can be contemplated. This, for example,' he said, showing a page covered with figures. Jack looked at it: the figures were in his own hand; the sheet was somehow familiar, though he could not place it. They were not astronomical calculations, nor anything to do with a ship's course, run, or position. Where had Killick dredged it up? Why had he preserved it? Then all at once everything was clear: these were his calculations of the food consumed by the squadron during his second visit to the Cape, kept all these years as something that might come in, something that formed part of that general sense of order and neatness that was part of his character as a sailor.

'These are victualling notes,' he said. 'Compiled according to a system of my own. You will see that they add up to a yearly consumption of one million eighty-five thousand two hundred and sixty-six pounds of fresh meat; one million one hundred and sixty-seven thousand nine hundred and ninety-five pounds of biscuit and one hundred and eighty-four thousand three hundred and fifty-eight pounds of soft tack; two hundred and seventeen thousand eight hundred and thirteen pounds of flour; one thousand and sixty-six bushels of wheat; one million two hundred and twenty-six thousand seven hundred and thirty-eight pints of wine, and two hundred and forty-four thousand nine hundred and four pints of spirits.'

The secretary wrote down the explanation: he and Brenton looked at one another and sniffed. 'Captain Aubrey,' said Brenton, 'do you expect me to believe that the *Leopard* consumed one million eighty-five thousand two hundred and sixty-six pounds of meat and one million one hundred and sixty-seven thousand nine hundred and ninety-five pounds of biscuits in a year?'

'Who the devil is talking about *Leopard*? And what the devil do you mean, sir, with your "do you expect me to believe"?' began Jack, then he broke off, his face turned to the window, listening intently. Was that distant gunfire, or thunder, or the rolling of a dray down there on the quays? He was absolutely unconscious of the officials, and his tense, remote expression impressed them strangely. Mr Brenton's eye fell on the razor, close by the Captain's hand; he checked his hasty answer and continued in an even voice, 'Well, we will leave that for the present. Now what have you to say to this?' holding out another paper. 'And pray what is the significance of kicky-wicky?'

Jack took it and his face grew paler still with anger: this was obviously, very obviously, a most private letter — he recognized that as soon as he recognized Admiral Drury's hand. 'Do you mean to tell me,' he said in a voice that filled the room, 'that you have broken the seal of a private letter, and that you have read what was clearly addressed to the lady alone? As God's my salvation . . .'

From this point on the tone rose higher and still higher. Stephen heard them hard at it when he was on the stairs and when he opened the door the volume of sound was very great indeed. They fell silent as he paced across the room and took Jack's pulse: then, 'You must leave at once, sir,' he said to Brenton. 'That is doctor's orders.' But Brenton had been called a miserable scrub-faced swab of a civilian and many other things; he had been compelled by sheer moral force to sit silent for minutes on end while Captain Aubrey listened for the guns; he had been humiliated in the presence of his secretary and the useless bailiff's man; and breathing hard he cried that he would not move a step until he had that document, pointing to the Admiral's letter in Jack's hand. Then he let fly a series of passionate and sometimes coherent remarks about his importance in the Department, the Department's unlimited authority over prisoners, and his powers of coercion.

'Leave the room, sir,' said Stephen. 'You are doing the patient serious harm.'

'I shall not,' said Brenton, stamping.

Stephen pulled the bell and desired Bridey to tell the porter to step up: a moment later, without a sound, the immense Indian appeared in the door, filling it entirely. 'Be so good as to show these gentlemen out,' said Stephen.

The Indian's cold eye, quite expressionless, moved over them; they were already standing, and now they walked out. But Brenton turned on the threshold and shaking his fist at Jack he cried out, 'You have not heard the last of me.'

'Oh go to the devil, you silly little man,' said Jack, wearily; and then, when the door had closed, 'Officials are much the same all over the world. That reptile might have come straight from the Navy Office to badger me about dockets I had forgotten to countersign in the year one. But I tell you what, Stephen, *President* and *Congress* have slipped out on the ebb, and I am very much afraid they have got clean away.'

'I really cannot have you worried like this,' said Stephen, to whom the sailing of the frigates was, at this moment, a matter of complete indifference. He was also very much afraid that in common civility Jack would ask after Diana, and in his present state of mind or rather of confusion he did not wish to speak of her. 'I shall go and have a word with Dr Choate,' he said.

He walked slowly down the stairs and stepped into the porter's booth to thank the Indian for his services. The Indian listened with something like approval on his face. 'It was a pleasure to me,' he said, when Stephen had finished. 'They were government officials, and I hate government officials.'

'All government officials?'

'All American government officials.'

'You astonish me.'

'You would not be astonished if you were a native of this country, an aboriginal native. Here is a letter for you; it came after you had gone this morning.' Stephen saw that the direction was in Diana's bold dashing hand and he put the note into his pocket; if he could as easily have put it out of his mind he would have been relieved, for although he knew very well that presently he should have to clarify his thoughts and resolve a number of conflicts and apparent contradictions, he did long for a period of calm before doing so. Fortunately the Indian seemed to be in a mood for conversation: he asked, 'Why do you say Ugh to me?'

'I looked upon it as a usual greeting in the

language of your nation — the Huron is represented as saying Ugh to the paleface in many authors, French and English. But if I am mistaken, sir, I ask your pardon: my intent was civil, though perhaps inept.'

'Most of the Hurons I know have every reason to say Ugh to the paleface, French, English or American: in the language that I speak — and I must tell you, sir, that there is an infinity of languages spoken by the original possessors of this continent — Ugh is an expression of disgust, repulsion, dislike. I had thought of resenting it, but it appeared to me that you meant no offence; and then I have a certain fellow-feeling for you; we are, after all, both defeated, both victims of the Americans.'

'Dr Choate has told me something of the unhappy Indian wars. He, at least, is very much opposed to them.'

'Dr Choate, yes: there are some good Americans, I admit. My grandfathers, who were at Harvard, at the Indian College, spoke of a Mr Adams as an excellent man. His mother, however, was a Shawnee — of the same nation, I may add, as the chief Tecumseh who is at present helping your people on the Canadian border. Here is Dr Choate.'

'Have you seen Dr Maturin?' asked

Choate. 'I am looking for him.'

'And I was looking for you, colleague,' said Stephen from the darkness of the booth.

'I have an urgent cystotomy,' said Choate, 'and as we were speaking of it at our Sunday supper, I am come to beg for your assistance.'

'I shall be delighted,' said Stephen, and in fact nothing could have been more timely: an exceedingly delicate operation, but one that he had often carried out — the intense concentration of mind and hand, the moral preoccupation with the bound patient, only too conscious of the knife — these would entirely absorb his spirit, giving it that inner tranquillity where it could work without being thrust and pulled by his reason and his wishes. Yet there was also the night, the unoccupied night, to be considered, and after he had spoken to Dr Choate abut the necessity for keeping the Navy Department away from Jack Aubrey, he asked him for a pint of laudanum.

'The laudanum by all means,' said Choate, 'you will find it by the hogshead in the dispensary. As to the Navy Department, I shall do what I can, but these officials have very extensive powers in war-time. I have had notes from them, sharp, peremptory and authoritative, not to say hectoring.'

The operation, performed on an immensely obese, timid patient, was far more intricate than they had expected; yet finally it was done, and not only was it successful in itself, but there was a real likelihood that the man might live.

Stephen went to Jack's room to wash his hands, and found him asleep, lying on his back with his injured arm across his chest, and still with that set look of physical suffering and moral shock, not unlike the fainting, earth-coloured patient who had so recently been wheeled away. Stephen knew that nothing but a change of wind would wake him, and having washed he took the whisky-bottle from its hiding-place and drank off half a glass, neat and fierce. No alcohol was allowed in the Asclepia, but the *Constitution*'s officers, particularly Mr Evans, were aware of this, and the space behind Captain Aubrey's books was filled with rye whisky, bourbon, and a thin, intensely acrid native wine.

He put the whisky back, dropped the glass — no change in that stern sleeping face — and withdrew, carrying his own laudanum bottle, green and labelled Poison. He had a small room on the inner courtyard, and here he found his lamp already lit and a fire glowing in the hearth: a green-shaded lamp that shone on his table and the papers spread over it, leaving the rest of the room in deep shadow. It was comfortable, the very picture of comfort; and he felt cold, desolate, extraordinarily lonely. Groping in his pocket he found Diana's note, tossed it on to the table, set his green bottle by it, threw his coat on the bed, and sat down, his chair turned half to the table and half to the fire.

For many, many years he had been unable to open his mind fully to any man or woman at all, and at times it seemed to him that candour was as essential as food or affection: during most of this period he had used his diary as a kind of surrogate for the non-existent loving ear — a very poor surrogate indeed, but one that had become so habitual as to be almost necessary. He missed it now, the close-written coded book, and having stared at the fire for a while he turned full to the table. His indifferent eye fell on the note, addressed in that familiar hand, and he drew a sheet of paper towards him.

'If I no longer love Diana,' he wrote, 'what shall I do?' What could he do, with his mainspring, his prime mover gone? He had known that he would love her for ever — to the last syllable of recorded time. He had not sworn it, any more than he had sworn that the sun would rise every morning: it was too certain, too evident: no one swears that he will continue to breathe nor that twice two is four. Indeed, in such a case an oath would imply the possibility of doubt. Yet now it seemed that perpetuity meant eight years, nine months and some odd days, while the last syllable of recorded time was Wednesday, the seventeenth of May. 'Can such things be?' he asked. He knew from examples that this had often happened to other men; and that other men also lost their minds or contracted cancer. Could it be that he was not, as he had implicitly supposed, exceptionally immune?

'Perhaps it is only an *intermittence du coeur*, no more.' That was extremely probable — a quasi-physical condition, allied to air and diet, anxiety, over-wrought anticipation, and a hundred other conspiring causes. He wrote another paragraph, with instances of strange, apparently inexplicable changes of set purpose, abdications, temporary loss of faith, that could in fact be set down to a vicious habit of body, mere body, the mind's dwelling-place — cowardice in brave men whose liver was disordered, the passing mental derangement of parturient women. He added some reflections on the effect of mind upon body too, such as eczemas, false pregnancies, and the actual production of milk, carefully sanded his last sheet, gathered the others, put them all into the dying fire, watched it flare up, turn and writhe, and fall into black, unmeaning ashes. He was not entirely convinced, and the contradictor in his mind observed that there were many men, and medical men at that, who palpated their tumours and pronounced them benign; but still it was a comfort to his undecided willing mind and with it he went to his bed. In the lower part of the building a man was singing 'Oh oh the mourning dove' as if his heart would break: Stephen listened to the song, until the rising tide of laudanum-sleep engulfed him.

The morning broke bright and clear, with a fine breeze in the north-north-west. Jack had been watching since dawn, and before breakfast he saw the expected sail stand into the bay; the light was exceptionally pure, the air transparent, and he soon identified the *Shannon*. She stood on and on, closer in than he had ever seen any of the blockading squadron, so close that he could see the officer up there with his telescope at the foretopgallant jacks. He could not swear to it, but he was almost sure that he recognized Philip Broke, who had had the *Shannon* these last five years. Closer still, until at last the gunners on Castle Island threw a high-pitched mortar-bomb right over her: at this she wore, but the little figure reappeared on her quarterdeck and mounted to the mizen cross-trees, the gleaming brass still levelled upon Boston harbour and the American men-of-war. A little later she filled and stood out into the offing on the larboard tack, while two hoists of signals broke out high above her topsails. Jack could not read them, but he knew very well what they had to say, and shifting his glass to the horizon he saw the *Shannon*'s consort bear up, crowd sail and run fast away east-south-east, right out into the Atlantic.

'Where is the doctor?' he asked, when breakfast appeared.

'Sure he's sleeping yet,' said Bridey, 'and we will let him lie. He had the cruel hard bloody operation yesterday, and is quite destroyed.'

Stephen was lying still when Mr Evans called on Jack, bringing a friend. 'I will not sit down,' said Mr Evans. 'Dr Choate says you are not allowed visitors. But I could not resist coming up just for five minutes with Captain Lawrence, who has a message for you. Allow me to name Captain Lawrence, formerly of the *Hornet*, now of the *Chesapeake*. Captain Aubrey, of the Royal Navy.'

The captains expressed their pleasure, but it was difficult to see much of it on Lawrence's shy, embarrassed face, and the name of *Hornet* struck all cheerfulness from Jack's. However, he assumed a decent appearance of cordiality and in spite of their protests called for coffee and sweet biscuits — 'or cookies, as I should say', looking at Lawrence with a smile. He liked the look of him, a big, open-faced man in a white coat, a man with a modest, well-bred air, and obviously a sailor. Lawrence returned the smile — there was clearly a mutual liking in spite of the awkwardness of the situation — and said, 'A little while ago, sir, I had the pleasure of meeting Lieutenant Mowett of your service, and he particularly desired me to wait on you, to bring his respects, to ask how you did, and to tell you that he was coming along very well in the hospital at New York.'

Mowett had been one of Jack's midshipmen many years before, and Lawrence had met him in the course of the murderous action in which the *Hornet* sank the *Peacock*. As they talked of the young man, who had had three ribs stove in by a splinter of the *Peacock*'s rail, it became clear that Lawrence and he had gone along very well together during their long voyage from the Demerara river and that Lawrence had been kind to the wounded lieutenant; Jack's heart warmed to him — he was much attached to Mowett.

The five minutes passed, another five, another pot of coffee, and eventually Choate came in and put them out. Jack returned to his telescope, Evans to the dismantled *Constitution*, and Lawrence to the *Chesapeake*.

The morning wore on, and part of the afternoon, a brilliant, cheerful day, and at last Stephen came in, still dull and heavy, frowzy from his sleep. 'You look much better, Jack,' he said.

'Yes, I feel it, too. *Shannon* looked into the port this morning, found the birds flown, all except *Chesapeake* and —'

'Did you hear that?' said Stephen, walking to the window.

'The glum-sounding bird?'

'The mourning-dove — there she flies. I dreamt of her. Jack, forgive me. I must go. Diana has invited me to dinner, with Johnson and Louisa Wogan.'

'I trust — I trust she is well?' said Jack.

'Blooming, I thank you: she asked after you most particularly,' said Stephen. There was a pause, but he said no more; and having waited until it was certain that no more would be said, Jack asked, 'Would you like my razor? I stropped it this morning until it would split a hair in four.'

'Oh no,' said Stephen, running his hand over his meagre bristly face. 'This will do very well. I shaved yesterday, or the day before.'

'But you have forgot your shirt. There is

314

blood on it — there is blood on the collar and the cuffs.'

'Never mind. I will pull up my coat. The coat is perfectly respectable; I took it off for the operation. A very pretty operation, too.'

'Stephen,' said Jack earnestly, 'be a good fellow for once, will you now, and humour me? I should be really unhappy if one of my officers dined in an enemy town, looking anything but trim. It could be taken that he was beat, and had no pride in the service.'

'Very well,' said Stephen, and took up the razor.

Trim, shaved and brushed, he hurried through the town: the sharp air cleared his foggy mind, and by the time he reached the hotel his wits were pretty well at his disposition. He was early, which was a relief to him, for a Presbyterian clock, differing as much in time as in doctrine from the many other clocks of Boston, had given him an unpleasant shock: indeed, he was so early that there was no one to receive him. They were still dressing, said the monumental slave, as she showed him into an empty drawing-room.

Here he stood for a while, looking at Johnson's pictures: the bald eagle, the Carolina chickadee, his old friend the black-necked stilt. Then he moved out on to the long balcony, to see whether it might command another public clock — neither he nor Jack possessed a watch. There was one, a great way down the street, but it was obscured by a group of workmen at the far end of the balcony, hauling up lime and sand for some repair, and having craned for some time he gave it up — what did the time matter, after all? From some way along in the other direction, where a curtain streamed from an open window, he heard Diana's voice raised in that familiar tone of reproach he knew so well: she was passing Johnson under the harrow. In a more gentlemanly mood Stephen would have moved away at once, but he was not feeling gentlemanly and after a moment he heard Johnson cry, 'My God, Diana, sometimes you are as loud as a hog in a gate.' The voice was strong and exasperated, and it was followed by the slamming of a door.

Stephen stepped silently back into the drawing-room and he was studying the turkey-buzzard when Johnson came in, cordial, welcoming, apparently unruffled. 'You are a tolerably good dissimulator, I find,' said Stephen to himself, and aloud, 'Surely this is a very able man. He gives us not the bird, for no bird ever had this brilliant clarity in every member, but the Platonic idea of the bird, the visible archetype of the turkey-buzzard.'

'Exactly so,' said Johnson, and they talked

of the turkey-buzzard and of the bald eagle whose nest Johnson hoped to see on Sunday — it was on a friend's land in the state of Maine — until Mrs Wogan and Michael Herapath arrived: at the same moment Diana Villiers came in through another door, and Stephen observed that although Wogan was dressed with particular care, Diana won hands down. She was wearing the lightest, purest blue, straight from Paris, and it made Wogan's Boston gown look painstaking and provincial: furthermore, she had such a *rivière* of blue-white diamonds around her neck as Stephen had rarely seen — a huge stone in the middle.

Even before they sat down to dinner it was clear to him that there was ill-will between Villiers and Wogan on the one hand and Villiers and Johnson on the other; and when they were at their soup, an admirable *bisque de homard*, it became equally clear that there was an attachment between Johnson and Louisa. They did their best to conceal it, but at times they were a little too formal and at others a little too free, the false note continually obtruding. Stephen was well placed to observe them, since the table at which they dined was rectangular and he occupied the middle of one long side alone, with Herapath and Louisa opposite him, Diana and Johnson at either end, and Wogan on Johnson's right. From Johnson's slightly constrained posture, Stephen was pretty sure that he was pressing Wogan's leg, and from Wogan's jolly, lively face it appeared that she did not dislike it.

Stephen was often rather silent and remote at meals; Diana knew this of old, and she spent most of her efforts during the soup and the course that followed on being agreeable to Michael Herapath. Stephen knew that she was barely acquainted with Herapath and he was surprised by the freedom of her conversation, its rallying, bantering tone, and by her telling an anecdote that was at the least ambiguous, a story either witless or indecent. Herapath too was surprised, but he was a well-bred creature and he concealed it, responding in much the same manner, as far as his habits and abilities would allow. This was not very far in the early stages of the meal, but she repeatedly filled his wine-glass and by the turbot he launched into a tale of his own, the only one of the kind he could remember. Yet half way through it seemed to occur to him that the end bordered too nearly upon the scabrous, and with an anxious glance at Stephen, he tailed away into a very foolish though innocuous conclusion. Discouraged, he said no more; and with both her neighbours nearly mute Diana was obliged to take

318

their entertainment upon herself. Her poise did not desert her for a moment; she filled their glasses yet again — Stephen noticed that she took no unfair advantage, but drank glass for glass with her guests — and gave them a detailed account of a journey to New Orleans. It was not particularly interesting, nor amusing, but at least there was a tolerably convincing appearance of conviviality at her end of the table — no awkward silences. Clearly she had had much practice in holding a party together throughout a long dinner: yet from the nature of her conversation it appeared to Stephen that these parties must have consisted of businessmen and politicians: and rather commonplace businessmen and politicians at that. Where was her quick, mordant, wholly spontaneous wit, her delicate turning of a wicked phrase, perfectly attuned to her company? Could *she* be reduced to anecdotes and set pieces, when neither he nor Herapath was a politician? She had also acquired a slight American accent, dead against her style. But, on the other hand, had she ever in fact possessed the particular excellencies whose absence he now so deplored, or had they existed only in his infatuated mind? No: she had possessed them. His memory was filled with objective proofs of that, and even if it had not been, her physical appearance was convincing evidence. To some degree every person's face was the creation of the mind behind it, he observed, thinking sadly of his own, and Diana's face and form and movement still reflected much of the fine dashing elegant spirit he had known.

It occurred to him that she had spent these last few years entirely among men, seeing no women apart from a few like Louisa Wogan; she spoke rather as men, and somewhat raffish, moneyed, loose-living men, speak when they are alone together. 'She has forgotten the distinction between what can and what cannot be said,' he reflected. 'A few more years of this company, and she would not scruple to fart.' A delicate distraction, that between true spirit on the one hand and boldness and confidence on the other: he was pursuing this line of thought when a fresh decanter appeared and Diana, visibly irritated by an indiscretion on the part of Johnson and Louisa, cried, 'God's my life, this wine is corked. Really, Johnson, you might give your guests something they can drink.'

Extreme concern on the black butler's face: a glass hurried down to the other end of the table. Silence, and then the verdict, delivered with studied mildness: 'Surely not, my dear: it seems quite sound to me. Take a glass to Dr Maturin. What do you say to it, sir?'

'I am no great judge of wine,' said Stephen. 'But I have heard that very occasionally the mouthful just round the cork may have an ill taste, while the rest of the bottle is excellent. Perhaps that is the case here.'

It was a poor shift, but enough for minds willing to avoid an *éclat:* the decanter was replaced and the conversation became more general. Herapath struck in with some considerations on the inevitable delays of the press: presently they were talking about the publication of his book, and it was pleasant to see Louisa Wogan's eagerness as they discussed the character in which it was to be printed, and the size and quality of the paper; she certainly had an affection for Herapath, but perhaps it was more the affection of a sister rather than of a mistress, a somewhat pharaonic sister.

Stephen too aroused himself to a sense of his social duty, and with the roast he told Diana and Herapath about the voyage in the cutter after *La Flèche* had burnt — their consuming hatred for a ship that passed without seeing them — their insatiable appetite for biscuit when they were taken aboard the ill-fated *Java* at last. 'Between breakfast and dinner,' he said, 'I saw Captain Aubrey eat three and a half pounds, taking a draught of water at eight-ounce intervals; and I kept pace with him, crying out at their perfect suavity, pitying Lucullus for not having known ship's biscuit before the high-weevil stage: for *Java* was only four weeks out.'

Diana asked him about Jack's present state of health, and when he had answered she said, in a momentary pause, 'Do please remember to give him my love.'

To his surprise Stephen saw Johnson stiffen, sit straight, presumably detaching himself from Wogan, and ask, 'Who is this gentleman to whom you are sending your love, my dear?' in a voice that endeavoured, without much success, to hide its strong displeasure.

'Captain Aubrey,' said Diana, raising her head with that fierce, beautiful gesture that Stephen remembered so well. 'A very distinguished officer in His Majesty's service, sir.' But then, breaking the tension, she added meekly, 'He is my cousin by marriage. He married Sophie Williams.'

'Oh, Captain Aubrey,' said Johnson. 'Yes. The gentleman I am to see this afternoon.'

The meal drew to an end: Diana and Louisa Wogan retired. 'I wonder how they will like each other's company,' thought Stephen as he held the door for them to pass. The men sat for a while, talking of Boston's subscription for the Muscovites who had suffered from the burning of their city, and of the attitude of the King of Prussia. 'It is shocking how little our public men know about conditions in Europe,' observed Johnson, and before they went into the drawing-room he said privately, 'Dr Maturin, if you are not engaged this evening I should very much like to have a word with you. This afternoon I must see Captain Aubrey — an official matter to do with his exchange — and some Frenchmen; but I do not suppose it will take very long. Could you perhaps sit drinking tea with Mrs Villiers until I return?'

'I should be very happy,' said Stephen.

He and Herapath walked into the drawing-room, where Diana and Louisa were sitting at some distance from one another; silently smoking long thin cigars. Herapath was a little unsteady on his legs, a little elevated in his spirits, and he thought fit to recite his version of a T'ang poem dealing with the emotions of a Chinese princess married for political reasons to a barbarian, the leader of a horde that lived brutishly in Outer Mongolia; and in his enthusiasm he had a tendency to stumble over the words. The women listened to him, Louisa with amused and kindly tolerance, Diana with a certain shade of contempt. Stephen did not listen at all.

He had felt a good many miseries in his

time, but none to be compared to this cold vacancy within. His observation of her had confirmed his suspicions of the day before and provided reasons for the first instinctive feeling. He did not love Diana Villiers any more, and it was death to him. Something in her essence had changed, and the woman who poured out the tea and talked was a stranger, all the more a stranger because of their former intimacy. The evident change was that anger and ill-humour, disappointment and frustration, had hardened her: her face was lovely, yet its expression in repose was not amiable. Louisa Wogan did not possess a tithe of Diana's style or beauty; she was on a smaller scale entirely; but her cheerfulness, her humour, and her willingness to be pleased made a painful contrast. The important change was far more profound, however: it was as though Diana's spirit had diminished and her courage had begun to fail, if indeed it had not already broken.

To be sure, her position was difficult and extraordinary courage would have been needed to deal with it; but then he had always looked upon Diana as a woman, a being, possessed of extraordinary courage. Without courage she was not Diana. But then again, he said (his mind changing direction), there was the physical aspect to be considered: if costiveness could affect a man's courage, how much more might an adverse phase of the moon affect a woman's? He looked secretly at her face for signs that would support this notion and indeed for encouragement, but to his dismay he found that his intelligence rejected the moon and all its influence, and merely recorded an impression that the high carriage of her head, the straightness of her back he had so much admired and for so long, now appeared slightly exaggerated, the effect of indignation, of a sense of ill-usage. If, as he supposed, her spirit had been damaged, and if from strong she had become weak, then the common vices of weakness would naturally ensue. It would not be surprising to find petulance, ill-temper, and even, God forbid, self-pity, falseness, a general debasement.

Herapath's voice had changed from the solemn mooing of recital: it must have changed some time before without Stephen's noticing it, since the present discussion or rather argument between him and Louisa about Caroline's feeding-time and the proper persons to be entrusted with it was already well advanced.

In time, Herapath, supported by Diana, prevailed, and there was a general move towards the door. 'Louisa is such a devoted mother,' said Diana. 'You would swear she was made for feeding babies: I am sure it must be her greatest delight. Is it not, Louisa?'

With some warmth Louisa observed that only those women who possessed babies could appreciate these things at their just value, and Stephen was tortured by the thought that Diana might answer with some reflection upon Louisa's manner of coming by her child; but she only said, 'Oh, my dear, before you go into the street I must just tell you that your petticoat is showing. It was disgraceful of me not to have mentioned it before dinner; though to be sure no one minds such things in a nursing mother.

'Lord, Stephen,' she said, returning, 'I am so sorry to have inflicted such a boring dinner-party on you. You have enough to bear as it is. But at least now we can talk.'

She talked with the absolute openness and freedom that Stephen had so envied, for there at her side, as she supposed, was the loving receptive ear: and certainly he listened with grave attention and concern. His friendship for her was quite intact, and it contained a large element of tenderness.

Her relationship with Johnson had been uneasy from the start: even if it had not been for the interminable business of his divorce their connection could never have lasted — he was violent, dangerous, and he could be perfectly ruthless; at ordinary times he was ill-tempered, far too rich for his own good; he was a philanderer, and his behaviour to his blacks was revolting.

'I suppose the actual sight, the daily experience, of slavery must be very hard to bear,' said Stephen, 'particularly on the industrial scale of a large plantation.'

'Oh, as for that,' said she, shrugging, 'it seems to me natural enough: there were quantities of them in India, you know. I should have said his black women. Any number of the mulatto children about the house in Maryland were his, and the older ones were his half-brothers or -sisters; and there were a couple of octaroon girls, cousins I dare say, who looked at me in such an odiously familiar, knowing way — I could not bear it — I felt like something that had been bought. The fellow was a perfect parish bull.'

'The parish bull slumbers in most of us, I fear.'

'It never slumbers in Johnson at any moment, I do assure you. And at the same time he is absurdly jealous, a perfect Turk. All he lacks is a beard and a turban and scimitar,' she said, with a ghost of her old smile. 'None of the black girls he has tossed the handkerchief to is ever allowed to marry, and he made me such scenes for talking to another man that you would never believe. I really think he would kill me and you too if he saw me do this.' She laid her hand affectionately on his. 'My God, Maturin,' she said, pressing it, 'what a relief it is to have somebody you can really trust and rely upon.'

It was after one of these scenes that she left him and came to London. He followed her: he was good, quiet, kind, full of promises of reform; he showed her lawyers' letters that made it seem that his divorce was very near. 'And he gave me these diamonds,' she said, unclasping the necklace and tossing it on to the couch, where it blazed and glittered like a phosphorescent wake. 'They were his mother's, and he had them reset. The big one in the middle is called the Begum. I suppose it is disgraceful to admit that they had an influence on me, but they did. Perhaps most women like diamonds.'

It was in London, or rather in their precipitate flight from London, that she learnt that Johnson was connected with American intelligence: but even then she had never imagined for a moment that what he did was in any way directed against England — she thought it was to do with stocks and shares and government funds in Europe, particularly as at that time there was a general idea that the United States would go to war with France. He terrified her, however, by saying that she was implicated, that Government would take her up and hang her for having passed papers on to Louisa Wogan, so like a fool she agreed to go back with him to America. She had received letters for Louisa, and she had passed them on; but she had thought it was only an intrigue until Louisa was arrested and she herself was taken to the Home Office and questioned for hours on end. She lost her head and ran off with Johnson.

It was the silliest thing she had ever done in her life. There she was in an enemy country, and the fellow had the infernal effrontery to expect her to help him in his work against her own people, and to be pleased when Royal Navy ships were taken. 'Oh, it went to my heart, Stephen, straight to my heart. Every one of those frigates we were so proud of, and there were three of them, without a single victory; and the Americans do so crow. And I see English officers walking about, prisoners of war: it is unspeakable.'

'Did you not become an American citizen?'

'Oh, I signed some foolish papers, because they said it would make the divorce easier, but how could a miserable bit of paper make any difference? Johnson is a very clever man, but sometimes he can be unbelievably stupid — to expect the daughter of a soldier who served the King all his life, brought up among soldiers, married to a soldier, to work against her own country! Perhaps he thinks he is Adonis and Byron and Croesus all rolled into one and no woman can resist him: he still thinks he can persuade me, because I write some of his letters to the Frenchmen. But he never shall, never, never, never!'

'Is his work important?'

'Yes. I was amazed. I thought he was just a rich man fooling about, a dilettante; but not at all. He is perfectly passionate about it — spends far more money than the government gives him — sold an outlying plantation in Virginia only last month. He advises the Secretary of State, and he has a whole swarm of people working under him. Louisa Wogan was one of them, and will be again. Oh, Stephen, I cannot bear it. I am desperate. How can I get out?'

He stood up, walked to the window, and stood there with his hands behind his back, staring down the balcony at the workmen. Her account was perfectly true: she was candid, but not entirely so — she said nothing about the fact that she was utterly at a loss, finding herself in the position of a woman who is being if not discarded then at least supplanted. Hitherto it had been she who gave the dismissal and the new role was beyond her; and she was so very much distressed, so deeply disturbed, that her intuition gave her no hint of his present state of heart. Then again, she was certainly afraid of Johnson. Her position was indeed quite desperate.

Turning he said, 'Listen, my dear. You must marry me: that will make you a British subject again, so that you can return to England. Jack and I are to be exchanged in a day or so, and you will come back with us as my wife. It will be a purely nominal marriage, a *mariage blanc,* if you wish.'

'Oh, Stephen,' she cried, springing up with such a look of gratitude and trust and affection that it filled his heart with guilt and remorse, 'I knew I could always rely on you.' She embraced him, pressing him close, and he concealed his lack of physical emotion by pressing her closer still. Then she stood away; her face fell, and she said, 'No. Oh, no. I was forgetting. They believe Aubrey had something to do with intelligence — that he palmed some papers off on Louisa when she was aboard the *Leopard.* God knows if they are right — I no longer know what to think about anybody — I should never, never have believed Louisa was a spy — but if they are, God help him, in Johnson's hands. There will be no exchange.'

Johnson could be heard, calling out in remarkably bad French, some way down the corridor, and they had time to recover an appearance of indifference before he came in. He excused himself for having been so long, and catching sight of the diamond necklace he picked it up. 'I was just going to put it away,' said Diana.

It flashed and sparkled as he poured it from hand to hand, and an infinity of tiny prismatic lights raced across the ceiling like swarms and swarms of shooting-stars. 'Yes, do,' he said. 'I am not quite satisfied with the clasp, and I should like the case to carry it in.'

Diana left the room without a word, carrying the necklace, and Johnson said, 'I saw Captain Aubrey this afternoon; he spoke so handsomely of you, Dr Maturin; and we got along very well together. There had been some unfortunate misunderstanding with the gentlemen who had questioned him before, but that was soon resolved. I rather think they were on the wrong track altogether, and that the business will soon be settled. Captain Aubrey is the most complete British sea-officer, the kind that taught our men their trade. But he puzzled me once or twice: would it be indiscreet to ask who the Admiral Crichton to whom he compared you may be? I cannot remember any such name among Lord Nelson's companions. And what can he have meant by saying that Napoleon was killing the golden calf in Russia? I did not like to linger, because really he has been so shockingly knocked about, and Dr Choate insisted that I should not fatigue him.'

'The Crichton in question was no doubt the ingenious Scotchman of some two centuries ago who spoke so many languages and who was called the Admirable for his shining parts: Captain Aubrey has long been persuaded that he served in the Royal Navy. As for the golden calf, I can only hazard the guess that there may have been some confusion between the error of the Israelites and the goose of our childhood that laid those golden eggs, poor bird.'

'Ah, I see, I see. Yes. So that he meant that Napoleon was ill-advised in attacking the Czar: just so. What is your opinion, Dr Maturin?'

'I really know so very little of these things. I only hope that all this useless slaughter and destruction will soon come to an end.'

'With all my heart,' said Johnson. 'You are a man of peace, and so am I; yet it does appear to me that if only there were a clearer understanding between the opposing forces — more true knowledge of the real aims and potentialities of each — that peace would come much sooner. And as I observed not long ago, we in the States are quite shockingly ignorant of the finer points of the situation in Europe. For example, it was only recently that we learnt of the existence of various organizations among the Catalans of north-east Spain who are determined to break away from the domination of Castile: we had supposed that there was only one. And then of course there is the state of affairs in Ireland. There are so many points of that kind where I should be so grateful for your advice.'

'I am afraid, sir, that the advice of a plain naval surgeon would be of little use to you.'

'You are not quite the plainest of naval surgeons,' said Johnson, looking amused. And after a pause he went on, 'I know something of your publications, your reputation, and your activities — your scientific activities. And Louisa Wogan has told me of your distress at the prospect of a war between the States and the United Kingdom, and of your let us say *impatience* at the English government's conduct in Ireland. But even if you were no more than a plain naval surgeon, you are a European, a much-travelled European, and your advice would be valuable. After all, our ends are essentially the same, the restoration of a just and lasting peace.'

'I fully take your point, and I have much sympathy with what you say,' said Stephen, 'but I must beg to be excused. In spite of my esteem for you personally, sir, I must point out that we are technically at war, and that if my advice should be of the least value to you, then I should be comforting the enemy, which, as you will agree, has a most unpleasant sound. You must forgive me.'

'A man of your intelligence will never be the prisoner of words, mere lawyers' words at that. No, no; pray reflect on what I have said. It is only on points quite unconnected with the Navy that I should like to consult you.'

'We have it on excellent authority that a man cannot serve two masters,' said Stephen, smiling.

'No,' replied Johnson, returning the smile, 'but he can serve an end that transcends both. Dear Doctor, I will not take your refusal.' He pulled the bell. 'Ask the gentlemen to come in,' he said to the servant, and to Stephen, 'Forgive me a moment. I just have to hand a letter to these Frenchmen.'

Dubreuil walked in, followed by the tall Pontet-Canet. Stephen recognized Dubreuil at once — he had after all watched the man in and out of the embassy at Lisbon, and from a maid's window opposite the ministry in Paris, although he was almost certain that Dubreuil knew nothing of him except by description. Dubreuil made a distant bow, which Stephen returned: Pontet-Canet asked him how he did. There were no introductions, and the Frenchmen, having received an envelope, retired.

'Did you notice that man?' asked Johnson. 'The small, unnoticeable man? You might not think so, but he is the most devilish creature. They had an agent on the Canadian border who thought it more profitable to be paid by both sides: they brought him down here, and what they did to him I will not even attempt to describe, although you are a medical man. The sight of the body, I do assure you, haunted me for weeks. They have notions I cannot possibly approve, although they may be efficacious, and it was a gross violation of our sovereignty; but in these critical times we cannot be as rigid with our French colleagues as I could wish. However, let us meet tomorrow: there are certain formalities to do with Captain Aubrey's exchange that we can deal with — I am sure he should not be worried in his present lamentable condition — and when you have slept upon it, I hope you will not object to my consulting you on a few points of purely European politics.'

CHAPTER SEVEN

Stephen was aware of Johnson's motives: they were tolerably obvious, for all love, obvious and tolerably clumsy. The man was not an artist, though the avoidance of any hint of material reward was a good stroke, and the mention of Catalonia was better still. What he did not know was just how much certainty Johnson and Dubreuil possessed. The Catalans might have been no more than a lucky shot in the dark: there had been a good many shots of one kind and another after dinner, sometimes directed towards regions utterly remote from Stephen's battlefield, such as Moscow, Prussia, and Vienna. A great deal would depend on what Johnson had learnt from Jack.

Their interview had been present to his mind throughout this afternoon with Diana, sometimes strongly present, sometimes no more than a cold worrying ghost or shadow far in the background, far behind her words; and now as he hurried back to the Asclepia he turned Johnson's account of it over in his mind. A true account, he was sure; no man could have invented the golden calf nor the phantom admiral. The implications of that Admiral Crichton made him feel colder still, and he increased his pace.

'There you are, Stephen,' said Jack. 'I am glad to see you. Did they give you a decent dinner? We had a Lenten dish of cod and beans.'

'Excellent, I believe. Yes, excellent, with a capital Hermitage. Diana sends you her love.'

'Why, that was kind in her, I am sure: indeed we are cousins, after all. And now, since I know where she is, I shall send her all proper acknowledgments for her goodness in writing to Sophie. Her — that is to say, Mr Johnson came to see me this afternoon. It seems that he is a great man under government in these parts: Choate was quite impressed.'

'How did you go along with him?'

'Surprisingly well. I was pretty reserved and distant to begin with, but he explained that the whole business had fallen into the wrong hands in the first place: he had looked into the matter of the brig, the *Alice B. Sawyer*, and he agreed that since the positions did not coincide it was nonsense to say that *Leopard* had brought her to — there had been a foolish mistake somewhere in the Department and he knew the man who would put it right.'

'Did he speak of your exchange?'

'Not particularly. He seemed to take it for granted that once the mistake was put right it would go through in the normal way, and I did not press him. I gathered that he was too great a man to look after the details. No: after we had dealt with the brig we mostly talked about Nelson — he is a great admirer of Lord Nelson — and the schooner he has down in the Chesapeake, one of those fast American schooners, I take it, that can lie so close to the wind, but even more about you. He thinks the world of Doctor Maturin.'

'Does he, indeed?'

'Yes, and he said such handsome things about your birds and your learning, your Latin and Greek; and not to be behindhand I added your French like a Frenchman's, and your Spanish and Catalan too, not to mention the outlandish languages you picked up in the East.'

'Brother,' said Stephen to himself, 'you may have dished me with your kindness.'

'He lamented that he never could contrive to speak the French,' continued Jack, 'and so did I, and we puzzled for a while over a paper someone had sent him from Louisiana: without boasting, I may say that I made out more of it than he did. By the way, what does Pong mean?' — writing it on a piece of paper.

'I believe it means a peacock.'

'Not a bridge?' Stephen shook his head. 'Oh well, never mind. Let us cross that peacock when we come to it. Then he was curious to know how you came to speak the Catalan, such an out-of-the-way sort of tongue; but knowing that there were some things you had rather keep under hatches, I said to myself, "Jack," I said, "*tace* is the Latin for a candle," and left him none the wiser. I can be diplomatic, when I choose.'

Nothing but Jack's diplomacy by land had been wanting to complete the picture: nothing could more effectually have fixed Johnson's attention on the one point that might determine Dubreuil in his identification. Yet on the other hand, the only Frenchmen who knew about Stephen's activities in Catalonia, who knew them at first hand and who knew him by sight if not by name, could (as dear Jack would put it) tell no tales. All was not lost, by any means: he might yet remain Dr S. Anon, a mere ornithologist.

'Jack,' he said, 'I am obliged to you for your good opinion, but in principle, my dear, you might avoid applauding what you are so kind as to call my parts to strangers when we are abroad; it might lead them to think that I was intelligent — even over-intelligent. In our service, on the other hand, you may say whatever you please: the more the better.'

'Lord, Stephen,' cried Jack, 'have I done wrong? I was diplomatic, as I say, as deep and mute as — why, anything you like to name.'

'No, no. I merely threw it out as a general observation. Tell, what news from the sea to-day?'

'*Shannon* looked into the port before breakfast, as I was telling you when you ran off, and finding *President* and *Congress* gone she sent her consort, probably *Tenedos*, away into the offing. Then Evans dropped in, bringing one of their officers, Lawrence, who had the *Hornet* when she sank our *Peacock*. He has *Chesapeake* now.'

'What kind of a man is he? Like Bainbridge?'

'No. Quite a different sort, much more open and unreserved — younger, too: about our age. I liked him extremely. To tell the truth, I liked him much more than Johnson, because although Johnson was so civil about you and a very gentlemanlike creature altogether, there was something I did not really care for: he was not the sort of man I should like to serve with, nor under, whereas I should be happy to ship with Lawrence. He brought a message from young Mowett, taken in *Peacock* and wounded, but doing well in New York.'

They talked of Mowett, a most engaging

young man with a literary turn, and Stephen recited some of his verse:

> While o'er the ship the gallant boatswain flies,
> Like a hoarse mastiff through the storm he cries,
> Prompt to direct the unskilful still appears,
> The expert he praises, and the timid cheers:
> Still through my pulses glides the kindling fire
> As lightning glances on the electric wire.

'What a memory you have,' said Jack. 'Like a . . .'

'Bull of Bashan?'

'Just so. Then after that Mr Herapath very kindly came and sat with me for a while after he had seen his sister. He told me what sad dogs the Republicans were, little better than mere democrats, and how he had fought for the King under General Burgoyne. He is a fine old boy, and he has promised to look in tomorrow, bringing me — here's *Shannon*,' he said, reaching for his telescope. 'See, she is just clearing the long island. Now he will put his helm down, to avoid the shoal. There is a nasty shoal just off the point; Herapath pointed it out to me; but by now Broke knows that channel like the palm of his hand. There: he rises, tacks and sheets — they will all be on tiptoe for the word — prettily done! She stays in her own length, nimble as a cutter. She is all alone now, with only *Chesapeake* to watch, *Constitution* being laid up; so we need not expect to see her throw out any signals.'

'Why alone? Surely two would keep the *Chesapeake* in far better than one.'

'That is the whole point,' cried Jack. 'He don't want to keep her in, of that I am very sure. He wants her to come out. She cannot be expected to come out against two frigates. That is why he sent *Tenedos* away the moment he saw that *President* and *Congress* was gone. There! She lays her foretopsail to the mast and brails up her driver, makes a sternboard, fills again, and she is round: prettily done . . .'

Jack kept up a steady commentary on the *Shannon*'s progress as she made her way in through the winding fairway, and while he did so Stephen wondered in himself, 'What shall I tell him?' Jack's physical state was fairly sound, but Stephen did not wish to interrupt his convalescence with any unnecessary agitation of mind; then there was the long-engrained habit of secrecy: and then again there was the uncertainty with regard to Dubreuil. On this occasion was he anything more than a property that Johnson moved on to the stage for his own purposes? As for Johnson, he was reasonably confident of being able to deal with him, although no doubt he was a dangerous man: Dubreuil, however, was quite another pair of sleeves; and he had suffered very, very much more from Stephen's activities.

He still had not made up his mind by the time the frigate reached the extreme range of the American batteries. 'She lies to,' said Jack. 'Just so. And there is Philip Broke at the masthead with his glass, staring at the *Chesapeake*. I was almost sure of him this morning, and now, with the sun in the west, I am quite certain. Should you like to have a look?'

Stephen aimed the telescope, found the distant figure, and said, 'I can make nothing of him, at all. But perhaps you know him well — can distinguish him at a great distance?'

'In course I do,' said Jack. 'Man and boy, I have known Philip Broke these twenty years and more. Surely I must have told you of Philip Broke a score of times?'

'Never,' said Stephen. 'Nor have I met the gentleman. I trust he is an able mariner?'

'Oh yes, yes, a capital seaman. To think that I should never have told you about him in all these years. Lord!'

'Pray tell me about him now. There is an

hour to go before our supper.' Stephen did not very much wish to know about Captain Broke, but he did want the steady background of Jack's deep, kindly voice while his mind revolved upon itself, waiting for the sudden flash that would tell him how to act.

'Well,' said Jack, 'Philip Broke and I are kind of cousins, and when my mother died I was packed off to stay at Broke Hall for a while, a fine old place in Suffolk. Their land runs down to the Orwell, the estuary of the Orwell, before it joins the Stour by Harwich, and Philip and I used to spend hours there in the mud, watching the shipping pass up to Ipswich, or fall down with the tide; a lot of those east-country craft, you know, that manage so amazingly well with short tacks in a tricky fairway, and colliers, barges from London river, and Dutchmen from across the way with their leeboards and fat arses, doggers, schuyts, and busses. We were both wild to run away to sea, and we tried once; but old Mr Broke came after us in a dog-cart, took us back, and whipped us till we cried like puppies — he was quite impartial. But still, we did have a misshapen sort of punt of our own, with a lugsail we were hardly strong enough to hoist: it was the most crossgrained brute that ever swam, and although it was so monstrous heavy, it would overset for a nothing. I used to save Philip's life three or four times a day, and once I said he should give me a halfpenny for each rescue. But he said no, if I could swim and he could not, it was clear duty as a Christian and a cousin to pull him out, particularly as I was already wet myself: still, he did say he would pray for me. Oh, those were happy days: you would have liked it, Stephen — there were all sorts of long-legged birds on the mud — we called 'em tukes — and bitterns booming away in the reeds, and those what-d'ye-call-'em big white birds with odd-shaped beaks — spoonbills — and the other kind whose bills turn upwards, and there was a dry place on the bank crammed with ruffs all fighting one another or pretending to, spreading out their neck-feathers like studdingsails. And we used to gather plovers' eggs by the bucketful. God knows how long it lasted, but it seemed like a small eternity, and it was always summer. But then he went off to school and I went off to sea.

'We wrote three or four times, which is a good deal for boys; but I am no great fist at a letter, as you know, and we rather lost touch with one another until I came back from the West Indies when *Andromeda* paid off. Then I found that he had been unable to bear his school, though he was quick at his book, and had persuaded them to send him to the Academy at Portsmouth. Well, of course, I did not like to be seen walking about with an Academite —'

'Were they a very wicked set?'

'Oh, I dare say they were as wicked as their means allowed, at twelve or thirteen or so, but it was not that: they were *low*. We looked upon them as a miserable crew of sneaking upstart lubbers, learning seamanship and gunnery out of books and pretending to set themselves on a level with us, who had learnt them at sea. Still, we were cousins, so I took him to the Blue Posts and gave him a decent dinner: I had seven guineas of prize-money in my pocket, and he had not a stiver — old Mr Broke was generous in big things, but he was precarious near with his ha'pence. And we went to the play, to see "Venice Preserved", and to a raree-show, where there was Cleopatra's asp, and some fleas that drew a coach, and for twopence more the genuine living Venus, without a stitch. I offered to treat him, but he said no, it was immoral.

'Then he joined *Bulldog*, Captain Hope: he must have been fifteen or sixteen then, very old to go to sea for the first time. But he was lucky in his captain, a first-rate seaman and a friend of Nelson's; he followed him into *L'Eclair*, and I saw something of him in the Mediterranean. Then he followed him into

Romulus, and we were shipmates for a while, when I took passage home in her. In those days I could not hold a candle to him in navigation; mine was all rule of thumb, until I came to love my conic sections quite late in life and to work out the theories for myself. His navigation did not surprise me, because he had always been good at mathematics as well as *hic haec hoc;* but I was amazed to find how he had come on in seamanship. We both passed for lieutenant at about the same time, but I did not see him again until St Vincent, when he was third of *Southampton,* and we waved as we passed, forming the line. After that we did not meet for years, though we heard about one another, of course, from common friends: he was in the Channel most of the while, and the German Ocean, made commander into that rotten old *Shark,* a miserable slug, only good for convoy-duty. He was posted well before I was, his father being a great friend of Billy Pitt's, but even so he could not get a ship and he was on the shore for years and years. He wrote me a very handsome letter after we took the *Cacafuego,* and he told me he was drilling the peasantry. He had married by that time, not very well, I am afraid.'

'Was the lady unsuitable? So many sailors take the strangest trollops to wife. Even drabogues.'

'No, no, she was perfectly suitable, in that sort of way: a gentlewoman, a connection, and a thumping dowry too — ten thousand, I believe. But she had the vapours, you know, a poor doer, weakly, always in need of repair; but above all she is always ill-used, always sorry for herself. I knew her as a little girl, and she was sorry for herself then, gasping and turning up her eyes. I am afraid it weighs upon him. I am sure he would have been better off with a jolly, good-natured wench without a farthing; a woman that takes herself seriously, and cannot laugh — Lord, it must weigh on him. I am sure it would weigh on me. I went down to Broke Hall soon after their first boy was born, and I wondered that he could bear it; but he did, just like one of your old Stoics; or a patient on the Monument, as they say. Still, he did get afloat as soon as ever he could after the peace, although he had inherited by then, a neat estate with some prime farming-land and the best partridge-shooting in the country: they gave him the dear old *Druid*, patched, wet, uncomfortable, cramped, and so weak she had to be doubled with fir, but how she could fly! I have absolutely seen her making fourteen knots with the wind on her quarter, under top-gallants, three reefs out of her topsails, and studdingsails aloft and alow. But he never had a chance of distinguishing himself in her, never met a Frenchman who was his match, which was a pity, because there never was a man who longed for glory more, or who worked harder for it — even Old Jarvie praised the order *Druid* was kept in, although the Brokes are Tories, and always have been. Then they gave him the new *Shannon*, built at Brindley's yard to replace the one Leveson Gower ran aground near La Hogue. That was in the year six, and I went aboard her at the Nore. You was in Ireland at the time, I believe. He had only just commissioned her and he had not had time to work her up, but she looked promising, and I hear she is in fine trim: certainly he always had the right ideas about gunnery and discipline.

'I had not seen him since my visit to Broke Hall, and I found him changed. Quieter, rather sad; I am sure it was his marriage. He always was a religious man and now he was more so: not one of your blue-light, psalm-singing, tract-and-cocoa captains, and there was no hint of turning the other cheek, or at least not to the King's enemies. You could tell that from his guns — he had fitted them with tangent sights already, out of his own pocket — and from the private powder and shot he had laid in by the ton; and anyhow he had a fine reputation for enterprise. No resounding single-ship actions, of course, since they had never come his way; but cutting-out expeditions and privateers by the score. But still, there was just a touch of the Puritan: no women aboard, the youngsters' grog cut on the first occasion, and no bawdy at his table.'

'I have known you stop the little boys' grog altogether, and you dislike women aboard: yet you are not a Puritan. It is true that you talk bawdy with other captains, and that you sing lewd songs when drunk.'

'Yes,' said Jack, leaving his songs to one side, 'but I do it for discipline and good order. Drunken youngsters or midshipmen are a nuisance, and quarrels about women can upset a whole ship's company, besides emptying their pockets so that they sell their slops and steal the ship's furniture, and ruining their health so that they cannot lay aloft or train a gun. Broke does it on moral grounds. He hates drunkenness in itself, and he hates adultery and fornication, because they are all three of them sins not against the ship but against God. When I say women, by the way, I mean common women, the hordes that put off in boats when a ship comes in.'

'This I have never seen.'

Jack smiled. There was a good deal in the Navy that Stephen had never seen. 'No, I do not suppose you have, since you have only sailed with me, and I will not have it in ships I command. But surely you must have noticed the swarms of boats, the hordes of brutes, round any man-of-war in port?'

'I had supposed they were visitors.'

'Some of them are. The men's wives and families, or sweethearts, but most of 'em are whores, two or three hundred whores at a time, sometimes more whores than men, and they lie with the watch below, doubling up in every hammock, sharing their victuals and taking their money, until the ship goes to sea again. It is a surprising sight, all that busy copulation — for there is never a screen, as you know — and not very pleasant for the married men's real wives and children. Most captains allow it, so long as the women are searched for spirits: they say it is good for the hands. And a good many of the officers and mids take girls in too. When I was a boy, I re-member the gunroom and the midshipmen's berth in the old *Reso* was full of 'em whenever we put in, and you were thought a miserable scrub and a holier-than-thou killjoy if you did not have your whack. It opens a youngster's eyes, I can tell you.'

Supper came, a single dish of cod, and Maurya said, 'Why, Doctor, sir, I thought you were in your room. I was going to take your tray in there. Did the gentleman find you, so?'

'What gentleman was that, my dear?'

'The foreign gentleman I told go up, I was so busy with the pots. Sure, he's sitting there yet, the creature.'

'I will go and see,' said Stephen.

The gentleman was not sitting there yet, but he had improved his time by going through Stephen's papers: it had been well done, barely discernible to an unsuspicious eye, except that the gentleman's professional skill did not extend to re-making a bed with the precision of a pair of nurses, and where he had searched under the mattress there was an unsightly bulge. But in any case Stephen's was a suspicious eye; it caught the unnatural neatness of the medical notes on his table and the rearrangement of his borrowed books.

'Jack,' he said, when they had eaten up their cod, 'things are not quite as I could wish. At one time they suspected you of being concerned with intelligence; now they suspect me. I do not believe the Americans will act without proofs, and there are no proofs. But there are French agents in America — one has just searched my room — and with them it is different. It is not impossible that the situation may turn ugly.'

'But surely they cannot do anything to you in the United States? This is not Spain.'

'Perhaps not: still and all, I have a suspicion

they might try, and I mean to take my precautions. When Mr Herapath comes tomorrow, please to give him this note: when he has read it, take it back and put it in the fire. It tells him I feel that further meetings between him and myself would be inopportune at this moment, and it begs him to procure us a pair of pocket-pistols. Do you think he will do so, Jack?'

'Yes,' said Jack, 'I believe so, if only I may mention the Frenchmen. He hates the French as much as I do.'

'Just touch upon them, then; a diplomatic hint, no more.' Herapath was not Johnson, not by a very long way indeed. 'I have already desired the porter to admit no man he does not know, and I have borrowed this from Mr Choate's instrument-cabinet.' He unwrapped his handkerchief and showed a catling with a heavy handle and a short double-edged blade. 'We use these for amputations,' he observed.

'It looks precious small,' said Jack.

'Bless you, Jack, an inch of steel in the right place will do wonders. Man is a pitiably frail machine,' said Stephen, looking attentively into Jack's face: perhaps he had been wrong to speak — the fever seemed to be returning. 'And many a one has been killed by a lancet, no more; though not always on purpose. But you are not to take what I have said as anything but a statement of suspicion. We have to take measures even against great improbabilities; and a pair of pocket-pistols will always come in.'

The suspicion, vivid throughout the night and morning, strengthened exceedingly as Stephen was walking through the little town to keep his rendezvous with Johnson. Coming towards him, on the other side of the busy main street, he saw Louisa Wogan: his eye was attracted to her by the men's heads turning on her passage, and he observed that two of her admirers were captured Royal Navy lieutenants, pleasantly named Abel and Keyne. She caught sight of him a moment later, gave him a queer look, difficult to interpret, though concern, fright, and enmity were there, and darted into the nearest shop, a tobacconist's.

'Thank you, my dear,' said Stephen. He kissed his hand to her and walked on, following the sailors at some thirty yards; he noticed how gaily they twirled their canes and saluted their acquaintance.

Carriages of one kind and another were picking up and setting down outside Franchon's hotel, or merely waiting, and from one of these, a little before he drew abreast of it, leapt Pontet-Canet, glaring about with a wild look upon his face and calling for a doctor. Seeing Stephen he ran to him, crying 'Quick, Doctor Maturin — the dame is in a fit — here in the coach — blood, blood!' He took him by the arm, urging him towards the open door. Two other men jumped out: two more came from the hotel porch. They were round him, pressing close, and all the time Pontet-Canet kept crying, 'Hurry, oh come at once. Hurry, hurry.' Quick low French muttered words, 'The other arm — club him quick — get his neck — fling him in.'

Stephen lunged back with all his force and threw himself to the ground, roaring and bawling, 'Stop thief, stop thief. Pickpockets. Keyne and Abel, a rescue, a rescue', making an infernal noise, lashing about, grasping arms and legs. He brought one man down and bit him till he screamed — they heaved him bodily up, but by now it was too late. There was shouting all around, a crowd, Keyne and Abel plying their sticks, and without a pause he kept up his 'Stop thief. Pickpockets.' Pontet-Canet's English deserted him. His 'Him robber' carried no conviction. The crowd was turning nasty. The Frenchmen crammed themselves into the coach with extraordinary speed and it thundered off, followed by angry shouts.

'Are you hurt, sir?' asked Abel, helping him to his feet.

'Did they rob you, sir?' asked Keyne, dusting him.

'All is well, I thank you,' said Stephen. 'Please to lend me a pin. Those ruffians tore my coat.'

'I am glad I broke my stick over the fat one's head,' said Keyne.

'How pleasant to see you,' said Johnson, when Stephen was shown in.

Stephen was pale and trembling with anger still but his mind was sharp and clear: he would play his hand as an outraged citizen. 'Mr Johnson, sir,' he cried, 'I wish to register an official complaint of the utmost gravity. I have just been set upon in the street, in front of this hotel, in front of your hotel, sir, by a band of ruffians, Frenchmen, led by Pontet-Canet. They attempted to abduct me, to force me into a coach. I shall register the same complaint with the British agent for prisoners of war first thing tomorrow morning. I demand the protection of your country's laws and the common security of person universally afforded to captured officers. I demand that Pontet-Canet be brought to trial and his followers identified and punished; and as soon as I have seen the agent he will make the same demand at the highest official level.'

Johnson was infinitely concerned. He begged Dr Maturin to lie on the couch, to take a little brandy, or at least a glass of water. He regretted the incident extremely, and he should certainly make the strongest representations to the Frenchman's chief.

Still playing the part of one who has received an outraged citizen's complaint, he then spoke in general terms for some considerable time, saying nothing with the practised ease of a politician — the iniquity of such proceedings to be deplored — the dreadful consequences of war — the desirability of peace, of a just and lasting peace. Stephen watched him as he spoke, and although he could control his impatience at the meaningless flow and his anger at the blundering attack, he was not so much the master of his eyes: their pale, unwinking, somewhat reptilian examination made Johnson nervous — it put him off his stroke. He brought his discourse to a lame conclusion, stood up, took a turn or two about the room, opened the window and called out to the workmen on the balcony to make less din, and then, recovering his poise, he went on in quite a different tone. Speaking confidentially, as man to man, he asked Dr Maturin to consider the difficulty of his position; he was only a small cog in a very large machine, and if in war-time those above thought fit to give French agents a greater degree of liberty, a freer hand than he for his part thought congruent with the national sovereignty, he could do nothing more than protest. And the reply would no doubt be that it was done for the sake of reciprocity — that American agents in the territories governed by the French were tacitly allowed an equal freedom.

'On the other hand,' he said, 'I can most certainly protect my own agents: of that you may be absolutely confident. So I do beg that for your sake you will allow me to enrol you as a consultant — What is it?' he cried, in answer to a knock.

'The carriage is at the door, sir,' said a servant, 'and Mr Michael Herapath is still waiting.'

'I cannot see him now,' said Johnson, going to his desk and taking a sheaf of galley-proofs. 'Give him these and say I hope to see him the day after tomorrow. No: stay. I shall give them to him myself on the way out.' The door closed, and he went on, 'To enrol you as a consultant, say on Catalan affairs. The barest minimum, a slight *aide-mémoire* on the situation there, the historical background, would suffice — just enough to satisfy Mr Secretary's conscience. I will not press you now; you are disturbed and I dare say very angry.

But I do beg you to give it the most earnest consideration, and to let me have your response on my return the day after tomorrow. Until then, I guarantee there will be no repetition of this morning's incident. And now, if I may, I will call a carriage for you. Though now I come to think of it, there is Herapath downstairs, if you prefer to go back with him: you certainly should not walk home alone, after such unpleasantness.'

Unless Michael Herapath was a perfect monster of duplicity, he was entirely ignorant of the whole affair; and Stephen had known the young man long enough and well enough to be sure that he was no monster of any kind, except perhaps of erudition. As they walked along he talked eagerly of his father's changed attitude towards the medical school, which he believed he owed to Dr Maturin's great kindness, and of his future studies; and he talked even more eagerly of his book, showed sample sheets, admired the print, gazed with loving eyes upon the title-page, and standing in the busy throng he read some passages aloud. 'Here is a version, my dear sir,' he said, 'that I flatter myself you will not wholly disapprove:

Flower: is it a flower?
Mist: is it a mist?

Coming at midnight
Leaving with the dawn.
She is there: the sweetness of a passing
    springtime
She is gone: the morning haze — no
    trace at all.'

Stephen listened gravely and applauded. He said, 'That may sum up the usual relationship between the sexes. Each tends to worship a being of its own creation. Women often expect oranges to grow on apple-trees, and men look for constancy to a purely imaginary ideal: how often a woman proves to be no more than the morning mist,' and slowly he edged Herapath along, sometimes as much as a hundred yards between the poems. In a decent interval he asked after Caroline, who was very well, apart from a slight rash, and after Mrs Wogan, who was somewhat out of sorts, mumpish, and off her food; but she would soon be cured by a sight of these proofs. Speaking as one medical man to another, Herapath offered a physical explanation for this state of mind and body; and going on from this they fell to discussing the books he should read.

'But more than any book,' said Stephen, 'I do most earnestly recommend a private corpse. Your school cadaver, tossed about in wanton play, your odd heads and parts, indifferently pickled by the porter's wife, are well enough for the coarse processes; but for the fine work, give me a good fresh private corpse, preferably a pauper, to avoid the fat, lovingly preserved in the best spirits of wine, double-refined. Here are eloquent volumes — *nocturna versate manu, versate diurna* — worth a whole library of mere print: there is your father on the other side of the road. I am sure he will help you to a corpse: he is a worthy man. Do you not perceive your father, Mr Herapath?'

They were approaching the Asclepia, and from it came the old gentleman, carrying a basket; but Michael Herapath was in such a pleasurable flutter of spirits with his book that he did not make him out until, in reply to Stephen's salute, he returned a distant bow. At the same time he shot Stephen a significant look, raised his finger to his lips, and although he did not actually do so, gave the impression of walking on the tips of his toes — a general impression of knowing stealth.

'He is carrying a basket,' observed his son, 'I dare say he has been taking Aunt Putnam soft-shelled crabs.'

'Should you not relieve him of his burden?' said Stephen. 'Enlightened self-interest, no less than filial piety, demands such a course.

Good day to you now, and I thank you for your company.'

'Jack,' he said, 'how do you do?'

'Prime, prime — but what's this, Stephen? Have you been in a mill?'

'Pontet-Canet tried to force me into a coach; Keyne and Abel came to my rescue. It amounted to nothing. Tell me, how did Mr Herapath respond to my request?'

'Are you really quite well, Stephen? No injury?'

'Quite well, I thank you. My coat is torn, but I have arranged it with a pin. What said friend Herapath?'

'He spoke up like a friend, like a good 'un; damned the French and all their works, stepped out directly, and came back with these in a basket.' Jack leaned over and brought up a case of pistols with their fittings. 'There. London-made, Joe Manton's best. As pretty a pair as you could wish; I have been playing with them this last half hour, getting the flints just so. Will you give me your coat?' he said, leaning over again for his hussif. 'It is only the sewing of the pocket.'

'I admire the way you sailors sew,' said Stephen, watching him.

'A pretty set of scarecrows we should look, if we were to wait for women to do it for us,' said Jack, stitching away. 'As a youngster I was in *Goliath* when she wore Admiral Harvey's flag, blue at the main, and we were expected to be uncommon trim: Hessian boots, white breeches, laced hats, black stocks; and anyone who did not pass the Admiral's inspection was put on watch and watch. Only four hours' sleep at a time comes very hard when you are a boy, so we plied our needles and our blacking-balls. But where I really learnt to sew was in *Resolution*, when Captain Douglas turned me before the mast, as I believe I told you.'

'I remember it. You were made a common sailor for a while, to cure you of lechery. A strange notion, from what you tell me of women on the lower deck; but perhaps it had an effect?'

'It had the effect of enabling me to make myself a suit of hot-weather slops. I will not say, to mend a friend's coat, for that might be ungenerous. We were given so many yards of duck, and we set to in our watch below; they were not your common purser's slops, neither, because we were a dressy ship — half the crew were dandy kiddies —and we topmen of the starboard watch sewed blue ribbons into our seams for church and divisions. And then I was sailmaker's crew as well, and that taught me a gallows sight more, including the use of my left hand, as you see. Tell me, Stephen,' he went on in quite a different tone, 'how do you see the situation at present, and what do you think we should do?'

'The situation, now? Well, I believe the French have smoked me. You know that in my line I have done them all the harm I could, and I think they will kill me for it if ever they can. On the other hand, I think Johnson can protect me.'

'Because of your friendship with Diana?'

'Not at all: I believe he knows nothing of its real nature: mere long acquaintance, no more, for him. And it would not answer if he did. They are not well together. She hates him as a man and as an enemy: Diana is very patriotic, Jack; she feels our reverses most bitterly.'

'Of course she does,' said Jack in a sombre voice. 'So must anyone who has a scrap of pride.'

'She wishes to leave him and to leave America. I have proposed that she should marry me, recover her nationality, and return with us when we are exchanged. If Johnson knew this, he would either provoke me, since he is a very jealous man and one who wishes to keep what I might describe as a harem — they are great duellers in the Southern states, and he has been out many times — or he would throw me to the French.'

Jack thought it better to make no remark on

Stephen's offer of marriage, though his consternation was plain enough to a perceptive eye: he said, 'He would protect you, then, out of liking, and because it is the right and proper thing to do?'

'He would not. He is an important man in American intelligence, and his liking would not weigh a feather: no, he believes that he may get some information out of me; and if I do not mistake, he supposed that from a little I may be led, by various forms of pressure, to give more and then more until at last he has turned me entirely. It is a common practice; I have often known it succeed. But I do not intend to be a party even to the first stages of the process. He has given me until Monday to make up my mind, and I mean to make use of that time. It appears to me that our safety lies in noise. I shall see our agent for prisoners of war, I shall speak to all our acquaintance, prisoners or otherwise, to all the foreign consuls in this town, perhaps to the civil authorities and the Federalist newspaper editors. Covert operations of this kind must be carried out in silence: noise is death to secret intelligence, above all in a town like this with an active, vocal public opinion, much of it strongly opposed to the war, and I mean to make all the public noise I can, just as I lay down in the street and bellowed and hallooed until a crowd gathered when Pontet-Canet set upon me. I believe it will answer in this case too; and that the shadowy charges against you having been abandoned, the exchange will take place in the usual way. That is how I shall spend tomorrow and what there is of Monday.'

'I hope to God you are right,' said Jack. 'But what about the bloody-minded Frenchmen in the meantime?'

'Johnson has given me assurances that they will not move before our next meeting: they are not in their own country, after all. He holds them over my head as a threat, you see, to compel me to acquiesce. It is reasonable to rely on his assurance, since he is not going to sacrifice a potentially valuable agent for the sake of gratifying Dubreuil's lust for revenge. It is in his interest to preserve me until our final interview on Monday; and after that we can sit here, never stirring out, protected by the public noise I shall have raised. And if, by any most unlikely chance, the French should make an attempt upon me here, we can now defend ourselves.'

Jack cut the thread and handed back the mended coat; he looked out of the window, where the *Shannon*'s topsails winked in the evening light, and said, 'Dear Lord above, how I do wish I could set you clear of all this

367

dirty, ugly, underhanded mess: how I long for the open sea.'

The dawn of Sunday did not break at all. The fog that had formed in the night only became a little lighter and more visible as it moved in quiet swathes along the quays, sometimes making silent whirlpools at the street corners, where it met a current of air. The slight increase in light was not enough to wake Dr Maturin, however, and the two nurses with whom he had contracted to go to early Mass were obliged to beat on his door to rouse him.

He hurried into his clothes, but even so the priest was on the altar by the time they reached the obscure chapel in a side-alley, and crept into the immensely evocative smell of old incense. There followed an interval on a completely different plane of being: with the familiar ancient words around him, always the same, in whatever country he had ever been (though now uttered in a broad Munster Latin), he lived free of time or geography, and he might have walked out, a boy, into the streets of Barcelona, blazing white in the sun, or into those of Dublin under the soft rain. He prayed, as he had prayed so long, for Diana, but even before the priest dismissed them, the changed nature of his inner words brought him back to the immediate present and to Boston, and if he had been a weeping man it would have brought the tears coursing down his face.

As it was, he felt a dry burning in his eyes, a constriction in his throat, while he waited for the priest to come out of the vestry. To him he stated that he was a prisoner of war, that he was likely to be exchanged in the next few days, that he wished to be married before his voyage, and that as soon as he could he would acquaint Father Costello with the day and hour, because the ceremony would have to be carried out with very little notice.

Then he left the misty, candle-lit chapel for the colder fog outside, and considered for a while. It would be no use calling on Diana at this time of the morning, since she often lay abed till noon, but there were many other things to do. Perhaps the first should be to see Mr Andrews, the British agent for prisoners of war: Stephen knew where he lived, and taking his bearings from the vague form of a clock-tower he set out. He had a fair knowledge of the town, and he was confident that presently he should cross the street with Franchon's hotel in it; the agent's house lay not far from the hotel, a couple of hundred yards behind it. But the broad street did not appear: instead he found himself at the harbour, with the far broader sea at his feet, stretching away into the greyness: high water, and scarcely a ripple. The wet quays were empty; drops fell from the yards and rigging of the ships tied up along them; no sound but the clopping of a few horses' hooves and the distant plash of oars as those few Bostonians who celebrated the Sabbath on Saturday or who did not celebrate it at all, rowed out to go fishing. On ordinary days there were a good many of these small craft: the *Shannon* never troubled them at all, but had been seen purchasing their lobsters, pollack, hake, and halibut in baskets.

At last he found a Negro on the waterfront, but the Negro was a stranger in those parts, and together they wandered in search of the street that ran down and opened on to the harbour itself. No street: only vile cobbles, puddles, dark warehouses and the encircling fog; and at one point Stephen thought they must soon reach the open country. But in time a light appeared, a row of lighted windows. 'Let us knock,' he said, 'and ask our way. We may be out of the town entirely.'

Yet before he had had time to knock he found he knew the place: although the fog removed it from its context and altered its perspective, it was the tavern where he had met Mr Herapath and his friends. The place was open, and as he pushed the door a rectangular flood of orange light lit up the fog. 'Come in and drink a cup of coffee, friend,' he said to his companion.

'But I am a nigra, sir, a black man,' said he.

'That is no very heinous crime.'

'Oh brother, you sure are a stranger here,' said the Negro, laughing, and he vanished into the fog, laughing still.

When Stephen came out, wiping his lips, it had thinned somewhat, and at times the red ball of the sun could be seen. The geography at least was plain; he walked briskly along to what he privately called the Rambla and up it to the hotel. There was some activity within, but as far as he could make out Diana's windows were blind: no lights behind the balcony along the whole first floor. From the hotel he took first one side-street, where a disoriented cock was crowing, then another, peopled by ghostly hogs; and not by hogs alone. He passed a couple of men lounging in a doorway, and an interminable family carrying prayerbooks, and as he drew near to Mr Andrews's house he saw a vague dark shape that very soon resolved itself into a coach. Four horses stretching out before it, gently steaming through their cloths. A black coach: Pontet-Canet's coach. No light in Andrews's windows, none in the fanlight of his door.

Deliberately he began to cross the road, but a head at the coach window cried *'Le voilà'*, the doors opened and men poured out. Stephen whipped round and raced back. A hog across his path very nearly brought him down and as he recovered he heard a whistle blown behind him and saw the two men leave their doorway. They ran to close the two side-alleys and both had their pistols out. The numerous family lay between him and them: did they amount to a crowd, a group numerous enough? They did not. Stephen was among them, the woman's outraged face turning towards him as he jostled her tallest boys, but even so the man on the left levelled his piece and fired, hitting a child just by him. After an infinitesimal pause of stupor the man of the family went for him like a tiger with his stick and Stephen ran left-handed past the fighting pair. The streaming hogs, the screaming children delayed the man on the right and those from the coach: Stephen had a clear start, but he also had a shocking stitch in his side. As he laboured on he looked right and left for a lighted house, a church, a tavern, and looked in vain, for this was a commercial district, gaunt warehouses with cranes protruding from their upper storeys, closed offices, shut-up shops, and the running feet were louder and louder behind. A weed-grown vacant lot

— an improvised pig-sty within it. He slipped through the ragged palings and crouched there with a gravid sow, near her time, timid, and new-littered for her farrowing. Bent double to overcome the stitch, he stared round for the dwelling of the man who had brought the straw: no cottage, no dwelling-house at all, only stark walls soaring up on all three sides, and no way out. In a few moments, when they missed him ahead, his refuge would become a hopeless trap; and the fog was growing patchy as a small breeze wafted it to and fro.

The stitch was gone. He moved to the paling, but already here were two men running back. He shrank down among the nettles, his pistol in his hand, a very wicked look on his face. They passed. He slipped out and ran directly after them, going free and fine, a bounding step. He passed a barefoot staring boy: the corner could not be far. But there were running steps, a single man, behind, and though now he ran at his greatest speed, even at the risk of overtaking those in front, the steps ran faster still. Closer, closer, and he could hear the panting breath: he could feel the pointing pistol. Closer still and the man was abreast, an Indian, a half-caste glancing sideways, a questioning dark face he had never seen, and here was the corner showing through the fog. '*Vite, vite,*' cried Stephen in a gasping croak, '*à gauche. Tu l'attraperas.*'

The man nodded, sped on, turned the corner at a shocking speed: the fog swallowed him. Stephen bore right and left and here was the coach again: still no light in Andrews's house, and cries behind him and in front, for one group had made the whole circuit. The coach doors still hung open, not a man there but the driver, dim in his box. Calling out '*Allez, allez,*' Stephen ran to the coach, slammed the near door, sprang on to the box, clapped his cocked pistol to the coachman's head and said, '*Fouette*'. The coachman changed colour, gathered his reins, cried '*Arré*' and cracked his whip. The horses lunged forward, the coach moved off, faster, faster and faster. '*Fouette, fouette,*' said Stephen, and the coachman plied his whip. The first group of men, tall Pontet-Canet with them, appeared ahead, stringing out across the road as they grasped the situation. '*Fouette toujours,*' said Stephen, grinding the pistol into the coachman's neck. They drove straight through the line and here was the side-road that led to the broad main street. '*À gauche. À gauche, je te dis.*' The coachman reined in to take the corner: the pursuers gained. The coach was round, rocking wildly on its springs; the broad street was just ahead. '*A droite,*' said Stephen, for the right-hand turn would take them fast away, galloping down the good road to the harbour. The coachman half-stood to heave upon the reins and swing his horses round: the pistol shifted as Stephen braced himself for the turn, and with a furious heave of his loins the coachman jerked him off.

He was up like a cat before the coachman could stop his team, before Pontet-Canet and his men were more than a vague dark mass coming towards him. He ran up the street, away from the coach: but he could not run much more — his head had hit the kerb and his feet were straying wild — and there was shouting in the fog ahead. Here was Franchon's hotel, and here, better than any public door with the Frenchmen so hot for blood, was the workmen's rope dangling from the balcony. Hand over hand he went up it, not indeed like a topman laying aloft but like a lithe dangerous wild beast trying one last ruse before turning on its equally dangerous and more numerous enemies: the balcony railing, and he was over, crouching there with his breath coming in enormous gasps, his heart beating as though it filled his breast, his eyes unable to focus clear.

He heard French voices below arguing about the way to take. 'He may have gone in here.' It would not be long before they saw the rope.

His breath was coming easier now, and he could see. He crept fast and low along the balcony, counting the windows to Diana's room. Hers was closed, and shuttered too. He rapped: no reply. He whipped out his catling, slid the blade into the crack and raised the bar, opened the shutter, tapped on the glass.

A voice below: 'I shall climb it.'

'Diana,' he called, and he saw her sit up in bed. 'Quick, for the love of God.'

The rope was creaking behind him now.

'Who is it?'

'Don't be a fool, woman,' he called, low but sharp, through the small gap he had forced in the frame — a broken pane would be sheer disaster. 'Open quick, dear Christ and all.'

She sprang up, opened the long window; he slid the shutter to without a sound, closed the window behind him, drew the curtain, and leapt into her bed, a huge bed, and he at the bottom of it. 'Get in on top of me,' he whispered through the sheets. 'Ruffle the clothes upon its foot.'

She sat there rigid, her toes warm upon his neck. Quiet footsteps on the balcony. 'No, that is Johnson's woman's room. Try the next but two.'

A long, silent pause; and at last a knock on

the door. Madame Franchon's voice: she was extremely sorry to disturb Mrs Villiers, but it was thought that a thief had taken refuge in the hotel: had Mrs Villiers heard or seen anything? No, said Diana, nothing at all. Might Madame Franchon look at the inner rooms? Mrs Villiers had the keys.

'Certainly,' said Diana. 'Wait a moment.' She slipped out of bed, threw some gauzy things over it, opened the door and returned to the deep rumpled nest of eiderdown and countless pillows. 'The keys are on the table there,' she said.

It took Madame Franchon only a few minutes to decide that the inner rooms, with their closed, unbroken windows and their unviolated doors, contained no flying thief, but in that time Stephen thought he must die of cramp and suffocation. The worst was the flood of apologies, and he felt an infinite relief when Diana cut them short, closed the door on Madame Franchon, and shot the bolt.

He came out into the air and gradually the drumming in his ears died away. 'You should have a drink, Maturin,' she whispered, reaching for a pretty little decanter by her bed. 'You don't mind drinking out of my glass?'

She poured him a stiff tot and mechanically he drank it off: the fire spread in his vitals. He recognized the smell, the same smell that mingled with Diana's usual scent there in the bed. 'Is it a kind of whisky?' he asked.

'They call it bourbon,' she said. 'Another drop?'

Stephen shook his head. 'Is your maid here? The tall one, Peg? Send her away, right away, until tomorrow.'

Diana went into another room. He heard the distant ringing of a bell and then Diana's voice, telling Peg to take Abijah and Sam to Mr Adams's house in the dog-cart and to give him this note. There seemed to be some low murmuring objection, for Diana's voice rose to a sharp, imperious tone and the door closed with a decided clap.

She came back and sat on the side of the bed. 'That's done,' she said. 'I have sent them all off until Monday morning.' She looked at him affectionately, hesitated, poured herself a finger of bourbon, and said, 'What are you at, Maturin? Flying from an angry husband? It is not like you to bound from one bed to another. Yet after all you are a man. You spoke to me from the other side of the window just like a man — just as though we were already married. You called me a fool. But perhaps I am a fool. I was truly desolated, hearing you with Johnson yesterday, and not seeing you after all. My God, Stephen, I was so glad to hear your voice just now. I thought you had deserted me.'

He turned his face to her, and her smile faded. He said, 'I was escaping from Pontet-Canet and his band. They mean to kill me if they can. They waylaid me in the street yesterday — that was what I was speaking to Johnson about — and they made a far more determined attempt just now. Listen, honey, will you dress at once and go to the British agent? Tell him I am beset and cannot stir from here. Pontet-Canet and Dubreuil live in this hotel, do they not?'

'Yes.'

'Any others?'

'No. But all the Frenchmen, officers and civilians, haunt the place. There are always half a dozen of them in the hall.'

'Sure, I saw them myself. Now Andrews may not be in Boston on a Sunday; there was no light in his house this morning. But he has a cottage by the sea, somewhere this side of Salem. Herapath knows it; he has been there. Could you see Herapath without Wogan?'

'Very easily. Louisa is in the country with Johnson.'

'Ah. Then if Andrews is not here, take Herapath with you to the cottage. Tell Andrews that if he can gather a party of our officers to cover us, all will be well. Dubreuil will never risk the flaring public scandal of an attack on the Asclepia, and by tomorrow I shall have raised such a noise that private murder will be out of the question. Call a chaise and wear a veil: there is no danger, but it would be as well for you not to be seen. Is there any likelihood of the people of the hotel coming to clean the room?'

'No. Johnson always insists upon his own house-slaves doing everything; but if you like you could go into his rooms. They do not open on to the corridor, and we have the only keys. There, on the table.'

She bent down, kissed him, and hurried out of the room. He heard her order the carriage — was it more than two posts to Salem? — and in less time than he had ever known a woman take to dress she was back in a travelling habit and a broad-brimmed veiled hat. They embraced. He said, 'I never doubted your courage, my dear. Tell the man to drive slow, in this wicked fog. God bless.'

She said, 'I will lock you in,' and she was gone.

He walked into the big drawing-room next door, unshuttered, and by contrast fairly light. The fog had thinned a little more, and standing on a chair he could see the dim form of her chaise move out into the roadway, turn to the right and right again, down the side-street he had so lately traversed, towards Mr

Andrews's house. If he were there she would be back in twenty minutes, if not, then in perhaps two hours or three. She had all the spirit in the world, all the courage, for this kind of thing, for a physical emergency; *guts,* as the seamen said; it was impossible not to admire her, impossible not to like her.

A French clock on the mantelshelf struck eleven, twice. He sat down, and while deep within himself he went on musing about Diana his medical side, his medical hands moved about his painful ribs, his far more painful head. He felt curiously exhausted, and his mind did not focus well but moved vaguely round and round the central point. The physician was in better shape, stating that the eighth and ninth ribs were probably cracked, no more; but that there was something very like a crepitation along the coronal suture, a little above the temporal crest, while the main seat of pain was on the other side, a clear *contre-coup* effect. 'I wonder that there was no concussion,' he observed. 'But no doubt nausea will ensue.' This was all the physician had to say since there was no remedy but rest, and Stephen's thoughts returned wholly to Diana. A glance at the clock showed him that she must by now have gone on to the Andrewses' cottage, and he pictured her haranguing the anxious, worried little man.

The half hour roused him to a sense of his duty. He returned to the bedroom, picked up the keys, and passed through the long suite of rooms to Johnson's private quarters, unlocking and relocking the doors as he went. The last true room was evidently his closet, with a large roll-top desk, a strong-box, and a quantity of files and papers: a door in the far corner led to a privy, which also contained a hipbath. It was just as well, because at this point the nausea that he had foreseen came on, and he knelt there, vomiting for a while.

Recovered now, and washed, he walked back into the study: the difficulty was to know where to start. On the scientist's principle of dealing with the easiest first, he went through the open files and papers. Most were the private records and accounts of a very wealthy man, but there were some interesting French documents with translations in Diana's dashing hand. These dated back to before the war: the more recent were in hands he did not recognize, except for Louisa Wogan's. Even so, Diana would possess useful knowledge about the background of the French connection. Memoranda about the military position on the Great Lakes and the Canadian land frontier: a coded list, presumably of agents there. A note about himself: 'Pontet-Canet confirms that Maturin has an inclination to retire to the States: a grant of land in a district of unusual interest to a naturalist might swing the scale.' More accounts and official correspondence, lists of prisoners, with remarks and interrogations. Nothing of the first importance, but useful material among the dross.

He turned his attention to the desk. None of the keys fitted it, which was significant. But roll-top desks in general presented no great difficulty to one who was used to these things, and once Stephen had found which of the ornamental knobs controlled the back-bar, one firm thrust of his catling released the bolt and the top rolled back.

The first thing he saw was the blaze of Diana's *rivière* in its open case, blazing even in this pale ghostly light, and beside it, under the heavy obsidian phallus that acted as a paperweight, a letter addressed to himself. The seal had been raised and he was not the first to read:

Dearest Stephen — I heard you talking and I expected you but I saw you go away without coming to me. Oh what can it mean? Have I vexed you? I did not give you a clear answer — we were interrupted — and perhaps you thought I refused your offer. But I did not, Stephen. I will marry you whenever you wish and oh so gladly. You do me too much honour, Stephen dear. I should never have refused you in India — it went against my heart — but now, such as I am alas, I am entirely yours — Diana. PS That gross fellow is taking his trollop into the country: come and see me — we shall have all Sunday together. Remember me to Cousin Jack.

He had barely grasped the full implication of this before he heard a sound at the door, a slight metallic grating at the lock. It was certainly not Diana. He seized the paperweight, silently closed the desk, and stepped behind the opening door.

It was Pontet-Canet, on the same errand as himself. The Frenchman obviously knew the place, and he was better equipped than Stephen. He selected one of the many skeleton keys on his ring and opened the strong-box, took out a book and carried it to the desk. His practised hand went straight to the master-knob, the top rolled back, and he sat down to copy from the book. He moved the diamond necklace to make room for the paper he brought from his pocket and in doing so he saw the letter. 'Oh, oh, *la garce,*' he whispered as he read it. 'Oh, *la garce.*'

Stephen had his pistol ready, but although this was an inside room, enclosed, he wished to avoid the noise. Pontet-Canet stiffened, uneasy, raising his head as though he felt the threat. Stephen strode forward and as the Frenchman turned he brought the massive obsidian down on his head, breaking both. Pontet-Canet was on the floor, limp but breathing. Stephen bent over him, catling in hand, felt for the still beating common carotid, severed it, and stood back from the jet of blood. Then he pulled the body to the hip-bath, placed towels and mats to prevent the blood soaking through to the floor below, and went through the dead man's pockets. Nothing of significance, but he did take Pontet-Canet's pistol and, since he did not possess one, his watch, a handsome Breuguet very like that which had been taken from him years ago, when he was captured by the French off the coast of Spain.

Changing the bloody chair for another, he sat down to the open book. Memoranda of Johnson's conversations with Dubreuil, copies of his letters to his political chief, day-by-day transactions, future projects, uncoded, perfectly frank: no wonder Pontet-Canet had gone straight to it. With this book before him he had his ally's secret mind wide open, without the last reserve.

On the most recent page, after a complaint about the Frenchmen's attack on Dr Maturin, Johnson had written, 'I shall have a further interview with him on Monday, when I propose to bring greater pressure to bear; if however he should still prove obdurate, I believe he must be discreetly resigned to Dubreuil in exchange for a free hand with Lambert and Brown, preferably in a place where this will excite no public comment. I have already repatriated virtually all the fit prisoners, to prevent any unpleasant incident.'

Had Johnson written this before or after he had read Diana's letter? If before, had he then given Dubreuil leave to go ahead, or had the Frenchman, fearing that Stephen would yield on Monday, decided to confront Johnson with a *fait accompli* once again? They were interesting points; but purely academic at this stage. He returned to the study of the book. It was easier to read now, the midday sun having partially dispersed the fog; and with the greater light the town had woken up — the noise of traffic in the street had reached something near its usual pitch, and someone at no great distance was letting off fireworks. Was this perhaps a holiday? Another American victory at sea? The pain in his head was growing and in spite of the greater light his eyes would not keep their focus long.

Lost in his reading and his conjectures and his pain he did not perceive the opening of the door that Pontet-Canet had left unlocked until it was already on the jar. *'Tu es là, Jean-Paul?'* whispered Dubreuil.

No choice this time; no question of silence now. Stephen rose, whipping round with the pistol already in his hand, thrust it against Dubreuil's recoiling chest and fired. The man jerked back against the edge of the open door and as it slowly yielded so he fell, the expression of amazement and malignity lasting until his head was quite down, dull and indifferent at last.

Stephen stood with the smoking pistol in his hand, listening to the immense report that seemed to fill the room and his head so lastingly. The smell of powder and scorched cloth. Slow, slow, the minutes passed; yet no one seemed to have heard the shot. No running feet, no hammering on the outer doors, no sound at all but for the clock striking the quarter; and outside some kind of a procession was passing the hotel — remote cheers, laughter, a squib or two.

The tension diminished to a tolerable pitch. He put the pistol down and dragged Dubreuil to the privy, to the hipbath. 'This is like the end of Titus Andronicus,' he said, with an affectation of callous brutality, as he heaved the body in.

But he was, he found, seriously disturbed, and he wondered why. He had not even searched Dubreuil. Why not? Corpses he had seen by the score, even by the hundred, in open and clandestine battle, yet this killing sickened him. It was unreasonable: he had had to kill or be killed, and Dubreuil was the man who misused Carrington and Vargas so inhumanly until they died. Yet there it was, and he found that he could do no more than read mechanically, scarcely retaining anything of significance . . . the squalor of his own conduct and of his enemies', all for the best of motives. The extreme violence of this morning, the physical and perhaps moral exhaustion, were obvious causes for his state, yet it was strange that he could not master his thinking mind and compel it to answer the question, What was he to do next? He posed the question again and again and the only answer was that it was impossible to leave the hotel with the Frenchmen waiting in the hall; that he must nevertheless get these documents and Diana clear; and that the Asclepia could be no sort of refuge once Johnson was back. A string of negatives, no more.

He heard Diana return. She was talking and for a moment he thought it must be Johnson, back before his time, perhaps warned by the traitor Peg; but then he realized that the other voice was Herapath's.

He went towards her, door after door, and she met him in the dining-room. Her face was anxious and downcast and as soon as she saw him she said, 'I am so sorry, so very sorry, Stephen darling, but Andrews was not there. He is gone back to Halifax in the cartel, with nearly all the prisoners of war.'

'Never mind it, my dear,' said Stephen gently — he felt an immense pity for her, he could hardly tell why. 'Herapath is with you?'

'In the drawing-room.'

'Were there any Frenchmen in the hall?'

'Yes, quite a crowd, laughing and talking, some in uniform; but neither Pontet-Canet nor Dubreuil.'

They walked into the drawing-room. Herapath greeted Stephen with a look of deep concern, but Stephen only gave him a vague howd'ye-do and said he must write a note. 'There is a writing-table in my room,' said Diana, opening the door and pointing.

He stared stupidly at the paper for some moments and then wrote: *Jack, I have been obliged to kill two Frenchmen here. There are other Frenchmen below and I cannot get out — they tried to kill me this morning. I must get*

Diana out of here at any cost at all, and some papers and myself if it can be done. Wogan will not do — do not tell Herapath this — nor the Asclepia. Choate might find Diana a refuge or Fr Costello, who is to marry me. I am not myself, Jack, do what you can. The big porter might prove a friend.

'Mr Herapath,' he said, coming back, 'might I beg you to give this to Captain Aubrey as soon as ever you can reach him? It is of the very last importance to me, or I should not trouble you.'

'With all my heart,' said Herapath.

They were alone, and Diana moved about the room, lighting candles, drawing curtains. She looked at him from time to time and said, 'My God, Stephen, I have never seen you look so down, or low, or such a wretched colour. Have you had anything to eat today?'

'Not a thing,' he said, trying to smile.

'I shall order a meal at once. And while it is coming, lie on my bed and have a drink. You look as if you could do with it. I shall have one too.'

He did as he was told — his head was furiously painful now — but he said, 'No food.'

'You do not like to see me drinking, do you?' she said, pouring out the bourbon.

'No,' said he. 'You are a fool to your complexion, Villiers.'

'Is whisky bad for it?'

'Spirits harden tissues, sure: that is a fact.'

'I only drink any when I am excited, as I am now, or when I am low. Still, as I have been low ever since I came here, I dare say I must have swallowed gallons. But I will not be low with you, Stephen.' A long silence, and she went on. 'Do you remember, years and years ago, you asked me whether I had read Chaucer, and I said "Filthy old Chaucer?" and you abused me for it? Well, at least he did say "In woman vinolent is no defence. Thus knoweth lechers by experience . . ." '

'Diana,' he said abruptly, 'do you know anyone in America — have you any sure friend that you can trust, that you can run to?'

'No,' she said, surprised. 'Not a single soul. How could I, in my position? Why do you ask?'

'You were so kind as to write me a letter yesterday, a very, very kind letter.'

'Yes?'

'It never reached me. I found it on Johnson's desk, next to your diamonds.'

'Oh my God,' she said, quite deadly pale.

'Clearly we must be away before he returns,' said Stephen. 'I have sent to Jack, to see what he can do. If he can do nothing, why, there are other possibilities.' Maybe there were: but what were they, apart from a wild flight in the dark? His mind could not, or would not, grapple with the problem hard and tight: clear, prolonged incisive thought was beyond his power.

'I don't care,' she said, taking his hand. 'I don't mind, so long as you are there.'

CHAPTER EIGHT

'Captain Aubrey, if you please,' said Michael Herapath.

'What name?' asked the porter.

'Herapath.'

'You are not Mr Herapath.'

Looking into those black implacable eyes Herapath replied, 'I am George Herapath's son. I have brought the Captain a message from Doctor Maturin.'

'I will take it up. No visitors are allowed.'

Shortly afterwards he reappeared with a nurse and said in a more human tone, 'Ascend. Miss will show you the way.'

'Mr Herapath,' cried Jack, holding out his hand, 'I am heartily glad to see you.' And when the door had closed, 'Come, sit close by my bed. Is the Doctor hurt?'

'Not that I could see, sir. But he was strangely slow: dazed, I might say.'

'Did you see any Frenchmen as you came away from the hotel?'

'Yes, sir. It is their general rendezvous, and there were eight or nine of them sitting about the lobby, soldiers and civilians.' His former captain had always been a formidable figure to Michael Herapath; he was still more so now, as he sat straight up in his bed, looking larger and broader and more angry than ever he had done aboard the *Leopard,* and when, after a dark, brooding pause, he said in that strong, decided voice of his, 'Reach me my shirt and breeches, will you?' Herapath did so without protest. He did cry out however when Jack plucked off his sling and thrust his injured arm into the sleeve. 'Surely, sir, Doctor Maturin would never allow . . .'

The only reply was 'My coat and shoes are in that tall locker. Mr Herapath, is your father at home?'

'Yes, sir.'

'Then be so good as to give me an arm down the stairs and to show me the way to his house. God damn and blast this buckle.' Herapath knelt to fasten it, reached Jack his pistol, and helped him down the stairs. 'Not,' as Jack observed, 'that I am not spry enough; but when you have been laid up a while, sometimes you are unsteady when it comes to a flight of steps. And I would not stumble now, by God.'

But in the hall the porter stopped them. 'You are not allowed out,' he said, his hand on the lever that controlled the door.

Jack compelled his face to assume what

amiability it could, and he said, 'I am only going to take a turn, to see Doctor Maturin.' His left hand clenched round the barrel of his pistol, and he measured the force of the blow he should have to give to disable such a powerful man. 'The Doctor is in some trouble,' he added, remembering Stephen's note.

The Indian opened the door. 'If he needs me,' he said without any change of expression, 'I am his man. I am free in half an hour: less, if necessary.'

Jack shook his hand, and they walked out into the fog, as thick now as it had been in the morning. 'Do you know, those damned French dogs set upon him this morning. They mean to kill him if they can. It is like attacking a ship in a neutral port. God rot their . . .' The rest of his words were lost in a deep growl of blasphemy.

Yet on the surface he was calm enough by the time they reached the house. He asked Herapath to go in first and tell his father he wished to see him alone, and when he was shown into the study he found the big man there, looking concerned, surprised, but welcoming.

'I am delighted to see you in my house, Captain Aubrey,' he said. 'Pray sit down, and take a glass of port. I do hope and trust that this is not imprudent, in such a fog, with your . . .'

'Mr Herapath, sir,' said Jack, 'I am come to your house, because you are a man I trust and esteem. I am come to ask you a service, and I know that if you cannot do it, if you must decline, you will not blab.'

'You do me honour, sir,' said Herapath, looking at him hard, 'and I am obliged to you for your confidence. Please to name the service: if it is a matter of discounting a bill, even an important bill, set your mind at rest.'

'You are very good, but it is far more than any bill that I could draw.' Herapath looked grave. Jack considered for a moment and said, 'You showed me two fine barques of yours, Mr Herapath, tied up not far from the Asclepia. Now when they were sailing, before this accursed war, I dare say your masters did not care to have all their best hands impressed. I dare say they had their hiding-holes.'

'That may be so,' said Herapath, his head cocked to one side.

'And knowing you, sir, I dare say they were about the best hiding-holes that could be devised.' Herapath smiled. 'Now I will not beat about the bush: I will tell you straight out, my friend Maturin is beset by a gang of Frenchmen who mean to kill him. He is gone to ground at Franchon's hotel, and he cannot stir. I mean to get him out, and with your leave, I mean to hide him in one of your barques.' He saw agreement and relief flood over Herapath's enormous purplish face. 'But that is not all. I must be quite open and candid with you. He has also knocked a couple of them on the head: the others do not know it yet, I am sure, but it cannot be long concealed. He also wishes to take an English lady with him, a cousin of my wife's, to whom he is contracted in marriage, Mrs Villiers.'

'Dr Maturin is to marry Mrs Villiers and take her away with him?' cried Herapath, perfectly aware that if Diana were to vanish Louisa Wogan would take her place; that Louisa was at present in the country with Johnson; and that Johnson would wish to have no part of his Caroline.

'Yes, sir. And what is more, Mr Herapath, what is more, I wish to go with them myself, to try to get them clear in a boat, when tide and weather serve, if you can let me have one: for you will observe, sir, that I have not given my parole. I am not a prisoner on parole. A dory would do. Stephen Maturin is a very learned man, but I would not trust him to cross a horse-pond in any kind of craft whatsoever, and I must go with him. There, sir: I have given you a plain, straight-forward account, and upon my honour I do not believe I have misrepresented anything, nor concealed any risk.'

'I am sure you have not,' said Herapath, walking up and down with his hands behind his back. 'I have a great respect for Doctor Maturin . . . I am amazed at what you tell me . . .'

'Do you wish to consider on it for a while?'

'No, no. I am only slow in answering because I cannot make up my mind which is best of *Orion* or *Arcturus* — the hiding-holes, I mean. A lady and two gentlemen: *Arcturus* it must be — so much more space. I have a fool of a ship-keeper aboard . . . that's of no consequence. But tell me, sir, how do you propose to get him out?'

'I thought of reconnoitring the place — backstairs, stables, servants' quarters and so on, before making any plan. All I know of the position is what your son has told me, and what I learnt from Maturin's brief note. I know that he is in Mrs Villiers's rooms — your son saw him there — but I do not know the nature of the terrain at all.'

'Let us have the boy in,' said Herapath. 'Michael, whereabouts in Franchon's are Mrs Villiers's rooms?'

'They are on the first floor, sir, in front, giving on to the long balcony.'

'The balcony?' said Jack. A light grapnel and a line could answer very well, on balconies. But there were other things to consider first. 'Tell me, did the Frenchmen below seem concerned, agitated, upset? Were they armed, busy with the people of the hotel or with officials?'

'Not at all, sir,' said young Herapath. 'They were laughing and talking as though they were in a café, or a club. As for arms, the officers had their swords, but I saw no others.'

Jack asked him to draw a plan of the hotel: a slow, unsatisfactory performance, as young Herapath had no gift that way, nor any visual memory. From time to time his father, who knew the hotel intimately, added a corridor or a flight of stairs, but after a while he left them to it while he paced up and down or stared out of the window at the fog.

'I have it,' he cried at last, interrupting them. 'I have it. It has come to me. The buck-basket and burnt cork. Doctor Maturin don't weigh above nine stone. Captain Aubrey, my ship-keeper in the *Arcturus* is a black man: let us cork your face and hands, so that you can take his place. I shall send him off to Salem or Marblehead, and no one will notice the odds or think twopence of it if they do. Othello!' he cried. His face was lit up, bright red with excitement and a kind of wild prospective triumph; his eyes, from oyster-like, had grown sparkling and young. Too young perhaps, thought Jack and his son, looking at him with astonishment; too young, and even drunk. Yet not a glass had been poured from the decanter; his hand and step were ready, if not his voice. 'Othello! And you have already smoked my Falstaff, sir, I am sure? Ha, ha, we shall confound the Frenchmen yet, God damn their knavish tricks. I have the greatest respect for Doctor Maturin.'

'I am not wholly with you, sir,' said Jack.

'Why, Falstaff and the buck-basket, don't you recall? They took him out in a buck-basket in the play, though he weighed five times the Doctor. We have just such a basket — huge. Michael, run and ask your aunt where the huge basket is. God love me,' he said, 'I feel like a young man again. We carry him out under their poxed French noses. From her . . . her acquaintance with Mr Johnson, I take it the lady is in no danger? I beg pardon, if I am indiscreet.'

'I believe she can walk in and out just as she pleases,' said Jack. 'At least until Johnson returns; and I understand he is engaged tonight.'

They understood one another, they understood the nature of Johnson's engagement, and they looked oddly false when Michael Herapath came back. The basket could not be touched: it was in the laundry, full of dirty clothes. 'Toss 'em out and bring it here,' said

Mr Herapath. 'No. First tell Abednigo I want the coach — I shall drive myself —and then run down to the *Arcturus* and send Joe to Salem: give him some urgent message to John Quincy, to be taken at once: see him out of the ship and take his set of keys. Tell him to go aboard the *Spica* and stay there till I send for him. There, sir, what do you think of my plan? Plain, simple, straightforward, eh? But then I am a plain man myself, and like things simple and straightforward: much as you do yourself, I believe.'

'A very pretty plan indeed, sir,' said Jack. 'And it has great advantages — a great deal to be said for it. But you will give me leave to alter it on a view of the terrain, if some new point arises. I have some notion that the balcony may serve, and perhaps we should be well advised to take a grapnel and say ten fathoms of stout line.'

'By all means, though I doubt you see your balcony at all, it is coming on so thick: why, now I can barely make out my neighbour Dawson's light from here, though half an hour ago it was quite sharp and clear. The only thing that worries me, is my blacks to carry the basket.'

'Do they have to be black men?'

'No. But it would seem more natural, pass unnoticed.'

'If I were blacked, as you suggest, I would do for one.'

'But your arm, my dear sir, your arm; and your general state of health.'

'My left arm has never been better, and it is certainly strong enough to carry half Maturin. Look.' He gazed about for some heavy object, pitched upon a tall marble stand, and raised it high. 'And yet, sir,' he went on, 'upon reflection, I believe we must first reconnoitre. A cutting-out expedition, without you know the harbour and the tides, is often a sad waste of life. Do by all means send your ship-keeper away, and until your son comes back we can weigh our measures, take counsel, and consider.'

'Very well. Michael, take the little mare.'

The interval was of no great length, and Mr Herapath filled it by drawing a better plan of the hotel, fetching the basket, several corks, some line and a pot-hook that would serve as a grapnel; he loaded a blunderbuss and three horse-pistols, double-charged and double-shotted. He was excited as a boy, and it was clear that he wished to be doing right away: he did not like the notion of a mere reconnaissance, but hoped to carry out the *coup de main,* as he often called it, in a single operation. His mind was much set on his second Negro and at one time Jack thought of the Indian porter. But how far was the man to be relied upon? There would be questions, and many of them, when the dead Frenchmen were discovered; and Jack had no wish for them to be discovered, all three, in the hiding-hole aboard *Arcturus*. Nor did he want Herapath to put his head into a noose. 'There is another small point to be considered,' he said, 'and that is the provision of someone to hold the horses, unless you stay on the box.'

'Oh, as for that,' said Herapath, 'any blackguard boy will do. There are always blackguard boys hanging around the hotel, to hold horses' heads.'

'Yes,' said Jack, 'but will not your blackguard boy recognize Mr Herapath?'

'Oh,' said Mr Herapath. 'Oh. Yes, indeed: I had best stay on the box, muffled up.'

Jack looked at his face: 'I had better not press that point,' he reflected, and he said, 'Might I trouble you for a civilian coat, Mr Herapath? Epaulettes are tolerably conspicuous, even on a foggy night.' He was indeed a conspicuous figure in a post-captain's uniform, complete but for his surrendered sword. 'Perhaps a serving-man's coat, or a frock, might be best: and a common round hat, if you have one at hand.'

'You think of everything,' said Herapath, and he hurried off. His enthusiasm, momentarily damped, blazed up again as he reclothed Jack in a choice of different coats, settling for a worn, sad-coloured gabardine. 'But we shall have to have your hair off, my dear sir, before we turn you into a convincing nigger.' Jack's hair was long and yellow, and he wore it clubbed, tied with a black ribbon between his shoulder-blades. 'I shall fetch scissors. And now I come to think of it, walnut-juice would be far better than burnt cork. You would not object to walnut-juice, Captain Aubrey?'

'Never in life,' said Jack. 'Once we have surveyed the field, and once we have fixed upon our plan, you shall dye me from head to foot, and clip my hair off too, if you wish.'

They fell silent, listening for Michael's return: Herapath fiddled with his buck-basket, blunderbuss, and the cordage, fetched one dark lantern and two plain, and a basket of provisions for the hiding-hole; Jack studied the plan. He did not regret his step — it was the only move open to him — but he did regret old Herapath's zeal. He was by no means sure how the old gentleman would behave when the expedition turned from something like play to earnest, perhaps very bloody earnest; and he much regretted the earliness of the hour. For such an operation the later the time and the fewer people about the better;

and keeping Herapath easy was going to be a task. Nor did he see the necessity for Negroes. The natural carriers were the hotel's men.

'Here he is,' said Herapath, and a moment later his son walked in. 'Is all well, Michael?' he asked.

'Yes, sir. Joe is on his way to Salem in Gooch's cart. And the coach is ready in the yard. I have sent Abednigo to bed.'

'Good boy. Now let us load these things aboard: they can all go into the buck-basket. Take care of the blunderbuss. Make haste, make haste. Now, sir, this way, if you please.'

'First,' said Jack deliberately, 'I will ask you to drive me to the barque. It is a cardinal rule of tactics, to ensure one's line of retreat.' His tone was so convinced, so authoritative, that Mr Herapath made no objection, although he did look a little discontented.

He climbed on to the box; they rolled out of the stable yard; and at once it became apparent to Jack that Mr Herapath was no great coachman. They gave the rounded stone at the corner into the street a long grinding scrape; and the driver's excitement communicating itself to the horses, the coach soon began to bound and rattle over the indifferent paving at such a pace, in spite of the fog, that those inside had to cling on, while Mr Herapath kept up a steady 'Hey now, Roger.

Easy, Bess. Easy, Rob. Hey there!'

They very nearly crushed two drunken soldiers, and they drove one gig fairly on to the sidewalk, but happily there was little other traffic in the streets, and the horses sobered as they neared the harbour. Herapath drove to his usual tavern — or rather the horses took him there — and they walked along the quays to the *Arcturus*, carrying a lantern and the basket of provisions.

'Now, sir,' said Mr Herapath, leading them below, 'I shall show you something that I reckon will surprise you.'

Below, with the smell of tar and cordage and bilgewater, aft to the bread-room and there they stood: the space, now empty, was entirely lined with sheet-metal, tinned, against the rats, and it still smelt of biscuit. Mr Herapath pressed the wooden slats that held these sheets, jerked them, and sounded the panels, all of which gave the same hollow boom. 'Where is it?' he muttered. 'Damn my eyes, I could have sworn . . . seen it a hundred times.'

'I believe it is this one, sir,' said his son, causing a slat to pivot. The metal sheet opened upwards on a hinge, showing a space where four or five hands could lie hidden while the ship was being searched.

'There! Look at that,' cried Mr Herapath.

'I said I should amaze you.'

Both father and son were so pleased that Jack had not the heart to say he had seen the device half a dozen times at least when, as a midshipman or lieutenant, he had been sent aboard merchantmen to press what men he could. But his sinking spirits rose a little when he reflected that it would baffle landlubbers, and that although officers of the Royal Navy might find it easily enough, those of the American navy had no practice in this sort of detection, since they never pressed men at any time, their crews being made up of picked volunteers. Yet on the other hand, many and many an American seaman had been hidden from impressment, either in barrels in the hold, or in places of this kind; and many an American officer had commanded merchantmen.

Mr Herapath showed him the catch inside that released the flap, stowed away the basket, and gave him the spare set of keys. 'Now, sir,' he said, looking at his watch by the light of the lantern. 'Now for our reconnaissance. It is growing late.'

It had grown later still by the time the coach reached the hotel. The first scrape on their setting out had injured the off-side trace, and it parted altogether when Mr Herapath involved the horses with a stationary handbarrow on the way up from the harbour.

The rope they had with them answered well enough, but it was a long, slow task: the ordinary lanterns took to going out, and they had to be relit inside the coach, while the dark lantern shed but a feeble gleam, and the restive horses gave trouble from the beginning to the very end. The accident happened on the corner of Washington Street, and although most of Boston was in bed, at one time a small knot of people gathered to give advice, and two of them addressed Mr Herapath by name.

In the first stages of the repair he was talkative, full of suggestions, eager to be done and off; by the time Jack had whipped and served the trace, with a stout preventer from the swingle aft, he had grown much quieter, though there was a tendency to find fault and take offence; and when at last they drove towards the hotel he was almost mute.

Jack knew the symptoms well: he had seen them often enough during the long pull towards a hostile shore, before the batteries opened fire. Young Herapath, on the other hand, was calm, steady, apparently unmoved: he bore his father's reproaches with admirable patience.

It was late; too late for any blackguard boys to hold the horses' heads. So late that there was little sign of life in the hotel, apart from singing in the bar: *Marlbrouk s'en va-t-en guerre, mironton mironton mirontaine* . . . and lights in the hall.

Jack lowered the glass and stared intently at the façade. A north-west breeze had sprung up while they were mending the trace and although the fog was still quite thick, between the drifting swathes he saw the lines of balcony across the front of the hotel. The coach came to a stop, not quite outside the door, but a little lower down the street. Jack stepped out, and said to Michael Herapath, 'You go in. See how the land lies, tell them we are here, and report back. You are all right, Herapath, are you not?'

'Yes, sir,' said young Herapath.

He went back along the sidewalk and into the hotel; and as the door opened light came out into the wispy fog and the singing grew louder: *Marlbrouk ne revient plus.*

Jack walked along by the horses — the offside leader was particularly restless and troublesome: the whole team seemed apprehensive and nervous and a cat crossing the street with a kitten in her mouth set them all capering — and from there he studied the hotel. His eye at once caught the workmen's pulley and its dangling rope: great possibilities there. Two men walked by and he busied himself with the trace as they glanced at the coach:

Mr Herapath plucked his coat collar round his face and pulled his hat still further down. A third, walking briskly, muttering to himself. Mr Evans of the *Constitution* and a colleague, deep in conversation. One black woman with a large flat covered basket on her head.

Mr Herapath found his tongue again, and talking half to himself, half to Jack as he stood near the step of the box, he kept up a continuous low stream of words: 'How long he is . . . I could have done it in half the time . . . always the same, dilly-dally, dilly-dally . . . we should have started far earlier, as I said . . . hush, there is a man crossing the street . . . I am not as young as I was, Captain Aubrey . . . these things are all very well for young men . . . how long he is, the God-damned fool of a boy . . . ain't it cold? My feet are like blocks of ice . . . you know, Captain Aubrey, I am a prominent citizen, a member of the town-meeting; anyone may recognize me . . . that was Reverend Chorley . . . it would be much wiser for me to sit inside the coach, if you will come up on the box.'

'So I will,' said Jack. 'But first I shall just step along to the corner, to see what the angle gives.' His mind was running fast and clear; that singing indoors did not speak of any state of siege, nor of an ambush; the balcony might prove a gift of God, even with his injured arm

— it was swelling most unpleasantly, and it had little strength, but still it would get him up. He had that fine contained feeling of going into action, heart beating high but well in hand, and the freshening breeze on his cheek as he stared up at Diana's shuttered window strengthened the impression: yet he kept his fingers crossed.

Behind the shutter, sitting by a pair of candles burnt almost to the sockets as Stephen read in Johnson's book, they heard a knock.

'Oh my God, it's Johnson,' whispered Diana.

The knock again, and she called out in a high sharp voice, 'What is it?'

'Mr Michael asks if Mrs Villiers can receive him,' said the ancient voice of the hotel porter, almost the only person still on duty.

'Yes, yes. Ask him to come up.'

Minutes, the minutes drew out, unnaturally long, and at last he was there. 'I am sorry to have been so long,' he said. 'I stood to watch the last French officers leave. They are just by the door, arguing and laughing: one at least is drunk. In a few minutes we may go. Captain Aubrey and my father are below, with the coach. I will go on to the landing, see them out, and tell you.'

'We shall be ready,' said Stephen, springing up. 'Diana, pack some clothes.' He hurried back to Johnson's room, made a quick, accurate selection of papers — by the wavering light of his candle Dubreuil's waxy face, white in the open privy door, seemed to move, losing the awful gravity of death — returned and sat with them on his knee, a heavy pile.

'Stephen,' whispered Diana, 'you said my diamonds were in Johnson's desk. Is it open, then?'

'It is. But do not go in there, Diana: you would see a very ugly sight.'

'Bah,' she said, 'I do not give a damn. They are mine. I have earnt them.'

She came back, carrying the jewel-case, and her footsteps left a diminishing trail of blood. 'I mean,' she said, 'by receiving his horrible political guests, and translating . . .'

He looked down. The Diana he had known could never have said the first words; or having by some impossibility said them, she would never, never have produced the explanation. She was obscurely aware of this: she said, 'I did not know you had anything to do with spying, Maturin.'

'No more I have,' he replied. 'But I know the army intelligence officer in Halifax, and these papers may be useful to him.'

Herapath put his head through the door. 'They are going out,' he said. 'They are in the outer lobby. Let us walk down.' He took Diana's small trunk and they went slowly down the stairs into the empty hall. The old porter was moving away from them, putting out the lights in the bar.

At the same time the Frenchmen, moved by some freak, burst out into the street with a concerted whoop, waving their hats. The coach instantly surged into motion; it was already going fast by the time it passed Jack on the corner. The Frenchmen hallooed, running past him after the coach for a little way, and then, still calling out and laughing, they faded into the fog. The horses could be heard breaking from a trot to a gallop.

Jack turned, saw his friends come out and stand, an uncertain group, looking right and left. He joined them as the light went out in the hall, and leading them round the corner he said, 'The horses bolted. Are there any Frenchmen left?'

'No, sir,' said Herapath.

'Cousin Diana, your servant. Stephen, how are you? Not hurt? Give me your bundle. Herapath, I am most uncommon obliged to you; by God, I am. Can you show us the way down to the harbour?'

'The quietest way is by this lane,' said Herapath. 'It leads by my house. Will you step in, and rest, or take some — some refreshment?'

'No, I thank you,' said Jack. 'The sooner aboard the better. But we must not hurry. We must walk naturally.'

Their steps echoed in the empty streets, and as they went the moon came through, faint at first and then quite clear as the fog fled with the breeze, until she showed most of the time, gibbous, hunched, sailing away northwest among the higher clouds and shedding her spectral light. A few cats, a sleeping hog, and from the back of Herapath's low and squalid house the fretful crying of a child.

'That is Caroline,' he said. He went in; the crying stopped; some time later he came out with a lantern, and by its light Stephen inspected Jack's wounded arm, bound it up and slung it with his neckcloth, taking the books and papers from him without a word.

In five minutes they were on the deserted moonlit quay, walking along by the ships, which creaked and groaned as they rocked on the rising tide. Herapath led them aboard the *Arcturus*, below, and to the bread-room. He opened the metal flap, and after a slight hesitation Diana climbed in, followed by Stephen: neither had said more than a few words since leaving the hotel and indeed the tension had mounted steadily from that point onwards.

'There is a basket in there, behind you,'

said Herapath, still speaking very quietly. 'I will bring you some more food tomorrow.'

Diana spoke up, and spoke handsomely: she thanked Mr Herapath extremely, more than she could say, for this evening; she could not tell him how she admired his coolness. She begged he would kiss that dear child Caroline for her, and she hoped she might see him again after he had had a good night's rest — no man had ever earnt it better. And if it should cross his mind to bring a little milk, she would be so very grateful.

Jack walked with him to the break of the quarterdeck, glanced at the sky, and said, 'Herapath, you have done nobly by us. Nobly, upon my honour. But we are not entirely out of the wood. There will be the devil's own hue and cry tomorrow, and I am not quite happy about your father. Do not suppose that I mean to make the least reflection upon him: after such kindness that would be a sad, shabby thing to do — base — contemptible. But he is an old gentleman: older than I had thought . And if they start to question him, what with the shock of tonight, and the horses bolting, he might be led — you understand me?'

'Yes, sir.'

'Now we spoke of a boat, your father and I — I think it was before you came in — so that when time and tide allowed I could get the Doctor and Mrs Villiers clear away. But now it seems to me that this is the time; and the tide will suit the moment it has reached the full. On the other hand, your father is out of the way at this moment; and tomorrow may be too late. Can you find me one?'

'There is Joe's boat alongside, sir. But it is only an old sawn-down scow he goes fishing in; it would never face the open sea, nor even a blow in the harbour. You could never reach Halifax in it, I am sure.'

'Grant reached the Cape in the cutter. But I hope I shall not have to go so far. May we have a look at it?'

Herapath crossed the deck to the starboard rail, found a rope and pulled: an ugly, slab-sided craft appeared from the gloom and ran alongside into the moonlight. A shrouded object lay fore and aft, and three cans gleamed in the moon like eyes. 'That must be his mast and sail,' said Herapath, 'and those are his bait-pots. I can smell them from here.'

Jack looked long and hard. 'At high water,' he said, 'I shall go into her and run out on the ebb. Will you not come with us, Herapath? I will rate you midshipman in any ship I command, and you could be the Doctor's assistant again. Things might be unpleasant for you in Boston.'

'Oh no, sir,' said Herapath. 'That would never do: though I am obliged to you for your care of me. I have ties here . . . and then, you know, we are enemies.'

'By God, so we are. I had forgot. I find it difficult to think of you as an enemy, Herapath.'

'Shall I give you a hand, stepping the mast, sir? It would be awkward, with your arm.'

The mast was stepped, young Herapath was gone. Jack stood there leaning on the rail, looking at the boat and out at the moonlit harbour, the vague looming of the islands and the powerful batteries. The tide flowed, perpetually mounting, the fenders strained and squeaked, and by imperceptible degrees the *Arcturus*'s deck rose above the level of the quay. He kept a continual watch on the shifting currents, the swing of the small-craft and their buoys, the changing sky — the seaman was all alive — and all the time his ear was stretched, however illogically at this hour, for some clamour in the town, parties hurrying along the waterfront, searching the ships. He also weighed a number of alternative courses of action if the breeze and his forecasts should fail. And beneath all this his mind strayed far away: to England and Sophie of course, but also to *Acasta*, his promised command, and the possibility of a meeting that might set the balance more nearly right, and lift the black depression that had been with him ever since his first hour in the *Java*. *Guerrière*, *Macedonian*, and *Java*; it was more than a man could bear.

Before this Stephen had called him a deeply superstitious man. Perhaps he was: he certainly had a strong belief in luck, as shown by various portents, some of them trivial enough, such as the presence of the star Arcturus overhead, and by a feeling, impossible to define, though a particularly steady confidence formed part of it, that told him when the tide was in his favour. He felt it now, and although from a primitive piety he dared not let the words form even in the remotest corner of his mind, he thought he should succeed.

On the other hand, he felt there was bad luck with Diana, bad luck hanging about Diana. He did not wish to be below with her. She was unlucky; she brought bad luck. Although he was deeply grateful to her and although he liked the way she had borne up so far — no mincing, no vapours, no complaints — for himself he wished her away. For Stephen he could not tell. He had seen him so tormented by her and for her these last years, that he could no longer tell. Perhaps it was right that he should have her at last. In the dead silence of the middle watch, the graveyard watch, he believed he could just make out their voices, far below.

But the long silence was coming to an end. The first Monday-morning wagons rumbled somewhere in the town, not a great way off, and far to the right he heard carts. The tide was very near the full; the flow had been diminishing this last half hour, and the small-craft — there were a great many of them, pleasure-boats, fishing-boats, and some yachts — no longer strained at their buoys. The moon was only a handsbreadth from her setting.

'Joe,' came a voice from the darkness under the *Arcturus*'s stern. 'Joe. Are youse a-going out?'

'I ain't Joe,' said Jack.

'Who are you, then?' asked the boat, now visible.

'Jack.'

'Where's Joe?'

'Gone to Salem.'

'Are youse a-going out, Jack?'

'Maybe.'

'You got any bait, Jack?'

'No.'

'Well, fuck you, Jack.'

'And fuck you too, mate,' said Jack mildly. He watched the boat scull clear, hoist its sail, quietly swearing, and glide away on the slack water. Then he went below, groping along aft to the bread-room. He saw light showing through the joints in the hinged sheet, tapped, and heard Diana's low voice, 'Who is it?'

'Jack,' he said, and the flap opened, showing Diana by the shielded lantern, with a pistol in her lap. The atmosphere was stifling, and the flame quite low. She put her finger to her lips and said, 'Hush. He has eaten everything in the basket, and now he is fast asleep. He had had nothing all day. Can you imagine that?'

Some part of Jack's mind had also dwelt on breakfast, since his stomach had been calling out for some time, and he was conscious of a piercing disappointment. 'Well, he must wake up now. We are going into the boat: the tide is on the turn.'

They tweaked and pulled him into a state of wakefulness and led him on deck, clutching his bundle.

For a vessel of her size, the *Arcturus* had no great plank-sheer, but even so the dim boat was a long way down. 'Must we change ships?' he asked.

'I believe we must,' said Jack.

'Would it not be better to wait for the tide to rise and float the boat a little higher, a little nearer to the deck?'

'Their relative positions would remain the same, I do assure you. Besides, the tide is already at the full. Come, Stephen, you have often jumped down into a boat deeper than that.'

'I am thinking of Diana.'

'Oh, Diana — she will skip down like a good 'un. You give her a hand over the side and I will receive her in the boat. Diana, where is your chest? Stephen, clap on to this line, and lower away handsomely when I give the word.' He swung over the rail, dropped to the mainchains, and with his left hand grasping a dead-eye he lowered himself into the boat. 'Lower away,' he called, and the little trunk came down. 'Now, Diana.' He guided her feet on to the chain-wale. 'Mind your petticoats and jump.'

'Damn my petticoats,' said Diana, and jumped. He received her full-pitch with his good arm. 'No one could call you a light woman, Diana,' he said, setting her down among the bait-pots and the pervading reek of decaying squid, and then blushed in the darkness. 'Come on, Stephen,' he called. There were wagons moving along the quay, and several lanterns, voices out on the harbour, bobbing lights.

'Jack, have you a piece of string in your pocket? I cannot climb down without doing up my parcel.'

'Poor lamb,' whispered Diana, 'he is still

half asleep.' She sprang up the side like a boy, took off her shawl, wrapped the papers in it, tied the corners, and tossed it into the boat.

'We shall get off some time, I suppose,' said Jack, more or less to himself, shipping the rudder. And when at last they were down, 'Diana, stow yourself right forward and do not get in the way. Stephen, there are the row-locks: pull right ahead. Give way.' He shoved off; the *Arcturus*'s side receded; Stephen made several effectual strokes.

'Boat your oars,' said Jack. 'Clap on to the halliard — no, the halliard. God's death — haul away. Bear a hand, Stephen. Belay. Catch a couple of turns round the kevel — the kevel.'

The scow gave a violent lurch. Jack dropped all, scrambled forward, caught two turns round the kevel and slid back to the tiller. The sail filled, he brought the wind a little abaft the beam, and the scow headed out to sea.

'You are cursed snappish tonight, Jack,' said Stephen. 'How do you expect me to understand your altumal cant, without pondering on it? I do not expect you to understand medical jargon, without giving you time to consider the etymology, for all love.'

'Not to know the odds between a halliard and a sheet, after all these years at sea: it passes human understanding,' said Jack.

'You are a reasonably civil, complaisant creature on dry land,' said Stephen, 'but the moment you are afloat you become pragmatical and absolute, a bashaw — do this, do that, gluppit the prawling strangles, there — no longer a social being at all. It is no doubt the effect of the long-continued habit of command; but it cannot be considered amiable.'

Diana said nothing: she had a considerable experience and she knew that if men were to be at all tolerable they must be fed. She was also feeling the first premonitory qualms of seasickness — she was a very bad sailor — and she dreaded what was to come.

The cut-down scow looked an awkward lump of a boat, but in point of fact, once Jack had grown used to its ways, he found that it behaved quite well, apart from its obstinate griping and its quite extraordinary leeway: its bottom was perfectly flat, and it skidded sideways from the wind almost as fast and far as it travelled forward. There was plenty of sea-room, however, and as he had no need to fear shoal water in a craft that did not draw six inches he set its head for Point Shirley in order to weather the long island.

They were not alone in the vast outer harbour: several other fishing-boats had put out, and now away to starboard, in the deep-water channel, lay the *Chesapeake* herself just looming into view. There were lights in her cabin — Lawrence was already up — and as Jack gazed the morning watch was called. More lights appeared in every scuttle and open half-port all along the berth-deck, and over a mile of water he could hear the voices of the bosun's mates, all the familiar din, so very like the ships he had served in.

Indeed the silence of the night was fading fast. Overhead the faint gulls were calling, and at the bottom of the bay Boston was waking up — lights showing the shape of the waterfront, when he glanced astern. But they would not be needed long: Saturn had set, following the moon to rise in Tartary, and already there was a lightening in the east.

On and on, steadily on, away from the land, the water rippling along the side, the sheet alive in his hand, the tiller under the crook of his knee. The breeze was nothing much, but with the help of the powerful ebb they were making four knots or five with relation to the shore; and now he could feel the beginning of the true ocean, the heave of the open sea, though much attenuated here by reason of the long island.

'What's amiss?' he asked suddenly.

'Diana is sick,' said Stephen.

'Well, well: poor soul. Let her lean out the leeward side.'

The lightness ahead increased and the long island was no longer a blur but a sharply-outlined black mass, well within gunshot. Diana had collapsed in the bottom of the boat. 'It will have to be worse before it gets better,' he reflected, glancing at her with a dispassionate eye. A string of gulls passed overhead, uttering their usual coarse cynical laughter; droppings fell aboard; and so they ran.

The breeze was drawing ahead: at this rate of leeway he would probably have to tack to clear the point. And as it drew ahead, so it slackened: the rising sun might swallow it entirely.

There was no breeze to be wasted. 'Lose not a minute,' he said: and tacking must lose many. Peering under the sail, he watched the island shore coming closer, quite clear now, with people walking about on it and white water off the point. Closer and closer still: he let fly the sheet and grasped an oar, trusting to the strong tide-run to carry them round. A couple of bumps, a rock fended off, and it had done so. A man called out to them from the island. Jack waved, hauled in the sheet, and now they met the swell, setting from the south-east and cutting up against the ebb. At once the scow began a lumbering dance, and a renewed sound of dry retching came from the bows.

'Put my coat over her,' said Jack, taking it off — an easy task with his arm slung outside. Stephen had already covered her with his, but she shivered still, gritting her teeth and clenching her fists, shivered convulsively.

Now there was Lovell's Island ahead, a cluster of fishing-boats, blue sky beyond, and brilliant rays shooting up into it from the east: and now the blazing rim of the sun himself, bearable for a moment, and then too powerful by far. The breeze, grown fitful and capricious, suddenly backed right aft, a stronger gust that thrust the scow's head into a rising wave. Diana was soaked: she neither moved nor groaned, flat in the bows.

'Bail with the bait-pots,' said Jack. 'That is Lovell's Island there ahead. I believe we shall weather it.'

'Aye? Very well. There is a glutinous substance in these pots: I see the head of a decapod.'

'Toss it out,' said Jack, 'and bail.'

'Those, I presume,' said Stephen, nodding towards the small-craft ahead as he bailed, 'are fishing-boats that set out before us. But what is that?'

Over the shining sea, from the south end of the long island, came a cutter, pulling double-banked, pulling hard and fast into the eye of the wind. Its course would intercept the scow's very soon indeed, the way those men were stretching out.

'Could you go a little faster, do you think?' asked Stephen.

Jack shook his head, stepped forward, and slowly lowered down the sail . The cutter was racing towards them: the men were armed — shoulder-belts, cutlasses, tomahawks and pistols — and in the stern-sheets an officer bent urgently towards them, bawling, 'Stretch out, stretch out.'

The coxswain at his side half rose and roared, 'Make a lane, there.' The small-craft scattered; the cutter dashed through them, turned left-handed in a long curve that took it past the northern point of the big island, and so vanished, still at a racing speed.

'That was Lawrence exercising his boarders,' observed Jack as he hoisted the sail again. 'He is a taut skipper, all right.' He found his heart beating double-time, and he said, 'They will be back aboard the *Chesapeake* in twenty minutes at this rate, in spite of the tide. How is Diana?'

'There is a certain degree of prostration, benign prostration.'

They looked at her: green, hair draggling over her clammy face, eyes closed, mouth clenched tight, a look of mingled death and stubborn resistance. Stephen wiped her cheek. Jack said, 'I shall favour the boat. You might move the bait-pots and that old sack under her head: perhaps she don't like the smell.'

He took the scow wide of Lovell's Island, south about, to ease the motion: south about, with the battery under his lee, through the channel, and there, as he cleared the southern tip, he saw what his soul had longed to see: topgallantsails and topsails beyond the northernmost of the Brewster islands, a ship standing in from the Graves.

Without his telescope he could not swear she was the *Shannon* yet, and he said nothing; but in his heart he had a beautiful calm certainty.

'You seem pleased, brother?' said Stephen, after a while, looking from the green-yellow to the red and beaming face.

'Yes, I am, to be candid with you,' said Jack, 'and so will you be, I believe. Do you see that ship, just clear of the northern island now?'

'I do not.'

'The northern island — the further island, the one on the left. Hull up, for God's sake.'

'Ah, I perceive it now. And for what my opinion is worth, I should say it looks quite like a man-of-war. There is a neatness, a certain air, that we associate with a man-of-war.'

Abandoning all opportunity for wit, Jack laughed aloud and said, 'That is *Shannon*, standing in for her morning look at the *Chesapeake*, ha, ha, ha!'

The *Shannon* stood on, stemming the tide; the scow, as close-hauled as it would lie, steered to cross her bows. Two miles had separated them at first: with their combined rates of sailing this distance lessened to half a mile in ten minutes, and Jack saw that he could not fetch her on this tack — the scow's leeway was too great — and that going about would leave him in her wake. 'Did I speak too soon?' he thought, and standing up he hailed as he had rarely hailed before. 'The ship ahoy. *Shannon* ahoy.'

A moment of the most intense anxiety, and he saw the frigate back her foretopsail: the way came off her just enough to let the scow run alongside. The awkward boat gave her a shrewd thump amidships, and from the deck above a thundering voice, a familiar voice, cried, 'Mind the paintwork, God damn your eyes. Mind the paintwork — fend off. I've a mind to put a round-shot through your bottom.' Then, in a milder tone, 'Well, Jonathan, have you any lobsters aboard? Paul, pass him a line.'

With the line firm in his hand and ease flooding through his heart, Jack could be facetious now. 'I must ask you to moderate your language, sir; we have a lady in the boat. Pray tell Captain Broke that I should like a word with him. And take your hands out of your pockets when you speak to me, Mr Falkiner.'

Blank consternation on the broad honest weather-beaten face above, the dawn of wrath, shocked silence, fore and aft, then a huge grin, and Falkiner cried, 'By — dear me, 'tis Captain Aubrey. I beg your pardon, sir. I will jump to the cabin directly. Will you come aboard, sir?'

Running feet on deck, orders, urgent cries, the rumble of Marines' boots, side-boys running down with baize-covered ropes, and Jack, poised on the roll, stepped across the gap and came up the side, piped aboard in style. The Marines presented arms, Jack took off his hat, and there was Broke, napkin in hand, egg dribbling down his chin. 'Why, Jack!' he cried. 'How glad I am to see you. How come you here? How do you do — your arm?'

'Philip,' said Jack, 'how d'ye do? I came in this boat, I do assure you. Might I beg for a bosun's chair? We have a lady aboard, somewhat indisposed, Sophie's cousin Diana Villiers. And perhaps my surgeon might use it too: he is a prodigious doctor, but no great seaman.'

Diana was hoisted up, limp, past caring, a

dripping dead rat, a dripping dead female rat, and carried into the absent master's cabin. Stephen came up after her and, bending low to his ear as he struggled out of the bosun's chair, Jack murmured, 'I can say it now: we have escaped — give you joy of your freedom, brother.' He then presented him, 'Doctor Maturin, my particular friend — Captain Broke. I say, Philip, you don't happen to be breakfasting, do you? Poor Maturin here is fairly clemmed, quite wasting away and fractious for want of food.'

It was extraordinary how naval routine took them in once more: they had not been aboard a few hours before they were entirely at home — they might have been in the *Shannon* these last weeks or even months, with all the familiar smells and sounds around them, and the familiar motion, unusually pronounced today. Not only had they several former shipmates before the mast, in the gunroom, and in the cabin, but almost every detail of the *Shannon*'s closely ordered life was the same as it had been in their other ships; and when the drum beat Roast Beef of Old England for the officers' dinner Stephen found that he salivated, in spite of his late and copious breakfast. Boston might have been a thousand miles away, but for the fact that it could still be seen, down there at the bottom of its great bay, as the frigate stood out to sea again, her morning's inspection done, to resume her long blockade.

She was nothing much to look at, just an ordinary thirty-eight-gun eighteen-pounder frigate of about a thousand tons that had been shabbily treated by the dockyard in the article of paint and that had been on the North American station for close on two years in all weathers, most of them unpleasant, with ice forming thick on the yards, rigging, and deck, playing Old Harry with what very little she possessed in the way of ornament or ginger-bread work or graces. But she was a happy ship: her people had been together, with few changes for a man-of-war, ever since Broke commissioned her; they were thoroughly used to one another, to their officers, and to their work; and they worked well, a willing, efficient crew of seamen.

Yet this happiness, at least as far as the gun-room was concerned, was overlaid by a heavy consciousness of defeat, a feeling that with the capture of three Royal Navy frigates in succession the service had fallen far, far below itself, and a most eager restless desire to avenge *Guerrière*, *Macedonia*, and *Java*. Stephen became aware of this when Watt, the first lieutenant, led him into the gunroom. Several officers were already there, and they made him very welcome. But once the introductions and the ordinary civilities were over he might have been in the *Java* again; the atmosphere was much the same — indeed, the officers were even more concerned about the American war. It was even more immediate to them, far more immediate, and they had been on the verge of action ever since it had been declared. From service gossip and the proceedings of the court-martial that acquitted Chads and the surviving officers of the *Java* they knew far more about the battle with the *Constitution* than did Stephen, but there were gaps in their knowledge and they plied him with questions: had the Americans used bar-shot? What effect did it have? Were there in fact many British deserters in the *Constitution*? At what range did she open fire? What did Dr Maturin think of their standard of gunnery? Did her round-shot break to pieces on impact? Was it true that the Americans used sheet-lead for their cartridges?

'Gentlemen,' said he, 'I was below throughout the battle. I regret my ignorance, but —'

'But surely,' said Mr Jack, the *Shannon*'s surgeon, 'surely you must have heard when the vangs parted? Surely some casualty must have spoken to you of the vangs?'

'The Captain's compliments to Doctor Maturin,' said a tall master's mate, hurrying in, 'and he begs the pleasure of his company at dinner.'

'Mr Cosnahan,' said Stephen, shaking his hand, 'I am delighted to see you again, evidently healthy, apparently sober. My compliments to Captain Broke, and I shall be happy to wait upon him.'

The higher the rank, the later the dinner. Cosnahan was already greasy from his pudding in the midshipmen's berth before the gunroom had sat down to their boiled cod, and the cabin's meal was still no more than a remote, though not unpleasing, smell in the galley: Stephen had salivated in vain. He quietly slipped a biscuit from the bread-barge into his pocket and returned to Diana.

She was more prostrate than ever, now that the *Shannon* was out in her natural habitat, the full Atlantic swell: a cold, glaucous, apathetic figure, racked from time to time by a spasm but otherwise mute and apparently insensible. He had already undressed and sponged her, and there was nothing more that his art could do, apart from warm blankets. He tidied her a little, gazed thoughtfully a while, gnawing on his biscuit, and then went below to the cabin that his old shipmate Falkiner had vacated for him. He checked his papers, now wrapped in sailcloth, and re-membering that he had spoken a little sharply in the night, he did what he could to make himself presentable, to do Jack credit in the cabin: clean and trimmed at last, he sat on Falkiner's cot, his newly-acquired watch in his hand, reflecting on Diana.

He had so very much to reflect upon, so very many aspects of a complex relationship, as well as marriage itself, that unknown state, that his thoughts had not run far beyond a long digression on the singular effects, physical and spiritual, of pregnancy, sometimes admirable, sometimes disastrous, before the elegant hands of the watch and a minute chime within told him that it was time to go. His night's sleep, short though it was, had been extraordinarily profound and restorative: his head still ached, he still found it hard to focus his eyes well enough to read, and his cracked ribs hurt abominably on the least false movement, but he was his own master for immediate purposes; he no longer had to struggle with a vacillating, uncertain, exhausted mind, incapable of decision; and although he could not see clearly as far as Diana was concerned, he was able to thrust his grief and sense of bereavement to one side.

On the way he met Cosnahan again, sent to fetch him, for Captain Aubrey placed no reliance on his surgeon's punctuality; but blameless for once and even commendable, he walked in with quiet triumph.

It was a good dinner — oysters, halibut, lobster, turkey-poult, and a massive roly-poly that gave the sailors at least a good deal of unaffected pleasure — and since most of the talk ran on nautical affairs Stephen had plenty of time to consider Captain Broke. He liked what he saw: a slight, dark man, reserved, quiet, grave, and even melancholy, not half Jack's weight but of much the same size in natural authority and determination. They were obviously close friends and at first glance this seemed paradoxical, their styles being so very different, the extremes of what was to be found in the service, as different as the centuries, Jack belonging more to the heartier, more flamboyant, hard-drinking eighteenth, Broke in the more discreet modern age that was spreading so fast, even in the conservative Navy. Yet they were both sailors, and on this plane they were as one; their ideas and their aims were both the same. Jack Aubrey was a fighting captain, made for the sea and violent action; so, in his different way, was Broke, and perhaps his sense of the Royal Navy's defeat was even stronger, if that were possible. He was a man of strong feelings, and although they rarely appeared the occasional gleam left

Stephen in no doubt. This was particularly apparent when he and Jack talked about the *Chesapeake*, now the sole object of the *Shannon*'s long blockade, the sole object of Broke's ambition and passionate desire. They had gone over every detail of her equipment before Stephen joined them, and Jack had been able to tell a great deal, from the exact nature of her carronades to a very close estimate of her crew, which he set at a little under four hundred. And now, when they discussed her commander Jack said, 'Lawrence is a very fine fellow, and I am sure that if his orders do not compel him to sit still, he will give you a meeting with all the pleasure in the world.'

'Oh how I hope so,' cried Broke with a fine flash. 'I have been waiting for him day after day, with our water running low — half allowance this last week, although I took all *Tenedos* could spare before sending her off — and the idea of being forced off the station, letting him out or leaving him to Parker, fairly tormented me. I sent in messages by various prisoners I discharged, inviting him to come out; but I dare say they never reached him. I was afraid he might be shy, or that he might share the feelings of so many people in New England.'

'Lawrence shy? Never in life,' said Jack emphatically.

'Well, I am heartily glad of it,' said Broke,

and he went on to speak of the feeling in Boston, as far as he had been able to learn it. He had frequently been in touch with the shore and he had gathered a good deal of information, some of which confirmed what Stephen knew while some went well beyond it. 'The Federalist party certainly wish *any event* which would tend to restore peace,' he observed, 'and that I had from an intelligent person. But just how my man would define *any event* is a question. It is all very well to subscribe to a general dislike of the war and to give general information on the state of public opinion; but when it comes to specific details that might bring about a defeat, why then, I suppose, one must reflect that it is one's own country that is concerned, however ill-governed it may be. Now I know they have a steam-vessel, armed with six nine-pounders: but when it came to information on that head — her power, her speed, her range of action, the possibility of cutting her off with the boats — my man grew shy. When you were on shore, Doctor Maturin, were you able to make any remarks on this steam-boat of theirs?'

Alas, Dr Maturin had had no notion of such a vessel: had she indeed a steam-engine mounted in her? What was her means of propulsion?

'The engine drives great wheels on either side, sir, like those of a water-mill,' said Broke. 'A precious awkward thing to meet with in a calm or in a narrow tideway, since she can sail, not only against wind and tide, but without any wind at all.'

'With one long twenty-four-pounder in the bows, such a machine could cut you up quite shockingly,' said Jack. 'I mean, in light airs or a calm.'

The conversation ran on paddle-wheels — on the jet-propulsion advocated by Benjamin Franklin — on the steamer that Broke had seen on a Scotch canal during the peace — those in service upon the Hudson River — their probable value in war — their short range likely to be improved — the dangers of fire — Admiral Sawyer's fury at the suggestion that one might be used in Halifax harbour for towing — the probability that sailors should soon have to turn into vile mechanics, in spite of the Admiralty's steady hatred of such a disgraceful innovation — the shortcomings of the Admiralty in general.

Captain Broke was a well-bred man and he often tried to make the conversation general, but with little success: Stephen was usually quiet at meals, given to long fits of abstraction: now he was quieter still, not only from his ignorance of nautical affairs but also because sleep kept welling up and threatening to extinguish him entirely. His night, though restorative, had been short; its effects were wearing off; and he longed for the swinging cot below.

Jerking himself from an incipient doze over his pudding, he became aware that Captain Aubrey was about to sing. Jack was the least self-conscious being in the world, and he would sing as naturally as he sneezed. 'I heard it in the Boston mad-house,' he said, emptying his glass. 'This is how it goes.' He leant back in his chair, and his deep, melodious voice filled the cabin:

'Oh, oh, the mourning dove
Says, where can she be?
She was my only love
But gone from me, oh gone from me.'

'Well sung, Jack,' said Broke, and turning to Stephen with his rare smile, 'He reminds me of that tuneful Lesbian

*qui ferox bello tamen inter arma
sive iactatam religarat udo
litore navim.*'

'To be sure, sir,' said Stephen, 'and as far as Bacchus and Venus are concerned, and even at a push the Muses, what could be more apt? Yet as I recall it goes on

> *et Lycum nigris oculis nigroque*
> *crine decorum*

and although I may well be mistaken, it does not seem to me that the black-haired boy quite suits, in a description of Captain Aubrey's tastes.'

'Very true, sir, very true,' said Broke, put out and disconcerted. 'I was forgetting . . . There are many objectionable passages in the ancients that are best forgotten.'

'Ha, ha,' said Jack, 'I knew it would never answer, chopping Latin with the Doctor. I have known him knock a full admiral on the head before this, with his ablative absolute.'

Broke gave a conventional laugh, but it was clear that he was unused to contradiction, that he did not possess his cousin's acute sense of humour, and that he disliked anything remotely approaching to bawdy; he was a graver, more earnest man altogether, and he returned to small-arms and great guns with all the earnestness and gravity the moral subject deserved. He described the exercises he had worked out for the frigate, and which the *Shannon*'s people had performed regularly for the last five years and more: Monday, seamen at target; Tuesday, swivelmen at target; Wednesday, swivels in maintop and all Marines at musketry; Thursday, midshipmen at target and carronades . . .

'Lord, Philip, that must stand you in a pretty penny,' said Jack, thinking of the tons of powder at eight guineas a barrel billowing away in smoke, half a hundredweight for every one of *Shannon*'s broadsides; to say nothing of the shot.

'Yes. Last year I sold the meadows over towards the vicarage, where we used to play cricket with the parson's boys, you remember.'

'No luck with prizes?'

'Oh, we have taken a fair number, at least a score this cruise; but I nearly always burn them. I did send in a couple of recaptures the other day, though it cost me a midshipman, a quartermaster, and two prime hands. But that was only because they belonged to Halifax. Otherwise I prefer to burn them.'

'That's heroic,' said Jack, deeply impressed, 'but don't it vex your people?'

'In ordinary times it would scarcely answer: but it is different now. After *Guerrière* I called them aft and told them that if we were to send prizes into Halifax we should have to man them and thus weaken the ship — we should have less chance of getting our own back if we met one of their heavy frigates. They are reasonable men; they know we are so short of ships on this station there is little likelihood of recovering our prize-hands before we put in ourselves; and they want their own back as much as I do. They agreed: no murmuring, no sullen looks, oh very far from it. They know I lose twenty times as much.'

Jack nodded: it was a most striking instance of abnegation. 'Well,' he said, 'and so you exercise your midshipmen separately? That is a very good idea: they cannot learn the men their duty, unless they can do it better themselves. A very good idea.'

'So it should be, Jack — I had it from you many years ago. You shall see them practising what you preached this very afternoon. Perhaps, sir,' — to Stephen — 'you would like to see them too, and to view the ship? I have made some changes in the gun-sights that might interest a philosophical mind.'

Swallowing a yawn, Stephen said that he should be very happy, and presently they walked out, up the ladder and on to the sunlit quarterdeck. The officers upon it at once moved over to the leeward side and Broke began the tour with a brass six-pounder in a port by the hances specially made for it. 'This is my own,' he said, 'and I use it mostly for the youngsters and the ship's boys; they can rattle it in and out without destroying themselves, and they can point it pretty well too, by now. And here you have my earlier quarter-sight . . .'

'But what is this?' asked Jack.

'A pendulum,' said Broke. 'A heavy pendulum. When it is at zero on this scale, do you see, the deck is horizontal, and at point-blank range a gun will hit its mark even if the captain cannot see it for the smoke. And behind each gun there is a compass cut into the deck, so that it can be trained round on a given bearing if the men are blinded — you know how the smoke lies when there is no great breeze, and what there is stunned by a heavy cannonade.'

Jack nodded, observing that in such cases 'you could hardly see your neighbour, let alone the enemy.'

Then came the carronades, ugly, squat, big-mouthed things, and the stern-chasers, long, elegant, and dangerous: a closely-reasoned discussion of the best breechings for carronades, the best way to prevent them from oversetting, and so forward along the gangway to the forecastle and its armament, more carronades and the bow-chasers. 'Here is my favourite,' said Broke, patting the starboard nine-pounder. 'With a two-and-a-half-pound charge she throws as sweet a ball as ever you could wish, true at a thousand yards.

She has my light-duty sight, because only the best crew fires her: you shall see the others on the maindeck.'

'I shall like that,' said Jack. They crossed the forecastle and he noticed a couple of hands slung below the bowsprit, busy about the figure that to the official mind symbolized not Agriculture nor Beer nor Justice but the River Shannon, carefully painting it with the same sad blue-grey that covered the frigate's sides. There being nobody within earshot, he said, 'Surely to God, Philip, you could afford her a touch of vermillion and a little gold leaf, prizes or no prizes?'

'Oh, as to that,' said Broke, 'we always were a very unostentatious ship, you know, not like poor old *Guerrière*, with all her putty and paintwork. Mind your step, Doctor,' he cried, catching Stephen's arm as the frigate's pitch threatened to fling him down the fore hatchway.

The long, low gundeck and the ship's main armament, the massive eighteen-pounders, bowsed tight up against their ports on either side, their carriages painted the same dull grey, so that they looked like powerful animals bound down, rhinoceroses, perhaps. To and fro along the lines among the busy parties of seamen, officers, and young gentlemen, Jack bowed from long habit under the beams,

Broke upright, full of contained enthusiasm as he spoke of each separate gun. They were all equipped with the Captain's simple, ingenious, robust brass sights and with flint-locks. Jack preferred the old slow-match to any lock, and as they argued the point, rooted to the deck, Stephen felt weariness rise to the flood: the pudding lay upon him like a pall. He said something about attending to his patient and withdrew, hardly noticed in the heat of the discussion. But instead of going directly to the cabin he walked aft, right aft along the quarterdeck to the taffrail and stood there for a while, staring at the wake and the boats towing astern — their disreputable scow, a launch, and Captain Broke's own gig.

He reflected on Captain Broke, an even more devoted, determined man than he had supposed. An austere man and no doubt rather shy in personal relationships: Stephen had the impression that he did not arouse quite the same affection among his crew as did Jack Aubrey, but there was not the least question of their great respect. It appeared to him that Broke lived in a state of unusual tension, as though he had an unusually heavy private cross to bear, and as though great concern with his guns and his ship helped him to do so. It would be interesting to meet Mrs Broke. The cross was there, whatever its nature: and obviously in a proud man the only sign of it would be the habitual reserve and tacit self-control that he had already re-marked in Broke. The *Shannon*'s surgeon joined him, and they talked of seasickness, the vanity of physical treatment on the one hand and the surprising effect of emotion on the other, at least in some cases.

'That man on the larboard gangway, there,' said the surgeon, 'the man in striped panta-loons chewing tobacco and spitting over the hammock-netting — he is the master of an American brig we took some days ago. She had just slipped out from Marblehead, and there she was, right under our lee at dawn, and we snapped her up in a trice.'

'In a what?'

'A trice. Now he was as sick as a dog — al-ways was, he told me, the first days at sea — and he had to be helped up the side, puking as he came. Hopeless case: could hardly stand: did not mind his capture. But the moment he sees his brig on fire, oh what a change! Colour returns, wrath and passion, a complete cure: stamps about the deck swearing — names the cargo — twenty-eight thousand dollars' worth and uninsured, ruin to his owners. Cured. Never a qualm since, and he is grown philosophical. I wish I could say the same.'

'Are not you philosophical, sir?'

'I am not, sir. I cannot bear to see the prizes burn. With half my share of these last four and twenty — four and twenty, sir, upon my honour — I should have bought myself a snug practice in Tunbridge Wells; and with the whole, I should not have needed to practise any more at all; I should have set up for a country gentleman. How I hope that wretched *Chesapeake* will come out, so that we may return to our legalized piracy.'

'You have no doubt of the event, then?'

'No more than did the surgeons of *Guerrière*, *Macedonian*, *Java* and *Peacock*. But in either case, it would be an end to this torment of seeing my fortune go up in hellish smoke and flames.'

'I must attend my patient, sir,' said Stephen. 'Give you good day.'

On the gundeck Captain Broke was also concerned for Diana Villiers. He said to his first lieutenant, a tall, round-headed man, rather deaf, who bent anxiously to catch his words, 'Mr Watt, it occurs to me that at quarters this evening, we should not make a clean sweep fore and aft. The lady in the master's cabin must not be disturbed. It is only seasickness, and she will no doubt be better tomorrow, but today she must not be disturbed; so let the cabin bulkheads stand. On the other hand, I should like to show Captain Aubrey what we can do, so pray let some targets be prepared.'

'Directly, sir,' said Watt, and he ran off: eight bells in the afternoon watch had already struck, and there was little time to spare. The hands who had not overheard the Captain's words observed the lieutenant's hurried pace and drew their own conclusions: in any case the whole ship's company knew what was afoot within two minutes, and the gun-crews gathered round their pieces, checking trucks and tackles and breechings, shot garlands, swabs, and worms, chipping and changing their flints. They knew Captain Aubrey's reputation as a tiger with the great guns, and his former shipmates among them had magnified his deadly accuracy and speed, reducing his factual three broadsides in three minutes ten seconds to three in two, and asserting that every shot went home. They did not quite believe it, but they wanted the ship to show well and they did what little they could: little it was, because the *Shannon*'s guns were never housed in anything much short of a perfect state, but still, a little slush from the galley could ease a block or a truck and perhaps strike a second off the time.

One bell in the first dog-watch, and Stephen sat down by Diana: a fairly heavy sea was still running and she was still motionless, a ghastly colour, but she opened her eyes when the drum beat for quarters and gave him a watery smile.

Quarters, and all hands ran to their action stations; and at once the ship took on much of her fighting appearance, her 330 people gathered in tightly ordered groups along her 150 feet of length. The midshipmen, the junior lieutenants, and the Marine officers inspected their men, reported to Mr Watt 'All present and sober, sir, if you please,' and Mr Watt, moving one step aft and taking off his hat, made the same report to Captain Broke, who then gave the expected order: 'A clean sweep fore and aft on the starboard side. Red cutter away.'

In a few moments all the bulkheads but Diana's had vanished, the cutter splashed down with its load of empty casks, and the bosun's calls uttered the shrill cutting pipe that hurried the sail-trimmers from their guns to wear ship as the *Shannon* began the long turn that would bring her starboard broadside to bear on the targets to windward.

The sun still high in the west, a fine topgallantsail breeze in the south-east, and the light perfect; but there was rather more sea running than Jack would have liked for accurate practice. She was round, and here was the first target, a cask flying a black flag on a pole, fine on the starboard bow, three or four hundred yards away. On the gundeck, the familiar orders 'Silence fore and aft — out tompions — run out your guns — prime', all purely formal, since the men moved automatically, having gone through these motions many hundred times, as Jack could see not only from their co-ordinated ease but also from the rutted deck behind each piece, scored deep by countless recoils, far too deep for any holystone.

'Three points, Mr Etough,' said Broke to the acting-master, and then, taking out his watch, 'Fire as they bear.'

The *Shannon*'s head fell off from the wind: the target came broader on the bow: the bow-gun went off, followed a split second later by the rest in a rippling broadside that came aft in one long roll of enormous thunder. White water sprang up all round the target; the smoke swept inboard and across the deck — the headiest smell in the world — and in the smoke the crews heaved furiously at their tackles, worming, sponging, reloading, and running out their guns.

'My God,' cried Diana, sitting straight up at the first great crack, 'what's that?'

'They are only exercising the great guns,' said Stephen, waving calmly, but his words if not his gesture were lost in the prodigious roar of the second broadside, the deep growl of the recoiling guns. The first had knocked away the flag, the second destroyed the cask entirely; but without the slightest pause the crews worked at their guns as the wreckage of the target swept down abaft the beam, whipping the two-ton cannon smack against the port-sills, training them round with handspikes, pointing them, the captains glaring along the sights. Then an unearthly hush as they waited for the top of the roll, the first hint of descent, and the third broadside shattered the remaining staves.

'By God, they will get in a fourth,' said Jack aloud. Already the guns were out again, trained hard aft. The bow-gun could not bear, but the remaining thirteen sent two hundredweight of iron hurtling into the sparse black wreckage of the target, far on the starboard quarter.

'House your guns,' said Broke, and turning to Jack, 'Four minutes and ten seconds. If you will grant me the bow-gun, that is four broadsides at one minute two and a half seconds apiece.'

If it had been any man but Broke, Jack would have told him he lied; but Philip did not lie. 'I congratulate you,' he said, 'upon my word, I do. A most admirable performance: I have never done so well.'

He did admire it heartily, but the less worthy part of Jack Aubrey felt somewhat put out: he had always felt a little superior to Philip, nautically superior, and Philip had equalled or even just beaten his most cherished record. Still there was the consolation that two of the locks had missed fire, which would never have happened with the slow-match, and that Philip had had five years to train his men, which had never happened to Jack. But it was most capital gunnery, and seeing the pleased, sweating faces looking at him from the waist and the quarterdeck in decent triumph, he added, with perfect sincerity, 'Most admirable, indeed. I doubt any other ship in the fleet could have done so well.'

'Now let us see what the carronades and chasers and small-arms can do,' said Broke, 'if you are sure it will not disturb Mrs Villiers.'

'Oh no,' said Jack. 'She is quite used to it. I have seen her handle a fowling-piece like any man. And I recall she shot tigers in India — her father was a soldier in those parts.'

Broke hailed the cutter, which laid out more targets, and the carronades, the chasers, and the small-arms men went to work. It was a beautiful sight to see them, the more so as Broke simulated all kinds of emergencies, calling away sail-trimmers, boarders, and firemen from the crews, which nevertheless worked on, unperturbed in the apparent confusion, and only a very little slower for the want of hands. A most impressive display, and one that could have been achieved only by the most intelligent and long-continued training, with good liking between officers and men; and it became even more impressive when Broke put his ship about and let fly with the larboard guns, the midshipmen, with their coats off and a look of concentrated eagerness and attention on their faces, fighting their brass six-pounder.

This was immediately above Diana's cot, within hand's reach of her head, and at its high-pitched, ear-splitting explosion she started up again. 'Stephen,' she said, 'close the window, there's a lamb. I must look utterly disgusting. I am so sorry to be such a spectacle, and such a bore. So very, very sorry . . .' But after the second crash he saw her smile in the half-light — the flash of her teeth. She took his hand, and said, 'Lord, Stephen dear, I am just beginning to realize it. We have escaped — we have run clean away!'

CHAPTER NINE

Jack woke at the changing of the watch to the familiar sound of holystones and swabs; he was aware that the wind had dropped in the night, but for a moment he could not tell what ship he was in, nor yet what ocean. Then once again the beautiful fact of their escape came flooding into his mind: he smiled in the darkness, and said, 'Clear away: we have got clear away.'

There was scarcely any light at all below, only just enough for him to make out the shape of Philip Broke moving quietly about the sparsely-furnished great cabin, where Jack's hammock was slung: and perhaps it was this that threw his sense of place and time out of beat — he had rarely slept in a hammock since he was a master's mate. Broke was already up and dressed — Jack could see the gleam of his gold epaulettes — and presently he tiptoed out, to the roar of the great double-handed stones just overhead and the thump-thump-thump as the afterguard flogged the quarterdeck dry. Jack heard him say good morning to the marine sentry at the cabin door and then again to the officer of the watch, young Provo Wallis the Nova Scotian, by the sound of his reply.

Smiling still he sank back into a rosy state between waking and doze. Not only was there a most restful lack of present responsibility, but the tension of yesterday had quite died away; it had persisted well into the night, lasting beyond all reason, but now he could look back upon that series of events as something already in the past. His fury at old Herapath's flight — and Jack had seen him whip the horses — had faded entirely, eclipsed by the contemplation of their luck. Luck all the way, luck at every turn. He considered old age and its mutilations and wondered what it would do for him: examples presented themselves to his mind, not only of mental decay, physical weakness, gout, stone, and rheumatism, but of boastful mendacious garrulity, intense and peevish selfishness; timidity if not cowardice, dirt, concupiscence, avarice. Old Mr Broke had been tolerably mean. Lord, there was nothing of that in his son! In the course of his career Jack had burnt or released a certain number of prizes in critical situations, so as to keep his crew up to strength, but four and twenty in a line was something beyond his experience and he honoured it extremely. True, Philip was comparatively well-to-do, but even richer men loved another ten or twenty thousand guineas: he remembered the nasty wrangle between Nelson, Keith, and St Vincent over their flag-shares in prize-money. And even more than Philip's disregard for cash, Jack admired the way he had formed his officers and men, so that they followed his opinion and shared his views: love of prize-money was so strong in sea-officers and man-of-war's men that it seemed almost contrary to nature. On the other hand all the Shannons, and not only their Captain, had had to swallow the taking of *Guerrière*, *Macedonian*, *Java* and *Peacock*: a very bitter string of pills. His mood grew dark at the recollection, and he clenched his fist. Precious little strength there: he felt his arm, bound tight across his chest — not much pain today, but no power either, scarcely enough to cock a pistol.

Broke had formed them very well, and he must have had good material to work upon. He was wrong about his flintlocks, but even so the *Shannon*'s gunnery was excellent: excellent, there was no other word for it. And Jack was particularly impressed by the small-arms men in the tops: the senior Marine officer had provided some of his best marksmen with rifled carbines, and they had done remarkable execution; while the swivel-guns, firing grape down on a hypothetical deck, had done even better. True murdering-pieces, well-plied. He had an uneasy feeling that he had never attended to the tops quite as he should have done . . . Nelson had never much cared for the use of fighting-tops in battle, partly because of the danger of fire, and until recently everything that Nelson said was Gospel to Jack Aubrey. But on the other hand, he had seen the *Java* carried into battle in obedience to the great man's dictum, 'Never mind manoeuvres: go straight at 'em', and it occurred to him that although Nelson was always right where the French and the Spaniards were concerned, he might have had other views if he had been at war with the Americans.

Broke walked in. 'Good morning, Philip,' said Jack, 'I was just thinking of you, and the splendid show of gunnery at quarters.'

'I am glad you were pleased,' said Broke. 'There is no man whose opinion I value more. But the question is, was it up to the *Constitution*'s standard?'

'Why, as to that,' said Jack, 'I cannot speak exactly for their rate of firing, since I did not have my watch in hand, but I know it was pretty fast — I reckoned something short of two minutes for their first broadsides, and they did better afterwards. Not as fast as *Shannon* at any time — perhaps in the ratio of three to four or even five — but pretty fast; and most uncommon true. They hit us very, very hard, you know. Yet accuracy for accuracy, I still think you may have the advantage; your men were firing with an awkward, uneven pitch and roll, whereas *Constitution* had a much more regular sea, right on the beam most of the time. Upon the whole, I should say *Shannon* would have outgunned *Constitution*; though it would have been a near-run thing, with their twenty-four-pounders. As for *Chesapeake*, I know no more than you; I never saw Lawrence do more than run his guns in and out, dumb-show. But he did that briskly enough, and he certainly sank poor *Peacock* off the Demerara river.'

'Well,' said Broke, 'I hope to put it to the trial today. We are on our last tun of water; I cannot stay; and I mean to send in to tell him so.' Broke's steward coughed discreetly at the door — what a contrast with Killick's way of bursting straight in, his coarse 'Wittles is up' and his jerk of the chin or thumb or both — and Broke said, 'First breakfast is ready when you are, Jack. I have had mine. And as I know you prefer coffee, I have ordered you a pot: I hope it will be to your liking.'

It was not. Philip's steward might be as discreet as a cat, but Jack would have given all his discretion and pretty ways for a pot of

Killick's coffee. He had not had a decent cup since the *Java*. The Americans had been kind, polite, hospitable, and their sailors thorough seamen, but they had the strangest notion of coffee: a thin, thin brew — a man might drink himself into a dropsy before the stuff raised his spirits even half a degree. Strange people. Their country was coming closer, he observed as he looked through the scuttle: pouring out another cup of the poor washy draught, he carried it out on to the quarterdeck.

The day was dawning fast, a day full of promise, with a steady breeze in the north-west, and the *Shannon* was standing in for her morning look at the *Chesapeake*, perhaps her last look, from what Philip had said. All the ritual of washing was over, and the ship presented a beautiful appearance of perfectly scrubbed wood, exactly coiled ropes, yards squared by the lifts and braces, masts and sheets gleaming with fresh slush; it would be an hour at least before the captain of the afterguard called for sweepers. Not a spit-and-polish ship — worn, indeed, and shabby, particularly in her sails — but clean and eminently serviceable. There was no brass that he could see, apart from the resplendent bell forward, the lambent quarterdeck six-pounder, and the sights all along; the busy deck-full of hands were doing something more directly connected with war than making metal shine. Some chipped corroded round-shot, others made foxes, paunches and seizings, and the forward pumps wheezed round, discharging a thin stream over the side. The hen-coops were already up. The proud cock crowed, clapping his wings in the first rays of the sun, and a hen cried out that she had laid an egg, an egg, an egg!

Philip himself was talking to an American ship-master, one of his prisoners; and over beyond him a score of men, a large party, stood dubiously round the carronades while some of their number slowly pushed them in and out under the guidance of two grizzled quarter-gunners with pigtails down to their waists. The Shannons knew that their Captain did not like the name of the Lord to be taken in vain and that he detested coarse expressions: the Captain was present, well within earshot, and the course of instruction had a somewhat unearthly air, with its supernatural patience and mild persuasion.

'Good morning, Mr Watt,' said Jack to the first lieutenant. 'Is there any sign of Doctor Maturin yet?'

'Good morning, sir,' said Watt, leaning his good ear towards him. 'I am entirely to your way of thinking.'

'I am glad of that,' said Jack, and in a rather

louder voice, 'Have you seen anything of Doctor Maturin this morning?'

'No, sir. But there is cocoa waiting for him in the gunroom.'

'That will set him up, I am sure. Pray, what are those men by the carronades? They scarcely look like Shannons.'

'They are Irish labourers, sir. We took them out of a Halifax privateer that had taken them from an American privateer that had taken them from a Waterford brig. The poor souls hardly knew where they were, but when we told them it was the *Shannon* and gave them some grog, they seemed pleased, and screeched out in their heathen way. The Captain let these fellows enter, though we find it very hard to teach them their duty, seeing that only three of them speak any English. But I hope they will be useful if it comes to boarding: they have terrible battles among themselves — you see those three with broken heads — and they understand the use of pikes and axes. Doctor Maturin, sir, good morning to you. I trust you found your cocoa hot?'

'I did, sir, and return all due thanks,' said Stephen, looking wistfully at Jack's cup: neither he nor Aubrey could love the morning until they had drunk a pint or so of true, freshly-roasted and freshly-ground boiling coffee.

The cock crowed again, and several of the Irishmen cried, *'Mac na h'Oighe slan.'*

'What do they say?' asked Jack, turning to Stephen.

'Hail to the Virgin's Son,' said Stephen. 'We say that in Ireland, when we hear the first cockcrow of the day, so that if we meet a sudden death before the day is out, we may also meet with grace.'

'They must keep that until we rig church,' said Watt. 'We cannot have Christian practices on weekdays, nor Christian precautions.'

'How is Mrs Villiers?' asked Jack.

'Somewhat better, I thank you,' said Stephen. 'Will I look at your cup, now? It has the curious pattern in its side.'

'Infamous hogwash,' murmured Jack, as the first lieutenant moved away to leeward on his Captain's approach.

'Listen, Jack,' said Stephen in the same low voice, 'Diana says that sea-captains can marry people. Is it true?'

Jack nodded, but no more, for Broke was at hand, politely asking for news of Mrs Villiers. Stephen said that the most distressing symptoms were over, that a tonic draught, such as coffee of triple or even quadruple strength, followed by a small bowl of arrowroot gruel, reasonably slab, would set her up by the afternoon. 'And then, sir,' he added, 'you would oblige me infinitely by marrying us, if you have the leisure.'

Captain Broke paused for a moment: was this a strangely-timed pleasantry? Judging from the Doctor's demeanour and his pale, determined face, it was not. Should he wish him joy of the occasion? Perhaps, in view of Jack's silence and Maturin's cool, matter-of-fact, unfestive manner, that might be inappropriate. He remembered his own wedding-day and the desperate feeling of being caught on a leeshore in a gale of wind, unable to claw off, tide setting hard against him, anchors coming home. He said, 'I should be very happy, sir. But I have never performed the manoeuvre — that is, the ceremony — and I am not sure of the forms nor of the extent of my powers. You will allow me to consult the Printed Instructions, and let you know how far I may be of service to you and the lady.' Stephen bowed and walked off. Broke said, 'Cousin Jack, a word with you.' And in the privacy of the after-cabin he went on, 'Is your friend serious? He looked grave enough, in all conscience; but surely he is a Romanist, is he not? He must know that even if I can perform this marriage it is meaningless to those of his persuasion. Why not wait until we are in Halifax, where a priest can do his business for him?'

'Oh, he is perfectly serious,' said Jack. 'He has wanted to marry her ever since the peace — she is Sophie's first cousin, you know.'

'But why the hurry? Don't he know we shall be in port before the week is out?'

'That is the very point, I take it,' said Jack. 'I gather there is some question about her nationality; she might possibly be considered an enemy alien, and a marriage on board would settle the matter out of hand.'

'I see. I see. You have never married anyone aboard ship, Jack, I suppose?'

'Not I. But I am fairly sure it can be done. The captain of a King's ship can do close on anything for a man except hang him without a court-martial.'

'Well, I shall look into the Instructions. But first I should like you to read this letter. It is addressed to Captain Lawrence. I have sent in several messages by word of mouth, saying I should like to meet him ship to ship, but from what you say about him I imagine they were either not delivered or that his orders kept him in port. Now it seems to me that the people ashore must know you are gone off by this, with *Shannon* as your obvious refuge; and since they were so eager to keep you they might be equally eager to get you back again and therefore more willing to send *Chesapeake* to sea. In any case, a written challenge has so very much more weight than anything verbal at second-hand. So with these two consider- ations in mind, I mean to send my letter in by an American prisoner, a respectable man called Slocum who lives in these parts. His boat is alongside and he has undertaken to deliver it. But you know Lawrence; you know what kind of letter is likely to have an effect. Please read it and tell me what you think. I have tried to put it in a plain straightforward manner — no rhetoric, no flourishes — the kind of challenge I should like myself. But I do not know if I have succeeded and I hope you will tell me without the least disguise.'

Jack took the letter:

His Britannic Majesty's Ship *Shannon*,
off Boston,
June 1813

Sir,

As the *Chesapeake* appears now ready for sea, I request you will do me the favour to meet the *Shannon* with her, ship to ship, to try the fortune of our respec- tive flags. To an officer of your character, it requires some apology for proceeding to further particulars. Be assured, Sir, that it is not from any doubt I can enter- tain of your wishing to close with my pro- posals, but merely to provide an answer to any objection which might be made, and very reasonably, upon the chance of our receiving unfair support.

After the diligent attention we had paid to Commodore Rodgers; the pains I took to detach all force but the *Shannon* and *Tenedos* to such a distance, that they could not possibly join in any action fought in sight of the Capes; and various verbal messages which had been sent into Boston to that effect, we were much disappointed to find the commodore had eluded us by sailing the first chance, after the prevailing easterly winds had obliged us to keep an offing from the coast. He, perhaps, wished for some stronger assurance of a fair meeting. I am, therefore, induced to address you more particularly, and to assure you that what I write I pledge my honour to perform to the utmost of my power.

The *Shannon* mounts 24 guns upon her broadside, and one light boat-gun; 18-pounders on her maindeck, and 32-pound carronades on her quarterdeck and forecastle; and is manned with a complement of 300 men and boys (a large proportion of the latter), besides 30 seamen, boys, and passengers, who were taken out of recaptured vessels lately. I am thus minute, because a report has prevailed in some of the Boston papers, that we had 150 men additional sent us from *La Hogue*, which really never was the case. *La Hogue* is now at Halifax for provisions, and I will send all other ships beyond the power of interfering with us, and meet you wherever it is most agreeable to you, within the limits of the undermentioned rendezvous, viz: — From 6 to 10 leagues east of Cape Cod Lighthouse, from 8 to 10 leagues east of Cape Anne Light, on Cashe's Ledge, in lat. 43 N. or at any bearing and distance you please to fix off the South Breakers of Nantucket, or the Shoal in St George's Bank.

If you will favour me with any plan of signals or telegraph, I will warn you (if sailing under this promise), should any of my friends be too nigh, or anywhere in sight, until I can detach them out of my way: or I would sail with you under a flag of truce to any place you think safest from our cruisers, hauling it down when fair to begin hostilities.

You must, Sir, be aware that my proposals are highly advantageous to you, as you cannot proceed to sea singly in the *Chesapeake*, without imminent risk of being crushed by the superior force of the numerous British squadrons which are now abroad, where all your efforts, in case of a *rencontre,* would, however gallant, be perfectly hopeless. I entreat you, Sir, not to imagine that I am urged by mere personal vanity to the wish of meeting the *Chesapeake*; or that I depend only upon your personal ambition for your acceding to this invitation: we both have nobler motives. You will feel it as a compliment if I say, that the result of our meeting may be the most grateful service I can render to my country; and I doubt not that you, equally confident of success, will feel convinced that it is only by repeated triumphs in *even combat* that your little navy can now hope to console *your* country for the loss of that trade it cannot protect. Favour me with a speedy reply. We are short of provisions and water, and cannot stay long here. I have the honour to be,

Sir, your obedient humble servant
P. B. V. Broke,
Capt. of HBM's Ship *Shannon.*

Jack skipped the postscript apart from the last words 'choose your terms — but let us meet' and handed back the letter. 'No,' he said, 'I think that is perfectly in order for a man like Lawrence. For my part I should have left out the fling about even combats and little navy — he knows all that as well as you or I — but I think it will certainly bring him out, unless he is under absolute orders to stay in port.'

'Very well,' said Broke, 'then I shall send it.' He stepped to the door, but then recollecting himself he called, 'Pass the word for my clerk.'

A small aged man in dusty black clothes and an ill-fitting tie-wig came in and said in a harsh shrill old voice, 'Is it to be re-wrote?'

'No, Mr Dunn,' said Broke. 'Captain Aubrey is so good as to approve it as it stands.'

'I am glad of that,' said the clerk, with no evident sign of pleasure. 'I have wrote it three times already, correcting the expressions, and there is a mort of work at a stand — complete-book, quarterly account and slop-book, all to be finished and wrote fair before we reach Halifax. Well, sir, what now?' He had no teeth, and as he fixed his testy, red-rimmed eyes on his Captain so he munched his gums, bringing his nose and chin close together in a way that had daunted post-captains before Broke was born.

'Well, Mr Dunn,' said Broke in a tone that lacked its usual authority. 'I should like you to look through the Printed Instructions or any other papers that may occur to one of your great experience, for information on marriage at sea in the absence of a chaplain, the powers of the captain, and the due forms to be observed.'

The clerk sniffed, took out his spectacles, wiped them, and peered at Jack; then, seeming to change his mind about some tart reply, walked out, muttering, 'Marriage . . . marriage . . . God preserve us all.'

'I inherited him from Butler when they gave me *Druid*,' said Broke, 'and have suffered under him ever since. It is much the same with my bosun. He served under Rodney, and we were shipmates in *Majestic* when I was a squeaker: he taught me how to make a midshipman's hitch, and he used to cuff me when I got it wrong. He was quite bald even then. They lead me a sad dance of it, between them; and if it were not that they know their duties through and through . . . however, we must get this letter off.'

The Captain Broke who emerged on to the quarterdeck with the letter in his hand did not look as though any man on earth could tyrannize over him, nor as though any subordinate could lead him a dance, however old: slim,

471

self-contained, and as it were invulnerable. He glanced eagerly at the land, automatically at the sky and the set of his sails, and turned to the American. 'Here is the letter, Captain Slocum, if you will be so good,' he said. 'All is ready, I believe, Mr Watt?'

'Yes, sir. The gentleman's boat is alongside, with his men and his dunnage already in it.' Leaning over the rail he added in a powerful voice, 'Mind the paintwork, there.'

'Good morning to you then, Captain,' said Slocum in a harsh nasal drawl, putting the letter away and preparing to leave. 'I reckon we may meet again, maybe a little later today; and I dare say my owners will be overjoyed to see you.' His face, with its sardonic expression and unwinking hostile gaze, vanished below the rail. The boat shoved off, hoisted its sail, and sped away close-hauled on the brisk north-westerly breeze, over the bright blue sea.

They watched it grow smaller in the distance, the sail shining in the brilliant day. Fine on the larboard bow lay Cape Cod, on the starboard quarter Cape Ann, and on the beam, right down at the bottom of the enormous bay, Boston and *Chesapeake.*

The master, or rather the acting-master, a young man named Etough, was the officer of the watch: to him the Captain gave orders that brought the *Shannon* round in the track of the boat, following it in slowly under topsails alone. Then he said, 'Mr Watt, would you care to breakfast with me?' and looking about among the young gentlemen on the quarterdeck he chose a lean midshipman and added, 'Mr Littlejohn, do you choose to join us?'

'Oh yes, sir, if you please,' said Mr Littlejohn, who had smelt the Captain's bacon this last five minutes, and whose soul was ravished away by the thought of the eggs that might accompany it — the midshipmen's berth had been on short allowance this many a day.

The breakfast was indeed magnificent. The steward, aware of Captain Aubrey's appetite and willing to do his ship honour, had broken out almost all his remaining stores: the third part of a Brunswick ham, kippered herrings, pickled salmon, seventeen mutton chops coming hot and hot, besides eggs, a kind of toasted scone, and two pots of orange marmalade, small beer, tea, and coffee as the Doctor had recommended it to be made. There was little conversation, however: Broke was silent and withdrawn, and by long-established naval tradition his first lieutenant could not speak without being spoken to. Yet this did not apply to Jack, and he addressed a few remarks to Mr Watt; but he was on the wrong side for the lieutenant's good ear, and after one or two attempts he confined himself to Littlejohn. 'Are you any kin to the Captain Littlejohn of the *Berwick*?' he asked.

'Yes, sir,' said the youth, quickly swallowing, 'he was my father.'

'Ah,' said Jack, wishing he had asked some other question. 'We were shipmates once, long ago, in *Euterpe*: a thorough seaman. I do not suppose,' he said, considering Littlejohn's age, his lack of emotion, and the year the French took the *Berwick*, 'I do not suppose you remember him very clearly?'

'No, sir: not at all.'

'Could you eat another chop?'

'Oh yes, sir, if you please.'

Jack thought of his own boy, still in coats: some day, would George reply to the same question in the same words, with the same decent but unmoved gravity, and continue eating with the same undiminished appetite?

'I am sorry to cut breakfast short, gentlemen,' said Broke, after a just-decent interval, 'but I hope we shall have a great deal to do today.' He stood up and they followed him out.

A certain odd nervous tension was evident on the crowded quarterdeck too; and indeed throughout the frigate men moved quietly, rarely speaking, often glancing far over the bay where Slocum's boat had vanished or at their Captain.

'Mr Etough,' said Broke, 'colours and best pennant, if you please, and lay her for Boston lighthouse.'

The *Shannon*'s ordinary pennant came down on deck for the first time for months, a frayed, windworn and now rather stubby object, although it was the mark of a King's ship in commission: the replacement soared up to the main-royal truck and there broke out, one of the *Shannon*'s rare luxuries, a long, long sapphire-coloured silk affair that streamed over her quarter, high above, while at the same time a worn blue ensign appeared at her mizen-peak and an equally shabby union at the jack-staff. The breeze had slackened, backing a little westward, and the frigate, as close to the wind as she would lie, scarcely made good two knots against the ebbing tide.

'Masthead, there,' called Broke, 'what do you make of the boat?'

The look-out's voice came down, 'It ain't in yet, sir; no, not by a long chalk.'

Almost imperceptibly the shore came closer, more distinct; the arms of the bay thrust very slowly further out to sea, so that Cape Ann crept towards the *Shannon*'s beam, bearing north by west, then past each several shroud to north by west a half north, and due north itself.

In the dim light of the curtained master's cabin Stephen said very softly, 'How are you feeling now, Villiers?'

No reply, no pause in the even breathing: she had gone to sleep at last, and with the quietness of the ship, the smoothness of the motion in this untroubled water, her whole person had relaxed. Her fists were no longer clenched; her face had lost the fierce, obstinate look of resistance; and although it was still pale it was no longer deathly. Her gruel had done her good; she had washed in what little water the *Shannon* could afford her; and above all she had done her hair: it streamed up, pure black on the pillow, showing the boyish fluting of her neck and an ear whose formal perfection surpassed that of any shell he had ever seen. He contemplated her for a while and then slipped out.

As he stood on the maindeck, blinking against the brilliance of the day, bemused, deep in his own thoughts, impeding the busy men, the captain of the maintop, a former patient of three ships ago, took him gently by the elbow, and saying, 'This way, sir. Clap on with both hands, now', guided him up the ladder to the quarterdeck.

Here he joined the purser, the surgeon, and

the clerk, who welcomed him, told him that they were lying to off the lighthouse, that there on the port bow were the Graves and then the Roaring Bulls, and that today they had great hopes of — their words ceased abruptly as Captain Broke desired Mr Wallis, the second lieutenant, to carry a glass up to the masthead and tell him what he saw.

Young Wallis sprang on to the hammock-cloths and ran up the ratlines as though up an easy flight of stairs, up and up; and from the jacks his voice floated down into the listening silence. 'On deck, there. Sir, *Chesapeake* is out in the road. At single anchor, I believe. She has had royal yards crossed.'

'Where is the boat?'

'Sir?'

'Where is Slocum's boat?'

'Still this side of the Green Island, sir,' called Wallis after a searching pause, and the silence fell again, broken by the sounding of seven bells in the forenoon watch.

'If she is in the outer road and if she has crossed her royal yards, she is most certainly coming out. She will win her anchor at slack water and sail on the first of the ebb,' said Mr Dunn, munching his gums with satisfaction. He had the Printed Instructions under his arm, and a sheaf of papers folded into the book, but his whole being was directed landwards, to the burial rather than to the marriage service.

'To what do you refer?' asked Stephen.

'Why, the *Chesapeake*, of course,' they cried, and the purser added, '*Constitution* won't be ready for sea this month and more.'

They fell to a close discussion of the state of the tide, the steadiness of the wind, and the new double-breeching of the carronades. Although Stephen's acquaintance with these theoretically non-combatant gentlemen had been short, he had already observed that they were even more martial than the rest — Dunn the clerk and Aldham the purser had commanded parties of small-arms men at quarters, blazing away themselves like fury, each with two loaders, and the surgeon had bitterly lamented that his post below the waterline always kept him from any action except the occasional boat-expedition — but even so Stephen was surprised by their steady flow of technicalities, their keen appreciation of the finer points, their heartfelt longing for violence and bloodshed.

Their flow was cut off short by another hail from the masthead. 'Sir, they are shipping the capstan-bars.' A pause. 'She drops her foretopsail. Main and mizen. Some trouble with her anchor.'

'A foul anchor won't take Lawrence long,' muttered Jack.

'He is coming out,' said Broke, turning to his officers with a smile. 'Mr Etough, we will dispense with the noon observation. Strike eight bells and let the hands go to dinner at once.'

All hands were prepared for this. The aged bosun already had his call to his lips as the Marine hurried past him to strike the bell — a sound almost invariably followed by the enormous hullaballoo of cooks bawling out mess numbers, men running and roaring with messkids, sailors beating on their plates and banging tables, but on this occasion strangely muted. It was as strange as the calmness with which the Shannons received their Captain's statement to his first lieutenant, made loud and clear, that today grog would be cut by half, to be made up some other time.

Having made this announcement, Broke hailed the masthead again for news of the boat: it was still well short of the *Chesapeake*. 'It is not my challenge that is bringing him out, then,' he said to Jack, 'but rather a desire for your company.' After a few moments he said, 'I am going aloft. I wish you could come with me, but I do not suppose you can use your arm.'

'For the masthead, no,' said Jack, 'but I can

manage the maintop, through the lubber's hole.'

They crossed the deck, and Dunn moved forward to intercept them. 'For this marriage, sir,' he said, 'I am afraid it is within your competence, and it seems that banns are not required at sea. Here are all the references, and I have marked the book of Common Prayer.'

'I really cannot attend to a marriage now, Mr Dunn,' said Broke. 'I am going aloft. But now I come to think of it, the lady must be moved. We are likely to clear for action very soon, and she must be moved. Mr Watt, tell me the state of the forepeak.'

'Well, sir, now that the pigs are all gone, it is pretty salubrious, apart from the rats and cockroaches.'

'Then as soon as the men have finished their dinner, let it be prepared. It may be sprinkled with eau de Cologne — there is an unopened bottle in my quarter-gallery — and a cot may be slung.' Then raising his voice, 'Mr Wallis, come down and wait for us in the top. Easy does it, Jack,' he said, as his cousin began to climb like an ungainly three-armed spider.

Between them Broke and Wallis heaved his sixteen stone into the sighting-top, and Broke carried on to the masthead, running aloft like a boy. Wallis passed Jack his telescope, arranged a studdingsail for him to sit on, and observed that 'it must be devilish awkward, with only one arm.'

'Oh, as for that,' said Jack, 'I am perfectly all right on deck. After all, Nelson boarded the *San Nicolas* and then the *San Josef* with only one eye, and won the Nile with only one arm. Will you leave me your glass, Mr Wallis? Thankee.'

The young man vanished: Jack glanced about the top — a spacious, convenient top, with a stouter armour of red-covered hammocks wedged into the netting between the stanchions than he had seen in a frigate, and two one-pound swivel-guns a side — and then settled to focusing the telescope, a difficult task with the fingers of his right hand only just peeping from the bandage and the sling.

The blur grew clearer: a cautious twist, and there was the *Chesapeake*, sharp and clear among a crowd of small craft. Jack could not see her forecastle — an island was in the way — but at the masthead Broke had a perfect view, and he called down. 'Anchor's apeak — they pawl and back —' At this moment the American frigate fired a gun, dropped her topgallantsails, and sheeted them home. 'Anchor's aweigh,' called Broke. 'He plucked it up in fine style.'

Now the *Chesapeake* cleared the island, full into Jack's sight, and he could see the hands laying aloft to rig out the studdingsail booms. The breeze was as fair as it could be, and as soon as Lawrence was clear of the last turn in the channel, clear of the light, he would set them on either side. Already the yachts and small craft had spread all the sail they possessed, the breeze being lighter in with the shore.

On the *Shannon*'s deck the hour of grog had arrived: the fife was squeaking 'Nancy Dawson', the master's mate stood by the tub, ladling the half-rations; but this high point of the seaman's day lacked all its wonted fire. The hands tossed off their half pints, barely savouring the rum, and hurried on to the forecastle and the starboard gangway and into the foremast rigging to stare at the *Chesapeake*: the whole watch below was high aloft.

Broke remained at his masthead for a while, saying nothing, watching with passionate intensity: Jack, having already seen the *Chesapeake* at much closer quarters, swept the harbour with his glass, and the town. He saw the Asclepia, and picked out his very window; the broad straight street running up to the State House, the street with the hotel in it; and he searched among the distant shipping for the *Arcturus* before returning to the frigate and her attendant crowd of boats. And now here was Broke, running down the topmast shrouds.

'Well, Philip,' said he, smiling, 'your prayers are answered.'

'Yes,' said Broke, 'but was it right to pray for such a thing?' He spoke very gravely, yet his face was lit up, almost transfigured. 'Come, let me give you a hand past the futtocks.'

On deck again, and Broke said to the officer of the watch, 'Course due east, Mr Falkiner; and we may keep under an easy sail.'

The backed topsail filled, the *Shannon* turned smoothly, brought the wind right aft, and stood out to sea. She had hardly gathered way before the *Chesapeake* rounded the light-house and set studdingsails aloft and alow, and they sheeted home together, while at the same moment her royals flashed out over all, a pretty piece of seamanship. From the *Shannon*'s deck she was hull-down, and indeed the lower part of her courses could not be seen except upon the rise; she was about ten miles away and even with royals and studdingsails abroad she would not be able to make much more than six or seven knots with this breeze, even with the ebbing tide. There was plenty of time to draw her right out into the offing, beyond the capes, where there was all the sea-room in the world.

Plenty of time, and since the *Shannon* made a clean sweep fore and aft almost every day at quarters — since the cabin furniture was so sparse and so contrived that it could be struck down into the hold in a very few minutes, while the officers' bulkheads and canvas screens vanished even sooner — and since she always had enough ammunition on deck for three broadsides, it seemed that there might be little to do to fill those necessary hours. Yet in even the most zealous ship there was a world of difference between clearing for action with a purely ideal enemy and preparing for battle with a large, formidable frigate that could actually be seen, that had the weathergage, and that showed every sign of a determination to close as soon as possible. Apart from anything else, no officers made their wills or wrote what might be their last letters home before quarters, whereas many, including both Jack and his cousin, now determined to do so as soon as they had the leisure. And then there was all the bosun's work, puddening and chaining the yards, and the gunner's, filling more cartridge, rousing up more shot, grape, round and canister; to say nothing of the wetting and sanding of the decks, the rigging of splinter-netting overhead, the spreading of damp fearnaught screens over the ways to the magazine, the placing of scuttle-butts of water for the men to drink between bouts; while as far as the surgeons were concerned, all instruments were to be thoroughly overhauled, and in many cases sharpened. And before the galley fires were put out, there was also the minor question of the officers' dinner. Jack was already longing for his, but when Broke proposed a last tour of the guns he walked along with him and the gunner and the first lieutenant without more than a private murmur.

As he had expected, not even the keenest eye could find anything amiss, but he was glad when, on reaching the forecastle, Broke asked him whether he had any suggestions to make. 'Since you ask me,' he said, 'I should like to see slow-match as well as flint-locks. Your locks can miss fire — scatter the priming — a match whipped across can save the shot. And I believe you cannot afford to waste a single shot with the gentleman over the way,' nodding towards the distant, but not so very distant *Chesapeake*, now under topgallant studdingsails as well — 'Besides, it is the old way; and I like old ways as well as new.'

The gunner coughed approvingly, and Mr Watt, who had caught the remark, said, 'Aye, indeed. The fathers that begot us.'

Broke considered, and then said, 'Yes.

Thank you, cousin: we must certainly not waste a single shot. Mr Watt, let it be so — but Lord, I am forgetting. How does the forepeak come along?'

'It is as trim and trim as we could make it, sir. It is not an abode of angels, like the master's cabin, but at least it smells as sweet as — as sweet as new-mown hay.'

'I must wait upon the lady,' said Captain Broke, glancing at the *Chesapeake* and then at the sun. 'Pass the word for Doctor Maturin. Doctor Maturin, how good of you to come: is Mrs Villiers well enough to receive me, do you think? I should like to pay my respects, and explain that she has to be removed into the forepeak, as we may very shortly be in action.'

'She is considerably better today, sir,' said Stephen, 'and would, I am sure, be glad of a short visit.'

'Very well. Then pray be so kind as to let her know that in fifteen minutes' time, I shall do myself the honour of waiting on her.'

The guns were finished; the officers were gone to their dinner in the gunroom; Broke tapped on the cabin door. 'Good afternoon, ma'am,' he said, 'my name is Broke, in command of this ship, and I am come to ask you how you do, and to say, that I fear we must ask you to change your quarters. There may be a certain amount of noise presently — indeed, an action — but I beg you will not be alarmed. You will be in no danger in the forepeak, and the noise will be much less; I regret it will be dark and somewhat cramped, but I trust you will not have to stay there long.'

'Oh,' said she, with great conviction, 'I am not at all frightened, sir, I assure you. I am only so sorry to be a burden — a useless burden. If you will be so kind as to give me your arm, I shall go along at once, and be out of the way.'

She had had time to change, to prepare herself, and when she stood up in her travelling-habit she looked more than usually elegant. Broke led her forward through lines of transfixed seamen, all of whom, after one quick, astonished glance, stared straight out through the open gun-ports: forward, then down and down to the forepeak, well under the water-line. It was a small three-cornered space, airless, reeking of eau de Cologne, and the dim light of a hanging lantern showed that a numerous party of rats had already joined the cockroaches on the cot. 'I am afraid it is worse than I had thought,' he said. 'I shall send a couple of hands to deal with the rats.'

'Please, please,' she cried, 'do not trouble yourself for me. I can deal with rats. And

Captain Broke,' she said, taking his hands, 'just let me wish you victory. I am sure that you will win. I put my whole trust in the Navy.'

'You are very, very kind,' he said with deep feeling. 'Now I shall have an even greater motive for doing all I can.'

'Jack,' he said, returning to the cabin, where Captain Aubrey was already deep into a sea-pie, 'you never told me Mrs Villiers was so beautiful.'

'She is a handsome woman, to be sure,' said Jack. 'Forgive me for starting, Philip; I was so damned sharp-set.'

'Handsome? She is much more than that — perhaps the most beautiful woman I have ever seen, although she was so pale. Such grace! And above all, such spirit! Never a question, never a complaint — walked straight into that foul forepeak, alive with rats, and only wished us victory. She puts her whole trust in the Navy, she said. Upon my life, that is a fine woman. I do not wonder at your friend's impatience. The kind of woman a man would be glad to fight for. I shall be proud to call her cousin.'

'Aye,' said Jack, thinking of Mrs Broke, 'Diana has the spirit of a thoroughbred: moves like one, too.'

Broke was silent for a while, prodding at his

sea-pie and then at the fried remains of yesterday's suet pudding, covered with purple jam.
'I am going to shift my clothes directly,' he
said. 'None of my uniforms would fit you, I
am afraid, but some of the officers are about
your size: I will send to the gunroom.'

'Thankee, Philip,' said Jack, 'and if you
could find me a pretty heavy sabre, that
would be even more to the point: or anything
with real weight and an edge. For the rest, a
brace of ordinary boarding-pistols will do.'

'But your arm, Jack? I had only thought of
asking you to look after the quarterdeck guns.
Their midshipman is away in that unlucky
prize — how I regret it!'

'I will lend a hand there or anywhere else
with all the pleasure in the world,' said Jack,
'but if it comes to boarding or repelling
boarders, it stands to reason I must have a go.
I shall get Maturin to bind my arm tight in.
My left is as good as ever it was — better, indeed — and I can look after myself pretty
well.'

Broke nodded. He had a grave, contained
look; most of his being was far away with all
the innumerable responsibilities of a commander, responsibilities whose crushing
weight Jack knew so well and whose absence
he felt so clearly now; but he dealt with various small immediate problems before the

meal ended — among other things, he sent the mate of the hold and a hand named Raikes, once a professional rat-catcher, into the forepeak. Then, the steward having brought an armful of clothes from the gun-room, they changed, Broke helping Jack with his awkward arm.

'Before we make a clean sweep,' he said, 'shall we exchange the usual letters?'

'Yes, certainly,' said Jack. 'I was about to suggest it.' He sat down at Broke's desk and wrote:

Shannon
off Boston Light

Sweetheart,

I hope and trust we shall be in action with the *Chesapeake* before the day is out. I could not wish for more, my dear: it has been a sad weight on my heart all this time.

But should I be knocked on the head, this is to bring you and the children my dearest, dearest love. And you are to know, a man could not die happier.

Your affectionate husband,
Jno Aubrey

He sealed it, handed it across, and Broke gave him his. They walked on to the quarterdeck without speaking: all the officers were there, and all had changed their uniforms, some, like Broke and his midshipmen, in the modern style of round hats and Hessian boots, some, like Jack, in the traditional gold lace, white breeches and silk stockings; but all wore finer clothes than usual, as a mark of respect for the enemy and for the occasion. And they were all gazing steadily astern where the *Chesapeake*, coming down with a fair wind and an ebbing tide, was well clear of the now distant land, hull-up, and throwing a fine bow-wave.

The senior Marine lieutenant, a tall, burly young man, came up to Jack with two swords. 'Would either of these answer, sir?' he asked.

'This will do admirably,' said Jack, choosing the heavier. 'I am very much obliged to you, Mr Johns.'

'On deck there,' hailed the look-out. 'She's hauling her wind.'

She was indeed. The distant *Chesapeake*, turning, turning until her studdingsails would barely set, showed her long side, fired a gun, and filled again. She was clearly inviting the *Shannon* to shorten sail and try the issue now, in this present stretch of sea. Many of the yachts and pleasure boats were still with her, or not far behind. ·

'Very well,' said Broke. 'Mr Watt, let us finish clearing the ship: there is little to be done, I believe.'

'Stephen,' said Diana, as he came into the forepeak with a can of soup, 'what is happening? I did not like to trouble Captain Broke, but what is happening? Are they chasing us? Will they catch us?'

'As I understand it,' said Stephen, crumbling biscuit into the soup, 'Captain Broke has sailed right into Boston harbour, directly challenging the *Chesapeake*, and now both ships are moving out into the open sea for the battle by common consent. It is not really a question of pursuit.'

'Oh,' she said, and absently she took three spoonfuls of the soup. 'Lord above,' she said, 'what is this?'

'Soup. Portable soup. Pray take a little more; it will rectify the humours.'

'I thought it was luke-warm glue. But it goes down quite well, if you don't breathe. How kind of you to bring it, Stephen.' She ate on until a cockroach fell into the can from a beam above, when Stephen took the pot and put it down among the other cockroaches on the deck.

They were sitting side by side on the cot and Diana linked her arm through his: she was not given to demonstrations of affection and perhaps she had no great store of affection to demonstrate — an unaffectionate creature, upon the whole, though passionate enough in all conscience — and the gesture startled him. 'Perhaps I spoke too soon when I said we had got clean away,' she said. 'I should have touched wood — clung to it. Tell me, Stephen, what are our chances?'

'I am no sailor, my dear, but the Navy lost the last three of these encounters, and as I understand it the *Chesapeake* has a far more numerous crew than our ship. On the other hand, the two are almost exactly matched in guns, which was not the case in the former actions, and Jack expresses great satisfaction with his cousin's attention to gunnery; while as far as I can judge, Mr Broke seems a most capable, energetic commander. Perhaps our chances may be nearly even: not that my opinion is worth a straw.'

'What will they do to us if we are taken? I mean you and me and Jack Aubrey?'

'They will hang us up, my dear.'

'I am sure Johnson is in that ship,' said Diana, after a silence.

'I dare say you are right,' said Stephen, his gaze fixed on the beady eye of a rat in the far corner, gleaming in the lantern-light. 'He is a passionate man, and he has a great deal to pursue.' He drew out a pocket-pistol and shot the rat as it advanced upon the soup. 'I brought these for you,' he said, taking the other from his left-hand pocket. 'And here are the little shot and powder flasks: I advise a quarter charge, no more. Picking off the rats as they appear will occupy your mind, besides diminishing the nuisance.'

'By God, Maturin,' cried Diana, 'you could not have had a better thought.' She dropped his arm, reloaded the smoking pistol and rammed home the wad. 'Now I need not be afraid,' she said, her eyes as fierce and proud as a falcon's.

It was the first time since he reached America that he saw the woman he had loved so desperately and he walked aft with his mind unsettled: aft to the cockpit, where the assistant-surgeons and the ship's barber were arranging their instruments. The *Shannon*'s surgeon himself was still on the quarterdeck, so keen was his delight in the prospect of a battle, and he was unlikely to be with them much sooner than the first casualty.

Jack came below to have his arm bound in, and Stephen, knowing that argument would be of no use in this case, chose three bandages of unusual length and a kidney-dish and took him aside. As the folds of the cingulum mounted to Jack's barrel-like chest, binding the dish firmly over his heart and his arm over that, he asked after Diana.

'She is very well, I thank you,' said Stephen. 'I took her a little biscuit and some portable soup from my colleague's comforts, and she found it went down gratefully. Her mind is occupied with the rats — I lent her our pocket-pistols — and with the forthcoming action. She is much restored: her physical courage was never affected at any time.'

'I am sure it was not,' said Jack. 'She always had plenty of bottom — I mean, she was always game.' And then in a low voice, 'Broke was very much concerned at not being able to marry you today: he hopes to do so tomorrow.'

Stephen only replied, 'When do you suppose it will start, at all?'

'In something like an hour, I think,' said Jack. But when he returned to the quarterdeck he found that he had been out: the *Shannon* had hauled to the wind and reefed her topsails: the *Chesapeake* was coming up fast, with three ensigns abroad, and now her bow-wave spread high and wide.

Broke called his men aft, and as he addressed them in his rather precise, formal voice, Jack saw that they listened with grave, fierce attention, some showing the emotion that their Captain concealed with a fair degree of success: there was evidently a total sympathy between them. The borrowed sword, hanging awkwardly at his right side, took Jack's mind off the brief address and in any case he was immediately behind the Captain; he only caught the words 'They have said that the English have forgotten the way to fight. You will let them know today there are Englishmen in the *Shannon* who still know how to fight. Don't try to dismast her. Fire into her quarters; maindeck into maindeck, quarterdeck into quarterdeck. Kill the men and the ship is yours . . . Don't cheer. Go quickly to your quarters. I am sure you will do your duty . . .' Jack did not catch all the words, but he did catch the answering growl of assent from the whole length of the crowded decks and gangways and it raised his heart like a trumpet-blast. A seaman on the starboard gangway, a former Guerrière, said, 'I hope, sir, you will give us revenge for the *Guerry* today?' And in this very particular atmosphere of freedom an old quartermaster spoke up, with a discontented look at the shabby blue ensign, the best the *Shannon* could do in the way of colours after so many months at sea, and said, 'Mayn't we have three ensigns, sir, like she has?' 'No,' said Broke. 'We have always been an unassuming ship.'

The sand in the half-hour glass ran out:

Boston was now twenty miles away. The glass was turned, eight bells struck, and Broke gave the orders that sent the *Shannon* slowly eastwards again, her foresail clewed up, her main topsail shivering: and so they ran, a good glass and more, the *Chesapeake* crowding sail in the *Shannon*'s wake.

Silence on the quarterdeck: silence fore and aft; only the quiet breeze in the rigging, and little of that with her sailing large; and the live water running along her side. And into this silence the voice of the midshipman at the masthead, reporting what every man could see: the *Chesapeake* was taking in her studdingsails, royals, and topgallantsails. She was striking her royal yards down on deck.

Watt glanced at his Captain. 'No,' said Broke, 'we will keep ours up. I do not trust this breeze — it may die away. Mr Clavering,' — to the midshipman high aloft — 'you may come down now. And Mr Watt, you may heave to and beat to quarters.'

The *Shannon* turned, the way came off her, and as she lay there, gently heaving on the swell, the drum volleyed and thundered. In a moment the men were at their stations, clustered in exact order round their familiar guns or in the tops or along the gangways, and the crowded quarterdeck thinned as the officers and midshipmen ran to their divisions, leaving only the master to con the ship behind the helmsman, the aide-de-camp midshipman, the first lieutenant, the Marine officers, and the Captain to direct all, with Jack a supernumerary behind him. The purser and the clerk, both wearing swords and pistols, were already with their small-arms parties.

The *Chesapeake* was coming down fast, hauling her wind as she came and steering for the *Shannon*'s starboard quarter. As well as her three ensigns she wore a large white flag at the fore with some marking upon it, apparently words. Broke raised his glass and read 'Sailors' rights and free trade'. He made no comment, but said to Watt, 'Let us have stopped ensigns at the mainstay and in the shrouds, ready to break out in case our colours are shot away.' Then he hailed the tops in turn, each under the command of a senior midshipman: 'Mr Leake, Mr Cosnahan, Mr Smith, is all well?' and each in turn replied, 'All's well, sir.'

Closer, and the *Chesapeake* was still heading for the *Shannon*'s starboard quarter. 'I hope to God he minds what Nelson said, and comes straight on,' thought Jack. 'Will he cross my stern, rake me, and range up alarboard?' murmured Broke, staring fixedly for the least movement of her rudder. Then without shifting his gaze, loud and clear, 'Second

498

captains and crews to the larboard guns. Flat on the deck if she rakes us: don't fire till she bears true.'

A patter of bare feet as the larboard sections of the gun-crews ran to the other side, and then silence again, with the smoke from the match-tubs drifting across the deck. A quick low order and the *Shannon*'s maintopsail filled, giving her a little way: then she shivered it and brailed up her driver, moving just enough to steer.

The *Chesapeake* was not going to cross the *Shannon*'s stern. Her wake was straight and true and now it was too late for her to turn. Lawrence had waived the advantage in order to bring his ship right into action in Nelson's way. 'Handsomely done,' said Jack, and Broke nodded. Watt said, 'That's what I like to see.' 'Starboard guns,' called Broke, and the men ran back: never a sound among them.

Closer: and closer still. The words on the flag were quite clear now: yet at this angle not a broadside gun on either side would bear. Closer, closer than musket-shot. And at fifty yards the *Chesapeake* luffed to run up parallel with the *Shannon* and fight it out, both ships with the breeze a little before the starboard beam, the *Chesapeake* to windward.

'Handsomely done,' said Jack again.

Still this silence, and Broke called down through the cabin skylight to his coxswain, the captain of the aftermost starboard maindeck gun, 'Mindham, fire when you bear on the second maindeck port from her head. And Shannons, no cheering till it's over. Do not waste a shot.'

The *Chesapeake* was ranging up, squaring her mainyard to check her way: her shadow, huge and ominous, fell across the *Shannon*, and in the silence Jack could hear the run of the water parting at her bow. He saw Lawrence plain, standing there on his quarterdeck, a tall figure in that same white coat. He took off his hat and waved it to him, but at that moment the *Chesapeake* gave three roaring cheers — a strangely British ring — and at the same time Mindham's gun spoke out. Splinters flew from the *Chesapeake*'s side just abaft the second port. A split-second's pause in which Broke said, 'Half past five, Mr Fenn,' to his note-taking youngster, and Mindham's neighbour fired, together with the aftermost carronade of Jack's division, followed by the bow-gun and then a prodigious rolling broadside from the *Chesapeake*.

From that moment on all was shattering din, the guns firing as fast as they could load, one broadside running into another, dense smoke from both ships sweeping over the

Shannon's deck, the whole air and the smoke in it quivering with the huge incessant concussions, with the orange stabs of flame jetting through the darkness — the bright sun quite veiled — and the crackle of small-arms from the two opposed gangways and the tops, the high bark of the swivel-guns.

The long waiting silence was utterly gone, the long tension — a kind of grave, quiet anxiety with each man very much alone — annihilated; and this was a continual enormously active present. Jack moved along behind the starboard quarterdeck carronades: there was little he could do as yet, for the crews were fighting their pieces beautifully, talking in quick jerked-out words, laughing, racing them in and out, sighting every shot with a quick, intent glance through the smoke at the pendulums that told them when the ship was on an even keel, cheering as the ball or grape or both went home. The confusion of noise was so tremendous that it was difficult to be sure, but he had the impression that *Shannon* was firing faster, truer than *Chesapeake*. The second captain of the aftermost carronade jerked round, staring straight at Jack: the fierce excitement was still blazing in his face but already his eyes were puzzled, astonished, wide. Jack dragged his body clear — a barshot had opened all his belly — and his mates ran the gun out, fired and sponged with no more than a single backward glance. Smashed blocks and stray rigging rained down on the netting overhead and splinters were flying inboard among the smoke in deadly swathes. The *Chesapeake* was hauling up a little to check her way, and in a gap through the smoke Jack saw her helmsman killed, her wheel smashed — her whole quarterdeck was strangely empty — had been from the very first broadside — and he no longer saw Lawrence at all.

At this point both ships had the breeze a little before the beam, but the *Chesapeake*'s motion suddenly increased and she came right up close to the wind — her headsails had probably been shot away as well as her helmsman killed — and there she lay, with no way on her at all, showing the *Shannon* her stern and larboard quarter.

And now the *Shannon* mauled her terribly, shattering her stern-ports, sweeping her decks in a long murderous diagonal, doing the most shocking execution; and blood ran thick from her lee-scuppers.

'She is going to haul away,' said Broke. 'Mr Etough, port your helm.'

'She has sternway, sir,' cried Watt. 'She's paying round off.'

This would bring the *Chesapeake*'s uninjured broadside into action, and, coming round, gathering headway, she could also board — a fatal move, perhaps, with her much larger crew.

Broke nodded, put the *Shannon*'s helm a-starboard, and roaring in his speaking-trumpet through the bellowing of the guns, ordered the mizen topsail to be shivered to keep her off the wind. But even as the sail-trimmers leapt to the braces from their guns, those few of the *Chesapeake*'s that could be brought to bear shot away the *Shannon*'s jibstay; and with no jib to swing her, she hardly moved, whereas the *Chesapeake*, her sternway still on her, was coming backwards towards the *Shannon*, and coming fast.

The lane of water between them narrowed, and all the time the *Shannon* kept up this tremendous fire, flinging hundredweights of iron and lead at the closest range. And still the *Chesapeake* came backwards. An overheated quarterdeck carronade overset on its recoil, breaking its breechings, and Jack was too busy helping to check it as it plunged among a mess of hammocks blasted from the nettings and of blood to see what was happening forward until he heard the crash as the *Chesapeake*'s quarter came grinding against the *Shannon*'s side, just amidships. But as he looked up he saw the *Chesapeake*, her sternway checked, beginning to forge ahead — she had dropped her forecourse. Yet scarcely had she made a few yards, still grinding along the *Shannon*'s side, but her quarter-gallery hooked in the fluke of the *Shannon*'s best bower anchor.

In an enormous voice for a man of his size, or of any size, Broke roared, 'Cease fire, the great guns. Maindeck boarders away. Mr Stevens, lash her fast. Jack, Mr Watt. Quarterdeck men forward to board.' Then, throwing down his speaking-trumpet, he cried, 'Follow me who can.'

He raced along the starboard gangway, drawing his sword as he ran and leaping over the bodies of his clerk, the purser, and several of their men. The moment the carronade was tripped, Jack followed him with the quarterdeck boarders through a violent plunging fire from the *Chesapeake*'s tops: but there along the gangway, outside the ragged bulwark and the torn hammock-netting, hung the old bosun and his mates, lashing the *Chesapeake* fast by a stanchion, and from the *Chesapeake*'s quarter-gallery and gunroom-port men were firing pistols at them, lunging with pikes, swabs, handspikes, and one, outboard himself, was slashing down at his arm with a cutlass. Jack checked his stride, tore his pistol free, and firing left-handed, missed his man. The bosun passed the turn — the knot was tied — the cutlass flashed down: Jack and Watt fired together and the man dropped between the ships. But too late: the arm was gone, severed, still clinging to the *Chesapeake*. They heaved the old man in. Jack shouted into a seaman's ear to clap his handkerchief tight round the stump and ease him down between the maindeck guns; the bosun said something with a ferocious grin, something like 'Damn the arm', but Jack did not catch it. He ran blundering on, awkward because of his bound arm, the quarterdeck boarders swarming past him on the gangway and below among the maindeck guns.

He reached the forecastle — many dead and wounded there — and saw that Broke had already boarded the *Chesapeake* with a score of hands. Jack followed him, jumping perilously on to the muzzle of a run-out carronade and so over what was left of the hammocks on to the American quarterdeck. Not a living man was there, though many dead, several of them officers; but as Watt came after him with a prodigious leap clear over the taffrail, so the lieutenant fell, shot from the mizentop. He was up at once, holding his foot and bawling across to the *Shannon* to fire a nine-pounder into the *Chesapeake*'s tops — 'Grape,' he shouted. 'Grape,' as more boarders, seamen and Marines made their way across by every point of contact and rushed past him, gathering at the mainmast.

'Forward, forward all,' cried Jack. He had his sword out — it felt good in his hand — and he drove at the men packed along the starboard gangway with a dozen boarders behind him, many of them Irish, screaming as they came. Little resistance on the gangway — the officers were dead or gone, the men disorganized — most skipped down to the maindeck and thence below, a few were killed. And so to the forecastle, which Broke and his men had already cleared except for some who were plunging over the bows or trying to force their way down the fore hatchway or fighting still, cornered against the bulwark. Jack's party came pounding up: the few men fighting, now far outnumbered, threw down their cutlasses and pikes and muskets.

Now most of the *Shannon*'s Marines were aboard, red coats along the decks, and while some of them helped the seamen as they fought to keep back the desperate rushes of the main hatchway, others returned the murderous fire from the main and mizentops.

But the ships were drifting apart, and there was no fresh stream of boarders. Broke stood for a moment. The whole issue was in the balance: if the Chesapeakes broke out from below, the Shannons on board were lost. Jack

glanced at the men who had surrendered on the forecastle and who stood, glaring stupidly, bewildered, savage. Four of them he knew — seamen, perhaps British, perhaps impressed Americans, he had sailed with; and if British deserters, certain of an ignominious death. 'Craddock,' said Broke to one of the boarders, a man with a badly wounded leg and a bloody forearm, 'guard the prisoners.' And raising his voice, 'Smith, Cosnahan, silence their tops. Mainhatch, all hands to the mainhatch.'

The men rushed aft, Jack blundering after them, Broke coming last, and as they ran so young Smith, commanding the *Shannon*'s foretop, made his way out on the yard, followed by his men, and thence to the *Chesapeake*'s mainyard.

'Sir, sir!' roared Craddock through the continuing fire of musketry and the shouting of men.

Broke turned. Some of the prisoners had caught up their weapons and they were right on him.

'Sir,' roared Craddock again. Jack caught the sound, whipped about and saw Broke parry a wicked pike-thrust, wound his man, and then fall, clubbed down with a musket. A third man was astride him with his cutlass high, but Jack's left-handed blow, delivered with all his strength and all his weight, flung the man's arm and cutlass into the sea and his body into the waist of the ship, and a moment later Broke's party laid the remaining prisoners dead. And during this quick, horribly bloody affray the men out on the *Shannon*'s yardarm stormed the *Chesapeake*'s maintop, while the nine-pounder's grape silenced her mizentop; and now all the boarders were swarming round the silent main hatchway. They clapped a massive grating over it and lashed it down, and apart from one last desperate shot from below resistance ceased. With a rending crash the *Chesapeake*'s quarter-gallery tore clear away, and she slewed round, lying helpless under the *Shannon*'s guns. A hoarse voice below cried out that they had surrendered.

'Are you all right, Philip?' cried Jack, loud although the tumult had quite died away.

Broke nodded. His skull was bared — white bone through the blood and perhaps still worse, with more blood welling from his ears. His coxswain tied a handkerchief over the shocking wound, and they sat him on a carronade-slide.

'Look aft, Philip,' said Jack in his ear. 'Look aft — she's yours. I give you joy.' He pointed aft, where the American colours were coming down. Watt was striking them. But now they were rising again, the white ensign undermost as if in defiance. To those in the *Chesapeake* it was clear that Watt had twisted the halliards. They shouted to him but he did not hear and the last gun from the *Shannon* roared out, scattering the small party on the *Chesapeake*'s quarterdeck and indeed killing Watt in his triumph and several of his men.

Broke stared from side to side, not fully comprehending: he fumbled for his watch, looked at it, and said, 'Fifteen minutes, start to finish. Drive them all down into the hold.' But now at last the colours rose again in their due order, soaring to the mizen-peak. Cheering, wild cheering fore and aft from the *Shannon*, and through the noise Jack cried again, 'Philip, look aft. She's yours — she's yours. I give you joy of your victory.'

This time Broke understood. He looked hard at the white ensign against the pure blue sky, the proof of his victory; he focused his dazed eyes; a sweet smile showed on his bloody face, and he said very quietly, 'Thank you, Jack.'

We hope you have enjoyed this Large Print book. Other Thorndike Press or Chivers Press Large Print books are available at your library or directly from the publishers.

For more information about current and up-coming titles, please call or write, without obligation, to:

Thorndike Press
P.O. Box 159
Thorndike, Maine 04986 USA
Tel. (800) 223-1244
Tel. (800) 223-6121

OR

Chivers Press Limited
Windsor Bridge Road
Bath BA2 3AX
England
Tel. (0225) 335336

All our Large Print titles are designed for easy reading, and all our books are made to last.